the Fantasy Writer's Assistant
and Other Stories

JEFFREY FORD

With an Introduction by Michael Swanwick

GOLDEN GRYPHON PRESS • 2002

"At Reparata," first published on-line on *Event Horizon*, February 15, 1999.
"Bright Morning," copyright © 2002 by Jeffrey Ford. Unpublished.
"Creation," first published in *The Magazine of Fantasy and Science Fiction*, May 2002.
"The Delicate," copyright © 2002 by Jeffrey Ford, revised from its original publication in *Space and Time*, no. 83, 1994.
"Exo-Skeleton Town," first published in *Black Gate: Adventures in Fantasy Literature*, 1, no. 1, Spring 2001.
"The Fantasy Writer's Assistant," first published in *The Magazine of Fantasy and Science Fiction*, February 2000.
"The Far Oasis," first published on-line on *SCI FICTION*, October 25, 2000.
"Floating in Lindrethool," first published on-line on *SCI FICTION*, June 13, 2001.
"High Tea with Jules Verne," first published in *Lady Churchill's Rosebud Wristlet*, no. 7, March 2001.
"The Honeyed Knot," first published in *The Magazine of Fantasy and Science Fiction*, May 2001.
"Malthusian's Zombie," first published on-line on *SCI FICTION*, May 31, 2000.
"On the Road to New Egypt," first published in *Aberrations*, no. 32, 1995.
"Out of the Canyon," copyright © 2001 by Jeffrey Ford. Unpublished.
"Pansolapia," first published on-line on *Event Horizon*, July 26, 1999.
"Something by the Sea," copyright © 2002 by Jeffrey Ford. Unpublished.
"The Woman Who Counts Her Breath," first published in *Northwest Review*, 32, no. 3, 1994.

Copyright © 2002 by Jeffrey Ford
Introduction copyright © 2002 by Michael Swanwick
Cover illustration copyright © 2002 by John Picacio

Edited by Marty Halpern

LIBRARY OF CONGRESS CATALOGUING-IN-PUBLICATION DATA
Ford, Jeffrey, 1955–
    The fantasy writer's assistant, and other stories / by Jeffrey Ford ; with an introduction by Michael Swanwick. — 1st ed.
    p.   cm.
    ISBN 1-930846-10-X (hardcover : alk. paper)
    1. Fantasy fiction, American.   I. Title: Fantasy writer's assistant. II. Title.
PS3556.O6997   F67   2002
813'.54—dc21   2001058488

All rights reserved, which includes the right to reproduce this book, or portions thereof, in any form whatsoever except as provided by the U.S. Copyright Law. For information address Golden Gryphon Press, 3002 Perkins Road, Urbana, IL 61802.
Printed in the United States of America.
First Edition

Contents

ix	INTRODUCTION: THE COMPREHENDING STRANGENESS OF JEFFREY FORD by Michael Swanwick
3	CREATION
15	OUT OF THE CANYON
27	THE FANTASY WRITER'S ASSISTANT
43	THE FAR OASIS
59	THE WOMAN WHO COUNTS HER BREATH
69	AT REPARATA
95	PANSOLAPIA
99	EXO-SKELETON TOWN
121	THE HONEYED KNOT

CONTENTS

- <u>137</u> SOMETHING BY THE SEA
- <u>157</u> THE DELICATE
- <u>163</u> MALTHUSIAN'S ZOMBIE
- <u>185</u> ON THE ROAD TO NEW EGYPT
- <u>195</u> FLOATING IN LINDRETHOOL
- <u>221</u> HIGH TEA WITH JULES VERNE
- <u>227</u> BRIGHT MORNING

This book is for Jack and Derek—
Some stories for all of the beautiful stories
you have given me.

Acknowledgments

I owe a great debt to Michael Swanwick for taking the time from a superhuman schedule to write the Introduction to this collection. There are so many reasons why any writer would be honored by his endorsement, not the least of which, for me personally, is that he is the author of *Jack Faust*, one of my favorite novels, and so many wonderful stories that have influenced my own short fiction writing. The most important reason, though, struck me one night when I happened to be sitting next to him at a dinner party in a restaurant. He asked me if I had ever read Fritz Leiber. I hadn't. He told me about Leiber and *Our Lady of Darkness*. Before this incident, Michael had always seemed somewhat of a conundrum, but in that telling, I witnessed an incredible enthusiasm and genuine excitement for the art and craft of writing that one would be hard pressed to find in the newest of writers. Later on, I thought to myself, *This guy has already written more great stories than five of me could write in a lifetime, won every major award at least once, and yet his passion for the endeavor remains wholly intact.* I count that as a very rare quality.

Any writer lucky enough to have the opportunity to do a book with Golden Gryphon can expect a first-rate, professional and enjoyable experience. Gary Turner and Marty Halpern are committed to turning out wonderful books. Special thanks to Marty. What can I say, the man is a perfectionist in the best sense of the word. If Marty were Moses, God would be seeing some red ink. I am indebted to his vigilance, dedication, and sense of humor.

Last but by no means least, I want to thank my agent, Howard Morhaim—trusted guide, committed reader, honest critic, magician.

Introduction: The Comprehending Strangeness of Jeffrey Ford

IT BEGINS WITH DREAMS. JEFF FORD TELLS ME THAT he gets a lot of his ideas for stories from dreams, and I believe it. They have that feel. They float a few crucial inches above reality. They obey a narrative logic that is not that of the waking world. They have that eerie beauty that the better sorts of dreams can have.

But though the translation of even the most generous dream into a sensible narrative is a prodigious task, if that's all these stories were, I would not be writing this introduction. A lucid intelligence is at work here as well.

Consider "At Reparata." It begins deep in the domain of Dream with Flam, titular High and Mighty of Next Week, standing on a cliff at twilight, fly-fishing for bats. This is a wonderful conceit, but a dangerous one. Immediately the story is situated so far from consensus reality that it threatens to break free entirely and float off into the empyrean of pure whimsy. Yet with craft and cunning Ford reels the story in and rationalizes it not all the way to the domain of the Real, perhaps, but certainly into the realm of Fantasy. A wealthy eccentric has established an absurdist monarchy at Castle Reparata, and there provides a haven for the outcasts and broken souls of the world. A prostitute is made a Countess, a madman becomes the Philosopher General, a highwayman is declared Bishop to the

Crown. But when the queen dies, His Royal falls into a melancholy that threatens the realm, and Flam goes in search of a healer.

At this point, we all know how this story is going to play out and the lessons (about people becoming the roles that they assume, mostly) that we're supposed to take from it. Except that's not the story being told. Ford has better images and more original lessons in mind for us. Images and lessons that exist somewhere between the fluid unreliability of pure imagination and the dull predictability of the conventional well-made story.

Sometimes the dreams are nightmares.

A salesman opens his sample case to reveal a human brain floating in a bottle. "Floating in Lindrethool" is ostensibly set in our near future, when new technology has made silicon-based computers obsolete. But the hard-bitten and cynical salesmen, with their hats and cheap hotels, come straight out of Depression-era America. It is a gritty noir scenario, and it comes complete with a gritty noir love story. But there's comedy there as well. Slackwell, the Sad Sack of a salesman who is this story's hero, undergoes a series of almost ritual humiliations, attacked by a bishop, hammered on the foot by a housewife with higher-than-average sales resistance. His nightmarish situation is comic, and so is his romance. But the comedy, rather than alleviating the horror, intensifies it.

A man trapped in his job, a brain trapped in a jar, a woman trapped in her dreams. How could they possibly be worse off than they are now? Well . . . they could lose the self-delusions that make their lives bearable. They could become aware of exactly how ridiculous they are. That, rather than death or dismemberment, is the Damoclean sword that hangs over this tale.

"Floating in Lindrethool" may be a horror tale or (for it has a perfectly unexpected happy ending) fantasy, or we can accept the initial rationalization and dub it science fiction. Ford's works evade easy categorization. Many could be fit into any of these three realms. Most would rest uneasily in whatever category they were placed. Genre boundaries melt in their presence.

In "High Tea with Jules Verne," for example, a nameless reporter interviews not the pioneering science fiction writer, but what seems to be a physical avatar of his subconscious mind. The master of rationality is turned inside out and remade into a dadaist ringmaster of the id. His characters infest his house like mice, and like mice must be trapped and exterminated. The founding father of a quintessentially rationalistic genre is made into a Maestro of Unreason. Surrealism, recursive criticism, simple literary playfulness— whatever this is, it is not SF, save by the loosest of standards.

Nor is "Exo-Skeleton Town." Though it takes place on an alien planet, whose atmosphere necessitates that humans wear protective exo-skeletons, it fails as science fiction in that it simply cannot be taken literally. I have heard Jeffrey Ford referred to as "the consummate inverter," and here he proves the validity of that title by turning everything inside out. In a neat reversal, his people physically inhabit movie stars, living within exo-skeletal simulacra of Marilyn Monroe and Humphrey Bogart and other cultural icons. They have colonized the stars that in our world have colonized our imaginations. Their true identities have become perilous secrets. The estrangement and interminable exile of modern urban life at its worst has been literalized in the deceitful pursuit of a product that is explicitly unworthy of such sacrifice.

You could write a thesis on this story's metaphoric take on the sins of late capitalism. Or you can simply let the dreamlike weirdness of the narrative carry you away. Whatever genre this might be, it is wonderful stuff.

Ford's fiction takes you by surprise. It undercuts all your assumptions. "Creation" begins with the Baltimore Catechism, that font of doctrinal certainty, and falls swiftly through the essential mystery of life to arrive smack-dab at the Unknowable. The young narrator, acting on a compulsion he does not understand, builds a log man out in the woods. "A large hunk of bark that had peeled off an oak was the head. On this I laid red mushroom eyes, curved barnacles of fungus for ears, a dried seedpod for a nose. The mouth was merely a hole I punched through the bark with my penknife." In a dream, a saint tells him his creation's name is Cavanaugh. Then Cavanaugh comes to life, and begins to haunt the boy.

Only, maybe not. The physical evidence is not compelling. Further, the lad is entering his adolescence, prey to subterranean ocean storms of emotion. He may be projecting his fear of a meaningless universe onto a literal stick figure. But while two separate readings of events are offered the reader, the story resolutely refuses to collapse its possibilities into one or the other. Believe what you will, the story says, in the fantastic or the workaday, in God or in Nothing, you're still looking at one and the same world.

This sort of effect—this dance of the literal and the figurative— is achievable only in prose. And Jeff Ford's prose is a highly idiosyncratic thing. Words come unstuck from their original meanings. The first name of Cellini's sister becomes the name of a castle. The adjective for a particular insight into the perils of overpopulation becomes an Armenian-American scientist. It is best not to pursue these meanings because they lead nowhere—not at any rate to the author's intentions. They are evocative, but what they evoke goes beyond the saying.

An extreme example of Ford's peculiar verbal alchemy is "Pansolapia," in which time has been abolished, at the cost not only of sequence but of causality. Dreaming of his fate-to-come, a sailor decides not to travel beyond the end of the world, and so gives birth to a dream-child. Simultaneously he drowns on his return from that ill-fated journey to a place where lion-men can speak but only in a language that has no meaning. Drowning, he enters a castle. Waking, he finds himself aboard the ship. These are not separate fates but aspects of the same thing experienced all at once. He is contained within a sorceress's dream, just as she is contained in his. But dreams can kill, and their consequences cannot be contained. Elsewhere, Ford writes, "Make no mistake, words have magic." Never more so than here.

If a lion could speak, Wittgenstein tells us, we could not understand it. More famously, he said, "That of which we cannot speak, we must pass over in silence." If I have made Ford seem cryptic and elusive, it is not because he is trying to mystify the reader but because he is in hot pursuit of truths that are extremely difficult to put into words.

"The Honeyed Knot" cuts right to the heart of that pursuit. It begins with a cascade of tales, story after story tumbling down the page, related by a protagonist who is Ford himself, teaching a writing course that is for his students more a means of self-discovery than a road to publication. One tale steps forward to achieve centrality, but its uncertainties and revelations do not trace a straightforward arc of revelation. The discoveries made by Ford, searching for the truth behind the tales, fold in upon themselves and reconnect in unexpected ways. The machineries of night are at work here, and if their mechanisms cannot be laid bare, their effects can at least be held up for examination.

Ford says that "The Honeyed Knot" is highly autobiographical. He held that job. The students were all real, as were the stories they wrote. One of them did indeed murder a little girl. He wrote this story as a kind of exorcism of his sense of disappointment in himself for not being able to foresee and prevent that death. "One of the things I think the story gets at is how a sense of responsibility can exceed its bounds and turns into a kind of destructive vanity or self-righteousness," he told me. "Maybe that's what I was going for there. Believing I should be able to do things I had no way of doing."

So there is serious stuff going on here. But I invite you to examine "The Honeyed Knot" on a more superficial level. In it, Ford's universe is revealed to be literally made up of stories. And the revelation at the end, the explication of the "honeyed knot" that is the story's central metaphor, leads us again both outward and inward, to life and to words.

If you were to require me to explain Ford's fiction with his own words, however, that's not where I would have you look. Rather, I would refer you to the last story in this volume.

"Bright Morning," original to this collection, is an audacious work that is on the surface an exercise in self-reference. The narrator might as well be Jeffrey Ford's *doppelgänger*. He gets the kind of blurbs and reviews that Jeffrey Ford gets. He has a publishing history not at all unlike that of Jeffrey Ford. But I wouldn't put too much weight on that, if I were you. Ford is a trickster, and not likely to be caught out as easily as that.

Right in the middle of "Bright Morning" comes a moment that touches upon the revelatory. "My sentences," writes Ford, who never seeks to obscure when it's possible to make manifest, "sometimes have the quality of Arabic penmanship, looping and knotting, like some kind of Sufi script meant to describe one of the names given to God in order to avoid using his real name."

Exactly. There is an inexplicable strangeness at the heart of this story, as there is in all of Ford's work. It is not, however, an alienating, but a comprehending strangeness, a means of coming to grips with something that can almost but not quite be put into words. Time after time, his protagonists come face to face with that instant of insight that might, even if only for that instant, reveal the hidden workings and secret connections of the universe.

But don't take *my* word for it. To understand the essential strangeness of Jeffrey Ford's world, you have only to dip into the stories contained herein. Experience the man's voice firsthand. Let him work his magic on you. Read. Marvel. Enjoy.

Comprehend.

Michael Swanwick
September 2001

The Fantasy Writer's Assistant
and Other Stories

Creation

I LEARNED ABOUT CREATION FROM MRS. GRIMM, IN the basement of her house down the street from ours. The room was dimly lit by a stained-glass lamp positioned above the pool table. There was also a bar in the corner, behind which hung an electric sign that read RHEINGOLD and held a can that endlessly poured golden beer into a pilsner glass that never seemed to overflow. That brew was liquid light, bright bubbles never ceasing to rise.

"Who made you?" she would ask, consulting that little book with the pastel-colored depictions of agony in Hell and the angel-strewn clouds of Heaven. Mrs. Grimm had the nose of a witch, one continuous eyebrow and teacup-shiny skin—even the wrinkles seemed capable of cracking. Her smile was merely the absence of a frown, but she made candy apples for us at Halloween and marshmallow bricks in the shapes of wise men at Christmas. I often wondered how she had come to know so much about God, and pictured saints with halos and cassocks playing pool and drinking beer in her basement at night.

We kids would page through our own copies of the catechism book to find the appropriate response, but before anyone else could answer, Amy Lash would already be saying, "God made me."

Then Richard Antonelli would get up and begin to jump around, making fart noises through his mouth, and Mrs. Grimm would shake her head and tell him God was watching. I never jumped around, never spoke out of turn, for two reasons, neither of which had to do with God. One was what my father called his "size ten," referring to his shoe, and the other was that I was too busy watching that sign over the bar, waiting to see the beer finally spill.

The only time I was ever distracted from my vigilance was when she told us about the creation of Adam and Eve. After God had made the world, he made them too, because he had so much love and not enough places to put it. He made Adam out of clay and blew life into him, and, once he came to life, God made him sleep and then stole a rib and made the woman. After the illustration of a naked couple consumed in flame, being bitten by black snakes and poked by the fork of a pink demon with horns and bat wings, the picture for the story of the creation of Adam was my favorite. A bearded God in flowing robes leaned over a clay man, breathing blue-gray life into him.

That breath of life was like a great autumn wind blowing through my imagination, carrying with it all sorts of questions like pastel leaves that momentarily obscured my view of the beautiful flow of beer. Was dirt the first thing Adam tasted? Was God's beard brushing against his chin the first thing Adam felt? When he slept, did he dream of God stealing his rib and did it crack when it came away from him? What did he make of Eve and the fact that she was the only woman for him to marry? Was he thankful it wasn't Amy Lash?

Later on, I asked my father what he thought about the creation of Adam, and he gave me his usual response to any questions concerning religion. "Look," he said, "it's a nice story, but when you die you're food for the worms." One time my mother made him take me to church when she was sick, and he sat in the front row, directly in front of the priest. While everyone else was genuflecting and standing and singing, he just sat there staring, his arms folded and one leg crossed over the other. When they rang the little bell and everyone beat their chest, he laughed out loud.

No matter what I had learned in catechism about God and Hell and the Ten Commandments, my father was hard to ignore. He worked two jobs, his muscles were huge, and once, when the neighbors' Doberman, big as a pony, went crazy and attacked a girl walking her poodle down our street, I saw him run outside with a baseball bat, grab the girl in one arm and then beat the dog to death as it tried to go for his throat. Throughout all of this he never lost the cigarette in the corner of his mouth and only put it out in order to hug the girl and quiet her crying.

Food for the worms, I thought, and took that thought along with a brown paper bag of equipment through the hole in the chain-link fence, into the woods that lay behind the schoolyard. Those woods were deep, and you could travel through them for miles and miles, never coming out from under the trees or seeing a backyard. Richard Antonelli hunted squirrels with a BB gun in them, and Bobby Lenon and his gang went there at night, lit a little fire and drank beer. Once, while exploring, I discovered a rain-sogged *Playboy*; once, a dead fox. Kids said there was gold in the creek that wound among the trees and that there was a far-flung acre that sunk down into a deep valley where the deer went to die. For many years it was rumored that a monkey, escaped from a traveling carnival over in Brightwaters, lived in the treetops.

It was midsummer and the dragonflies buzzed, the squirrels leaped from branch to branch, frightened sparrows darted away. The sun beamed in through gaps in the green above, leaving, here and there, shifting puddles of light on the pine-needle floor. Within one of those patches of light, I practiced creation. There was no clay, so I used an old log for the body. The arms were long, five-fingered branches that I positioned jutting out from the torso. The legs were two large birch saplings with plenty of spring for running and jumping. These I laid angled to the base of the log.

A large hunk of bark that had peeled off an oak was the head. On this I laid red mushroom eyes, curved barnacles of fungus for ears, a dried seedpod for a nose. The mouth was merely a hole I punched through the bark with my penknife. Before affixing the fern hair to the top of the head, I slid beneath the curve of the sheet of bark those things I thought might help to confer life—a dandelion gone to ghostly seed, a cardinal's wing feather, a see-through quartz pebble, a twenty-five-cent compass. The ferns made a striking hairdo, the weeds, with their burrlike ends, formed a venerable beard. I gave him a weapon to hunt with: a long, pointed stick that was my exact height.

When I finished putting my man together, I stood and looked down upon him. He looked good. He looked ready to come to life. I went to the brown paper bag and took out my catechism book. Then kneeling near his right ear, I whispered to him all of the questions Mrs. Grimm would ever ask. When I got to the one, "What is Hell?" his left eye rolled off his face, and I had to put it back. I followed up the last question with a quick promise never to steal a rib.

Putting the book back into the bag, I then retrieved a capped, cleaned-out baby-food jar. It had once held vanilla pudding, my little sister's favorite, but now it was filled with breath. I had asked my father to blow into it. Without asking any questions, he never looked away from the racing form, but took a drag from his cigarette and blew a long, blue-gray stream of air into the jar. I capped it quickly and thanked him. "Don't say I never gave you anything," he mumbled as I ran to my room to look at it beneath a bare light bulb. The spirit swirled within and then slowly became invisible.

I held the jar down to the mouth of my man, and when I couldn't get it any closer, I unscrewed the lid and carefully poured out every atom of breath.

There was nothing to see, so I held it there a long time and let him drink it in. As I pulled the jar away, I heard a breeze blowing through the leaves; felt it on the back of my neck. I stood up quickly and turned around with a keen sense that someone was watching me. I got scared. When the breeze came again, it chilled me, for wrapped in it was the quietest whisper ever. I dropped the jar and ran all the way home.

That night as I lay in bed, the lights out, my mother sitting next to me, stroking my crewcut and softly singing, "Until the Real Thing Comes Along," I remembered that I had left my catechism book in the brown bag next to the body of the man. I immediately made believe I was asleep so that my mother would leave. Had she stayed, she would have eventually felt my guilt through the top of my head. When the bedroom door was closed, I began to toss and turn, thinking of my man lying out there in the dark woods by himself. I promised God that I would go out there in the morning, get my book and take my creation apart. With the first bird song in the dark of the new day, I fell asleep and dreamed I was in Mrs. Grimm's basement with the saints. A beautiful woman saint with a big rose bush thorn sticking right in the middle of her forehead told me, "Your man's name is Cavanaugh."

"Hey, that's the name of the guy who owns the deli in town," I told her.

"Great head cheese at that place," said a saint with a baby lamb under his arm.

Another big bearded saint used the end of a pool cue to cock back his halo. He leaned over me and asked, "Why did God make you?"

I reached for my book but realized I had left it in the woods. "Come on," he said, "that's one of the easiest ones."

I looked away at the bar, stalling for time while I tried to remember the answer, and just then the glass on the sign overflowed and spilled beer onto the floor.

The next day, my man, Cavanaugh, was gone. Not a scrap of him left behind. No sign of the red feather or the clear pebble. This wasn't a case of someone having come along and maliciously scattered him. I searched the entire area. It was a certainty that he had risen up, taken his spear and the brown paper bag containing my religious instruction book and walked off into the heart of the woods.

Standing in the spot where I had given him life, my mind spiraled with visions of him loping along on his birch legs, branch fingers pushing aside sticker bushes and low-hanging leaves, his fern hair slicked back by the wind. Through those red mushroom eyes, he was seeing his first day. I wondered if he was as frightened to be alive as I was to have made him, or had the breath of my father imbued him with a grim food-for-the-worms courage? Either way, there was no dismantling him now—*Thou shalt not kill.* I felt a grave responsibility and went in search of him.

I followed the creek, thinking he would do the same, and traveled deeper and deeper into the woods. What was I going to say to him, I wondered, when I finally found him and his simple hole of a mouth formed a question? It wasn't clear to me why I had made him, but it had something to do with my father's idea of death—a slow rotting underground; a cold dreamless sleep longer than the universe. I passed the place where I had discovered the dead fox and there picked up Cavanaugh's trail—holes poked in the damp ground by the stride of his birch legs. Stopping, I looked all around through the jumbled stickers and bushes, past the trees, and detected no movement but for a single leaf silently falling.

I journeyed beyond the Antonelli brothers' lean-to temple where they hung their squirrel skins to dry and brewed sassafras tea. I even circled the pond, passed the tree whose bark had been stripped in a spiral by lightening and entered territory I had never seen before. Cavanaugh seemed to stay always just ahead of me, out of sight. His snake-hole foot prints, bent and broken branches, and that barely audible and constant whisper on the breeze that trailed in his wake drew me on into the late afternoon until the woods began to slowly fill with night. Then I had a thought of home: my mother cooking dinner and my sister playing on a blanket on the kitchen floor; the Victrola turning out the Ink Spots. I ran back along my path, and somewhere in my flight I heard a loud cry, not bird or animal or human, but like a thick limb splintering free from an ancient oak.

I ignored the woods as best I could for the rest of the summer. There was basketball; games of guns with all the children in the neighborhood, ranging across everyone's backyard; trips to the candy store for comic books; late night horror movies on Chiller Theatre. I caught a demon jab of hell for having lost my religious instruction book, and all of my allowance for four weeks went toward another. Mrs. Grimm told me God knew I had lost it and that it would be a few weeks before she could get me a replacement. I imagined her addressing an envelope to Heaven. In the meantime, I had to look on with Amy Lash. She'd lean close to me, pointing out every word that was read aloud, and when Mrs. Grimm asked me a question, catching me concentrating on the infinite beer, Amy would whisper the answers without moving her lips and save me. Still, no matter what happened, I could not completely forget about Cavanaugh. I thought my feeling of responsibility would have withered as the days swept by, instead it grew like a weed.

On a hot afternoon at the end of July, I was sitting in my secret hideout, a bower formed by forsythia bushes in the corner of my backyard, reading the latest installment of Nick Fury. I only closed my eyes to rest them for a moment, but there was Cavanaugh's rough-barked face. Now that he was alive, leaves had sprouted all over his trunk and limbs. He wore a strand of wild blueberries around where his neck should have been, and his hair ferns had grown and deepened in their shade of green. It wasn't just a daydream, I tell you. I knew that I was seeing him, what he was doing, where he was, at that very minute. He held his spear as a walking stick, and it came to me then that he was, of course, a vegetarian. His long thin legs bowed slightly, his log of a body shifted, as he cocked back his curled, wooden parchment of a head and stared with mushroom eyes into a beam of sunlight slipping through the branches above. Motes of pollen swirled in the light; chipmunks, squirrels, deer silently gathered; sparrows landed for a brief moment to nibble at his hair and then were gone. All around him, the woods looked on in awe as one of its own reckoned the beauty of the sun. What lungs, what vocal chords, gave birth to it, I'm not sure, but he groaned; a sound I had witnessed one other time while watching my father asleep, wrapped in a nightmare.

I visited that spot within the yellow-blossomed forsythias once a day to check up on my man's progress. All that was necessary was that I sit quietly for a time until in a state of near-nap and then close my eyes and fly my brain around the corner, past the school, over the treetops, then down into the cool green shadow of the woods. Many times I saw him just standing, as if stunned by life, and many times traipsing through some unknown quadrant of his Eden. With each viewing came a confused emotion of wonder and dread, like on the beautiful windy day at the beginning of August when I saw him sitting beside the pond, holding the catechism book upside down, a twig finger of one hand pointing to each word on the page, while the other hand covered all but one red eye of his face.

I was there when he came across the blackened patch of earth and scattered beer cans from one of the Lenon gang's nights in the woods. He lifted a partially crushed can with backwash still sloshing in the bottom and drank it down. The bark around his usually indistinct hole of a mouth magically widened into a smile. It was when he uncovered half a pack of Camels and a book of matches that I realized he must have been spying on the revels of Lenon, Chocho, Mike Stone, and Jake Harwood from the safety of the night trees. He lit up and the smoke swirled out the back of his head. In a voice like the creaking of a rotted branch, he pronounced, "Fuck."

And most remarkable of all was the time he came to the edge of the woods, to the hole in the chain-link fence. There, in the playground across the field, he saw Amy Lash gliding up and back on the swing, her red gingham dress billowing, her bright hair full of motion. He trembled as if planted in earthquake earth, and squeaked the way the sparrows did. For a long time, he crouched in that portal to the outside world and watched. Then gathering his courage he stepped onto the field. The instant he was out of the woods, Amy must have felt his presence, and she looked up and saw him approaching. She screamed, jumped off the swing, and ran out of the playground. Cavanaugh, frightened by her scream, retreated to the woods and did not stop running until he reached the tree struck by lightening.

My religious instruction book finally arrived from above, summer ended and school began, but still I went every day to my hideout and watched him for a little while as he fished gold coins from the creek or tracked, from the ground, something moving through the treetops. I know it was close to Halloween, because I sat in my hideout loosening my teeth on one of Mrs. Grimm's candy apples when I realized that my secret seeing place was no longer a secret. The forsythias had long since dropped their flowers. As I sat there in the skeletal blind, I could feel the cold creeping into me. "Winter is coming," I said in a puff of steam and had one fleeting vision of Cavanaugh, his leaves gone flame red, his fern hair drooping brown, discovering the temple of dead squirrels. I saw him gently touch the fur of a stretched-out corpse hung on the wall. His birch legs bent to nearly breaking as he fell to his knees and let out a wail that drilled into me and lived there.

It was late night, a few weeks later, but that cry still echoed through me and I could not sleep. I heard, above the sound of the dreaming house, my father come in from his second job. I don't know what made me think I could tell him, but I had to tell someone. If I kept to myself what I had done any longer, I thought I would have to run away. Crawling out of bed, I crept down the darkened hallway past my sister's room and heard her breathing. I found my father sitting in the dining room, eating a cold dinner and reading the paper by only the light coming through from the kitchen. All he had to do was look up at me and I started crying. Next thing I knew, he had his arm around me and I was enveloped in the familiar aroma of machine oil. I thought he might laugh, I thought he might yell, but I told him everything all at once. What he did was pull out the chair next to his. I sat down, drying my eyes.

"What can we do?" he asked.

"I just need to tell him something," I said.

"Okay," he said. "This Saturday we'll go to the woods and see if we can find him." Then he had me describe Cavanaugh and when I was done he said, "Sounds like a sturdy fellow."

We moved into the living room and sat on the couch in the dark. He lit a cigarette and told me about the woods when he was a boy; how vast they were, how he trapped mink, saw eagles, and how he and his brother lived for a week by their wits alone out in nature. I eventually dozed off and only half woke when he carried me to my bed.

The week passed and I went to sleep Friday night, hoping he wouldn't forget his promise and go to the track instead. But the next morning, he woke me early from a dream of Amy Lash by tapping my shoulder and saying, "Move your laggardly ass." He made bacon and eggs, the only two things he knew how to make, and let me drink coffee. Then we put on our coats and were off. It was the second week in November and the day was cold and overcast. "Brisk," he said as we rounded the corner toward the school and that was all he said until we were well in beneath the trees.

I showed him around the woods like a tour guide, pointing out the creek, the spot where I had created my man, the temple of dead squirrels. "Interesting," he said to each of these, and once in a while mentioned the name of some bush or tree. Waves of leaves blew amidst the trunks in the cold wind and, with stronger gusts, showers of them fell around us. My father could really walk and so we walked for what seemed like ten miles, out of the morning and into the afternoon, way past any place I had ever dreamed of going. We discovered a spot where an enormous tree had fallen, exposing the gnarled brainwork of its roots, and another two acres where there were no trees but only smooth sand hills. All the time I was alert to even the slightest sound—a cracking twig, the caw of a crow—hoping I might hear the whisper.

As it got later, the sky darkened, and what was cold before became colder still.

"Listen, " my father said, "I have a feeling like the one when we used to track deer. He's nearby, somewhere. We'll have to outsmart him."

I nodded.

"I'm going to stay here and wait," he said. "You keep going along the path here for a while but, for Christ's sake, be quiet. Maybe if he sees you, he'll double back to get away, and I'll be here to catch him."

I wasn't sure this plan made sense, but I knew we needed to do something. It was getting late. "Be careful," I said, "he's big and he has a stick."

My father smiled, "Don't worry," he said and lifted his foot to indicate the size ten.

This made me laugh, and I turned and started down the path, taking careful steps. "Go on for about ten minutes or so and see if you see anything," he called to me before I rounded a bend.

Once I was by myself, I wasn't so sure I wanted to find my man. Because of the overcast sky the woods were dark and lonely. As I walked I pictured my father and Cavanaugh wrestling each other and wondered who would win. When I had gone far enough to want to stop and run back, I forced myself around one more turn. Just this little more, I thought. He's probably already fallen apart anyway, dismantled by winter. But then I saw it up ahead, treetops at eye level, and I knew I had found the valley where the deer went to die.

Cautiously, I inched up to the rim, and peered down the steep dirt wall overgrown with roots and stickers, into the trees and the shadowed undergrowth beneath them. The valley was a large hole as if a meteor had struck there long ago. I thought of the treasure-trove of antlers and bones that lay hidden in the leaves at its base. Standing there, staring, I felt I almost understood the secret life and age of the woods. I had to show this to my father, but before I could move away, I saw something, heard something moving below. Squinting to see more clearly through the darkness down there, I could just about make out a shadowed figure half-hidden by the trunk of a tall pine.

"Cavanaugh?" I called. "Is that you?"

In the silence, I heard acorns dropping.

"Are you there?" I asked.

There was a reply, an eerie sound that was part voice, part wind. It was very quiet but I distinctly heard it ask, "Why?"

"Are you okay?" I asked.

"Why?" came the same question.

I didn't know why, and wished I had read him the book's answers instead of the questions the day of his birth. I stood for a long time and watched as snow began to fall around me.

His question came again, weaker this time, and I was on the verge of tears, ashamed of what I had done. Suddenly, I had a strange memory flash of the endless beer in Mrs. Grimm's basement. At least it was something. I leaned out over the edge and, almost certain I was lying, yelled, "I had too much love."

Then, so I could barely make it out, I heard him whisper, "Thank you."

After that, there came from below the thud of branches hitting together, hitting the ground, and I knew he had come undone. When I squinted again, the figure was gone.

I found my father sitting on a fallen tree trunk back along the trail, smoking a cigarette. "Hey," he said when he saw me coming, "did you find anything?"

"No," I said, "let's go home."

He must have seen something in my eyes, because he asked, "Are you sure?"

"I'm sure," I said.

The snow fell during our journey home and seemed to continue falling all winter long.

Now, twenty-one-years married with two crewcut boys of my own, I went back to the old neighborhood last week. The woods and even the school have been obliterated, replaced by new developments with streets named for the things they banished—Crow Lane, Deer Street, Gold Creek Road. My father still lives in the same house by himself. My mother passed away some years back. My baby sister is married with two boys of her own and lives upstate. The old man has something growing on his kidney, and he has lost far too much weight, his once huge arms having shrunk to the width of branches. He sat at the kitchen table, the racing form in front of him. I tried to convince him to quit working, but he shook his head and said, "Boring."

"How long do you think you can keep going to the shop?" I asked him.

"How about until the last second," he said.

"How's the health?" I asked.

"Soon I'll be food for the worms," he said, laughing.

"How do you really feel about that?" I asked.

He shrugged. "All part of the game," he said. "I thought when things got bad enough I would build a coffin and sleep in it. That way, when I die, you can just nail the lid on and bury me in the backyard."

Later, when we were watching the Giants on TV and I had had a few beers, I asked him if he remembered that time in the woods.

He closed his eyes and lit a cigarette as though it would help his memory. "Oh, yeah, I think I remember that," he said.

I had never asked him before. "Was that you down there in those trees?"

He took a drag and slowly turned his head and stared hard, without a smile, directly into my eyes. "I don't know what the hell you're talking about," he said and exhaled a long, blue-gray stream of life.

This story is somewhat about growing up Catholic during the fifties and early sixties. My catechism teacher's name was really Mrs. Grim and that about says it all. She'd dole out the candy apples while laying a rap on you about the agonizing fires of eternal damnation. It was a long time before I ran into anything quite as lurid as the pastel illustrations in that catechism primer. Only when I finally read Bram Stoker's Dracula *did I find something that came close in sensibility. The woods always offered me great comfort against such weirdness, and I spent a lot of time exploring them on my own when I was a boy. I wrote this story for my father who, through the good times and the crappy times, always said "Thank you" to life.*

Out of the Canyon

ALTHOUGH MANY OF MY YOUNGER COLLEAGUES here at *The Gazette* do not feel it necessary to retain a sense of objectivity in their reporting, I still hold to the credo that my job is not to make the news but to relate it to the public. The following story was the first time I had to work hard not to speculate about the facts.

I was sent some years ago to do a piece on the murder of a co-ed at Preston University. It was a very tragic incident, but not one I expected would consume my time the way it has. What began with the body of a young woman, a seemingly straightforward case of unrequited love gone sinister, slowly opened outward like an ever-expanding blossom of infinite petals.

The damn thing has still not stopped growing, for recently I have noticed I am being followed when I go out at night. My phone will ring and there will be no answer, just the sound of one vibrating note. Don't ask me how I know, but I am certain it has to do with the Tooms case. All of this plus what I have already come to learn tells me it is time now to pluck the evil flower in hopes that it will begin to whither before it overtakes me. I present it to you as objectively as possible, and leave it to your own discernment to reach a conclusion as to its importance.

Tooms Canyon is a God-sized thumb gouge in the earth a hundred miles east of the Rockies and twenty-five miles north of the historic Horace/Griffin line. The declivity is steep and treacherous. Nothing grows therein—not a weed. In the midday sun the red rock and powder become like the walls of a furnace, and the rippling of the atmosphere caused by the rising heat has been known to conjure visions of paradise almost too intricate to be a mirage.

In the western wall at the southern entrance to the canyon lie the radioactive sulfur springs which, year after year, draw the weak, the lame, and the terminally ill. Although some well-documented, remarkable cures have taken place at the springs since their healing powers were first discovered in 1860 by Elijah Tooms (visionary and animal-carcass sculptor) the poor accommodations, the harsh sun, have made it one of the best kept secrets among miraculous environments.

When Tooms died in 1930, at the age of ninety, he had just completed a three-hundred-yard boardwalk that ran from the old stage trail to the cave in order to accommodate patients who would find walking in the deep red sand too exhausting. Although its handrails are splintered and some of its planks staved in or missing, it is still very much in existence. It had been patched once in 1945 when the area was made part of a federal preserve and then later in 1968 after the area lost its protected land status and was occupied by a commune of draft-dodgers, ex-prostitutes, and college dropouts from Southern California.

In his day, Tooms frequently took out ads in the newspapers back East and in California to herald the amazing properties of the springs and to announce that the use of them was free, but only five known individuals visited the site in the time that he was its self-proclaimed proprietor. His diary attests to the full recovery of each of the patients. In fact, he, himself, bathed in the springs regularly and attributed his lifelong vigor to this daily ritual.

To this day, standing sentry within the cave of the glowing, yellow-green waters, are those sculptures that Tooms created from the remains of animals he had either discovered dead in the canyon or had shot, himself. The idea of making them came to him after he ingested a certain red-capped mushroom that appears along the upper rim of the canyon following a heavy rain. He was gazing at the sun-bleached skeleton of an armadillo when he envisioned it rising up into a two-legged stance. Instead of its own insignificant head, he saw the skull of a coyote balanced on its negligible neck. Its paws were now bird talons dried like beef jerky by the sun. It said, "Build me" to him, in the voice of the woman who had broken his heart and sent him West in search of his fortune.

Because so many of the cures have, in recent years, been verified and confirmed by scientific research, the religious community came to believe that there must be some part of God swirling in those strange pools. In 1970, Hawaiian pearl divers were hired by the Vatican to explore the depths of the Tooms Canyon Curative Springs. Hundreds of feet deep, at the phosphorescent heart of the magic, they found a book half-buried in the snowdrift sand. When it was brought to the surface, the experts discovered that even the ink had been completely preserved by the inherent chemistry of the waters. It was clear that they had resurrected Elijah Tooms's own diary.

Hardly anyone noticed the story, a mere 150 words, which appeared in the *Horace/Griffin Examiner* of January 1, 1971. It was reported that in an unusual show of generosity, the Vatican bequeathed the diary outright to J. T. Mortenson, the famous neo-Freudian fundamentalist critic. "Le Mort," as he was known by those who feared him in the academic world, immediately took a sabbatical from his teaching duties in order to begin poring over the unusual find.

During that year off, the critic became estranged from his wife of twenty years. Lilian Mortenson was said to have told her friends that the book was the cause of all their problems. She confided that he had become obsessed with it, not just the story, but the actual letters of the words, the ink that formed them, and the paper they were written on, as if some grandiose secret lurked just below the surface of the physical object.

During the divorce proceedings, she stated for the official record that Mortenson had begun to consult ancient texts of magic and could be seen in his study hopping on one foot and reciting things backwards. "The day he drew a big circle on the Persian carpet with chicken grease and sat at its center for eight hours, playing some viciously annoying little instrument, was the last straw," she said. "After that I packed my bag and went to my sister's place." All Mortenson could say in his defense at the deposition was, "Time is of the essence," and with this he lost the Mercedes and house to his wife.

The following year, when Mortenson returned to teaching at Preston University, his colleagues found him a changed man. Whereas Le Mort had always cut a trim, daggerlike figure, as seemingly deadly as his reputation for slashing the works of those who disagreed with his *protosexual sublimation* theory, he was now grossly overweight and perpetually reeking of tobacco. "His eyes were like the openings to deep dark pits," said his department head, Joshua Hyde-Summers. "He was always clutching his briefcase to his chest and darting looks over his shoulder. I found him in the hallway that runs beneath the Fine Arts building one night well after the last class had let out, lying on the floor in an alcove, staring blankly at the ceiling. On another occasion, he nervously confided to me that he was being stalked."

In late October of that year the body of a female student was discovered in that very alcove, lying in a pool of blood. The autopsy confirmed that she had her throat slit by a sharp instrument, most likely a razor. Students reported having seen a tall, thin figure, either with a very large head or wearing a huge hat, lurking in the shadows of the campus at night. This was the center of the investigation for a short time before Mortenson's colleague came forward with new information. Because of the location of the body, Hyde-Summers notified police as to Mortenson's strange behavior. "I went with the officers to find him," said the department head. "I knew he would be heading for his night class just then. We caught up with him as he entered the alley between the Chemistry and Physics towers. The policemen called to him and he ran. They gave chase, but never found him. It was as if he disappeared somewhere between those two structures."

To this day, no one knows for certain what fate befell the enigmatic J. T. Mortenson, but a year after his disappearance, when the university was having his office cleared out, a young scholar by the name of Ned Dyson found photocopies of ten entries from the Tooms diary. Without telling anyone, he removed them from the archive box and took them to his own office and then home after work. That night, he read them to his wife as they got progressively drunk on merlot.

It was Mrs. Dyson's idea to burn the pages one by one over the sink. "Think of it," she had said, and he stood by and laughed, watching Elijah Tooms's words ripple into brown and disappear. The next morning he awoke with a terrible hangover and a recollection of ashes in the sink. He groaned, but his wife told him, "Don't worry, I have it all inside me."

Over the course of the next two years, the young man and his wife conducted hundreds of sessions of automatic writing. She claimed that a spirit named Thilliada would enter her while in the trance state and direct her hand to reproduce the exact words of

Elijah Tooms. Since the penmanship that resulted from these sessions was often nearly illegible, Professor Dyson would immediately take the pages from her and begin to translate them into readable script. What resulted from their work was, supposedly, a complete and true replication of the text of the diary.

Notwithstanding the fact that Meg Dyson was eventually committed to a mental institution for pyromania and for having held long conversations with the crows in her backyard, the diary was believed to be, by the few notable Tooms scholars who were given a brief glimpse of it, an authentic replication of the original work. It revealed the everyday mind of Tooms—the searing heat of the canyon, memories of an unrequited youthful romance in the city, coyotes along the eastern rim at dusk, experiments with the red mushroom, the bone sculptures (or osteomorphetes as Tooms referred to them), the visitors, the cures.

After his wife was committed, Professor Dyson, having felt that the book was in some way responsible for unhinging her, burned the only extent copy in his kitchen sink while drinking two magnum bottles of merlot and ingesting his entire prescription of valium. He lies in a hospital bed now on perpetual life support, wasted to the appearance of one of Tooms's osteomorphetes with but a thin scrim of flesh. His last words to the 911 operator were, "I have done the unspeakable."

Many mysteries swirl about Mortenson and the Tooms diary. In trying to sort them out, I went to visit Meg Dyson one morning at the State Mental Institution in Barkersville. At the time, Mrs. Dyson was sedated, but her mind seemed quite clear. She sat in a chair on the veranda, strapped down with restraints. I introduced myself and asked if she could shed any light on the history of the diary. Over the course of the next two hours, she revealed to me one portion of Tooms's life as she knew it from his writings. At times, she would close her eyes and quote verbatim from the text she had helped to reproduce, at other times she would gibber incomprehensibly. I can only now give you in narrative form what I had obtained from her. The absolute truth must remain a distant, rippling mirage, a feverish heat dream of the canyon.

On a breathlessly cold Sunday night in the month of August 1885, Thilliada Bass, then seventeen and suffering biyearly bouts of lust, which the specialists of the time had deemed hysterical in the extreme and her parish priest had attributed to possession, stepped off the late stage coach and into the starlit desolation at the southern mouth of the canyon. The lights in Elijah's second-story bedroom window guided her. Past giant cactus sentries, thorns and tumbleweed, she found the house the man had built with his own hands. He met her on the porch, holding a lit candle.

Tooms's first impressions of the girl were recorded in his diary:

> It is shocking to see Miss Thilliada without her kerchief. I have never before seen a bald woman. She told me that her hair had fallen out due to the treatments she was subjected to by the therapists back in New York. Still, she is quite attractive and seems a gentle creature. I like that she speaks up and is not afraid of conversation.

For the first week of Miss Bass's stay there were blue skies and cool temperatures. Tooms would escort her each morning to the springs for her treatment. Sometimes the sand would be too much for her, and he would have to carry her part of the way. *She was light in my arms*, he writes, *like a large doll or some baggage stuffed with cotton balls.* When they arrived at the entrance to the cave, he would place her gently on her feet. Then he would walk down farther into the caves where they gave way to unexplored passages and chambers. Once he was out of sight, she would undress and slip into the waters of the springs.

While Thilliada let the chemistry of the pool leech into her trouble spots, Elijah was deep in the earth, sitting cross-legged in a chamber that had long ago been painted by the cave man whose skeletal remains lay in the dust strewn with flower petals thousands of years old. Tooms refers to this place in his diary as the ancient man's grave. The wall paintings depicted the hunting of an upright, horned creature that had left many men dead in its wake. Very lightly etched into the wall holding the scene was a spiral that encompassed the action, the center of which was the left eye of the beast.

She told him on the second day of her stay at the canyon that her mother had paid doctors to concoct her illness so that she could be sent away. It seems her mother was conducting an illicit affair with a very wealthy gentleman and did not want it ruined with Thilliada spying on her every move. "The spring will help that too," Tooms had told her. In the evenings she would cook for him, elegant meals derived from the native flora and fauna: possum and potato stew, crow with lemon glaze. Tooms recorded some of the recipes in his diary.

Thilliada had been with Tooms for a little over a month when he wrote in, as he put it, "a trembling hand," *I have done the unspeakable and there is no turning back.* In a troubled confession, taking up three closely written pages, Tooms revealed that early one Monday morning, he snuck a peek at Thilliada as she slipped, naked, into the spring. *I saw it all, and I ran down into the cave. In my fit of debauchery, I felt license to snatch up the bones of the ancient man and work them over thoroughly.*

In the privacy of a small shack that stood a hundred yards behind the house, Tooms assembled the ancient man's bones, giving him a cow skull and the shins of an ass. He lacquered and drilled and pounded for hours at a time, and Thilliada wanted to know what he was making. "When it's finished," Tooms told her. He confessed in his writings that he must lower his gaze in her company now. After dinner one night, as he was about to take his plate to the sink, he found a note beneath it, on the place mat. *I saw you looking,* it said. He shoved the note in his pocket and left the kitchen.

As the days passed, she never mentioned the note nor gave any sign that there was some secret between them. Instead she spoke at great length about the current theories of a lost continent populated by exotic flying people at the center of the Earth and that the entrance to this land was at the North Pole. "I don't see it," Tooms admitted to her, and she laughed at him for his lack of sophistication. Every day her excitement about seeing his latest sculpture grew, and he admitted how this fired his desire for completion.

Then came the torrential rains. Both Tooms and Thilliada stayed inside for two days for fear of flash floods and mudslides. She read a book about famous castaways, and he sat by the fireplace playing his jaw harp. He recorded on the second night, as lightning and thunder ripped through the canyon, how it was the first time he noticed that Thilliada's scalp had begun to sprout a dark fuzz. The next morning the rains had vanished and so, mysteriously, had his jaw harp.

On the following day, as much as he attested to wanting to spend time working on his pile of bones, he left the house early and went exploring for mushrooms up on the rim of the canyon. It was a quarter of a day's journey, but before he left, he saw Thilliada to the spring. *The harder the rain, the more magnificent the crop,* he wrote. He knew he had to eat the hallucinogen right on the spot or its properties would diminish, so he searched long and hard for the most succulent disk.

He reported that at noon he found a most pleasing specimen

and sat down with his back against a boulder to nibble on it. *Its meat is soft and sweet like chewy confection,* he said of the mushroom. When he was finished, he swallowed half the contents of his canteen and, immediately, brilliant colors shot across the sky. A crow on the other side of the canyon called to him something about the ancient man's bones. Then, from out of thin air, ten feet past the rim, a figure with horns approached him. *It came out of a cloud, playing my jaw harp. The rest was vague, but I remember the creature whispering in my ear, and it sounded like wind in the canyon. Then I nodded in agreement.* With this the entry ended.

Tooms again picked up his pen three days later in order to record the afternoon on which he revealed the sculpture to Thilliada.

> *We stood out behind my work shack beneath an overcast sky. The weather was exceptionally cool for the canyon at that time of day. She wore a loose-blowing dress with a colorful pattern of daisies, and her green eyes appeared lit from within with excitement. The work stood before us draped in an old sheet, and I told Miss Thilliada, "I call it Ogatai—a name the vultures screamed to me when I journeyed along the rim." She clapped her hands like a child.*

The sculpture Tooms referred to is still in existence to this day. It stands alongside the old boardwalk at precisely the halfway point to the springs. The cow skull is tilted back slightly as if it watches the movement of the clouds, and its left hand is thrust out, palm up, proffering payment. The workmen who replaced some of the timbers and planks back in '45 testified to being haunted for many years by the statue's diabolical grin. Some members of the '68 commune recall that the thing was known as "Thief," because occasionally they would wake in the morning and find it draped with their jewelry and holding in its right hand the straight razor that the men passed around for shaving.

Thilliada was so impressed, she threw her arms around Elijah and kissed him. *When she touched me,* he wrote, *I could hear the canyon groan and the lizards leaping out of the water pail next to the well.* She led him back to the house and, as he put it: *We had a feverish assignation on the kitchen floor. Later, in the parlor, she showed me something new.* They eventually fell asleep and Tooms had a nightmare of Ogatai creeping through the darkened house.

She was still sleeping soundly when Tooms woke late in the

night. He got up and immediately dressed. *The moon was in the open window*, he wrote. *It was so cold there was frost.* He went downstairs and got his rifle from over the fireplace. As quietly as possible, he slipped out the front door and headed for the canyon.

> *I trembled, and though it was cold, the sweat ran into my eyes and poured down my back. My very heart was chilled.*
>
> *I came across him exactly where I had been told he would be, standing in the dried-out streambed a hundred feet south of Fat Rock. He was clutching a leather satchel of some kind and wearing a brown suit that shone sickly in the moonlight. A heavy man, not likeable at first glance.*

Upon seeing Tooms, the man called out, "Where are we?"

"The canyon," Tooms told him.

The man spluttered nervously, telling Tooms, "I know this much—it has something to do with the intersection of Fate and Desire."

"Stop talking nonsense," said Tooms as he brought the rifle up to aim.

> *I hesitated, watching him hold his satchel up to protect his head. He called out for his mother. Then I heard one note, the twang of the jaw harp, and with this I fired a bullet into his heart.*

The stranger died immediately. Tooms went to inspect the body, but . . .

> *Before I could lean over to check the wound, Ogatai was there in a starry whirl, holding the corpse over his shoulder. I carried the satchel and we headed for the springs. The osteomorphete creaked horridly along behind me, and I could hear it breathing.*

Tooms and his weird companion deposited the dead man's clothing, his satchel and the book it contained into the springs. Enormous bubbles rose as if the waters were belching. Then they proceeded down into the caves, to the chamber that had held the ancient man's bones. They carefully laid the body out and covered him with the leatherized petals of prehistory. *Out on the desert sand, I watched Ogatai dance in the moonlight*, writes Elijah. *When the morning came, I was alone in bed.*

Thilliada Bass left the canyon a week later on the evening stage. Tooms never recorded his feelings about the departure. All he wrote was, *She left behind for me her book of castaways, and I read it ragged as if it was the Bible.* Two months later, he received a letter from her in which she stated that her mother had forced her into an arranged marriage with a young banker named Reginald Mortenson and that she was due to have a child before the year was out.

This was all I got out of Mrs. Dyson before she again reverted to complete gibberish. I thought I had taxed the poor woman enough for one day, so I called for the attendant to come and take her back to her room. When the young man arrived with a wheelchair, Mrs. Dyson became suddenly lucid again and asked me, "Why do you want to know all of this?"

I told her I was writing an article for a newspaper.

She started to laugh, and said, "If you're smart, when you are done writing it, you'll burn it. Don't give it a chance to keep growing."

I assured her I would consider her suggestion.

"No you won't," she said, and the attendant wheeled her away.

There is one final article of evidence pertaining to this story that might help you decide what it all means. Near the end of his life, after nailing the last plank onto the boardwalk, Tooms stopped writing in his diary because, as he told Thilliada (by then the widow Mortenson) in a letter, the book was stolen. That missive had apparently been folded once by the old woman and hidden away in a copy of Poe's *The Narrative of Arthur Gordon Pym of Nantucket*. A few years ago the edition of Poe and the letter were discovered among the volumes of her grandson's, J. T. Mortenson's, library when his ex-wife sold the entire collection to the archives of Preston University for a tidy sum. The following is an exact transcription of Tooms's only remaining words:

> *Dear Thilliada:*
> *Not a day has gone by that I have not thought of you. Although I resolved long ago not to interfere with your life, things have changed now that death is close at hand. I was awakened from a dream of you and me the other night by the sound of something moving in my house. At first, because of my dream, I hoped it might be you, returning. Then, as I came fully awake,*

I thought it must be a strong wind blowing out of the canyon. As I listened more intently, though, I heard a distinctive creaking like a great wheel of bones endlessly turning and the labored breathing of a creature trapped by Time. The next morning I discovered that my diary had vanished and in its place I found my old jaw harp. Back in the days when your youthful beauty graced the waters of the spring, I gave away everything to love you for a few brief hours. Now I know that what I agreed to set in motion will never end. So, I send these words to you from out of the spiraling canyon, and beg that you protect them from the flames.

Elijah

A story that devours itself about an ancient curse that perpetuates itself in a spiral through time. I always wanted to create osteomorphetes, but here, in suburban South Jersey, the skeletons are insubstantial and usually remain hidden away in closets. My only western story, and as yet, unpublished.

To protect yourself from the curse after reading this piece, make a circle with chicken fat on your best carpet, stand in the middle on one foot and repeatedly chant the first word that comes into your mind until your spouse, significant other, child, or close friend calls the shrink.

The Fantasy Writer's Assistant

WHAT WOULD YOU EXPECT A FANTASY WRITER TO look like? In your mind you see a man with a white Merlin beard and long lithe fingers that spark magic against the keyboard, or perhaps a plump woman with generous breasts and hair so long it spreads about the room, entwining everything like the many-tentacled spell of a witch.

Picture instead Ashmolean, my fantasy writer, the one whose employ I was in for more than a year. Whatever power of enchantment he possessed was buried behind his eyes, because his description lent itself more to thoughts of other genres. Like one of Moreau's creatures, he appeared the result of a genetic experiment run amok—a giant sloth whose DNA had been snipped, tortured together with that of a man's, and then taped and stapled. His stomach was huge; his arms short and hairy; his rear end, in missing the counter weight of the tail, had improvised with a prodigious growth in width. The head was a flesh pumpkin carved with a frown. Vacant, windowlike eyes were rimmed by shadows, and the scalp was as devoid of hair as was Usher's roof of shingles. Even his personality was a conundrum that might have driven Holmes to forsake his beloved cocaine for the crack pipe. The only "fantasy" I noticed was when he sat at his computer. Then he pounded the keys like he was hammering nails into a wooden cross and gazed at the monitor as would the Evil Queen about to utter, "Who is the fairest of them all?"

I came to Ashmolean through an ad in the local newspaper. It said: *Wanted—clerical assistant devoid of interest in literature or ideas.* He told me at the interview that he wanted someone who would not think, but merely to do research. Well, I fit neither of the criteria, but being seventeen and without a college degree, I thought it might be more interesting than selling hamburgers, so I lied and acted as blank as possible. He stopped typing for a moment, which he had been doing continuously through all of his questions, turned, and looked me up and down once. "Welcome to Kreegenvale," he said.

Contrary to my job description, I had been a reader and a thinker. Even back in the lower grades, when the other children in my school would go out to the playground with their balls and bats and field-hockey sticks, I would take a book and sit beneath the oak tree at the far boundary of the field where sounds from the adjacent woods would cancel that riot of competition in which society was desperate to inculcate me. In high school, I suppose I could have been popular. There were boys who wanted me for my long hair and slim figure, but the only climaxes I was interested in were those offered by Cervantes and Dickens. I had a few dates, but the goings-on in bowling alleys and the back seats of cars always seemed inelegant narratives, the endings of which could be predicted from the very first page.

Perhaps things couldn't have gone any differently for me, seeing as I grew up, an only child, in a house where success was measured by the majority vote of the world at large. Both of my parents had been driven to achieve in school, at work, and in their personal tastes. My father, a well-respected contract lawyer, never discussed anything, but when speaking to me always closed his eyes, pulled on his left ear lobe, and held forth on some time-honored strategy for defeating whatever problem I might bring to him. My mother, on the other hand, though a busy CPA, had always professed a desire to be a writer. Her favorite author could have been none other than Nabokov. In the beginning, I read to please them, and then somewhere along the way, I found I couldn't stop.

I read the greats, the near greats, the stylists, the structuralists, and then I read Ashmolean. His works filled and spilled from the bookcases that lined his study. He had written short stories, long stories, novels, and even a poem or two. All of it, every word he had birthed from electrons on that computer screen, had gone toward advancing the career of Glandar, the Sword Wielder of Kreegenvale. Those thousands of pages contained more sword wielding than you could fit in a stadium.

That rugged thug of mountainous muscles, sinews of chain link, and spirit that was the thundering of eight and a half wild horses, had slain dragons, witches, elves, giants, talking apes, and legions of inept, one-dimensional warriors whose purpose of creation was to be mown down like so much summer hay. When Glandar wasn't wielding he was wenching, and occasionally he wenched and then wielded. He was always outnumbered, yet always victorious. No one in the realm rode or drank or satisfied the alluring Sirens of Gwaten Tarn like Glandar, and no one so completely bored me to the brink of narcolepsy.

In comparison with the fiction I was used to reading, my fantasy writer's writing seemed like redundant, cliché-ridden hackwork. Say what you will of Glandar, though, his wielding pleased Ashmolean's readers no end. My fantasy writer was richer than the Pirate King of Ravdish. After his fourth novel, he could have lived comfortably for the rest of his days, existing extravagantly off the interest that Glandar's early adventures had generated. Ashmolean continued on, even though, as one unusually insightful article told, his wife had left him long ago and his children never visited. His house was falling down around him, but still he worked incessantly, pounding on the keys with an urgent necessity as if he were instead administering CPR. It was not like anything new ever happened at Kreegenvale. Sooner or later it was a certainty there would be generous portions of wielding and then Glandar would end the affair with a phrase of warrior wisdom. "One must retain a zest for the battle" was my favorite.

The critics raved about Glandar. "Thank God Ashmolean is alive today," one had said. About *The Ghost Snatcher of Kreegenvale*, the famous reviewer Hutton Myers wrote, "Ashmolean blurs the line separating literature and genre in a tour de force performance that leaves the reader sundered in two with the implications of a world struggling between Good and Evil." His fellow authors blurbed him with vigor, each trying to outdo the other with snippets of praise. I believe it was writer P. N. Smenth who wrote: "I love Glandar more than my own mother."

My part in all of this was to keep Ashmolean from committing inconsistencies in his fantasy world. There was nothing he hated more than to go to a conference and have someone ask him, "How could Stribble Flap the Lewd impregnate the snapping Crone of Deffleton Marsh, in *Glandar Groans for Death*, when Glandar had lopped off the surly gnome's member in *The Unholy Battle of Holiness?*"

Ashmolean would never turn around from his computer, but shout his orders to me over his shoulder. "Mary," he would say, "find out if the horse with no mane has ever been to the Land of Fog." Then I would scramble from the lawn chair in which I sat, book in hand, boning up on the past adventures, and search the shelves for the appropriate volumes that might hold this information. The horse with no mane had been to the Land of Fog on two separate occasions—once while accompanying Glandar's idiot first cousin, Blandar, and the second instance as part of the cavalry of the famous skeleton warrior, Bone Eye.

This process was rather tortuous at first, as I struggled to learn the world of Kreegenvale the way a new cabbie learns the layout of a foreign city. After a time, though, by taking books home to peruse at night and with the speed I had accrued as a well-practiced reader, I had been over almost every inch of the mythical realm and probably knew better than Ashmolean where to get the best roasted shank of yellow flarion in the kingdom or the going price of a shrinking potion.

The one thing I didn't know at all, even after so much time had passed, was Ashmolean himself. He was always brusque with his demands and would offer not so much as a thank you no matter how obscure the tidbit I dredged up for him. When he would rise from his throne at the computer to go to the bathroom (he drank coffee one cup after another), he would pass by me without even a nod. On payday, the second and fourth Monday of every month, my money would be sitting for me in an envelope on the seat of the lawn chair at the back of his office. It was a paltry sum, but when I would try to broach the subject of a raise, he would call out, "Silence, Kreegenvale hangs in the balance." The surreal nature of my employment was what kept me returning, Monday through Saturday, for such a long stretch of time.

When I would leave in the afternoon, I often wondered what Ashmolean did when he wasn't writing. There was no television in his house as far as I could see, and no one except his agent ever called him. He hid from his fans for the most part save when there was a conference, and then I had read that he would not sign books and would not hold conversations once he had stepped down from the podium.

It was a puzzle as to when he shopped or did his laundry or any of the other mundanities that the rest of us take for granted. He seemed somewhat less than human, merely an instrument through which Glandar could let this world know of his exploits. The one clue that he was actually alive in the physical sense was when he would break wind. After each of these long, flabby explosions, which prompted me to begin thinking again of the merits of selling hamburgers, he would stop typing for only a moment to murmur Glandar's famous battle cry, "Death to the unbeliever."

You couldn't find two greater unbelievers than my parents during this time. They wondered why I hadn't raced off to college, what with my excellent grades. "How about a boyfriend?" my mother kept asking me. "It's time, you know," she would say. My father insisted I was wasting my life, and I needed a *real* job, something with benefits. All I could tell them was what I felt. I wasn't quite ready to do any of that, although I was sure someday it would happen. Working for my fantasy writer was the closest I could get to that feeling of sitting at the boundary of the field by myself, away from the riot, and still pretend to be doing something useful.

Then one day, a year and a half into my employment, Ashmolean was hammering the keys in service of his latest work, *Glandar, the Butcher of Malfeasance*, and I was in my lawn chair skimming through a novella entitled, "Dream Fountain of Kreegenvale," which had appeared in the March 1994 issue of *Startling Realms of Illusion*, when the typing abruptly stopped. That sudden silence drew my attention more completely than if he had taken a revolver from his file drawer and fired it at the ceiling. I looked up to see Ashmolean's hands covering his face.

"Oh, my God," I heard him whisper.

"What is it?" I asked.

He spun his chair around and, still wearing that finger mask, said, "I'm blind."

Out of habit, I moved toward the bookshelves, initially thinking some scrap of research would ameliorate his problem. Then the weight of his words struck me, and I could feel myself begin to panic. "Should I call an ambulance?" I asked, taking a step toward him.

"No, no," he said, removing his hands from his face. "I'm blind to Kreegenvale. I can't see what Glandar will do next. The entire world has been obliterated." He stared at me, directly into my eyes for the first time. Through that look I could feel the weight of his fear. All at once, I remembered that I had read that his real name was, of course, not Ashmolean but Leonard Finch.

"Maybe you just need to rest," I said.

He nodded, hunched over in his chair, looking like a lost child in a shopping mall.

"Go home," he said.

"I'll be back tomorrow," I said.

He waved his hands at me as if my words worsened his condition. I wanted to ask him if I would still be paid for the rest of the day, but I didn't have the courage to disturb him.

On the four-block walk back to my parents' house, I had metaphorical visions of Ashmolean as an abandoned mine, a tapped-out beer keg, a coin-operated drivel dispenser long since dropped from the supplier's route. He had plumbed the depths of vapid writing and actually found the mythical bottom. As the day wore on into evening, though, I had a change of heart. I don't know why, but after dinner as I was sitting alone in my room, making poor progress with Camus's "Myth of Sisyphus," I suddenly had a vision of the defeated Leonard Finch still sitting in his office with his hands covering his face. I threw down the weight of Camus and went to tell my mother I was going for a ride.

I went everywhere on my bike, hoping people would think me a health nut instead of realizing the embarrassing fact that I had not yet tested for my driver's license. It was early autumn and the night was cool with a Kreegenvale moon—like the blade of a scimitar—as Ashmolean would have it time and again. I covered the four blocks to his house in minutes, and, as I pulled into his driveway, I noticed that all the lights were out. For the longest time I sat there, trying to decide if I should knock on the door. I think what finally made me get off my bike and go up the steps was that same desire that always drove me onward with any story I was reading. I wanted to find out how it ended.

For all my innate curiosity, I knocked very softly and took a step backward in case, for some reason, I had to run. I waited a few minutes and was about to leave when a light suddenly went on inside. The door slowly pulled back halfway and then Ashmolean's head appeared from behind it.

"Mary," he said and actually smiled. He pulled the door open wider. "Come in."

I was more than a little taken aback by his good humor, unable to remember ever having seen him smile before. Also, in that moment, I realized there was something very different about him. All of that frustrated energy that released itself daily in his punishment of the keyboard now seemed to have vanished, leaving behind a meek doppelgänger of my fantasy writer. I was reminded of his novella "Soul Eaters of the Ocean Cave," and momentarily hesitated before stepping inside.

"One second," he said and left me there in the foyer. I wondered what he had been doing in the dark. He soon returned with a manuscript box in his hands.

"Take two days and read this. On the third day, come to work. I will pay you for the time," he said.

I took the box from him and just stood there not knowing if I was to leave or not. He looked to me as if he needed someone to talk to, but I was mistaken. That vacuous demeanor that had put me off on my arrival now crumbled before my eyes. The redness returned to his face, the arch to his eyebrows. He stooped forward and, with true Ashmolean fury, blurted out, "Go."

I did, quickly. By the time I was on my bike, the lights had again been extinguished inside the house. There was no question in my mind that he was a maniac; what bothered me more was his obsession for creative honesty. He truly could not continue unless he saw for sure in his mind what would happen next in Kreegenvale. This was a practice I had always associated with writers of a different caliber than my fantasy writer. It was with this in mind that I began that night to read *The Butcher of Malfeasance*, and, for the first time, I found I cared about Glandar.

When Ashmolean wrote a novel, it was always a doorstopper, and *Malfeasance* was no exception. It was different in one respect, though. For the first time in any of Glandar's adventures, the hero had begun to show his age. There was a particular passage early on, following the beheading of an onerous dwarf, where he even complained of back pain. Also, while lying with the beautiful Heretica Florita, green woman of the whispering wood, he opted for long conversation before vegetable love. Moments of contemplation, little corkscrew worms of uncertainty, had burrowed into the perfect fruit of wielding and wenching that had been Kreegenvale.

I thought perhaps these changes had come because of the nature of the story. In this adventure, Glandar's enemy was a product of himself. It had been well established way back in *A Flaming Sword in the Nether Region* that the Gods of Good smiled upon Glandar for his heroic deeds. To keep him healthy and able to work their positive will against the forces of evil in the world of men, the Gods would send the blackbird, Kreekaw, to him at night. The bird would snatch Glandar's nightmares from him as he dreamed them, and then fly them to the Astral Grotto where Mank, the celestial blacksmith, would incinerate them in his essential furnace.

In the new novel, Stribble Flap the Lewd seeks revenge for

having had his member lopped off in an earlier book. Taking his bow, he waits outside the palace at Kreegenvale one night and, as the blackbird leaves Glandar's window with a beak full of nightmares, slays it with an arrow to its heart. The bird plummets into Deffleton Marsh, releasing the nightmares, which coalesce in the rancorous bottom mud and form, through a whirling, swirling, glimmering, and shimmering mumbo-jumbo reminiscent of Virginia Woolf, the monster Malfeasance, a twelve-foot giant with an amorphous rippling body and a shaggy head the size of seven horses' rumps set side by side. This horror begins to roam the countryside spreading its ill will. Glandar avoids a confrontation with the giant until he learns that it has killed Heretica Florita and sloppily devoured her green heart.

On the third day I returned to Ashmolean. He was waiting for me in his office, looking again rather pale and meek. I was surprised to find my lawn chair had been moved up next to his writer's throne. He greeted me by name again, and motioned for me to sit beside him.

As I handed him the manuscript box, he asked me if I had read it.

I told him I had.

I thought he would ask me what I thought of it, but I should have known better. Instead, he said, "Did you see it? In your mind, like a movie? Were you there?"

I told him I was there, and I had been. Although the writing was Ashmolean's usual halting, obvious subject/verb, subject/verb style, the whole adventure, right up to the end where the final battle was about to take place, had truly been more vivid than life.

"Please," he said, and then paused for a moment.

Please? I said to myself.

"Just as you would find on the shelves those instances from the history of Kreegenvale I required, now I need you to find something for me in the future of the realm."

I knew what he was asking, but still I shook my head.

"Yes," he said. "You must. There is no one else who knows the saga as well as you. I chose you for this. I have slowly been losing my vision of Kreegenvale for the last two books. I hired you because I knew you were bright. I could see you were a dreamer, a loner. What kind of girl as pretty as you would apply for a stupid job like this? I knew the day would come when I would go completely blind to the story."

"You want me to write the end of the book?" I asked.

"You don't have to write it," he said. "Just tell me what you see. Tell me in as much detail as possible what Glandar does in his final battle with the Malfeasance. Not just how he slays it, but how he moves the sword, how he dodges the monster's acid belches, what kind of oaths he showers upon it."

"How?" I asked.

"Close your eyes," he said.

I did.

"See it here," he said, and I felt his finger touch my forehead between my eyes. "Go back to the adventure. See it step by step. What did they look like? How did they sound? What was the exact shade of green of Heretica's flesh? When you fall into the story, when you are there, follow what they do. Speak it to me, and I will write it down."

"I'll try," I said. At first it was hard to get to the story, because all I could think about was his telling me he knew all along I was bright and why would a pretty girl like me want such a stupid job.

"One must retain a zest for the battle," I heard him whisper, more, it seemed, to himself than to me. Like a shard of glass this phrase made a small tear in my thoughts of me, and the light from Kreegenvale shown through. With great concentration, I widened the hole in the fabric and eventually struggled free into the realm of Glandar.

The beginning of the story played itself out before my eyes like a video on fast forward. I was everywhere I had to be, like an actual subject of the realm, in order to see the key moments of the story speed by. I watched Stribble Flap fire his arrow, saw the dwarf's head roll onto the ground with a gush of blood, and turned away as Heretica reached toward Glandar's loin cloth at the end of their lengthy dialogue. When I looked back, I was standing beside the hero himself. The wind was blowing fiercely, the sky was, of course, cerulean, and we were very near the edge of the cliff that overlooks the ocean.

Glandar held his sword, the mighty Eliminator, in his left hand. In his right, he clutched the octagonal shield, Providence, given to him by his dying father. Sweat glistened on his tan, muscled body. His long black hair was tied back with a vine of Heretica's hair—all that was left of her. Fifty feet away, near the very edge of the cliff stood the Malfeasance, its towering blob of a body birthing faces here and there that called insults to the king of Kreegenvale. The head of the monster was like an enormous clod of earth come to life. Its yellow mane hung down in a tangled greasy mess, stained with blood and spleen. Its mouth opened wide enough to swallow a cow, displaying numerous rows of jagged teeth.

"Smell my bile, the perfume of your own night terrors," it bellowed, licking its lack of lips with a boil-ridden whale tongue.

The Malfeasance released a ball of gas, a miniature violet sun that sailed on the breeze toward Glandar. He lifted his shield and held it up to block the bomb of acid breath. I watched as the noxious blast bubbled the paint that had been the heraldic design of Kreegenvale. Glandar grunted, and fell to his knees.

"I think that burnt the hair in my nose," he whispered from where he knelt on the ground. Then he looked right at me. I saw a glimmer of recognition in his eyes as if he was actually seeing me standing there. He smiled at me and slowly stood up.

"Hold up, Mal," he called to the monster. "She's here."

As the hero walked toward me, I saw other characters from Kreegenvale come out of hiding from behind the rocks and trees that were about fifty yards behind us.

"Somebody give me a drink," called the monster, "I've got to get this taste out of my mouth."

"Everybody take a break," called Glandar over his shoulder. He shoved his sword into the ground and dropped his shield.

"What's happening?" I asked.

"Mary, right?" he asked.

I nodded.

"We've been waiting for you."

The others, all of whom I recognized from other stories, gathered around him. The Malfeasance was now leaning over us, swaying in the wind.

"Hello, darling," the monster said to me, reaching down with an arm that grew from its side for a wineskin from Stribble Flap.

"Mary," said Glandar, "there's not much time. I'll explain. We had Heretica put a spell on Ashmolean a few books back so that he would eventually lose touch with our world. It took a while to work, because he's so powerful. I mean, he's God, if you know what I mean. At first we thought he might just give up on us, but then, when he hired you, we realized what his plan was."

"You mean, to finish the book?" I asked.

"Right," said a woman to my left. I turned and saw the beautiful green face of Heretica Florita.

"I thought you had been devoured?" I said.

The Malfeasance laughed. "We made up a woman out of grass

and sticks and such and I ate that in her place. How could I really eat her?" he asked.

"Don't ask," said Glandar. The assembled characters started laughing and Heretica leaned over to punch the hero in the arm.

"Why are you telling me this?" I asked.

Glandar waved the others away. "Let us have a moment, here," he said. They all took a few steps back, and sat down on the ground. In seconds, what appeared to be flagons of wine and mead were making the rounds. The Malfeasance sipped from its wineskin and let the children use its back as a slide. Every time one of the little ones laughed, so did the creature with a wheezing cough.

Glandar led me away toward the edge of the cliff. When we were out of earshot of the others, he turned to me and said, "It's got to be over, Mary. I can't take any more of this."

"You miss Ashmolean?" I asked.

"No, not at all. I thought you would understand. What I'm telling you is *I* can't go on. If I have to kill one more thing, I don't care if it's a mosquito, I'm going to lose my mind."

"You are unhappy with Ashmolean," I said.

"Some of the others call him Ash-holean. I have more respect for him than that, but I've been with him from the first page. There were times in the beginning where it was all very exhilarating, but now, man, life in Kreegenvale is a tedious thing. There's nothing new here. I know, when every adventure begins, that I'm going to be killing. Imagine waking up every day and knowing you are going to have to kill something or someone, maybe a whole army of men you have no quarrel with."

"But there are other aspects to Kreegenvale than the killing," I reminded him.

"I'm not a drinker. Every time Ashmolean has me quaff flagons, I'm sick as a dog for the next fifty pages. All that wenching too—sickening. You'd think the guy never saw a woman with normal size breasts. All I ever wanted was a few minutes of love, but that's more exotic to the big man than the three-faced cat boy of Ghost City."

"Do you want me to make him write love into the plot?" I asked.

"It's too late for that. I just want to help free the others now. I want an end to it, so that they can go back to the lives they had before I happened to them."

"I used to feel the same way about Kreegenvale when I first started reading about you," I said. "But now, I don't think I've ever read anything that has been so alive to me."

"Ashmolean would be a sham if not for one thing. He truly feels it. That's a miraculous thing. I'm doing this because I want to help him out as much as the others."

"You want me to sacrifice you to the Malfeasance, don't you?" I asked.

He nodded and I could see tears in his eyes. "That's what heroes are for," he said.

"I don't know if I can do that. He probably won't let me," I said.

"He will," said Glandar. "He can't prevent it. You're too powerful."

"Too powerful?" I said.

"Please," said Glandar, and his voice shifted through an odd transformation into Ashmolean's. "Do you see it?" asked my fantasy writer.

I looked to my left and there he sat, fingers poised above the keyboard, ready to start hammering. I turned back to my right and saw Glandar and the Malfeasance in their battle positions by the edge of the cliff.

I could feel the power that Glandar had mentioned welling up inside of me. "Okay," I said, "get ready." My words came forth with an energy of their own, flowing straight up from my solar plexus, colored with vivid description, crackling with metaphor and simile. I spoke without hesitation the battle of Glandar and the Malfeasance, monster born of the hero's own ill thoughts.

The Eliminator flashed in the sunlight, and there was rolling and running and gasping for air. Wounds blossomed, blood ran, bones shattered. Great chunks of the monster's amoebic body flew on the ocean wind. And the invective was brilliant: "May you burn in Mank's essential furnace until the scimitar moon sews your soul to eternity." Acid breath and biting steel, the two fought on and on—now one getting the upper hand, now the other.

To my left, Ashmolean was white hot, typing faster than the computer could announce the words that jumped from me to his fingers. "Death to the unbeliever," he murmured under his labored breath.

In the end, Glandar, so brutally wounded that he was beyond recovery, gave one final suicide charge forward, burying himself in the viscous flesh of the monster, forcing both of them over the edge of the cliff.

Ashmolean cried out, "It can't be!" as I described them falling, yet his fingers continued typing.

"No," he moaned as they hit the rocks hundreds of feet below, but the action on the keyboard never slowed.

He wept as the ocean waves washed over them. After he typed

the final period, he turned away from me to cover his face again with his hands. With that last dot, Kreegenvale went out like a light in my own mind. I pushed back the lawn chair and stood up. Ashmolean's body was heaving, but all of his grief was silent now. Saying nothing, I left the room, left the house, and never went back.

As devastating as the death of Glandar might have been for Ashmolean, it left me with a sense of determination about my own life that even the sword wielder had never exhibited. When thinking what to do next, I remembered Leonard Finch putting his finger on my forehead and saying, "See it here." In rapid succession, I took the job at Burgerama and registered for classes at the local college. I often thought about what I had done to my fantasy writer, but reconciled it by telling myself it was the best for everyone.

Still, memories of Kreegenvale would sometimes blow through my mind, especially when I sat in the literature lectures and the profs would fall into theoretical obscurity. Then I prayed Glandar would kick in the door and start wielding. For the most part, though, I loved learning again. I took a lot of English courses, but I knew I didn't want to teach. As for the job, it was greasy and hot for little pay, and when I'd slide those horse-fat sandwiches across the counter to the eager customers, I'd whisper, "Death to the unbeliever." For all the Gwaten Tarn horrors of Burgerama, I enjoyed getting to know the other workers that were my age.

Things were going very well, and my parents were pleased with my progress, but for me, something was missing. I realized one night that what I wanted was to be a writer. Even to be back in Ashmolean's study, where words breathed life into the impossible, would have sufficed. I bought a notebook and began trying to tell a story, but from some lack of courage or an overabundance of self-criticism, I never got further than the first few lines. "If only Kreekaw would come," I thought, "and snatch this frustration from my troubled sleep."

I was into my second semester of college and succeeding in the time-honored tradition, when one day UPS delivered a package for me at my parents' house. My mother called me, and I came downstairs, rubbing the sleep from my eyes. I had been up late reading Swift's "Battle of the Books" for an exam. She handed me the brown parcel, planted a dry kiss on my cheek, and then left for work.

Opening the mailer, I slipped out the contents—a brand new, fat, hardcover book. A thrill ran through me when I saw that it was a copy of *The Butcher of Malfeasance*. Of course, I dropped the mailer and paged frantically to the end of the novel, to the part I had been responsible for. Five pages from the end, I picked up the narrative where Glandar faces off against the monster by the edge of the cliff. Reading it was an experience I will never forget, for Ashmolean had used my exact words. I ran my fingers over the print on the page and when it didn't brush away, I thought to myself, *I created this.*

I saw the battle take place before my eyes just as I had seen it in Ashmolean's office the day I dictated it to him. The oaths and all were there, perfectly rendered. But when I read to where the ocean washed the fallen bodies out to sea, there was another whole page of writing.

Puzzled, I continued to find that Glandar returns that night to Kreegenvale. Soaking wet, with urchins in his hair and seaweed wrapped around his neck, he steps into a room of mourners. They rejoice, the flagons are passed, and he tells how the elastic body of the Malfeasance saved him from the fall. Although he almost drowned, he managed to fight the current and come ashore three miles down the coast. Then the novel ends on a high note, promising more drinking, wenching, and wielding to come.

"What the hell is this?" I said aloud. A few minutes later, after reinspecting the mailer, I found my answer. In my rush to see my words in print, I had missed the letter from Ashmolean that was addressed to me:

> Dear Mary:
>   I'm sorry, but I had to change your ending a little. Think of all the future royalties I would have lost had I let Glandar die. I'm not ready to kill him off just yet— everyone needs a fantasy. He sends his best and apologizes for his part in the fiction I created for you. I knew from the day I met you that you were smart, that you loved books and ideas. I would have realized that even if I hadn't made a phone call to your school before you even came to the interview. They told me about your place on the edge of the field. I know that place. There are other places you need to go as well. Sometimes an act of destruction can be an act of creation. I felt you needed that to begin your journey. I believe that as your obsessed, blinded, fantasy writer, I was the best character I ever created. What good is the illusion of fiction if it cannot show us a way to become the people we need to be? Glandar says, "Be courageous, squeeze every

ounce out of life, and live with honor." Simple but still not a bad message to sometimes remember in this complex world. I did this because I knew someday you might become a writer, but that you needed a little help. Glad to be of assistance.

Ashmolean

At first I was confused, but I read the letter again and laughed like a believer. I never took my test on Swift that day, but instead went to the kitchen and made a pot of coffee. Then, I returned to my room and over the course of two days, my mother and father calling to me from the other side of the locked door, I wrote this story.

This was the first story I published in The Magazine of Fantasy and Science Fiction—*the realization of a life-long dream. "The Fantasy Writer's Assistant" was nominated for a Nebula Award and is probably my best known story. Gordon Van Gelder, in his concise editorial style, made two pinpoint suggestions that cut directly to the heart of the matter. Incorporating them made all the difference.*

The story is about Fantasy and genre and literature and writing, but for me it is most importantly about two individuals and their relationship, how they help each other. Both the characters of Ashmolean and the narrator, Mary, are in some ways autobiographical and in more ways not. Why is it written in the voice of a young woman? I don't know, it's just the way I saw it, as Ashmolean might say. I think it is important to keep in mind that at the end, Mary does not adopt the older writer's style, but writes her own story in her own way.

Glandar's phrase, "One must retain a zest for the battle," comes directly from my father and is part of his personal philosophy of life.

This story has always been for Bill Watkins, author of "The Beggar in the Livingroom," Centrifugal Rickshaw Dancer, Cosmic Thunder, Going to See the End of the Sky, *and* The Last Deathship Off Antares, *who gave me great encouragement and insight into the writing of Speculative Fiction.*

The Far Oasis

IN THEIR EXQUISITE SELF-CENTEREDNESS OUR ANCEStors believed that they were alone in the universe. At the same time, they had convinced themselves that Earth was the blue apple of God's eye and the sole reason for all of creation. This two-headed fallacy caused humanity both delusions of grandeur and a paranoiac sense of loneliness. Although we eventually achieved the ability of space travel at speeds exceeding that of light and discovered a proliferation of planets along with the near-infinite diversification of species inhabiting them, we could never flee far enough to escape those ingrained disabilities of ego and the angst of isolation but carried them with us like ghostly stowaways to the most remote corners of the universe. The drama caused by the tension between these two psychological conditions born of the same impulse played itself out on a million far-flung stages. As a historian, I can tell you that in studying the history of mankind, this is, though it dons a multitude of disguises, the sole phenomenon one studies. At least a thousand instances come readily to mind, but allow me to apprise you of a single case, and it will be for you like a mirror. One glance and you will be assured that you are not alone in your willful loneliness.

※ ※ ※

The celestial city of Aldebaran had pirouetted through the limitless vacuum for centuries, and its population, whose original purpose was to find a habitable world to colonize, had grown so at home in the star-studded blackness of space that the group mind could not conceive of leaving its clear-domed vessel for the natural atmosphere and sunlight of any planet no matter how blue. The citizens of Aldebaran had done well, not only in maintaining their systems, both mechanical and organic, but also in maintaining their society. To their credit they remembered the concept of love and kept it alive all the long years they aimlessly drifted.

In order to ensure survival it was absolutely necessary that their laws be strict. Those of the original population, who had written the precepts for the city, knew the dangers of allowing chaos to get a foothold in a closed system. Justice on Aldebaran was humane, but it was also swift and given a place of utmost importance. When a citizen too egregiously violated the code, he or she was viewed as a plague virus and banished, with the greatest expediency, to the surface of the closest habitable planet. The citizens viewed this punishment in the same manner that their ancient Earth ancestors did the consignment to Hell.

Somewhere in the fifth century of the history of Aldebaran, a little less than halfway to its annihilation in the maw of a black hole, there lived within the city a man named Honis Sikes. He was just one of a hundred other agricultural workers who tilled the soil that lay between the boundary of the dome and the structural complex that was the city at its center. He was a hard worker, and although he was by nature shy, he was well known for his expertise at a popular strategy game played with corn kernels on a board that carried a labyrinthine design. The name of this entertainment was Maize. In his time away from the fields, he designed boards for this game and recorded some of the more interesting points of strategy from famous games he remembered having played or seen. There were very few players who had ever beaten him, and the lucky ones who did never repeated the feat. In this fact, he enjoyed a modest notoriety all throughout Aldebaran.

Once when he was playing in the city park, a large group of onlookers present, he called for his next opponent and a young woman stepped up to the table. She was carrying a board of her own making, and when she placed it down on the table for all to see, the crowd gasped at the complexity of the design. Sikes smiled at her, for the only thing he wanted more than to be admired for his play at Maize was a real challenge. The game began and right from the very start, the young woman took the lead. Play was heated and corn kernels came and went from the labyrinth so fast that many of the onlookers couldn't follow what was happening. Near the end, when it looked like Sikes was about to lose, he put into effect a secret strategy that rapidly depleted the woman's store and closed down the labyrinth around her. He had trapped her only remaining viable pieces, causing them to (in the parlance of the game) rot.

Sikes knew that he had met a formidable opponent, but it was not until after he was finished playing the game that he noticed how beautiful she was. Her hair was long and light, the color of the beams from the artificial growth lamps that were positioned throughout the fields. Her face was unusual in that it was not as pale as that of the predominance of citizens but still held the tone of some ancient Earth ethnicity. The eyes also were startling in their exotic almond shape and deep green like the fabled wandering star, Karjeet. He quickly packed up his board and pieces and followed her out of the park. On the street that ran past the entrance to the underground generators and gravity replicators, he caught up to her.

"Hello," he called.

She turned, her hair whipping in a bright wave over her left shoulder, and he knew he would never forget the sight of it. As he approached, he felt weak, but held himself together and inquired as to her name.

"Methina," she said.

They exchanged some comments about the game. He told her about his job in the fields, and she said to him that everyone who played Maize knew about him. She volunteered that she was a laborer in the fission plant.

"And can you tell me that strategy you used at the end of the game?" she asked, smiling.

"That is my secret," he said. "It must be initiated in the second move of the game or it will not work. I call it the Winner's Conceit."

They walked on for a time down the street together, conversing, and when they came to the place where their intended paths diverged, Sikes, who had always been very shy with women, very much a loner, set his courage and asked if she would join him on the upcoming holiday when the city governors allowed the gravity replicators to be turned way down and everyone gained, for an hour's time, something akin to the power of flight. To this she agreed, told him where and when to meet her and then turned away, leaving him standing on the corner. It took a few moments for her acceptance to sink in, and when it did, he dropped his board and box of pieces, his kernels scattering everywhere.

On the day of the holiday, they met as agreed upon at the outdoor café in the center of town. Methina wore a long, white dress that billowed around her, and when she leaped and swept through the skies above the city she embodied for Sikes the ancient concept of an angel. It was a custom of good luck that one must jump upward from the smaller buildings to the tallest, Shiva Tower, and from there kick off and ascend to touch the inner apex of the dome. This they each did, encouraged and applauded by the other. Methina and Sikes held hands and performed midair somersaults together. They flew, laughing, arms flapping, like Earth birds above the fields.

After the gravity replicators had been restored to their standard settings and the city lights had been turned down to the merest glow, the two found themselves alone in a clearing of a small thicket of woods, an island of green out in the golden wheat field. They lay on the ground while above, way out past the clear boundary of the dome, a spiraled galaxy turned slowly like a milky pinwheel in a cosmic breeze. Pieces of space debris occasionally collided with the invisible force field surrounding Aldebaran and these shards of creation disintegrated in showers of orange sparks.

The two Maize players had long since lost interest in using their tongues for speech and were now twining them heatedly; their bodies locked in a tight embrace. Off came their clothes. But just at the moment of fruition, Sikes panting like a robot worker suffering a power surge, Methina put her palms against his chest and held him back.

"First, you must give me the secret of the Winner's Conceit," she whispered.

Sikes, who had imagined himself taking the technique smugly to the grave, who had long daydreamed of future generations puzzling over the riddle of the move, spewed forth the strategy with its placement of kernels, its series of moves and when to perform them with each of the basic types of labyrinths. "You must distract the opponent," he grunted, "by letting her take the lead, clouding her mind with the winner's conceit."

"All right," she said and removed her palms, but it was too late. Sikes lurched inelegantly forward once with bad aim, his kernels scattering everywhere.

She dressed quickly and left him there on the ground weeping, for now it had become clear to him that he had squandered the treasure of his secret and never so much as entered the labyrinth.

In the days that followed, Sikes could not return to Maize. The game was finished for him. When he would try to force himself to contemplate strategies he had been assiduously building in his mind for months, they were crowded out by the image of Methina's beauty and the somatic memory of her naked body. He did not know where she lived, but she had told him that she worked at the fission plant. One afternoon he left the fields early without telling his superiors and went to wait for her outside the plant's entrance.

He watched the workers exit, filled with the excitement that he would again see her. But she never materialized. Going down into the plant, he found the office and gave her name, inquiring as to what shift she worked. Since the secretary was a devotee of Maize and was impressed to be speaking with Sikes, she told him that there was no one with that name among the workers. Methina had lied to him. For a moment he felt lost, but then reassured himself with the thought that Aldebaran was an island from which there was no escape.

He began looking for her everywhere in the city, at the café, in the museums, along the shore of the lake. He had forsaken his job in the fields, dodging calls from his superiors. With each passing day, he succumbed more and more to a growing sense of melancholy. He began to believe that she had been merely a figment of his imagination generated by his own loneliness until, one day on the observation deck of Shiva Tower, he ran into Porleman, another aficionado of the game.

"Where have you been, Sikes?" asked the thin, horse-faced man.

"I'm out of the Maize," he said.

"Just in time," said Porleman. "There is a new champion, a woman, who is hacking through the ranks of players with what appears to me to be that famous tactic of yours."

"You've seen her?" asked Sikes.

"She crushed me the other day over at the Provident Club. She's taking on all opponents. No one has been able to stand up to her."

Sikes stood, hidden down an alley, across the street from the Provident Club. He waited patiently for hours until the city lights had been dimmed and the players and fans began to file out and head home to their apartments. Finally, he saw Methina, if indeed that was her real name, exit the club and head down the street. She walked alone through the shadows cast by the buildings. The governors had opted for a windy night and the breeze machines had been set at three-quarter speed. With a stealth born of his desire, he snuck quietly up behind her and grabbed her by the shoulder. She gave a sharp cry and turned quickly, her hair whipping over her left shoulder as it had the day he had met her.

"Sikes," she said, and seemed relieved it was not someone more threatening. "Good to see you again."

"You tricked me," he said. "You stole my move."

She shook her head and laughed softly. "I had my own strategy," she said, "and beat you with it. You were too foolish to see that the game extends beyond the boundaries of the board. I broke no rules."

"I don't care," said Sikes, "have the strategy. What I want is to see you again. I haven't been able to think of anything but you," he said.

"Feel free to think of me," she said, "but I have as little interest in you as I might a single kernel on the twenty-ninth space of a spiral labyrinth riddled with rot."

"What about the holiday?" he asked. "The clearing in the trees?"

"You, Sikes, were a victim of the winner's conceit," she said. "Goodnight." She turned to leave.

He could not let her go and so employed a new intuitive strategy, one devoid of intellect and logic. His only goal was to touch her again. He put his hands around the soft flesh of her throat and held on with all his strength until her arms stopped flailing and she slumped, lifeless, against him. When the city lights were brought up again hours later, the citizens on their way to work found him in the same spot, clutching her to him in a vicelike embrace. The security officers were called out, and the game closed down around him.

Honis Sikes was found guilty and sentenced to banishment. On the day of his sentencing, he begged the magistrate that he simply be executed on Aldebaran and not be sent out into space to some nameless planet. The good man on the bench felt the horror of Sikes's situation and, never having had to banish someone from the city before, had a difficult time refusing him. But in the end, after consulting with the other magistrates, they all concluded that his crime was too heinous and if their ancestors insisted on one thing that would ensure the perpetuation of the celestial city, it was the upholding of the law as it was written.

The probe that was to be Sikes's new island in the void for what would end up being the next four hundred years was not much larger than he was. Inside was a suspended animation chamber called a cocoon, for the process that was used to preserve human life on long space flights was one borrowed from the chrysalis stage of Earth caterpillars. Those insects wrapped themselves in a cocoon and then through their own organic chemistry changed into a liquid state only to be reformed from that mucous later into the guise of a butterfly. Through the use of technology and inorganic chemistry, so too was the case with the body of the traveler in this device. Sikes's bone and muscle, flesh and blood, would again cohere out of the liquid sleep, the only difference being he would not come forth a resplendent winged creature but merely the same old Sikes.

Along with the criminal were stowed a microwave rifle with rechargeable pack, a knife, a handheld fire starter, a single set of clothing, and a heavy coat. There was also a small, six-by-six cube sealed in a bag that when released would draw in the ambient water vapor and grow to become a modest boxlike shelter with a door and a window. The prisoner was allowed to request a personal belonging and Sikes requested his favorite labyrinth board and set of kernels. All of this was done with the understanding that, surely, the outcast had little chance for survival on an alien world. Still, it eased the consciences of the people of Aldebaran and was in keeping with their humane philosophy.

Sikes was stuffed, screaming for the mercy of death, into the cocoon cylinder of his temporary space tomb. In minutes he was deep in the liquid sleep, his physical being sloshing back and forth within as the small vessel was wheeled to the launch pad in the underground of the city. The controls had been set so that the probe would wander through the universe until its sensors, acute spectrographs that used a technique called light dissection, picked up signs of a habitable planet. Then the navigational devices would take over; the single rocket would fire and send him to his new home.

Criminal probe #87659 was shot into the absolute zero of space in the wake of the turning city, a gleaming chrome kernel cast into a game without boundaries. One would think that Sikes's mind might be a complete blank, but no. There was, even in that suspended state, a dim sort of consciousness; a psychedelic inner realm of intermittent ghost life and insect memory, like pieces of a shattered mirror taking wing.

Then Time was a maniac scattering dust, and miles had no

meaning until, suddenly, for what seemed like an eternity, those shards of the shattered mirror flew together like pieces of a puzzle, assembling themselves, and Sikes awoke, reformed from the chemical soup that was himself. The panel of the cocoon slid open, the door of the probe drew back and he beheld his prison. He gasped frantically, trying to recall the process of respiration, and once he did, he screamed from the pain of the sunlight in his eyes. For the first hour on his new world, he lay where he was, dizzy and nauseous. These ill affects soon passed, and though he was weak, he managed to crawl out of the probe and onto the burning sands.

Sikes found the clothes where, four centuries earlier, they had told him they would be. Dressing quickly with shaking hands, he finally got his feet into the heavy boots that protected them somewhat from the searing heat of the red desert. He looked into the sky and saw that the sun was at midday. What he was unsure of was how long a day would be. Scanning the flat terrain, he saw no signs of life, not even the merest scrap of vegetation. His mind was still cloudy from the liquid sleep, but he managed to make a plan. He would retrieve the rifle and knife and shelter cube from the probe, pack the smaller items in the sack they had sent with him, and strike out in one direction. As long as his strength held out he would search, but if he did not find a more inviting landscape in his travels before he became too weak to continue, he would turn the rifle on himself and end his misery.

"Habitable planet, indeed," he said aloud as he struck out due west from the probe. He went only a few yards before remembering the Maize board and pieces, and because of the comfort they provided, being a link to his previous life, returned to fetch them.

Walking on a planet with a yellow sky above him and not the reassuring scoop of the dome was frightening at first. He felt very much as if he had died and gone, a spirit, to another realm as in the religious Earth myths of old. Then he remembered more clearly his reason for being there, and he thought back through the thousands and thousands of miles and hours to Aldebaran and the image of Methina. Now with so much distance from her murder, he wondered what he had been thinking to have done something so unspeakable. The why of things was totally lost to his memory, but try as he might he could not forget the feel of her body and the long, bright wave of her hair.

Sikes journeyed far. His mouth was parched and perspiration rolled off him and evaporated before hitting the sand. He halted, wondering if it was time to use the rifle, and that is when he saw in the heat-rippled distance the definite outline of what he believed to be trees, a wide swath of them sprouting from the unforgiving sand. He made his way toward them, and at first they seemed to be receding as he approached. Eventually, he closed his eyes against the brightness of the day and doggedly continued to put one foot in front of the other. When he stopped to rest some time later, he opened his eyes and beheld before him an enchanted scene like something from a child's picture book of long ago.

He found himself standing on the edge of a forest whose trees were straight, blue-trunked giants topped with silver leaves. A little way in beyond them, he saw a meadow of long violet grass blowing in a wind that seemed only to exist within the boundary of the trees. Rushing forward, he ran in under the canopy of silver leaves and the second he was beneath their shade, he felt the heat in the soles of his boots subside and a breeze against his face. He had not yet thought about what his reason was to survive, but for the first time he had an inkling that it might be possible.

As it was, Sikes did survive, for within the borders of the roughly three-hundred-acre oasis he had stumbled upon there were three good-sized lakes, fruit-bearing trees, and wildlife in all its various and intricate forms. Surrounding his living prison was a vast sea of impassable red desert. This place was just large enough for him to feel comfortable in. Aldebaran had been no more than an island in a forbidding void, and so he was used to a life within definite boundaries. He thought of the oasis as a large Maize board, and as he went through his quiet days there he dreamed of strategies that would allow him to outsmart his crafty opponents, Boredom and Death.

He set up his camp next to one of the lakes. The water-vapor-absorbing structure they had sent with him only partially inflated since the climate of that area was so very dry. Still there was enough room for him to lie down inside and to store his belongings. The water in the lake was not only clean and satisfied his thirst, but it was composed of some other element than hydrogen and oxygen that gave it a sweet flavor.

The first thing that Sikes became aware of was the length of the days and nights. They were not too different from the artificial ones that had been imposed on Aldebaran. The night always seemed a little longer than the day, if that was possible, and there was, with regularity, the hulking presence of a large ringed planet in the southern sky. The star that was the sun of this world burned much whiter and hotter than his childhood learning implant had said Earth's sun had, but it also appeared somewhat farther away.

Sikes surmised that the entire desert must have at one time been a forest, but because of some climate change or erosion the sands had overtaken the flora and dried up rivers and streams. Only in rare places like the oasis, where the water most likely came up from deep in the ground, were there pockets of life, miniatures of how things had once been on a grand scale. He also knew that somewhere on the planet, not farther away than birds would want to migrate, there must have been a different terrain since flocks of different types of small winged creatures infested the trees for a week or two and then were gone.

In addition to the strange life forms of armored insects, large stupid fish with piglike faces he caught with his hands, and chittering little things that were a cross between lizards and chipmunks, there was a species of larger animal with which he shared the residence of the oasis. He was surprised at their number, given the surrounding hostile environment and the long time they must have existed within the boundary of the three hundred acres. They were disconcertingly bipedal, going almost upright with the same basic body form of two arms, two legs, a torso, and head, as humans. They were covered with long hair of various different shades, yet they were not human at all, not even primate.

The flesh of these creatures was soft, almost like plant meat, and they were so lacking in intelligence it seemed to Sikes that even the fish of the lakes were more cognizant. Hairy, walking asparagus was how he thought of them. At night, he heard their calls—the sound of a sickly old woman wheezing. They were, luckily, not aggressive. In fact, Sikes could walk right up to them and blow their brains out with the rifle. He found them an excellent source of sustenance, but found he could not cook them without first removing the head. Once they were dead, their eyes gave the illusion that all had finally become clear to them. Sikes killed them indiscriminately, sometimes for food and sometimes for sport to counteract boredom.

So this then became Sikes's life, the existence of the castaway. He had conceived of all manner of diversions in order to try to retain his sanity. At night he studied the stars, trying to determine in what quadrant of space his planet resided. During the day he hunted, practicing with the rifle so often that his aim was perfection itself. He replaced the kernels of corn from his Maize box with pebbles and played against himself every afternoon before the sun set. With nothing but time on his hands, what amazing strategies he came up with. The least of them made the Winner's Conceit look like the tactic of a dimwitted child. The kernels of corn he planted, in four neat rows and watered consistently every day. On the morning that he first saw the small green sprouts poking through the soil, he felt a sense of accomplishment like none he had experienced in his entire life.

Once he had established his presence in the oasis, he went on half-day journeys of exploration. The landscape of the entire expanse was fairly uniform in its composition. There were groves of the silver-leafed trees, small clearings and meadows of violet grass, and then the three lakes. Only in one spot at the northernmost extent of the oasis were there outcroppings of rock that jutted up from the soil in small hills. There were caves carved by erosion into the faces of these stony eruptions, and it was here where the two-legged creatures—the Geets, as he had come to call them, after the inventor of Maize—lived. On a particularly tedious afternoon, he sat a little way off from their colony and took target practice, drilling young and old alike with blasts from the rifle.

Though the seasons changed, they were but minor ripples in the natural routine of the land. They came every few weeks it seemed, and he could note them by transformations in the leaves of the blue-trunked trees. In one season the silver leaves shone at night, in another they dropped off, in the next the ones that had dropped off disintegrated into a kind of fuzz that blew on the breeze all over the oasis. Then the leaves sprouted and grew again and this cycle continued without fail.

The only other marker of the change in season was that with each permutation of the leaves, the Geets would give birth to a new brood of young. He could not tell if there were male and female Geets, for they all had two womanly breasts, or how they mated, but it was a certainty that, although they were short-lived, they were incredibly prolific. *I may very well utterly deplete the capacity of this rifle before all is said and done,* thought Sikes after putting a neat hole through the head of one a hundred yards away. Soon after this, he noticed that they had begun to flee when they knew he was nearby.

The corn had apparently retained its distant genetic memory of Earth, because it ignored the seasons of the new planet and grew at its own slow speed. Sikes lavished attention on the stalks as if they were his children, and eventually silky-topped ears began to sprout. He looked forward to a meal of orange-eyed pink bird stuffed with corn. Every morning he checked the progress of the precious fruit, and then one day he discovered that some of the ears were missing. He knew immediately, from the footprints in the soil, that the Geets had come at night and stolen from him.

That night he did not go to sleep but kept himself awake by designing in his mind a new Maize board he would carve out with his knife on a section of blue bark. This kept him well awake and so entranced he did not hear the first stirrings in the corn stalks outside his shelter. When the noise finally became clear to him, he grabbed the rifle and crept outside. Up in the sky, the ringed planet lightened the night with its reflected glow. He moved cautiously around the corner of the rows and saw before him a good-sized Geet reaching for a second ear of corn. He brought the rifle up to aim and pressed the wave generator button at the side. The creature heard the subtle click and, startled, turned to look. By then, Sikes had his finger on the trigger, but he did not fire. The Geet clumsily plucked the second ear of corn and lumbered away into the night with it.

Back in the shelter, Sikes lay on the floor, the same scene repeatedly playing in his mind's eye. He saw the Geet turn to look at him, and when it did, its long blonde hair whipped in a wave over its left shoulder just as Methina's had back on Aldebaran a lifetime before. Since he had begun his struggle to survive, he had not allowed himself to think of her once, but now the memory of their night together came flooding back to him. In his mind he again touched the soft skin of her legs and stomach, and his loneliness became a momentary pain in his chest that nearly killed him. It was also in that moment that his most incredible and diabolical strategy of all was born. He would later come to call it the Lover's Conceit.

In the next ten days, Sikes mercilessly murdered all of the Geets he could find whose hair was not the same color as the beams of the growth lights positioned in the fields of Aldebaran. The extent of the killing sickened him, but he would not stop. By the time his rampage was over, there were very few of the Geets left living in the caves at the north of the oasis. To these chosen blonde creatures, he brought all but an armful of the corn he had grown. Although they fled when he arrived with it, he watched from a blind as they later snuck out of the forest and feasted on his offering. When the silver leaves fell from the trees, there were now many more young with hair the color of Methina's. Even the babies with lighter hair, but not the exact shade, he murdered.

The microwave rifle was rarely given a chance to cool down in the seasons that followed. Sikes no longer thought of it as an instrument of death but now as a tool of creation. After the blonde color was achieved, he began to select for a lack of body hair. This process took the equivalent of two full Earth years and many Geet generations, but Sikes was patient and focused. The days passed more quickly now and he was never bored. He had a purpose that, for him, bordered on the religious.

In the years that followed, he selected for nakedness, skin tone, the shape of the eye, weight and height. The Geet populations dwindled as they grew more and more to resemble Methina. He knew he could never hope, in the span of his life, to achieve her intelligence and personality in them, but something had changed in their ability to think for they had become increasingly difficult to hunt. They seemed to know when he was coming, and they abandoned the caves altogether a year or two after he had created a brood whose soft flesh was the color of weak tea. Although he had nearly forgotten Aldebaran, the image of Methina remained crystal clear in his mind, and like a depraved sculptor whose medium was an innocent species, he carefully carved his way toward his concept of perfection.

The silver leaves fell, turned to ghosts and were resurrected so many times that the new blue-barked Maize board, chipped and cracked in half, had twice been replaced. I need not describe at length the horrors Sikes's experiment had visited upon those poor creatures throughout this long age of slaughter, but one day when he was out in the woods searching for their new hiding place, he saw, at a distance, one of the adults of the species. She must have heard him approaching and froze in a crouch. He looked through the telescopic sight of the rifle and nearly lost his breath. There, two hundred yards away stood, for all intents and purposes, Methina. Sikes was an old man now, wrinkled, stoop-shouldered, bald, and bad in the knees, but the sight of her made his passion stir. The only work left to be done was to produce eyes the color green of the fabled wandering star, Karjeet.

He continued to grow corn, and had increased his yearly output by ten times what the first crop had yielded. Besides having been a main staple of his diet, the Geets loved the taste of it more fervently with each altered generation, and he would use it as a lure to draw them into the open. This is what he was doing one day, hiding in a blind behind a fallen tree fifty yards from a pile of corn, when he heard something behind him. He turned quickly only to catch the sight of Methina charging at him. She opened her mouth to display a row of sharp teeth, an item of anatomy he had not before seen in the Geets. Lunging for his rifle, he inadvertently knocked it out of his reach. She lunged for him, pinned him to the ground and sunk her fangs into his shoulder. Even with the pain, having her lying on top of him confused his thinking, mixing desire in equal parts with fear. At the last moment, before she could disengage and go for his neck, he reached for his knife and cut her throat.

As he knelt over the beautiful body he had created, he shook his head, wondering how he had managed to overlook the Geets' increasing aggression. He remembered how, not but a few days earlier, he had witnessed a pack of his special Methinas attack and eat an imperfect one with throwback hair on its face that he had wounded in the arm with a bad shot. So immured had he become to the death of the lesser Geets that at the time it had not struck him as anything worth noting. But now he saw that as they approached perfection, they were becoming more dangerous. He then heard others in the woods around him and fled back to his camp by the southern lake.

The color of Karjeet eluded him, but he continued to try to render it. More incidents of the Methinas' aggression had taken place, but now he kept the rifle perpetually with him and powered on. He hated to have to shoot some perfectly good specimens, whose eye color was now tending toward that of a ripe lime, not perfect but moving in the right direction. As he went about his gruesome work, he began to have more and more memories from his days on Aldebaran.

One night, after playing what he considered to be perhaps the most perfect game of Maize against himself, he fell asleep in the structure and dreamed of flying above the spires of the bottled city with Methina. They stood atop Shiva Tower, and when it was his turn to leap up to touch the inner dome, he did not ascend but halfway. With each subsequent jump he made, he flapped his arms harder and felt within as though he were approaching some kind of total climax. She stood on the observation deck beneath him and yelled louder and louder with each successive thrust that took him closer to his goal. Just as the tip of his finger was about to touch the center of the inner dome, he awoke.

The glow of the ringed planet shone in the one small window above where he slept on the floor. He became immediately aware that he was not alone in the structure. He cleared his eyes and saw the gleam of their hair and the shadowed curves and soft contours of their naked bodies.

"Methina," he said and held out his arms.

As she came toward him, the final move of the Lover's Conceit, she smiled sharply in her myriad forms.

There you have it, one kernel of human history to serve as an example of the whole twisted game. The planet that Sikes had been stranded on is now called Fereshin, and the oasis that held him captive still exists. The Geets are still there and yet more changes have been wrought in them, leading on from the work he had accomplished. There are those who still bare a strong resemblance to Methina, and irony of ironies, their eyes are now the exact green of Karjeet. This development came not directly from Sikes but from their acquired cannibalism of those born differently without their selected beauty. Some chemical in the heart, I believe.

Sikes's unnatural stress on the species moved them to a sharper level of cognizance. The Methinas who became violently ill from the consumption of his flesh now had the wherewithal to remember never to devour another like Sikes again. His looks had become imprinted upon their newly vibrant minds and, in their eating of the ugly others of their species, they avoided those Geets who carried any of his physical traits. Follow the progression of this practice over generations. Now, if you were to travel to Fereshin and the far oasis in the red desert, you would find it predominantly populated with a multitude of Sikeses and Methinas, like a single couple trapped in a labyrinth of mirrors.

The old saw in writing fiction is show it, don't tell it, but there are those writers who tell it and do so to wonderful effect—Borges, Chekhov, Steven Millhauser, sometimes Kipling. This is a story in the "tell it" vein. I was influenced in writing this piece by the book, Ka, a reconfiguration of the stories of the Gods of India, by Roberto Calasso. These amazing myths take all kinds of wild and wacky plot twists without warning. They waste little time on devices that contemporary fiction insists upon to suspend disbelief. The concept at the end of "The Far Oasis" that deals with the radical altering of a species through unnatural selection came to me through an essay in Carl Sagan's collection Cosmos. *In this essay, he tells about a place in the Sea of Japan, where a princess and her Samurai retinue drowned themselves instead of being captured by the enemy. Local crab harvesters, in the ages that followed, sometimes found crabs with a mottling on their shells that somewhat depicted the face of a Samurai and would throw them back in honor of that ancient sacrifice. Now, there exists in those waters a species of crab whose shells carry precise portraits of those noble warriors.*

The Woman Who Counts Her Breath

DOROTHY HIMMELREICH, AS I KNOW HER, HAS A stocky build, generous of bosom and gut, a rear end in the Rubens-meets-gravity line, and rather thin limbs. She wears her hair cut short, a bleached-blonde skullcap that is never quite perfectly combed. All of this is of little consequence, existing merely to frame her face. It is a meaty face, jowly, and thick in the lips. Her nose is short and pushed in a bit. The eyes are deep-set and always on the move, scanning the room to see that everything fits into her expectation of how it all must be. Should she come across, say, a child acting out or a person expressing a complex thought, her top lip curls ever so slightly and her nostrils flare. A slight grin that has nothing to do with merriment is the sure sign that she is about to set things straight. Her overall air is one of constant suspicion, an ever readiness to take offense.

It is well known that Dorothy Himmelreich counts everything. The telephone poles she passes while walking, the steps from the house to the mailbox at the end of the driveway, the spots on a ladybug's back, the number of rings before someone picks up the telephone, the stars in the night sky, her husband's sneezes. When the day is done and she is lying in bed, her eyes closed but not yet asleep, my mother-in-law, Dorothy Himmelreich, counts her breaths. The very experience of life for her is a running tally. Perhaps when it comes time for figuring the total, she wants to make sure she is not being overcharged. She is pathologically cheap, even to the point where I once heard her express joy at the purchase of a garden hose because it was probably the last one she would ever have to buy before she died. Her favorite story to tell is one in which a salesgirl had mistakenly undercharged her for an item.

For one so concerned about money, it would seem logical that she would not be very interested in spending it on unnecessary items, but this is not the case. She will buy anything if it is cheap enough, and she will buy a lot of it, whether it is something she needs or not. Every weekend during spring and summer, she leaves her house early and travels to the local garage sales and flea markets. "I only spent ten dollars for all of this," she will say to her husband while pointing to a box jammed full of rusting gadgets, single dinner plates from discontinued sets, old tools, ash trays (she doesn't smoke), party decorations, shirts from the seventies with gravy stains. In response her husband simply stares in disbelief, his mouth open, thinking of the third stall of the garage, so heaped with possessions that it resembles the proverbial "Dark Side of the Moon." Give the woman some credit, though; at the end of each summer, she has her own garage sale and tries to unload it all for more than she paid for it. Parting with these things causes her little anguish because she knows that the following spring other detritus will be hers again.

Her belief system is a gumbo of stoicism and superstition. If you try to rest while the sun is up, she bangs the pots and pans in the kitchen, slams the door, calls out in a loud voice. Naps are tantamount to public masturbation. If you try to tell her about a supernova recently discovered at the edge of the universe, she will shake her head, squint her eyes, and ask you to show her in writing where you saw such a story. Since you don't have the magazine with you, she simply smiles, self-satisfied. She has told me that she would never want to win the lottery, because that would make her famous and great catastrophes only happen to famous people. Her children have, to a degree, accepted her superstitious system. They recount a story about a young boy in the neighborhood whom she didn't like because he was impolite. When he reached the age of twelve, he climbed a water tower in town and leaped to his death. She told her family back then that she had put a hex on the boy. Now when the story is told in her presence she does not admit to the hex, but in her eyes there are small fires burning and she can't help but laugh.

Her attempts at showing affection are similar to a well-trained soldier breaking down his rifle for inspection. The usual counsel of wise elders, namely, "Don't worry, it'll work out," becomes metamorphosed on her lips to, "You have acted in a ridiculous manner once again." For all of Dorothy's inability to display emotion, my wife did tell me about having seen her cry once. On the hutch in the living room, Dorothy displayed her zoo of crystal animals. They were expensive little knickknacks and, in lieu of having to actually think of a gift, her husband would give her money at each holiday to purchase another. There were dozens of them, arranged in concentric circles around her favorite, a delicate dragonfly, which she had purchased years before with her first paycheck from her first job. Every month she would perform the ritual of dusting each piece with a small chamois cloth the size of four postage stamps. During one of the dustings, the dragonfly slipped from her hand and smashed into slivers against the hardwood floor. Her reaction only lasted a moment, but there were tears in her eyes, and a small, muffled sound of anguish escaped from her mouth. Years later I interrupted her once when she was staring into the empty center of the zoo. Her eyes were unusually vacant and her lips slightly parted.

My mother-in-law's cold nature has had an adverse affect on both her husband and children. The children are all grown now, married, and live on their own, but she keeps all four of them trapped tightly in orbit around her. It is her fuming silence—her never-voiced but obvious disapproval—that works the trick for her. My wife has been in therapy for some time now, trying to figure out how to please her. The eldest son is a live wire of nerves. He can't leave anything alone. If he develops a wart on his foot, he must dig at it with an X-acto blade. My wife's older sister seeks solace in status, and veils the disappointments of the past in catalog silks and designer sunglasses. The baby brother has become a cop who, when confronted with emotional situations, stares silently into the distance. All of them are tight with a dollar. All of them can spot a garage-sale sign while doing sixty on a busy road. She does not approve of their marriage partners or the way they are raising their children. It is hard to tell how much responsibility Dorothy can claim for her husband's dark mood. At one time, he had been creative, an artist who had attained some level of recognition. Now he is a grouch who can barely lift a paintbrush without cursing his very existence. Because of her scorn for naps, he sleeps until noon every day. Then he has lunch and works until after dinner when he begins on the martinis. Each night, he sits in his chair in the den, gazing listlessly at the television while flipping through the forty-six channels, trying to find some soft-core porn that will take him through the night. When you ask him how it's going, his only reply is, "Grim."

In times of crisis, the mind of the woman who counts her breath runs flawlessly, as if filled with the whirring gears of a Swiss watch instead of the usual, easily flustered gray matter. Her solution to most problems is to restore order at any cost and then mete out a swift, harsh punishment to the responsible individual or individuals. There is no such thing as an accident to our subject; even the inherent chaos of normal change has a culprit lurking behind it, more often than not a member of some minority. Occasionally, she feels it necessary to remind even Nature that she will not tolerate any monkey business.

My wife's younger brother told me that one night he discovered a raccoon inside a garbage can and was quick enough to trap it by slamming the lid down tightly and placing a large brick on top. Just then, as if she knew she was needed, Dorothy appeared in her nightgown. Assessing the situation with a look that might have cracked rock, she immediately began barking orders. "Get me a light," she said. "Go to the laundry room and bring me a bottle of Clorox and a bottle of ammonia." When he returned, he found that she had taken a ski pole from her collection of junk in the garage and punctured a hole in the top of the plastic garbage can. For some reason, she was also wearing a black ski glove on the hand she used to grasp the pole. He was ordered to hold the light above and behind her, and was admonished when its beam strayed from the opening she had made. "Ammonia," she said like a surgeon demanding a scalpel. Her son handed it over. The entire bottle was emptied into the hole. The procedure was repeated with the Clorox. In seconds a yellowish-gray mist began emanating from the opening, as if it were a chimney on a winter's night, and, from within the can, he heard the creature's claws scrabbling against the hard plastic. She stood and listened for ten minutes, her nostrils flaring. He could tell she was counting. A little while later all was silent inside the can. She turned to her son and said, as if giving the last few instructions for a recipe, "Get it out of there and beat it with a shovel. Then cut the tail off and bury it."

❖   ❖   ❖

She was born during the depression, an only child. The family was poor and both her parents had to work. Her mother was a seamstress in a sweatshop, and her father a painter of houses. I have seen photographs of them. They are a tall and willowy pair. The mother wore small circular glasses that rested at the end of her nose, and her hair was put up in a bun that, in its tightness, appeared a perfect rock for hurling at a window. The father was lanky with thick wrists, and in every picture wears a look that verges on both horror and puzzlement. The mother's favorite pastime was ironing. As Dorothy has said, "She loved to iron. She could iron all day." Next to drinking beer, her father's favorite hobby was cross-stitch. They lived on the bottom floor of an old two-story house. An Italian family, the Calabrias, lived in the flat above them.

The woman who counts her breath had a lonely childhood. Her parents worked six days a week, leaving home before sunrise and not returning until well into the night. The child would wake to an empty house each day, and at night crawl under the covers with no one there to read her a story or give her courage against the dark. She had her meals with the Calabrias upstairs and, now, willingly states that it was Mrs. Calabria who really raised her. When she was not with this surrogate family for dinner or lunch (breakfast she ate in her own apartment, usually a piece of bread), she spent her days alone. She walked the neighborhood by herself, and her greatest joy was kneeling on the pavement, studying insects. Her favorites were the ants, the way they marched in single file with proper determination, the way they returned for their dead when she would thumb one into oblivion, the way they would band together to remove the pebbles with which she had plugged their holes. Most of the time she sat at home staring out the window, counting off the seconds as Sunday approached, the day her parents did not have to work.

Sundays were days of chores. She would clean the apartment with her mother. Then they would prepare food, put up jam, bake bread. The place was not very big but the tasks continued from sunup to dinner. The times when she felt closest to her mother were when she would be allowed to sit and watch her iron. Three hours in silent communion, the old woman's glasses fogged with steam, shrouding her eyes. On Sundays her father would wake early and go out to the bar to buy beer. He would return late in the afternoon, bringing a pail of suds home with him, and, from then till dinnertime, would sit by the front window drinking and cross-stitching initials on handkerchiefs, making wall hangings that read "A Fat Cupboard, A Lean Will." The plan was that he would sell these creations, but in reality they just kept piling up. Before bed, the child would lift the back of her nightgown and her father would scratch her back, not with his nails but with the rough palps of his calloused fingers. Even today when Dorothy tells about this, her lips clamp together in a grin like a closed vise.

One day, during one of her lonely journeys through town, she discovered an odd looking *something* growing on the branch of an oak sapling. It was shiny brown and looked like a miniature brain. She broke the branch off and brought it home and put it in her room. The seconds leading to Sunday came and went twice, and then one morning she woke to find her room filled with what she thought to be fairies. They were busy everywhere, crossing the expanse of bare wood that was her floor, scaling the curtains, traversing the ceiling, hopping about on the dresser, peeking from her shoes, reconnoitering the topography of her mounded comforter. They were tiny and dark and for much of the time stood on two legs like little men. When she crawled out of bed and her foot touched the floor, they all immediately stopped what they were doing. On closer inspection, she saw that they were baby praying mantises and that the strange little brain had been their nest. She sat down and began to count them, and, in the silence, they grew used to her presence and once again resumed their activity.

That morning she skipped her meager breakfast and began setting up her dollhouse for them. She built forts from blocks and arranged the fleet of little wooden boats, carved by her father, on the lake that was a blue braided rug. By lunchtime, she stood in the midst of a bustling insect city. At night when she would go to bed, they would climb the bedpost and infiltrate the covers. In the mornings she would wake with dozens of tiny red bites all over her body. These little wounds itched and tormented her, but she said nothing to anyone. She never felt alone during this time.

This all lasted till Sunday when her father, preparing to work her back, discovered, through his beer haze, the hundreds of insect bites. The slaughter that followed remains a blank spot in Dorothy's memory. But from the way her usually wide nostrils constrict when telling the story, I can envision her mother painstakingly seeking out each little citizen of the mantis civilization and crushing it with the same patience she displayed when ironing. Here, the record becomes silent and whatever transpired remains locked away in the past.

One Sunday afternoon, while in the middle of ironing, Dorothy's mother removed her spectacles and announced that she was going to have a baby. Instead of imagining a partner with whom she could share the burden of counting, Dorothy saw only a rival for her parents' already limited attention. Before her mother put her glasses back on, she added that Dorothy's bedroom would be needed for the nursery and that her father had gotten permission to build her a room at the back of the house. Her father, who had grown more reticent than usual of late, exhibiting a kind of general confusion in both his daily routine and cross-stitching, began at once on the room extension, working at night and on the weekends. He had always been handy with tools and had done construction before, but this job lacked his usual tenacious perfection. It was impossible to know at the time that he was suffering from the first stages of lead poisoning. The room at the back of the house was finished within a month. It was so poorly made that its walls would sway slightly in the autumn wind, and there were many gaps where the planks were supposed to fit together but, like her father's thoughts, did not. The only substantial aspect to the room was a vault-like door that would need to be kept closed so that the cold could not creep down the hall and affect the expected baby.

The child was promptly moved into the dark, cramped addition so that the nursery could be set up. Lying beneath mountains of covers, her nights were filled with terror. When the wind would blow through small chinks in the walls, it made the sound of someone murmuring. In her mind, the noises became words, and she imagined the voice to be that of the Devil, spewing out a steady string of threats and curses. When she told her parents about this they told her not to be foolish, but when she confided her fears to the Calabrias, a family of devoted Roman Catholics, they nodded silently and made the sign of the cross. When she would go upstairs for lunch and dinner, Dorothy was asked to sit at a separate table from the rest of the family. At night, if she was finally able to sleep, she dreamt that a flood came and washed away her room or that a terrific gust of wind toppled the weak structure, burying her alive. Even though the child had become a nervous wreck, she knew that much of what she feared was only in her mind. But when something began galloping across her bed in the middle of the night, she discovered that her room had become haunted by a flesh-and-blood creature. She would awaken to footfalls on her covered legs and scream, but the wind passing through the sieve that was her room would snatch her cry and carry it away before anyone could hear.

Determined to find out what it was that paid a nightly visit, she forced herself to stay awake. When she felt its presence, she quickly lit a candle. The sudden light revealed an immense black rat sitting at the end of her bed. She thrust the flame toward it and it screeched and dove onto the floor. Only when the rat had invaded the other part of the house, and was seen by her mother, did anyone believe in its existence. By this time she had spent many sleepless nights warding the thing off with the candle. Of course, traps were set. It was on a Sunday that the entire family heard one of the traps snap shut and then the place filled with the rat's agonizing screams. They ran to the kitchen and saw it flopping around in the trap by the garbage can. The rat was so huge and vicious looking that no one knew what to do. They simply stared in disbelief as the rat chewed its own leg off and then fled, running on a bloody stump, into the bathroom. Dorothy's father slammed the bathroom door shut, trapping it inside, while her mother ran upstairs to the Calabrias to fetch Mr. Whitey.

Mr. Whitey was a deaf, long-haired cat as big as a small dog. He had a fierce reputation in the neighborhood for never losing a fight, and was well known for leaping onto the back of a certain German Shepherd, digging his claws in and riding down the block. Mr. Whitey was thrown into the bathroom with the rat and almost instantly a battle ensued. They could tell by the noises that the rat had taken refuge in the big old bathtub that stood atop four porcelain lion paws. The Calabrias made the sign of the cross, Dorothy's mother stared rigidly at the door, and her father forgot more than once what he was doing. Dorothy herself has said that at one point she broke down and began screaming along with the screams of the beasts. In the end, the rat was dead and Mr. Whitey emerged, three-quarters dead himself.

Mr. Whitey died soon after the war in the bathtub and, unfortunately, so did Dorothy's father. The lead poisoning, contracted by working with paint for most of his life, infected his blood and swabbed three layers of enamel on his reasoning. He had grown more and more demented, wandering off jobs and winding up three towns away not knowing how he had gotten there, spilling his beer down the front of him, and cross-stitching thin air instead of his craft. When there was nothing left of him but a shell that walked and mumbled, he stayed home with the child during the day and the job of caring for him was given to her. She fought a hard battle, leaping on the back of death and riding for weeks. In the end, her father died in his chair one night, his skin having turned slightly green from the blood dyscrasia. That spring, her mother, only weeks away from giving birth, lost the baby to a miscarriage. So

Dorothy moved back into the finished nursery that was her old bedroom.

Times were very bad then and existence was always hand-to-mouth. It was at this time, I believe, that her counting continued on past the goal of Sunday, the tally stretching outward indefinitely.

At the time I wrote this story, I was reading Freud. While doing so, I was not overly concerned with whether I believed or disbelieved his theories concerning the workings of the human mind. Freud, for whatever merit (or lack there of) his theories have, is a terrific writer with a real flair for the dramatic and the unexpected. The book Three Case Histories *was one that took hold of my imagination. It offers case histories of "The Wolf Man," "The Rat Man," and "The Psychotic Doctor Schreber." All three of these cases are broken down into the same structure. First, the "problem" is presented (or the individual's mania and how it manifests itself), and then Freud lays out his analysis. The funny thing is that the analysis, in its reasoning, is often more bizarre than the strangeness of the given patient's condition. In "The Woman Who Counts Her Breath," I applied Freud's structure to the investigation of a character's personality. One thing Freud was definitely right about is that there are always mitigating circumstances, powerful forces from our early lives that have made us what we are. To delve into them, to study the* why *of people, often leads to understanding more about their (and our own) humanity.*

At Reparata

EVERYONE REMEMBERS WHERE THEY WERE WHEN they first heard that Queen Josette had died. I was standing in twilight on that cliff known as the Cold Shoulder, fly-fishing for bats. Beneath me, the lights of the palace shone with a soft glow that dissolved decrepitude into beauty, and a breeze was blowing in from the south, carrying with it the remnants of a storm at sea. I had just caught a glimpse of a star, streaking down behind the distant mountains, when there was a tug at my line followed hard by a cry that came, like the shout of the earth, up from the palace. I heard it first in my chest. Words would have failed to convince me of the fact, but that desperate scream told me plainly she was dead.

Josette had been an orphan left at the palace gates by a troupe of wandering actors. She arrived at a point in her life between childhood and maturity, wondrously lithe and athletic with green eyes and her dark hair cut like a boy's. I suspect she had been abandoned in hopes that her beauty and intelligence might work to make her a better life than one found on the road. This was back in the days when Ingess had just begun to build his new court from society's castaways. Upon seeing her, he pronounced she was to be the Lady of the Mirrors, but we all knew that she would some day lose the title to that of Queen. The drama that brought her to this stately affair was ever the court's favorite spectacle and topic of conversation.

Her hair grew long and entangled us all in her charm and innocence. Ingess married her on a cool day in late summer five years after her arrival, and the Overseer of Situations released a thousand butterflies upon the signal of their kiss. We all loved her as a daughter, and the younger ones among us as a mother. She never put on airs or forced the power of her elevated position, understanding better than anyone the equanimity that was the soul of the Palace Reparata. Her kindness was the perfect match for Ingess's comic generosity.

With her passing, His Royal, as he had insisted on being called, came apart like light in a prism. I sat four nights in succession with him in the gardens, smoking my pipe and listening to him weep into sunrise. The quantity of tears drained him of his good looks and left him a haggard wreck, like some old crone, albeit with shining, blonde hair.

"See here, Ingess," I told him but could go no further, the logic of his grief too persuasive.

He'd wave his hand at me and turn his face away.

And so the world he had managed to create with his pirate ancestor's gold, his kingdom, suddenly lost its meaning. Before Josette had succumbed to the poison of a spider bite, Reparata was a place where a wandering beggar might be taken in at any time and made a Court Accountant or Thursday's High Astronomer. Every member of the palace had a title bestowed upon them by His Royal. There was no want at Reparata, and this made it an oasis amidst the sea of disappointment and cruelty that we, each in his or her own way, had found the world to be.

Never before had a royal retinue been comprised of so many lowly worms. The Countess Frouch had been a prostitute known as Yams in the nearby seaside town of Gile. His Royal welcomed her warmly, without judgment, as he did Tendon Durst, a round, bespectacled lunatic who believed beyond a doubt that he was joined at a shared eye with a phantom twin. In a single day's errant wandering, Durst had set out as a confirmed madman and ended the evening at the palace with a room of his own and a title of Philosopher General. We had never before seen someone speak simultaneously from both sides of the mouth, but that night he walked in his sleep and told us twice at once that he would never leave Reparata. We all shared his sentiment.

Even Ringlat the highwayman, hiding from the law, performed

his role of Bishop to the Crown righteously. Our lives were transformed by a position in society and whatever bizarre duties His Royal might dream up at his first encounter with us, standing before him at the palace gates, begging for a heel of bread or the eyes from that morning's marsupial dish. Times were bad everywhere, but Ingess was so wealthy, and Reparata was so far removed from the rest of the world, no one who wandered there and had the courage to ask for something was sent away. We lived long bright days as in a book and then, with a fit of narcolepsy, the reader closed his eyes and fell asleep.

If we ever had intentions of fleecing His Royal, the time of his mourning was the perfect opportunity. Instead, we went about our jobs and titles with even greater dedication, taking turns keeping an eye on our melancholic leader. My full title was High and Mighty of Next Week. Ingess, beneath his eccentric sense of humor, must have known that it was the only position vague enough to tame my impulses. On my own, I, who had never done an honest day's work in my life, created and performed a series of ritual tasks that gave definition to my importance at court. Gathering bats in order to exterminate the garden's mosquitos was only one of them. Another was dusting the items in the palace attic.

On Mondays I would usually spend the mornings making proclamations, and on the Monday following the death of Josette, I proclaimed that we should seek some medical help for His Royal. He had begun to see his young wife's spirit floating everywhere and was trying to do himself in with strong drink, insomnia, and grief.

"I see her next to the Fountain of the Dolphins as we speak, Flam," he said to me one night in the gardens.

I looked over at the fountain and saw nothing, but, still, the frantic aspect of his gaze sent a shiver through me.

It turned out to be the first proclamation of mine that was ever acted upon. I got high and mighty on the subject and didn't wait until the following week. Carrier pigeons were sent out to all the surrounding kingdoms inquiring if there was anyone who could cure the melancholy of loss. A small fortune in gold was offered as the reward. I changed my own title to Conscience of the King and set about to do all in my power to cure Ingess, if not for his own good, then for the good of the state.

While we waited for a reply, His Royal raved and stared, only stopping occasionally to caress the empty air. His mourning reached such a state of hysteria that it made me wonder if it was natural. I had the Regal Ascendiary, Chin Mokes, a five-time convicted forger, take over the task of signing the royal notes of purchase in order to keep the palace running smoothly. A plan was hatched in which one of the women, well-powdered and bewigged, would dress up like Josette and, standing in the shadows of the gardens, tell Ingess to stop grieving. After the Countess Frouch laughed at us in that tone that could wither a forest, though, we saw the emptiness of our scheme.

Two harrowing months of sodden depression slithered by at a snail's pace before word finally came that a man from a distant land, a traveling practitioner of medicine, had recently arrived by ship in Gile. Frouch and I went in search of him, traveling through the night in the royal carriage, driven by none other than Tendon Durst. Though I was wary of the philosopher's sense of direction, his invisible brother was usually trustworthy. We arrived at daybreak by the sea and witnessed the gulls swarming as the fishing boats set out. "Do you think it is a good idea that you came back?" I asked her as we left the carriage.

"It's a test," she said, as she adjusted the position of her tiara atop her spiraling platitudes of hair and stamped out her cigarette. Heels were not the best footwear for the planks and cobblestones of Gile, but she wore them anyway. I thought the mink stole a little much, but who was I to say? To look the Conscience of the King, I wore one of his finer suits, a silk affair with winged collar and matching cape. In addition, I borrowed a large signet ring encrusted with diamonds. We left the Philosopher General in deep meditation and went forth as royalty, past the heap of fish skeletons, toward the boardwalk that led to the tavern.

The tavern keeper had known the countess in her earlier life and was pleased to see her doing so well. We asked if he had beheld the foreign healer and he told us he had.

"A short fellow," he said, "with a long beard. All he wears is a robe and a pair of boots." The tavern keeper laughed. "He comes in every day a little after sunrise and has me make him a drink he taught me called Princess Jang's Tears. It ends with a cloud of froth at the top and a constant green rain falling in a clear sky of gin toward the bottom of the glass. I'd say he knows a thing or two."

I ordered two of them for us, using gold coin as payment. The tavern keeper was ecstatic. We sat by the large front window that looked out across harbor and bay. Neither of us spoke. I was contemplating my transformation over the past years from unwanted vagrant to the executor of a kingdom, and I am sure by the look in Frouch's eyes, she was thinking something similar. The strange drink was bittersweet, cool citrus beneath a cloud of sorrow. Then the doorbell rang and our healer entered.

The tavern keeper introduced us, and the healer bowed so low as to show us his star-shaped bald spot. He told us his name was unimportant but that his reputation was legendary even on the remote Island of the Barking Children.

"You are far flung," the countess said to him, "but can you cure loss?"

"I can cure anything, Countess," was his reply.

"Death?" I asked.

"Death is not a disease," he said.

He agreed to accompany us back to the palace if we would have a drink with him. The tavern keeper created a round of Princess Jang's Tears on the house, and we sat again at the table near the window.

"I feel you have a strong connection to this place, Countess," said the healer.

"You're as sharp as a stick of butter," she said and lit a cigarette.

"Do you regret your days here?" he asked her.

"If I did, I would have to regret life," she said, turning her face to the window. Princess Jang's Tears were not the only ones to fall that morning.

The healer nodded and took his drink in a way that showed me he might have a regret or two himself. My hope was that these disappointments did not stem from the health of his patients.

We rode back to the palace in perfect silence. The healer sat next to Frouch, and I across from them. As the carriage bounced over the poorly maintained road from Gile, I studied the man we had hired. His face, though half-hidden by a gray beard, showed its age yet still shone with a placid vitality. I knew he was smiling, though his lips did not move. On the palms of each of his hands were tattoos of coiled snakes. The robe he wore did not appear to be some form of foreign dress but in all reality a cheap, flannel bathrobe that might be worn by a fisherman's wife. Around his neck hung an amulet on a piece of string—an outlandish fake ruby orbited by glass diamonds set in a star of tin-painted gold. His small burlap sack of belongings squirmed at my feet.

"The young man's grief will consume him if I don't take drastic measures," the healer said to me after he had spent a day studying His Royal. We sat in the dining hall at the western end of that table which was so long and large, we at court called it the island. It was late and most of the palace was asleep. I sipped at coffee and the healer crunched viciously away at a bowl of locust in wild honey that the palace chef, the Exalted Culinarity, Grenis Saint-Geedon, once a famous assassin, had been so kind as to leave his bed to prepare.

"What do you mean?" I asked.

"Do you see what I am doing with this bowl of holy sustenance?" said the healer, a locust leg sticking out of the right corner of his mouth. "It will eat out his soul."

"Will he die?" I asked.

"That's not the worst part of it," said the old man.

"What are these drastic measures?"

"Let me just say, once I have begun, you will wish you hadn't requested I do so," he said.

"Can you cure him?" I asked.

"That," he said, lifting the bowl to lick it, "is a certainty that has roots in the very first instant of creation."

Either this man was an idiot or so great a physician that his method and bearing were informed by some highly advanced foreign culture. His dress and the manner in which he ate did not suggest the latter, but my most recent glimpse of Ingess trudging like a somnambulist along the great hall was enough to convince me that the healer's diagnosis was correct. His Royal had shriveled miserably and was totally despondent. Even that blonde hair was now disintegrating into salt and floating away in his lethargic wake.

I feared the countess would lash me with her laughter when she heard of my decision, but I told the healer right then, as he set his bowl back on the table, "Do what you must."

Then the old man's lips moved into a wide grin to reveal a shattered set of teeth. He lifted the amulet from his chest and kissed the audacious ruby at its center. "You'll live to regret this," he told me.

"I already have," I said.

The next morning I had to address the assembled royalty of the court of Reparata on the subject of Ingess and his treatment. We met in the palace theater, all fifty-two of us. I took the stage, again dressed in the fine clothes of His Royal as a way of adding authority to my words. Miraculously, Frouch spared me as I apprised them of my decision, but the others were very skeptical. How could they not be — they had seen and met the healer.

"He's a fake," Chin Mokes cried out, and this got the others going because who better to know a forgery than the Regal Ascendiary?

"Eats insects," said the Exalted Culinarity, spitting as the stories told he had once done on the foreheads of each of his victims.

The Chancellor of Waste went right for the jugular. "He's no physician, he's Grandfather Mess. He couldn't cure a pain in the ass unless he left the room."

"He is legendary even on the remote Island of the Barking Children," I told them.

"Probably for keeping the sidewalks clean," someone shouted.

All of the jewelry of the assembled members of the court dazzled my eyes, and my head began to swim. Perspiration formed along my brow, and for the first time since coming to Reparata, I had that feeling of abandonment which had haunted my wandering for so many years.

Then the countess stood up and the others instantly quieted down. "You've all had a chance to pass wind. Now its time to get on with the necessity of saving His Royal. Unless one of you has a better plan, we will all follow the healer's advice and see his treatment through."

The Chancellor of Waste opened his mouth wide to speak, but Frouch, without even turning to look at him said, "If you don't want me to laugh at you, you'd better reserve that part of your title that is about to issue from your tongue."

The Chancellor relented and sunk down in his seat as if to duck a derisive giggle.

Before sunrise the next morning, the treatment was begun.

His Royal lay completely naked on a bare table in the palace infirmary, rocking slightly from side to side and muttering all manner of weirdness. Frouch and I were present to represent the court during the medical procedure. Beside the healer, the young lad, Pester, Prince of the Horse Stalls, was in attendance, sitting on a stool in the corner, ever ready to do the physician's bidding. We also called for Durst, the Philosopher General, to see if he could decipher what might be Ingess's last message to us. It was a generally held belief in those days that one madman could easily interpret the ravings of another. The healer was anxious to begin, but we forestalled him, explaining how important a message from Ingess might be to his loyal subjects.

Durst came in dragging the invisible weight of his twin, and performing the impossible feat of discussing two different subjects simultaneously from either side of his mouth.

"My dear Philosopher," said the countess. "You give sanity a bad name."

He bowed as far as his stomach would allow, and then stood and listened with something verging on attention to our request. It was heartwarming to see how proud he was to have been of some use in the crisis. He strode with an official bearing over to the table where Ingess lay and leaned down to listen to the feverish stream of words.

While the Philosopher General was performing his duties, Frouch poked me in the side with her elbow and we both had difficulty holding back our laughter at the sight of him. The healer, witnessing the whole thing, merely shook his head and sighed impatiently.

When Durst finally turned around, we asked him what Ingess was saying.

He looked puzzled and told us, "It all sounds like gibberish to me."

The countess and I broke out laughing.

"But," he continued, holding up his right index finger, "my brother says that His Royal is concerned with a stream running under a bridge."

"Fascinating," said the healer as he ushered Durst out of the infirmary.

Upon his return, the old man lifted his burlap sack onto the table next to Ingess's head. From within it, he retrieved a pair of spectacles whose lenses were long black cylinders capped with metal. He fit the arms of these over His Royal's ears and adjusted the tunnels so that they completely covered the eyes. The moment this strange contraption was in place, Ingess let loose a massive sigh and went completely limp.

"What's this?" I asked.

The healer undid his bathrobe tie, wrapped the flaps around him more completely and retied it securely. "At the ends of those two tunnels there is a picture that appears, because of the way our sight overlaps, to have a third dimension. It is so endlessly fascinating to behold that the viewer thinks of nothing else. Time, pain, regret, are pushed out of the mind by the intricate beauty of the scene."

"What does it show?" asked Frouch.

"I can't explain," said the healer, "it is too complex."

"Why is it necessary?" I asked.

"Because," said the healer, "what I am about to do to your liege would otherwise be so painful that his screams would threaten the sanity of everyone within the confines of the palace." With this, he reached into that bag of his and pulled forth a wriggling green creature the size of a man's index finger.

The countess and I stepped closer to see exactly what he was holding. The creature was a segmented, jade green, centipede-like thing with a lavender head and tiny black horns.

"Sirimon," he said with a foreign inflection in his voice.

"It looks like a caterpillar," said Frouch.

"Yes, it does," said the old man, "but make no mistake, this is Sirimon."

"His Royal's not going to eat that is he?" I asked, swallowing hard the memory of the healer's midnight snack.

"Perish the thought," the healer said, and with great care he brought his hand down to Ingess's left ear. He gave a high, piercing whistle, and the diminutive creature marched forward across his palm and into the opening in His Royal's head.

Frouch laughed at the sight of it in an attempt to control her horror. I turned away feeling as though I would be sick.

"Now we wait," I heard the healer say. He pulled up a chair and sat down.

Somewhere into our fourth hour of silent waiting, the old man jotted down the ingredients to Princess Jang's Tears and gave it to Pester.

"Tell the barkeep not to forget the bitters," he said.

The boy nodded, and before he could leave the room, I called out, "Make that two."

"Just tell him to keep them coming," called Frouch.

Pester returned, carrying a tray with three glasses and the largest pitcher in the palace, which contained a veritable monsoon of liquid sorrow. Frouch lit a cigarette and the healer poured. We made small talk, and, in the course of our conversation, the healer regaled us with a tale of his most recent patient, a man who, through the obsessive reading of religious texts, had become so simple and crude that he had begun to revert back into the form of an ape.

"His wife had to coax him down from the trees each evening with a trail of bananas."

"Did you change his reading habits?" asked the countess.

"No, I shaved his body and then prescribed three moderate taps on the head with a mallet at breakfast, lunch and dinner."

I was about to ask if the poor fellow had come around, but before I could speak, I noticed an irritating, disconcerting little sound that momentarily confused me.

"What is that?" I asked, standing unsteadily.

"Yes, I hear it," said Frouch. "Like the constant crumpling of paper."

"That is Sirimon," said the healer.

I walked over to Ingess and listened. The diminutive noise seemed to be coming from inside his head. Leaning over, I put my ear to his ear. It was with dread that I realized the sound was identical, though quieter being muffled by flesh and skull, to that of the healer working away at his bowl of locust.

"What's the meaning of this?" I yelled.

The old man smiled. "Sirimon is rearranging, creating new pathways, digesting the melancholy."

I had fallen asleep and was wrapped in a nightmare memory of childhood when a hand came out of the shadows and smacked me on the back of the head. Coming to, I rubbed my eyes, and standing before me was the healer holding forth his infernal green worm, now bloated and writhing in its obesity.

"Sirimon has finished," he said.

Frouch was over by the table that held Ingess. Her powdered hair had deflated and now hung to the middle of her back. She stared blankly down at His Royal and was laughing as though she was weeping. The healer's optical contraption was gone and Ingess's eyes were rolled back to show only white. His mouth was stretched wide as if trying to release a scream that was too large to fit through the opening.

"Quickly," said the healer, "to the kitchen."

Just then Pester came in leading a group of men—Chin Mokes, Grenis Saint-Geedon, Ringlat, and Durst. There was a whirl of frantic activity in which we were told to lift His Royal and carry him to the kitchen. Once there, we were instructed to tie him to the huge rotisserie spit on which the Exalted Culinarity would turn whole hogs at feast time. When His Royal was lashed securely to the long metal rod, the healer told Grenis to turn the handle and set it so that the patient's left ear was toward the floor. Then the old man called for Pester to bring a large pot and set it down in the ashes, where the fire usually burned, directly underneath His Royal's ear.

A moment after the boy set the pot down, a dollop of viscous white fluid dripped from His Royal's ear and splattered inside it. The assembled company all took a step back at the sight of this. Then a steady stream of the goo began to fall, like beer from an open tap, filling the pot.

"He said we must let no harm come to this substance, no matter what happens to it," said Frouch, who had just arrived in the kitchen.

"What in the Devil's name is it?" asked Ringlat.

I turned to ask the healer the very same question, but he was no longer in the room.

"Nice work, Flam," said Chin Mokes, "you've turned the king into a flagon of goo."

"Where is that physician?" said Grenis Saint-Geedon, pulling a butcher knife from his rack. He left the room with a murderous look on his face.

Over the course of the next two hours, the pot filled nearly to the brim, and the healer was searched for everywhere but never found. At daybreak, Ingess opened his eyes and yawned.

The Palace Reparata rejoiced at the fact that His Royal had been returned to full health. It had been necessary to help him see to his needs for a week or so, but as soon as this period of convalescence had passed, he was up on his feet and performing his royal duties. Much of the hair he had lost had already begun to grow back, and he regained nearly all of his muscular vitality. The deep melancholy, though gone, had taken some small part of him with it, for now, in his face, there was a series of subtle lines that made him look more mature. No longer did he weep for hours on end. In fact, I did not witness one tear after the ordeal. Neither did he laugh, though, and this small formality was like a troublesome pebble in my shoe.

I went one night to the gardens to release the bats and found him, sitting on the bench across from the Fountain of the Dolphins, staring up at the moon.

"Durst gave a lecture today on the nature of the universe. His belief is that it began with a giant explosion," I said and laughed too hard, trying to get him to join me.

Ingess merely shook his head. "Poor Durst," he said. "I never told you but I had sent for some word about him to the asylum that he wandered away from. It seems he had a twin brother who drowned when he was ten. He might have saved him but he was too afraid of the water."

"His Royal," I said, exasperated with his response, "why do you stare at the moon?"

"Don't call me that anymore, Flam. I'm not a king. Just a pirate's grandson who was left far too much gold."

"As you wish," I said.

He turned then and forced a smile for me. "I want you to have Saint-Geedon prepare a feast. I need to thank everyone for their efforts to save my life."

I nodded and left him.

Later that night, I sought out Frouch and found her on the terrace that overlooks the reflecting pond. She was sitting in the shadow of a potted mimosa, feeding breadcrumbs to the peacocks.

I pulled up a chair and told her about the feast that would be held in another two days. She brightened at the prospect of this.

"I have a gown I've been waiting to wear," she said.

"How do you feel now that everything is back to normal?" I asked.

"You were brilliant as the Conscience of the King," she said.

"I'd rather put that entire affair behind me," I said. "But there is one thing that I still wonder about."

"The picture at the end of the healer's strange spectacles?" she said.

I shook my head, "What became of that muddle that dripped from Ingess's ear?"

She clapped her hands to send the birds scurrying away and sat forward. "You mean you haven't seen it?" she asked.

"No."

"Come now," she said and stood. "You've got to see this."

She actually took my hand as we walked through hallways, and it made me somewhat nervous to find myself behind the protective field of her dangerous laughter.

We ended our journey in the small chapel at the northern end of the palace. The Ministress of Sleep, old Mrs. Kofnep, was just lighting a last votive candle as we entered. Beyond her, resting on the altar atop a satin pillow of considerable size was a huge ball with fine white hair growing all over it.

"There it is," said Frouch.

"That thing?" I asked, pointing.

Mrs. Kofnep greeted us and then turned her own gaze on the strange object. "I haven't decided if it's an egg or a testicle or a replica of the world," she said with a self-mocking smile.

"It took that form of a perfect sphere the day after it came from His Royal's head," said the countess.

"The white hair wasn't there two nights ago," said Mrs. Kofnep.

"I had it moved here to protect it," said Frouch.

We stared at it for some time, and then the Ministress of Sleep left us with the usual complaint about her insomnia.

The next day I was busy with preparations for the feast, but before turning in, I went back to the chapel to have another look at the oddity. Changes had obviously taken place, for now it was stretched out and tapered at either end with a large bulge in the middle. The white hair had grown profusely, and wrapped itself around to swaddle whatever was there gently undulating at its core.

The feast was held in the grand ballroom and the Exalted Culinarity had outdone himself with the exotic nature of the dishes served. Crow-liver pâté on paper-thin slices of candied amber was the appetizer. For the main course there was fowl, hog, beef, and even crocodile done up with fruit and vegetables to appear like tropical islands floating in calm seas of gravy. On each table was placed a punch bowl of Princess Jang's Tears, the drink that had of late become all the rage at Reparata.

Ringlat gave a benediction in which he likened the loss of Josette to highway robbery and our combined efforts to revive Ingess as the true power of the Law. With the exception of Mrs. Kofnep, none of us was overly religious. I looked around as Ringlat finished to see bowed heads and all manner of halfhearted religiously symbolic hand gesturing. When Durst took the podium, I was relived, knowing his drivel would cast out the seriousness of the Bishop's sermon. He did not disappoint. His gift to Ingess, as he put it, was the discovery of the meaning of Time. To represent his tangled ball of musings in a nutshell, he surmised from one side of his mouth that Time existed to make eternity pass more quickly, and from the other side that it served to make it pass more slowly. We gave him a standing ovation and then started drinking.

Through the entire gala, His Royal sat on the dais, neither eating nor drinking, but nodding with a mechanical smile to one and all. By my third serving of the Tears, I forgot about my concern for him and stepped out on the dance floor with the countess. For that evening, she had applied a false beauty mark to her upper lip, and I found it remarkably alluring. At some point in her life, she had been beautiful, and on that evening, dressed in a cream-colored gown, her hair done up in two conical horns and decorated with mimosa blossoms, she approached her former radiance like a clock frozen at only a minute to midnight.

"Flam, your dancing leads me to believe I will have to guide you to your room later with a trail of bananas," she said and whisper-giggled into my left ear. The sound of that laughter did not frighten me, but instead made my head spin as though it were Sirimon opening a new pathway to that portion of the brain that houses desire.

Chin Mokes walked on his hands. Pester spun like a dervish. The Illustrious Shepherd of Dust sang an aria about the unrequited love of a giant. The Majestic Seventh did impressions of farm animals until she passed out beneath the table which held the island of roasted hog. The ballroom was a swirling storm of good will and high spirits while at its center sat Ingess as though asleep with his eyes open. Not once did his smile disappear, not once did he miss a chance to shake hands or give a thank-you kiss, not once did he laugh.

Then, sometime well after the dessert of chocolate balloons, there was a shrill cry of distress and the room went absolutely silent. I looked up from my drink to see what had hushed the crowd and saw the Ministress of Sleep, Mrs. Kofnep, standing just inside the northern entrance to the ballroom, working madly to catch her breath.

"Come quickly," she cried, "something is happening in the chapel." She turned and left in great haste and we all followed.

The small chapel was just large enough to accommodate all of us as long as Pester sat atop Durst's shoulders. We crowded in, panting and perspiring from our dash through the Hall of Light and Shadow, across the rotunda of the Royal Museum, and then down the steps just past the observatory. Upon the altar, the white entity, which I now knew to be a cocoon, rippled wildly, rocking and emitting sharp cries high and thin enough to pass through the eye of a needle.

There was an awed silence among the members of the court, and only Ingess had the wherewithal to draw his long dagger in case the expectant birth came forth a terror. People clutched each other as the white fabric of the thing began to tear with a sound like a fat man splitting his trousers. Ingess audibly groaned and his dagger clanked to the floor as the thing began to unfurl itself. An explosion of fine white powder was released at the moment of birth and then immediately blown away by some phantom breeze. When that cleared, I saw it above the altar, hovering in the air, a huge, diaphanous moth with wings as big as bed sheets. It looked only a hair more substantial than a ghost, glimmering in the light from the flickering votives.

The crowd became a chorus and voiced a gasp and then a sigh as the thing flapped its huge wings and flew above our heads toward the entrance. Pester, his face a mask of wonder, reached up toward it from where he sat on Durst's shoulders. His index finger ran along its underside as it passed into the hallway, and then his finger, like a flame going out, disappeared from his hand. The boy's mask of wonder became one of horror and he screamed. We meant to help him but by then the powder that had fallen from the moth reached our eyes. It caused in me a feeling of sorrow more deep than the one I experienced upon my mother's death when I was five. The entire court was reduced to tears. Only Ingess had not been affected. I saw him retrieve his dagger from the floor with the same stoic look he had worn at the feast.

When the effects of the moth's powder had worn off, we gathered round Pester to inspect his hand.

"There was no pain," he said. "Only inside, a sadness."

Some touched the spot where the digit had been, still unable to believe it was gone. Ringlat, knowing that as the bishop he should do something profound at this point but having no clue as to what, took the boy's hand in his and kissed the nub. Mokes actually turned to Tendon Durst for an explanation, and the Philosopher General mumbled something about insect fear and the ringed planet. Chin nodded as if he understood. The strange powder that had fallen now covered Frouch's beauty mark and somewhat disintegrated her power of enchantment. All jabbered like magpies, and the one thing that was finally decided upon was that strong drink was required. Before we left the chapel, Ingess apologized to us, especially Pester, since it had been his royal mind that had been responsible for the moth.

The evening ended with everyone, including the king, drinking themselves into oblivion. We wondered where the creature had wafted off to, but no one wanted to go in search of it. Sometime near daybreak, I and the others trudged like the walking dead to our sleeping chambers to feast on bad dreams. My last thought as I dozed off was of Frouch and her fleeting beauty.

Three days passed without a sign of the moth, and the court began to breathe easier, thinking that it was now time to put aside the tragic saga of Josette's death. I know that Ingess was approached by Saint-Geedon and some of the others about perhaps starting a project that might recapture the old spirit of Reparata, but His Royal very kindly put them off with promises that he would consider the suggestions.

On the night of the third day, while sitting in the garden with my cage of bats, I spotted the moth. It lifted slowly up like a dispossessed thought of ingenious proportion from behind a row of hedges, causing me to drop my pipe into my lap. I considered running, but its fluid grace as it moved along the wall of green hypnotized me. When I finally adjusted to the shock of its arrival, I noticed that same sound Sirimon had made when cavorting in

Ingess's head. In less than a minute it had left a good span of hedge completely devoid of vegetation. Only a mere skeleton of branches remained. I nervously lifted the latch on the bat cage, thinking that their presence might frighten it away. As always they swarmed frantically out and around the garden, but none of them would dare go near the moth. Before I moved from my seat, I saw it consume an entire rose bush, a veritable mile of trailing vine, all of Josette's tiger lilies, and the foliage of an immense weeping willow.

The next morning, the moth having disappeared again, the court gathered in the garden, or I should say where the garden had been. Its destruction was so complete that I could count on my hands the number of leaves still clinging to their branches. There was a certain sadness about the destruction of that special place, but for the time being it was blanketed by a stronger sense of amazement at the enormity of the thing's appetite and its efficiency in satisfying it.

"Do we have a large net?" asked the Chancellor of Waste.

"Why, do you want to be the one to wrestle with it?" asked Pester, holding up his hand for all to see.

"It must be destroyed," said Ringlat, "it's far too dangerous."

"But it is beautiful," said the Illustrious Seventh.

"The garden was beautiful," countered the bishop. "This thing is evil."

Ingess stepped into the middle of the crowd and turned to look at each of us. "The moth is not to be harmed," he said.

"But it is not righteous," said Ringlat.

"The moth is not to be harmed on pain of death," said Ingess without anger and then turned and strode away toward the palace.

The members of the court said nothing, but each looked at his or her shoes like scolded children. A death threat from Ingess was like an arrow through the heart of Reparata. In that moment, we felt its spirit dissolve.

"Death?" said Chin Mokes when His Royal was out of earshot. He shook his head sadly. The others did the same as they wandered aimlessly away from the missing garden.

I called to Frouch to wait up for me, but to my surprise she turned and continued on toward the palace.

As we soon learned, the garden was only the beginning. On the next evening the ethereal glutton invaded the closets of the southern wing and, moving from room to room, devoured all of the linens and finery of those who resided there. All that remained by way of clothing was the outfits those court members had arrived at Reparata in, which had long ago been stored away in trunks. The next day I met the Chancellor of Waste at breakfast, and he was wearing the clown outfit that, in his previous life, had been his uniform. The shoes were enormous, the tie too short, the jacket striped and the pants checkered. In a loud voice, he desperately tried to explain and his embarrassment was contagious. It was a disarming sight to see half the royalty of court traipsing about in threadbare attire.

Ingess assigned the royal accountant to bring gold so that new fashions could be sent for immediately, but when the doors of the counting house were opened, allowing the sunlight access, the moth was startled into flight and brushed past the accountant. When he was finally able to clear his eyes of the insect's powder and his mind of its resultant depression, he discovered that the creature had a taste for more than just leaves and clothing. A good half of that immense trove of gold was gone.

All were skeptical of the story the accountant told, suspecting him of theft, since he had actually been a pickpocket earlier in his life. A few nights later, though, when the moth returned, more than one witnessed its consumption of jewelry, and Saint-Geedon vouched that it had, in minutes, done away with every place setting of the royal silverware. Ingess had even lost his crown to it, but still, in the face of strident requests that it be exterminated, he refused to relent on his command that it not be harmed.

I went to visit Frouch in her rooms the morning after it dined in our quadrant of the palace. My own wardrobe had vanished through the night along with just about everything else I owned. When I knocked on the countess's door I was wearing my old jacket missing an arm and the trousers I had wandered a thousand miles in, whose gaping knee holes made the bottom half of each leg almost superfluous. Putting these things on again was very difficult, and for a moment I considered simply going about in my bathrobe as the healer had.

There was no answer from the countess, and I was about to leave when I heard something from beyond the door that I at first mistook for the sound of Sirimon. I listened more closely and it came to me that it was Frouch, weeping. In a moment of madness, I opened the door and entered anyway.

"Countess," I called.

"Go away, Flam," she said.

"What's wrong?" I asked, though I already had a good idea.

"Don't come in here," she said, but I had to make sure she was all right.

She stood in the middle of her room, wearing the short, revealing dress she had worn ten years earlier when walking the streets of Gile. Her hair was down and unpowdered to show its true mousey brown and gray.

"The dream is finished, Flam," she said, looking up at me with a face that showed every hard moment she had ever lived.

I wanted to comfort her, but I did not know how.

"Countess," I said, and took a step forward.

"Countess," she said, and laughed in a way that drilled my heart more thoroughly than Sirimon could have.

"Come walk with me," I said. "Let's get some air."

"Get away from me," she said.

Her response angered me greatly. I left her there and went to walk the corridors, talking to myself as if I were Durst. Passing the large oval mirror outside of the library, I caught a glimpse of a fool, jawing away, dressed in my old rags, his hair undone and wild. I knew now what I had looked like years earlier to the inhabitants of those towns I had visited and been evicted from. I needed to get a hold on reality, and so decided to go to the palace attic and do some dusting. I trudged up the long flight of steps, assuring myself that work was the cure for my woes.

I threw back the door of that hidden sanctuary, and saw instantly that the moth had visited. The creature had cleaned the place out completely, leaving not one candelabrum, not the slightest feather from the eagle decoration that had been made for the holidays five years earlier. All of the old objects I had so scrupulously cared for over the years were gone.

"No," I said, and the word echoed out to the far reaches of the empty expanse. Then it struck me that the moth had devoured my very title. The gardens no longer needed bats, the things in the attic did not require dusting, and as for my Monday proclamations, I had been making them long before I ever came to Reparata. At least when I was the High and Mighty of Next Week, the promise of the future always loomed ahead, calling me on. Now, all that was left was the past.

When the moth began devouring the very marble structure of the palace, Ringlat, Chin Mokes, and the Chancellor of Waste hatched a conspiracy to do away with it. Many of the others had agreed to help them. As it was put to me when they attempted to conscript me into their plot, "Ingess is not in his right mind. We have to save him again." I was told that Saint-Geedon had been chosen, because of his skills as an assassin, to form a plan to strike the insect down. What was I to do but agree?

I had often wondered what the link was between the professions of hired killer and chef, because Grenis had made the transition from one to the other almost overnight when he chose Reparata as his home. After I watched him create the bomb, though, I no longer had any questions. The outer casing of the device was made from a thick crusted peasant bread called Latcha, which was a main staple of the farmers in the surrounding countryside. Through a small hole he cut in the top of the loaf, he dug out the dough, leaving it as hollow as a jack-o-lantern. Next came a strange mixture of chemicals and cooking powders, each of which he measured out in exact amounts. To this he added boxes of nails and pieces of sharp metal. For the finishing touch, he asked Pester to bring him the vanilla.

"What does that do?" I asked.

"For sweetness," he said.

To create the fuse, he pan-fried over a low fire a long piece of string in some of the same ingredients that were used in the main course. When the string had cooled, he inserted one end into the bread, replaced the cap of crust he had cut, and then garnished the outside with radishes cut into florets. We gave him a round of applause to which he clicked his heels and nodded sharply.

The moon couldn't have been brighter the night we put our plan into action. It had been decided that we would lay the trap outside the walls of the palace so as not to chance destroying anymore of the quickly diminishing structure. Just beyond the gates, there was a deep moat that ran the circumference of Reparata. We crept cautiously out across the drawbridge, which, since there was little threat of invasion in those times, was always left down.

Ten yards off the bridge, and twenty yards to the surrounding tree line, we heaped up a pile of whatever belongings still remained to us. Those who had nothing to give removed curtains from the few rooms that had not been visited yet by the moth. Within this hill of things, we planted the bomb, and then ran the long fuse over to the tree line where we took up positions, hiding in the shadows at the edge of the woods.

There were more than twenty of us in the group. Because I was nervous that Ingess might discover our treachery or that we might fail, I didn't notice that the countess was among the conspirators until we stood beneath the trees. She had somewhere gotten a set of men's clothing and her hair was tied back.

"Frouch," I whispered, "I didn't know you were part of this."

"I hope that bomb blows the damned bug to tatters, the same

way it did my life," she said. There was an edge to her voice I had never heard before.

I reached out and put my hand on her shoulder, but she shrugged it off and lit a cigarette. I meant to ask her what I had done to make her cross with me, but just then the Philosopher General whispered a duet of, "Behold, the floating hunger."

It flew slowly out past the open gates of Reparata, its wings quietly beating the air. The powder it threw off caught the moonlight and created a misty aura around it. Its antennae twitched at the scent of curtain silk, gown muslin, old shoes, strings of pearls, and the deadly loaf at their center. When it landed with the lightness of a dream feather and began to dine, Saint-Geedon turned to Frouch and nodded. She flicked the ash off her cigarette, puffed it hard three times and then put the burning end to the tip of the fuse. The tiny spark was away in an instant, eating the treated string faster than even the creature could.

Frouch licked her lips, Ringlat rubbed his hands together, and the Chancellor of Waste wheezed excitedly as that dot of fizzling orange raced toward explosion. When it was exactly halfway to the heap where the moth was busy vanishing an old topcoat, who should appear at the palace gates but Ingess dressed in full battle armor and mounted on Drith, his nag of a warhorse. The moment we saw him there, it was obvious he had finally come to his senses and decided to slay the creature as his subjects had begged him. He drew his long sword, pointed it at the moth and then spurred the old horse in the flanks.

As His Royal reached the middle of the drawbridge, the spark reached the loaf. We braced ourselves for apocalypse but all that followed was a miserable little pop, weaker than a champagne cork, and the issuance of a slight stream of smoke. The moth flapped upward in a panic, unharmed, but this sudden motion frightened Drith and he reared on his hind legs, throwing Ingess from his back and into the deep waters of the moat.

The ridiculous course of events left me standing with my mouth open wide. Everyone was stunned by the misadventure.

Then Frouch yelled, "He'll drown in that armor."

She took two steps past me, but I saw that someone else had already begun sprinting toward the moat. It was Durst, and I had never seen his lumpen form move with such speed in all the years I had known him. He did not hesitate at the edge, but awkwardly formed his hands together into an arrowhead in front of him, kicked up his heels in the back, and dove into the water. At the sight of this, we all started running.

I don't know how he found him in the dark at the bottom of that moat, nor do I know how he lifted him to the surface and brought him to the bank. Ringlat and I reached down and pulled His Royal up onto dry land. Pester and Chin Mokes did the same with Durst. In seconds we had Ingess's helmet off, and much to my relief found that he was still faintly breathing.

"He's alive," yelled Ringlat, and the assembled company shouted.

Frouch helped us remove the rest of the armor as the others gathered round Durst, patting his head and slapping him on the back. I stole a look at him in the middle of my work and saw that he had lost his spectacles. When I noticed he was no longer bent by the weight of his twin, I had a feeling he would not be needing them.

Whereas the night had brought a miraculous opportunity to the Philosopher General, His Royal had not fared so well. We freed him of his armor, but no manner of nudging, tapping, massaging, could wake him from unconsciousness. My fear that he had been too long underwater without air seemed now to be a fact. Still, we gathered him up and brought him back inside the palace. The structures of the buildings were no longer sound because of the work of the moth, so we carried one of the last remaining beds out into the courtyard and laid him on that. Then we gathered around him like dwarfs around a poisoned princess in a fairy tale and waited with far too much hope than could reasonably be expected.

The other members of the court who were not part of our ill-fated plot now came out of the palace to join us, bringing reports of what little remained in the wake of the moth. Ingess's fortune was now completely gone, the food stores, with the exception of an old pot of moldy cremat, were thoroughly decimated.

"The place is as empty as my heart," said the Illustrious Seventh, who in her ripped tunic from yesteryear was looking none too illustrious.

We stayed in that courtyard through the remainder of the night and the following day, standing around, watching His Royal's every faint breath. From off in the distance came the occasional sounds of some piece of the architecture crumbling and falling with a thunderous crash, having been undermined by the moth's earlier dining. I witnessed with my own eyes the fall of the eastern parapet. It slouched and fell, tons of marble, like a sandcastle in the surf.

When the young ones began to complain of hunger there was nothing to give them. None of us had been at Reparata long enough to forget that feeling of utter need. Frouch and some of the others discussed possibilities of where to find food, but nothing came readily to mind. Then Ringlat removed his Bishop's robe, throwing it to the ground. Beneath, he was dressed in the black costume of the highwayman. He borrowed a scarf from one of the ladies and tied it around his face just beneath his eyes.

"Flam," he said. "If I'm not back by nightfall, you will have to think of something else." We watched him run across the courtyard to where Drith stood drinking from a small fountain. With one leap, he went atop the back of the horse and landed in its saddle. Grabbing the reigns, he spun the mount to the left, whipped it and gave it his heels. The old nag responded and, together, they were off like a shot through the gates of Reparata.

The day was as long as any I have ever witnessed. The afternoon dragged on as our expectations of His Royal's recovery grew more faint than his breathing. When things became almost intolerable and some of the very young had begun to cry, the Chancellor of Waste gathered them all together and, borrowing some small objects from the crowd (my pipe, a pocket watch, a knife), began juggling. Occasionally, he would allow one of the things to hit him on the head before he caught it and sent it back into the cycle. This drew some laughter from the children. For we who were older, the transformation of the chancellor himself, from fatuous ass to merry buffoon, was marvelous enough to bring a smile in spite of the predicament our king was in. He juggled, acted idiotic, and performed pratfalls for hours, until he finally slumped down onto the ground in exhaustion. The children ran to him and, climbing upon his back, used him as a boat while he slept.

"What are we going to do?" Frouch asked as we stood together at twilight, staring down at Ingess, whose condition hadn't changed all day.

I shook my head. "I'm lost," I said.

"We can't stay here any longer," she told me and I wasn't sure by the tone of her voice if she was talking about the entire court or just the two of us.

There was no time to question her about this because, just then, Ringlat came charging across the drawbridge on Drith. With one hand he clutched the horse's reigns and with the other he held tightly to a bulging cloth gathered up at one end and thrown over his shoulder.

"Dinner," he called as he leaped down from his mount. When he spread the cloth out at our feet, we saw it was filled with all manner of food.

"It seems the lord provides, Bishop," I said to him as everyone crowded around to take something.

"In this case, the lord taketh away. Righteous robbery, Flam," he said. "That road to Enginstan always was a favorite of mine."

"In broad daylight?" I said.

He shrugged, "I wouldn't make a habit of it, but it seems my reputation still lives. When all I demanded was food, they were more than happy to comply. How many do you know who can claim to have been robbed by Ringlat and lived to tell of it? Something to pass down to their grandchildren."

"You're a generous man," I told him as he searched around for where he had dropped his bishop's robe.

There was just enough to eat in that sack to quiet the children and calm the adults. The last crumb of the last loaf was finished just as night settled in. We knew the moth was about, because as soon as darkness was upon us we could hear pieces of the palace coming down. I called for everyone to gather in close to Ingess in case any of the surrounding facades might give way. It was cold and we huddled together on the ground, a human knot around His Royal. The answer to the question I never got to ask Frouch earlier was answered when she took a place beside me and leaned against my shoulder. I put my arm around her and she closed her eyes.

Some slept but I stared numbly into the dark and listened to the destruction of Reparata. It was just after I was sure I heard the southern colonnade drop into the reflecting pond that Pester stood up.

"It's coming for us," he screamed in a shrill voice, pointing up above with his missing finger.

I looked up at what I at first mistook for the moon, but soon saw was the moth, slowly descending from a great height. The powder was falling toward us, and I roused everyone as quickly as possible so as to have them escape its ill effects. Groggy and scared, the company moved quickly back away from Ingess, since it appeared precisely there that the moth would land.

"Will it eat him?" asked Frouch as we looked on in horror, totally powerless to stop it.

"It took Pester's finger with no problem, it devoured solid marble," I said.

The others around us started to yell and wave their arms in an attempt to frighten it away, but the moth, as lovely as a delicate blossom on the breeze, continued its descent, showering His Royal with its powder. Frouch turned away as it came to rest, laying its body upon the entire length of Ingess. A groan went up from the assembled court as the moth wrapped its wings around him like a pale winding sheet. I watched through tears, expecting at any moment to see the huge insect lift off and leave behind an empty bed. Instead, it gave a long mournful cry and before our eyes, like magic, dissipated into a light fog that continued to hang about the body. Then Ingess roused, filling his lungs with an enormous gasp, and the airy remains of the moth entered him through his mouth and nostrils. He opened his eyes and sat up, and when he finally exhaled, it came as a blast of laughter.

As I approached him, he held his hand out to me, and I could see in his eyes that mischievous look from before the tragedy. He told us that while he was unconscious, he had been with Josette in the garden. She told him to stop grieving or she would never be happy. "We must slough off the cocoon of Reparata," he said.

"That won't be difficult," said Chin Mokes, "there's nothing left."

At this, Ingess laughed again as he had on the day when he bestowed upon me the title of High and Mighty of Next Week. We gathered around him for the last time, penniless, homeless, facing an uncertain future.

The next day, after tearful goodbyes, we left the broken shell of Reparata and scattered out across the countryside like a brood of newborn insects. Without a word between us, Frouch and I decided to travel together. Life on the road was hard, but we had each other to rely on. For no good reason, we made our way to the coast and ended our journey in, of all places, Gile. I became a fisherman on one of the boats and Frouch took a job serving drinks in the tavern. It was a funny thing, but no one ever recognized her from her earlier days. The only one who remembered was the tavern keeper, and he told the customers who asked that she was royalty in disguise.

I had heard that Ingess eventually married again and took up farming. He became famous far and wide for the prodigious nature of his crops and the generous prices at which he sold them. It became known by all those who might have fallen on hard times that his home was a place of refuge. Although I think of them often, I can not say what became of the rest of the royal court of Reparata. All I know is that years later, when an evil tyrant arose in the north and threatened war on the entire territory, he was found one morning with his throat slit, a gob of spit on his forehead, and smelling strangely of vanilla.

As for that healer, Frouch overheard, at the tavern one evening, a visiting merchant speak of an old man in a bathrobe he had encountered in a drinking establishment in the distant port of Mekshalan. "It seems the old man had arrived with a flea circus that he was sure would cure the Great Pasha's crippling disease of exquisite boredom," said the merchant. "He showed me the circus and I saw nothing but meager black specks hopping about. When I asked him if he thought they were so entertaining they would lift the great one out of his boredom, he shook his head and said, 'Of course not, but when they get loose in his beard and turban, he'll have plenty to do.' "

In the evenings when I come in off the bay, Frouch is waiting for me at the table by the window of the tavern with plates of food and two glasses of Princess Jang's Tears. As night falls we head home to our little shack in the dunes, light a fire and lay together, conversing and watching the play of shadows on the ceiling. In those shifting projections, I have had glimpses of Reparata, and Ingess and Josette. An image of the moth also frequently appears there, but the persistent beating of its wings no longer frightens me now that I have learned there are some things in this world that can never be devoured.

Ellen Datlow was the first editor who ever asked me to send her a story. In meeting her I got the feeling that she wanted me to write something I really wanted to write. I'm not sure where this slant-wise fairy tale came from, but I had a great time concocting it. I remember I received her e-mail accepting the story on Christmas Day. During a follow-up correspondence of about twenty e-mails, Ellen helped me revise it. That was like a crash course in writing short fiction. Ellen has published a number of my stories since this first one, and with each, I continue to learn things. The most important lesson has always been to take risks.

Some details about this story: the image of the main character fly-fishing for bats in the beginning of the story is a direct rip-off from Washington Irving's The Alhambra, *in which a character fly-fishes for sparrows. Reparata was the name of the sister of the famous Italian goldsmith and sculptor Benvenuto Cellini. And Princess Jang's Tears is an actual drink that was made for me by an illegal Chinese immigrant, who was the bartender at The House of Yu, a restaurant attached to a motel I lived in for a while. Some years earlier, one of my favorite writers, Jack Dann, labored for a while as the night clerk on the graveyard shift at this same motel.*

Pansolapia

THE WOMAN OF THE PALACE, VASHMENA, MOVES with the grace of the hornbills hunting in a sunset lake. Her black gown, like melting night, is studded with chips of quartz that catch the light of the torches and recreate the heavens. She is deep in meditation—now pacing, now swaying slightly, now standing still. When at rest, it is impossible to tell if she is breathing. The only signs that she is more than a statue are the twitch of a nostril and a quivering at the ends of her silken black hair. Then, like an illusion, she moves—slow as thick mist rolling—wide, arcing arm strokes and high, backward steps. She falls through space where speed has lost all meaning, and holds her long middle fingers curled to her palms. When she lands, back into perfect stillness, it is as if she has never moved at all.

Behind her green eyes roars an iron-colored ocean. The waves are mountains and the troughs, quick trips to hell. The sky is the color of dirt and the wind has a voice. "Sleep," it howls at the men lashed to the rigging of a lone, double-masted ship. Nothing could be more frightening to them than its exquisite elocution, for its command is the voice of the woman they saw dance in the courtyard at Pansolapia. It follows them down beneath the waves, swamping their thoughts as the brine bursts their lungs. Their long hair rises up in wavy points toward the distant storm as the ship drifts into darkness. All hands grin. All hands stare at the woman in black, now moving like an eel, now posing like a rock upon a rock.

The stars shiver down her stomach as her hips swing with fluid speed, and the lion-pawed guard at the gates of the palace knows to let the sailors pass. He growls a command to proceed, which the long-haired foreigners take to be a challenge. They draw curved, serrated knives and wait for a fight. The old beast-man, Kilif, laughs at their weapons and steps aside. "Gusmashnease," he says, his only word, which means nothing, and the broadest of the men sheathes his blade and smiles. "Pansolapia?" asks the traveler, scanning the crumbling turrets of the impossible structure. Vashmena breathes out slowly through her nose as she watches, at an incredible distance, Kilif nod and brush away a tear.

Her voice vibrates, filling the courtyard and frightening the vultures into flight. One word, one syllable, gets beneath the bricks and loosens them. Imperceptibly, her ears prick up in response to the echo just as they do when the sailor calls to her down the long hall of columns leading to the carnivorous gardens. Her memory of running is played out in her pulse. A hundred yards away, she feels his breath at the back of her neck. His pursuit is the gentle tapping of her left foot. She crouches and then as quickly stands and begins to spin as the bearded foreigner suddenly wakes before dawn on the day he is to begin his journey to Pansolapia. Ardnith is his name, and he looks at his sleeping wife, wondering if he will return.

They hear a sound, like a sigh, as they pace quietly, so not to draw ghosts, through the corridors of the deserted palace. How could they know it is the sweep and swirl of her dress as she comes to rest in the courtyard of Pansolapia? The place is nothing like what they had wondered when the Shaman commanded them to go in search of the future. Ardnith's wife had wept at the order, for her recent nightmare had shown her their demise. "What is it?" asked Ardnith as he held her. "Gusmashnease," says the loyal Kilif sometime eight years hence, and the widow soon-to-be says less. Ardnith draws his blade as the first hungry blossom descends to devour him.

Her nipples harden as she recalls his touch, creating a new constellation across her chest. The sailors look up one night on their return journey and realize they are lost. "This is not our ocean," they cry after studying the stars. Young Freg holds tightly to the lock of hair he has stolen from the murdered Kilif, as if a lion's courage would now breathe through him. Ardnith knows immediately that they have been cursed by Vashmena. In the courtyard, she again breathes out, this time through her mouth, and the winds begin to trouble the ocean.

As the ship founders, he remembers taking her from behind in a mirrored chamber, and all he remembers is the illusion of her. She hides and watches as he couples with her image, but when he loses his seed it seeps into her reflection and then into her through her eyes. So now, as she dances, her stomach swells with the deception of the foreigner. She dances as she had for the company before they retreated through the phantom palace toward the harbor. As Ardnith sprints for his ship, the snail-streaked walls and frayed tapestries disintegrate, bleeding atoms.

Vashmena falls suddenly back on the stones of the courtyard and opens her legs. She breathes now, only through her mouth, rapid, determined breaths. Her cries wake Ardnith's wife as he is preparing to leave. "Please, don't go," she whispers to him. "The Shaman is a fool," she says. "There is nothing beyond the rim of the world." He tells her he must go and heads for the door. He turns back to look at her as his lungs give their last breath to the rising ocean. Vashmena is dancing, she is giving birth. The Shaman is in his cave, chanting a lion-man to life from a scrap of hide, a tooth, a claw.

As the seaweed wraps around Ardnith's neck, his life plays itself out before his eyes. He sees his childhood, his father's battle scars, caribou moving through the early morning frost, icebergs colliding off shore, his wife's long blonde braid like a maze, his decision not to go. In that instant, Pansolapia is born, and Kilif shouts, "Gusmashnease," loud enough to wake the sleeping sailor. Ardnith rubs his eyes and opens them to see the Shaman, cradling the dream child in his arms. The sly old man spins like a woman dancing and steps away into the night. Then Ardnith hears the masts splinter and crack. The blossom consumes him with a maw of thorns, in a mirrored room, at the bottom of the ocean, next to his sleeping wife.

I get a lot of place names and character names from my dreams. "Pansolapia" came to me one night after just having read Italo Calvino's Invisible Cities. Who the hell knows what it means? I stored the name away in my memory, and it kept nagging at me to become part of a story. In order to shut it up, I wrote a lousy poem with a simplistic rhyme scheme, good for jumping rope to but not much else, about a city at the end of the world called Pansolapia. As soon as the poem was done, I filed it away.

My brother-in-law Mike Gallagher is a comic book artist and writer. You can see his work in the pages of Mad magazine from time to time these days. A few years ago, Mike worked for Marvel Comics. He wrote for the books Mad Balls, Alf, Heathcliff, Mighty Mouse, and a series called Guardians of the Galaxy. When he'd go into the city to see his editor at the Marvel offices, he used to get free comics. Every month, he'd score me the latest Conan books. Conan was a running joke with us. We admired our favorite barbarian's methods of problem solving, his way with the ladies, his dialogue (sort of a mix between Elizabethan English and Bizarro). Some of the artists who worked on these books were truly amazing. Anyway, I'd get them and use them for bowl reading and then chop them up and make collages out of them. At one point they were all over my house.

One winter day when I was making a collage out of Conan, I took a break and started reading a book called Time: The Familiar Stranger. One thing that struck me about the nature of time, as was stated in the book, was that it has been proven by physics that the passage of time is an illusion. All time is really happening at the same time. This blew me away. I had to wonder how we can know stuff like this and just keep on with our lives in the manner we always have—not that it stopped me from doing exactly that.

So I decided to write a kind of barbarian story where everything was happening at the same time. In it there is a city at the edge of the world. I cast around for a name for that place, and just as I was, the Pansolapia poem in the file drawer cried, "Me," in that minute voice of Vincent Price as The Fly. I dedicate this piece to Mike, for without the Conans, I never would have thought of it.

The story was published by Ellen Datlow on Event Horizon, which I thought was pretty courageous on her part. I had a feeling that most who read it would shake their heads and say, "What the fuck?" And that's pretty much what they did.

Exo-Skeleton Town

AN HOUR AGO I CAME OUT OF SPID'S SMOKE house and saw Clark Gable scoring a couple balls of dung off an Aphid twice his size. It was broad moonlight, and Gable should have known better, but I could see by the state of his getup and the deflation of his hair wave that he was strung out on loneliness. I might have warned him, but what the hell, he'd end up taking me down with him. Instead I stepped back into the shadows of the alleyway and waited for the Beetle Squad to show up. I watched Gable flash his rakish smile, but frankly Scarlet, that Aphid didn't give a damn. When he gave up on the ancient film charm and flashed the cash instead, the bug handed over two nice little globes, sweating the freasence in droplets of bright silver. Love was in the air.

Then they descended, iridescent in the dim light of the streetlamps, circling in like a flock of Earth geese landing on a pond. The Beetles were always hot for action and they had a directive that allowed them to kill first and ask questions later. The Aphid they just kicked the crap out of until it looked like a yellow pancake with green syrup, but Gable was another story. Because he was human, they shot him once with a stinger gun, and when the needle pierced his exo-flesh, the real *him* blew out the hole with an indelicate *frrrappp* and turned to juice on the street. The dung balls were retrieved, Gable's outer skin was swiped, the bluebottles swooped in for a feeding, and twenty minutes later there was nothing left but half a mustache and a crystal coin good for three tokes at Spid's. I crossed the street, picked up the crystal and went back into my home away from home away from home.

This is Exo-Skeleton Town, the dung-rolling capitol of the universe, where the sun never shines and bug folk barter their excremental wealth for Earth movies almost two centuries old. There's a slogan in Exo-town concerning its commerce—"Sell it or smell it," the locals say. The air pressure is intense, and everything moves in slow motion.

When the first earthlings landed here two decades earlier, they wore big, bulky exo-suits to withstand the force. It was a revelation when they met the bugs and by using the universal translator discovered that these well-dressed insects had smarts. I call them Beetles and Aphids, etc., but they aren't really. These terms are just to give you an idea of what they look like. They come in a span of sizes, some of them much larger than men. They're kind of a crude, no-frills race, but they know what they want, and what they want is more and more movies from Earth's twentieth century.

In trying to teach them about our culture, one of the members of the original Earth crew, who was an ancient movie buff, showed them *Casablanca*. What appealed to bugs about that pointless tale of piano playing, fez wearing, woman crying, I can't begin to tell you. But the minute the flick was over and the lights went on the mayor of Exo-Skeleton Town, a big crippled flealike specimen who goes by the name of Stootladdle, offered to trade something of immeasurable worth for it and the machine it played on.

Trying to work détente, the crew's captain readily agreed. Stootladdle called to his underlings to bring the freasence and they did. It came in a beeswax box. The mayor then whipped the lid off the box with three of his four hands and revealed five sweating bug turds the size of healthy meatballs. The captain had to adjust the helmet of his exo-suit to get a closer look, not believing at first what he was seeing. "Sure," he said in the name of diplomacy, and he forced his navigator, the film buff, to hand over the *Casablanca* cartridge and viewer. The navigator, wanting to do the right thing, also gave the mayor copies of *Ben Hur* and *Citizen Kane*. When the captain asked Stootladdle, through the translator, why he liked the movie, the big flea mentioned Peter Lorre's eyes. The earthlings laughed but the mayor remained silent. When the captain inquired as to what they were supposed to do with the freasence, the answer came in a clipped buzz, "Eat it." And so began one of the first intergalactic trading partnerships.

I know it sounds like we humans got the messy end of the stick on this deal, but when the ship returned to Earth and scientists tested the freasence, it proved to be an incredibly powerful aphrodisiac. A couple of grains of one of those spherical loads in a glass of wine and the recipient would be hot to go and totally devoted for half a day. The first test subjects reported incredible abilities in the love act. Those original five globes disappeared faster than cream puffs from a glutton's pantry, and none of it even made it out of the laboratory. So another spaceship was sent, carrying *Gentlemen Prefer Blondes*, *Double Indemnity*, and *Gone with the Wind*. Ten balls of dung came back at warp speed, and the screwing started in earnest.

Two decades of this trade went on, and by then we had bartered copies of every movie we could find. Private corporations started making black and white, vintage original films by digitally resurrecting the characters of the old films, feeding them into a quantum computer, and putting them in new situations. The bugs got suspicious with the first couple of batches of these, especially one entitled *We Dream* with Bogart, Orson Welles, Trevor Howard, Carmen Miranda and Veronica Lake. It was about a love pentagon during the Nazi occupation of Brooklyn. In the end Welles explodes, Trevor Howard poisons Bogart and then is shot by Carmen Miranda, who runs off with Veronica Lake. The problem with the film was that it was too damn good. It didn't have what the ancients called that "B" quality.

To offset this problem the specialists came up with a batch of real stinkers, starring the likes of Mickey Rooney, Broderick Crawford, and Jane Withers. One in particular, *Lick the Devil*, was credited with having saved the precious dung trade. I've seen it and it's terrible. Crawford plays an Irish Catholic priest, Withers is the ghost of the Virgin Mary, and Rooney plays a slapstick Chinese waiter in the racist fashion of the old days with a rubber band around his eyes. I've always said I'd like to shake the hand of the insidious mother who made that one.

Anyway, as the ships kept coming, trading their bogus movies, technical advances were made on Earth in the exo-gear that humans would have to wear on the bug planet. The geniuses at the Quigley Corporation came up with a two-molecule-thick suit that hugged the body like a second skin. Everything that one needed was shrunk down to nano-size and made part of the suit. It breathed for you, saw for you, heard with a built-in translator for you, ate for you. The only task that was necessary was emptying the exhaust twice a day through a three-inch-long circular spigot in the crotch area. The device you emptied the spigot into was a vacuum, so that when the pipe opened for its instant, the crushing weight of the atmosphere couldn't splat you. This new alloy the designers used was so flexible and strong it easily withstood the pressure.

The first of these exo-skins, as they were called, gave Earth traders back their human form, so that they now had false faces and eyes and smiles and skin color and hair. The exo-skins were made to resemble the people that they encased like so much sausage. Then some ad exec got the idea that they should make these suits in the guise of the actors of the old movies. Bogart was the prototype of these new star skins. When he showed up on the bug planet, they rolled out the brown carpet. Stootladdle was beside himself, calling for a holiday. The dung rollers came in from the luminous veldt that surrounds the town and there was a three-day party.

As time went on, the exo-skins improved, more authentic with greater detail. They made a Rita Hayworth that was so fine, I'd have humped it if Stootladdle was wearing it. Entrepreneurs started investing capital in an exo-skin and a ticket to the bug planet. They'd bring a couple of movies with them, score a few turds and head back home to cut the crap up into a fortune. At first, one trip was enough to set up an enterprising businessperson for the rest of his life. Back on Earth, the freasence was so sought after that you could only buy it with bars of gold bullion. For the wealthy it was the death of romantic love, but the poor still had to score with good looks and outlandish promises.

The bugs rationed how much freasence could be sold in a year, and on Earth the World Corporation did the same, because the rich didn't want the poor screwing out of their class. In Exo-Skeleton Town, if you were caught trafficking without a license, like poor Gable, you were disposed of with little ceremony by the Beetle Squad. Anyone could come to the bug world and try to get a license, but they had to go through Stootladdle and he operated solely out of whim. If you had an exo-skin resembling a star he admired, you had a good chance, but sometimes even that didn't guarantee anything.

So a lot of people made the space flight, which took a year each way even at three times the speed of light, and got stranded on the bug world with no way to raise the money to finance the return trip.

If you brought a hot movie, something the bugs were into, you could make enough money to survive by showing it to individual bugs at a time for a few bug bucks, which were actually mayflies that when dried and folded resembled old Earth dollars. Twenty mayflies could be exchanged for a crystal chip.

Some unlucky bastards brought movies they were positive would get them some action on the freasence market. I can see them on their trip here as the stars stretched out like strands of spaghetti during the warp drive, thinking, "Oh, baby, I've got a Paul Muni here that's gonna make those cold-blooded vermin do a jig, or Myrna Loy has got to be worth at least a turd and a half." But when they got here, they found the fickle tastes of the population had changed and that of all people, it was Basil Rathbone and Joan Blondell who were making the antennae twitch that year. So they were stranded with an old movie not even a mosquito would watch and no means of support. The bugs didn't care if these interlopers starved to death. I remember seeing Buster Keaton sitting in a dark corner at Spid's for a week and half. Finally, one day a Mantis figured out the silent comic had died and took him away for his private collection.

I got into it probably at the worst time, but I was young and so determined to get rich quick, I didn't heed any of the warnings. I didn't have a lot to spend on my skin, so instead of trying to get a top-shelf actor suit, I figured it would be wise to go for someone who was only on the verge of super stardom but who showed up in a lot of the old movies. The company I bought from showed me a nice Keenan Wynn, but after becoming a student of the old films in preparation for my journey, I knew Wynn was strictly television movies and light heavies in the full-fledged flicks he had done. Then they showed me a Don Knotts, and I told them to go fuck themselves. I was about to leave when they brought out a beauty of a Joseph Cotten. I knew better than the people who made the suit how cool Cotten was. *Shadow of a Doubt, Citizen Kane, The Third Man.* I plunked down my money and before I knew it, I was walking home with a bag full of suave and vulnerable everyman.

I would have rather sat on the bowl backwards for a year than take that space flight. It seemed endless, but I spent my time reading books about ancient movies and dreaming what I would do with all my gold after I scored my load. My ace in the hole was that I had a great movie to trade. This was a real one too. It had been handed down over generations on my father's side. To tell the truth, I stole it from him the day I left for the spaceport. It was a little low budget job called *Night of the Living Dead*. My old man would dust it off for holidays and we'd watch it. Who knew what the hell was going on in the film? It was in black and white, but supposedly, from what I had read, it was a cult classic in its time. I remember once, as a kid of about ten, my old man leaned over to me where I lay on the floor one Christmas watching it with the rest of the relatives. He said to me, "You know what the deeper implications are here?" pointing to the monitor. I shook my head. "The director is trying to say that the dead will eat you." My old man was as profound as a stone. All I saw was a bunch of stiffs marching around. For years I thought it was a parade. If I were to see that movie today, it would probably still get me in the holiday spirit. Anyway, it wasn't as early as I would have liked, but I thought the whole anti-Hollywood, independent movie scene, a late-twentieth-century phenomenon, might be ready to explode on the bug planet.

I still remember the day when we landed at the little spaceport next to Exo-Skeleton Town, and I looked out the window at a village of one-story concrete bunkers in the dark lit by streetlights. It was like a nightmare. Putting on the Cotten was the only thing that saved me from crying. Climbing into those skins is a painful experience at first. There's a moment when you have to die and then be revived by the suit's biosystem. The one thing nobody told me about was how it itches when you first get in. I thought it would drive me wild. Then another guy who had been to the bug planet before stepped into a smart little Nick Adams getup and warned me, "Whatever you do, don't think about the itching. It can seriously drive you insane." I was in agony when I stepped through the airlock and into the slow, heavy world of insects.

It cost me a fortune but I managed to arrange a meeting with Stootladdle only a few days after my arrival. He was a sight to behold. Hairy, too many arms. His eyes were round as saucers and a thousand mirrors each. I became momentarily dizzy trying to watch each and every *me* he was seeing all at once. The voice that came through the translator was high and thin and full of annoyance.

"Joseph Cotten," he said. "I've seen you in a few things."
"*Shadow of a Doubt?*" I asked.
"Never heard of it," said the flea.

Now, as I gaze through the pale orange haze into the mirror behind Spid's smoke bar, I realize all that was a long time ago. Five, ten years may have passed since I came to the bug planet. The smoke has a way of paralyzing time, blotting out its illusion of progress, so that yesterday might as well be today and vice versa. Whatever this stuff is that Spid burns to make the smoke, it looks like big handfuls of antennae. The mind spins with a logic as sure as a spider web. Real memories intrude now and then as do self-admonitions for a wasted life, but the smoke's other feature is that it lets you not give a shit about anything but taking in more smoke.

The smoke has turned my brain to cotton, so that now I am cotton(en) inside and out. Yes, the Cotten went rotten a long time ago. So now I give old Spid, that affable arachnid, the crystal chip Gable dropped, and he says, "The usual, Joe?" I nod and bare my exhaust pipe. He fits the tube to my opening and I set the vacuum on intake by touching my left pinky finger to my right earlobe. The nano-machinery does its thing and sucks a bolus toke of the orange mist. With the smoke, you never exhale.

It wasn't long after I arrived that I got hooked on the smoke and ended up selling my movie for a ridiculously low price in order to get high one night. An elegantly thin cricket gave me ten crystal chips for it, and I spent the next three days dozing and smoking at Spid's. When my credit ran out, and a few hours passed, I came to and began to panic. That was how I became Stootladdle's flunky.

"How do you feel about living?" he asked me when the Beetle Squad brought me to his office. I had been caught on the street trying to score a turd without the proper papers. Even in my orange haze, I was surprised they hadn't plugged me.

"Tomorrow is another day," I said to him.

"I'm going to slap you around and you're going to like it," he said. Then he did, all those arms working me over at once. The blows were like a stinging swarm of locust and the nano-technology, true to its guarantee, registered every one. When I was thoroughly dazed, he gave a little jump in the air and kicked me right in the nuts, or where they would have been if the suit makers had bothered to render them. I fell forward and he caught me with his mandibles by the neck.

"I've got a spot for you in my private collection right between Omar Sharif and Annette Funicello," he said.

I promised I'd do anything he wanted if he let me live. He loosened his grip and I stood, rubbing my throat. He laughed loud and long, the sound of teeth scraping concrete, and he put two of his arms around me.

"Now, Joseph," he said, "I have a little job for you to do."

"Anything," I said.

Stootladdle waved away the Beetle Squad, and I was left alone with him in his office. He sat down at his desk and triple motioned for me to take the chair across from him.

"Feeling better?" he asked.

I looked into his eyes and saw myself nodding ad infinitum.

"Yes," he said. "Very well. Have you ever heard of a film called *The Rain Does Things Like That?*"

"Will it go badly for me if I haven't?" I asked.

He laughed. "It will go badly for you no matter what," he said.

"No," I admitted.

"It doesn't matter," he said. "I saw this movie once, years and years ago, very early on in our trade relationship with your planet."

"How is it?" I asked.

"It's the butterfly's dust," he said.

"If it's that good, how come I never heard of it?" I asked.

"The actors were unknown, but I tell you there is a young woman in it named Gloriette Moss, who is nothing less than startling. It's a love story. Poignant," said Stootladdle, scratching his hairy stomach.

"I'll have to catch it some time," I said.

"No, Joseph," he said, "you're going to catch it now. The only copy of the film on the planet resides out in the luminous veldt with the widow of Ambassador Lancaster. His widow, who still lives out there on the estate, is none other than Gloriette Moss. I've tried to buy the movie from her for my collection, but she refuses to sell. It was her husband's favorite film because she starred in it. Sentimental value, as you earthlings say. I want that movie."

"Why don't you just send out the Beetle Squad and take it?" I asked.

"Too delicate a situation," he said. "She has ties to Earth's military. How would it look if we started roughing up an ex-ambassador's wife? It could interrupt our thriving trade."

"If you send me back to Earth, I'll tell them to make her give you the film," I said.

"Ready for another beating, I see," he said. "No, I want you to go out there and get it for me. I don't care how you get it short of stealing it, but I want it. You can not harm her. She must willingly give it to you and then you will give it to me and I will let you live."

"How am I going to do that?" I asked.

"Your charm, Joseph. Remember how you were in *The Third Man*, bumbling yet sincere, but altogether charming?" he said.

I nodded.

"Succeed or suffer a slow, painful death."

"I think I hear zither music," I said.

Stootladdle put his slackey (like an ancient rickshaw conveyance) and driver, an ill-tempered termite, at my disposal for the trip out of town. Once beyond the dim glow of the streetlights of Exo-town, things got really dark. Our only guide was the ragged moon all jumbled and bashed. The driver kept complaining about the pests, miniscule mammals with gossamer wings, bats the size of Earth mosquitos, that traveled in clouds and stung viciously. He at least had a few extra appendages at his disposal with which to keep them away. I was frightened of him, frightened of the dark and my grim future, but the thing that scared me more than anything was the thought of going without the smoke for more than a day. The mayor had assured me that Gloriette Moss was a smoke fiend herself and had her own setup, keeping a huge supply on hand of whatever that stuff is that one burns to make it. I prayed he wasn't playing with me on this score. He said that the reason she never went back to Earth was because she was hooked.

After a jostling, potholed, nightmare of a journey, we came in sight of the luminous veldt—an immense pasture of long wind-blown grass that glowed against the dark with the resilient yellow-green of cat's eyes. The light from it eased my fear and its slow ocean movement was very relaxing. In the face of its beauty, I almost forgot my predicament. The driver turned onto a path that cut through the grass, and we traveled for another mile or so with me in a kind of stupor.

"Out, earthworm," he said, and I came suddenly to my senses.

"Where are we?" I asked.

"This is it," he said. "Get out."

"Where is the Lancaster estate?" I asked.

"Look," he said, and pointed out with three of his arms that we were at a crossroad of paths. The grass was high over our heads.

"Take that path. Up there a way, you'll see an Earth house. I can't take you any farther. If the lady sees me, she'll know you have come because of Stootladdle."

"Thanks," I said as I got down from the slackey.

"May maggots infest your nostrils," he said. Then he turned the hitch around and was gone.

There I was, Cotten, three light-years from Earth, on a bug planet of perpetual night. The stars were brilliant above me, but I did not look up for fear of the loneliness and recrimination I might feel at seeing the sun, a blinking dot in the distance. I thought of my parents, thinking of me, wondering what had become of me, and I saw my old man, shaking his head and saying, "That jerk-off took my movie."

The Lancaster house was a creaky old retro affair from the part of Earth's history when they used wood to build dwellings. I'd seen pictures of these things before. The style, as I had read in one of my many film books, was Victorian. These baroque shelters with lace-like woodwork and myriad rooms were always popping up in the flicks from the thirties and forties. Pointed rocket-ship-looking turrets on either side of a big three-story box with a railed platform that went all the way around it. As I made my way toward the steps that led to a door, I quickly, out of desperation, mind-wrote the script for the next scene.

I knocked once, twice, three times, and waited, hoping the lady of the house was home. There was no way I would ever make it to Exo-town on my own. Eventually the door pulled back and a young woman appeared behind an inner screen door.

"Can I help you?" she asked, almost in a whisper.

"I'm lost," I said. "I wandered away from town, hoping to see the luminous veldt, and although I've found it, I don't think I can return. Something has been chasing me through the tall grass. I'm scared and tired." Having said this, I had a feeling my words had come out too stiffly to be believed.

She opened the screen door and looked at me. "Joseph Cotten?" she said.

I nodded and looked as forlornly as possible.

"You poor man," she said, and motioned for me to enter.

As I crossed the threshold, it became clear to me that old Joe was on the job. If it had been only me, she most likely would have locked the door and called the Beetle Squad, but since it was Cotten, the consummate professional of ingratiating *Third Man* haplessness, she immediately felt my pain.

Inside the bowels of the old Victorian, standing on an elaborately designed rug, amidst the spiraled wooden furniture, in the face of an ancient stand-up clock, I took in the beauty of Gloriette Moss. Stootladdle knew his film, because here was obvious star quality in the supernova range—an exotic hybrid of the young Audrey Hepburn and the older Hayley Mills. She was this and more than this, with a midlength blonde wave, a face so fresh and innocent, a smile that was straight grace until the corners curled into mischief. She wore a simple, cobalt-blue dress and no shoes. She was Jean Seberg with hair, Grace Kelly minus the affectation.

"I rarely have visitors now that my husband has passed away," she said, her hands clasped behind her back.

"Sorry to trouble you," I said. "I don't know what I was thinking, coming out here into the wilderness on my own."

"It's no trouble, really," she said. "I rather enjoy the idea of company."

"Well, just let me get my bearings and I'll be off," I said, and though I spoke this plainly, I could feel Cotten creating a look of half-hidden dejection.

"Nonsense," she said. "You've come all this way to see the veldt. You can't go back to town by yourself, you're lucky you made it here alive. There are things in the grass, you know. Things that would just as soon eat you."

"I'm sorry," I said. "I had come all the way from Earth to scout locations for a film about the bug planet. I'm thinking of reviving the art of cinema back on the home world, and I thought what better place to make a movie than the only place in the universe where movies are still appreciated for their art and not how much freasence they will bring."

"That's wonderful," she said, her face brightening more than ever. "Stay here with me for a while and I will show you the veldt. This house has so many empty rooms."

"Are you sure I won't be putting you out?" I asked.

"Please," she said. "I'll have my man show you upstairs and get you situated."

I began to speak, but she said, "I'll hear nothing to the contrary," and that ancient, elegant phrase, issuing from that smooth face made me weak.

"Vespatian," she called out, and a moment later a pale green grasshopper as tall as me, dressed in a black short-coat and trousers, appeared at the entrance to a hallway leading left.

"We have a visitor," she said. "Mr. Cotten will be staying for a time. See him to the large room on the third floor, the one with the view of the veldt."

"As you wish, madame," said the bug with the obsequious air of a David Niven. "This way, sir."

As I was delivered to the door of an upstairs room, Vespatian informed me that dinner would be at eight. I thanked him and he gave a pained sigh before deftly spinning and walking away.

The minute I was in my room, I became the Cotten of *Shadow of a Doubt*. I laid down on the bed, a view of the glowing waves of grass out beyond the floor-to-ceiling window making it feel as though I were on a ship sailing a sea of light, and began to scheme.

At dinner, we ate charbroiled centipede steaks and sipped at fermented roach mucous from fine crystal Earth goblets. I'd always thought if I had the money, I'd bring pizza to the bug planet, but that is something else again.

"Now, Joseph," said Gloriette. "I know you from your films, but I bet you have never heard of me before."

"But I have," I said, taking a chance of revealing too much. "I've never seen it, but anyone interested in film knows of *The Rain Does Things Like That*. After meeting you, I can now see why it is such a cult classic."

She laughed like a girl and then as suddenly a look of sorrow came over her. "My husband, the great Burt Lancaster, loved that movie," she said. "That is all that is important to me about it."

"Yes," I said. "I was sorry to hear about the ambassador when I arrived from Earth."

"He was a great man," she said, and the nano-technology produced delicate tears true to her obvious feelings.

We ate then in silence. I dared not speak and interrupt the memories clearly she was reliving. She sat motionless for some time, a piece of centipede on her fork, staring down at the table.

When I finished, I quietly got up and left the dining room. I went to bed and tried to sleep, but now that my situation was fixed and the nervous tension generated from an uncertain fate had worn off, my desire for the smoke began to scratch at my brain. I was so strung out I thought I smelled it wafting about my room. It became impossible to lay still any longer, and I got up and paced. There came a death scream of some prey from out on the veldt, punctuating the ambient drone of crickets. I let myself out of the room and quietly snuck downstairs.

I crept through the darkened house from room to room, wondering at all of the twentieth-century gewgaws that lined the shelves. The ambassador, it was evident, was a real fan of ancient Earth. Then, I truly did smell the smoke, and at the same time saw a light coming from a room at the end of a long hallway on the first floor. As I approached, I heard soft music—Ella Fitzgerald, I believe. At the entrance, I looked in and saw Gloriette sitting on a couch. Before her on a low table were a huge bottle of the concoction we had at dinner, a full glass, and a smoke pot, smoldering away, the orange mist hovering about the room. The long tube from the pot draped down and then up beneath her dress, between her open legs.

At that moment, she turned and saw me. Her half-opened eyes registered no alarm or embarrassment. She smiled, now much older than before, a smile devoid of mirth.

"Smoke?" she asked.

"If I may," I said twitching inside my exo-suit.

She patted the couch cushion next to her, and I went over and sat down.

Reaching beneath her dress, she unhooked the tube that led to the pot. The *woosh* sound of her spigot closing followed. She handed me the tube, and I pulled down my zipper, maneuvered myself into position and hooked up.

My God, what a relief. I still remember it even through the haze of all the intervening years of smoke. When I had finished, we sat in the orange cloud, listening to the heavenly music.

"Who are you, Joseph?" she asked in a whisper.

I knew what she meant, but it was too dangerous to speak of such things. On the bug planet, the charade of the exo-suits had not quite been figured out. Stootladdle and his minions really thought we were the stars we appeared to be. They were so enchanted by our personas, they had not bothered to apply the necessary logic to the situation. It was like the secret of Santa Claus, and I didn't want to be the one to blow it.

"A friend," I said, amazed at myself for having the wherewithal not to prattle under the influence of the smoke.

"Do you miss Earth?" she asked.

"Yes," I said. "I miss the sunlight."

"I could go back any time I wished," she said. "But there is nothing for me there. When the ambassador died, in a way, so did I."

"A good man," I said.

"A very good man," she said. "He loved his work. No one could wrap Stootladdle around their finger like my husband. The freasence market owes him such a debt. And not only his work, he was so good to me too. We always talked and joked, and twice a year, using his own wealth, we would go to town and, I hope you don't mind me mentioning it, visit the box."

"The box?" I asked.

"Stootladdle has a pressurized chamber you can get into and remove your exo-skin. It costs a great deal to use, but my husband thought nothing of the expense."

"But didn't that give the secret away?" I asked.

"No, Joseph," she said and laughed. "They think when we enter it, we are merely molting. They think of it in bug terms. A place for us to shed our outer skins and mate." She blushed and her giggling overtook her for a time.

"Imagine what their concept of humanity must be," I said, and laughed.

"A man from Earth invented the box and paid to have it brought here. It was popular for a time among the expatriates because he did not charge so much, but when Stootladdle saw that there was wealth to be made from it, he had the inventor meet with an accident and confiscated the box. Now he charges exorbitant rates for little more than an Earth half-hour."

"He is a bastard," I said.

"I shouldn't be telling you this, but I don't care now. In the box, we knew each other as the people that we truly are." Here, she set herself up for another toke, and after that the conversation died. The old phonograph finished the black platter and the music became a *scratch, scratch, scratch* that in its insistence blended with the crickets outside. I dozed and when I awoke, Gloriette was gone. I stumbled upstairs to bed.

The next day, which of course was always night, Vespatian brought the truck around. Gloriette and I sat on the open platform in the back on lounge chairs bolted to the metal deck. We had a pitcher of drinks and a picnic lunch.

"Into the veldt, Vespatian," she ordered.

"As you wish, madame," said the grasshopper from the cab.

She showed me the sights of that illuminated flatland, and I could tell she felt a vicarious wonder through my own astonishment at its beauty. In the afternoon, we came upon a dung ranch. Out in the tall grass, behemoth insects, called Zanderguls, elephant-sized water bugs, moved slowly through the veldt. Gloriette explained that these lumbering giants ate the grass, which was set aglow by tiny microbe-sized insects that carried their own luminescence. As the huge beasts dined, they excreted, in near equal proportion, globules of the freasence. A chemical reaction of the microbes mixing with the digestive juices of the Zanderguls gave freasence its special love qualities for earthlings. Behind each organic aphrodisiac machine followed a flea, one of Stootladdle's brethren, with a cart in which they would place the lumpen riches of the bug planet.

Just being out there near so much freasence turned my thoughts to sex. Gloriette, I noticed also had a certain flush about her, and I detected the presence of her nipples from beneath her demure pink party dress. When she saw me noticing, she called out to Vespatian, "That's enough for today."

The dutiful insect started the truck and took us back by way of a river path. Its waters were blacker than the night, but in its depths pinpoints of light darted about.

"There is Earth," said Gloriette, pointing out into space at a star that was smaller than one of the river mites.

"So it is," I said, but did not look.

That night, after dinner, after Vespatian had retired, Gloriette and I sat in the parlor staring through the orange fog at *The Rain Does Things Like That*. Earlier, when we had come in from the porch, an antique projector and a portable screen had already been set up. After a few good tokes, she turned off the lights and flipped the switch on the movie machine.

To be honest, the film was awful, the plot was what was known as a tearjerker, but Gloriette Moss was so radiant even in black and white, so honest, that the other lousy actors, the poor cinematography, the creaking scenario, didn't matter. It was about a young woman who, because she had been abused by her first husband, had become an alcoholic. We see her stumble out of a bar in the middle of a rainstorm and make her way along a city block. She is drenched when a young man approaches her with an umbrella and asks if she would like to share it with him. As it turns out, he too has a drinking problem. To make it short, they fall in love. Then they decide to help each other overcome their respective addictions. There is much overacting in relation to delirium tremors consisting of, among other things, swarms of insects, but finally love prevails. After the couple has succeeded, we see them married, living in an apartment building, modest but cozy. Life is wonderful, and then it starts to rain. The young husband tells her he is going across the street for a pack of cigarettes. From the window she watches him leave the building. As he crosses the street a car, driven by none other than the perpetually annoying Red Buttons, careens around the corner. The brakes are slammed, the car skids, and Gloriette's lover is killed. In the last scene of the movie, she is back at the bar. The bartender says that he hasn't seen her in some time and that she looks awful. She sips her drink, takes a puff of her cigarette and says, "The rain does things like that."

When the movie ended and the tail of the film slapped the projector with each spin of the spool, Gloriette turned to me and said, "You know, I have almost come to believe that this is an actual memory and that I am watching the real me when I was younger."

I told her she was fabulous in it, but she waved her hand in a manner that told me to leave the room. At the doorway, I turned back and told her she was beautiful. I don't think she even heard me, so intent was she rethreading the film as if intending to watch it again.

The days passed and I forgot completely about my assignment from Stootladdle. I had unwisely fallen in love with my mark. At every turn I had expected her to see through me, but each and every flaw in my design was masked and made charming by Cotten, so that I began to become aware, through the long hours we spent together, that she also had feelings for me. It was as if I were in a movie, some grade-B flick that, with its exotic backdrop of the veldt and the alchemy of its stars, transcended the need to aspire to "A" status and would live in the hearts of its viewers.

Or so I dreamed, until one day I passed Vespatian in the hall. He grabbed me by the arm, squeezing hard, and whispered, "Stootladdle sends a message. You have two days to deliver the film or on the third, if you do not, you will be hanging slack with Omar Sharif."

Suddenly the house lights went up, as they used to say, and again I was buried up to my neck in nightmare. I entertained the idea of coming clean with Gloriette and telling her of my predicament. Out of the kindness of her heart, she might turn the movie over to Stootladdle to save me, but at the same time she would know I had betrayed her. I did not want to lose her, but I did not want to die either. Even Cotten, expert thespian that he was, couldn't disguise my quandary. After dinner the night that Vespatian had delivered the dreaded message, Gloriette asked what was troubling me.

"Nothing," I told her, but later, after we had taken the smoke, she asked again. The drug weakened me and my growing fear forced me to rely on her mercy. I was sitting next to her on the couch. I reached over and took her hand in mine. She sat up and leaned toward me. "I have a confession to make," I said.

"Yes?" she said, looking into my eyes.

I did not know how to begin and sat long minutes simply staring at her beautiful face. From out across the veldt came the sound of thunder, and then an instant later the rain began to fall, tapping lightly at the parlor window.

I opened my mouth to speak, but no sound came forth. She took this as a sign and moved her face close to mine, touching her lips against my own. We were kissing, passionately. She wrapped her arms around me and drew me closer. My hand moved along the thin material of her dress, from her thigh to her ribs to her breasts. She made no protest for she was as hot as I was. We fondled and kissed for an unheard of length of time, more true to the manner of the twentieth century than our own. When I could stand it no longer, I reached beneath her dress. My hand sailed along the smooth inner skin of her thigh, and when I was about to explode with excitement, my fingers came to rest on the cold steel of her exhaust spigot. I literally groaned.

The suit makers, in all of their art and cunning, had left out that which may be the most important aspect of human anatomy. Think of the irony, a suit made to enhance a commerce dealing ultimately in sex, but having no sex itself. At the same moment I groped her steel pipe, she was doing the same to mine. We released each other and sat there in a state of total frustration.

"The box," she said. "Tomorrow we will go to town, to the box."

"Are you sure?" I asked.

"We have to," she said.

"But can you afford it? I haven't the money," I said, still slightly trembling.

"No, I can't afford it either, but there is something that Stootladdle wants that I can trade for a half-hour in the chamber," she said.

Then it struck me, just like in Gloriette's movie, love would prevail. She was going to trade the film for me, and I would live and not be found out by her. Frank Capra himself couldn't have conceived of anything more felicitous.

Vespatian woke me from a warm, bright dream of summer by the sea. "Mrs. Lancaster is waiting for you in the truck," he said. I hurriedly got dressed and went downstairs.

As I climbed into my chair, I saw that Gloriette was holding the movie tin in her hand. She tapped it nervously against her knee.

"Good morning, Joseph," she said. "I hope you are well rested."

"I'm ready," I said with a lightness in my heart I had not felt since landing on the bug planet.

She wore a yellow dress and a golden bee pendant on a thin cable around her neck. Her hair was done in braids, and she shone more vibrantly than the veldt itself.

"Exo-Skeleton Town," she called to Vespatian.

"As is your pleasure, madame," said the grasshopper, and we were off.

We rode in silence through the dark. Somewhere, after we had left the veldt far behind and I couldn't see two feet in front of me, I felt her hand touch mine and we intertwined our fingers. All went well until we reached the outskirts of Exo-town, and there, beneath a streetlamp, we witnessed a despondent Judy Garland, in blue gingham, put a stinger gun to her head and pull the trigger. Her exo-skin must have been poorly made because, instead of her leaking out, it blew apart like a bursting balloon, spewing blood and guts of her true self across the passenger door of our truck.

Gloriette covered her eyes with her hand. "I wish I hadn't seen that," she said. "This is surely Hell."

"It's alright," I told her. "She's better off."

The bluebottles immediately appeared and began devouring the remains.

"Drive faster, Vespatian," she called.

The grasshopper hit the gas pedal and we were driving down the main street of Exo-Skeleton Town no more than three minutes later.

Stootladdle was beside himself with cordiality when he finally understood the deal that Gloriette was putting before him.

"An old movie and not well known," he said, taking the film tin from her. "But, in deference to your late husband, and because you are so delightful, I will take this token in exchange for a half-hour in the box for you and your friend."

"When you see me in the scene at the end of the film, where I am in the bar," she said to him. "Always remember that at that moment, as I am saying my final line, my left high heel is flattening a roach beneath my bar stool."

"It will thrill me to the very thorax," said the mayor.

"The box," she said.

"Yes, follow me," said the flea. As we left his office, he turned to me and whispered, "Cotten, you damn rascal."

The box was in an otherwise abandoned building down the street from the mayor's office. He unlocked the door with the end of a long thick hair that jutted from his cheek. We stepped into the deep shadows behind him. There before us, almost indistinguishable from the rest of the darkness, was a large black box, ten by ten by ten. Stootladdle moved to the front of it and appeared to be pressing some buttons. There was a sound of old gears turning slowly, and a panel slid back revealing bright light, as if from my dream of summer.

"Remember," said the flea, "you must wait until the gong sounds inside before you can molt your outer skin. Also, when the gong sounds for the second time, you must replace your skin within five minutes or you will die when the door opens again. All this was told to me by the dear Earth man who invented it."

"Joseph?" asked Gloriette.

"Let's go," I said.

"This is surely paradise," said Stootladdle as he swept out his arms to usher us into the box of light.

I could hear the door slowly closing behind us but could see nothing, my eyes temporarily blinded. It was warm, though, and there were sound affects—a stream running, birds singing, a tinkling wind chime, and the rustling of leaves.

Just as my vision cleared, I heard the gong sound.

"Isn't it perfectly lovely," said Gloriette.

"The most beautiful place I've ever been," I said. I looked around and there was nothing inside, just the floor and walls padded with deep foam rubber covered in crimson silk.

"Come, Joseph, make me forget about the veldt," she said.

I put my arms around her. She gently pushed me away. "Let's molt," she said with a nervous laugh.

Four successive taps at the center of the forehead made the exo-skin peel down like the sectioned hide of an orange. We reached out and tapped each other.

Imagine wearing a pair of ill-fitting shoes, shoes far too tight. Imagine walking for months in them with no relief. And then imagine finally taking them off, and you will know one hundredth the relief of shedding an exo-skin. This sensation itself verged on orgasm. Cotten fell away and lay rumpled around my ankles. I kicked him into a corner of the box. When I looked back at Gloriette, she had her back to me. I was pleased to see her real hair was a perfect color match for that of the actress. Stepping up behind her, I put my hands on her shoulders.

"Scratch my back," she said, and I did.

"That feels so good," she said, with a sigh.

Then she turned and I took a step away from her. My eyes went wide as did hers. I noticed a sudden hollow feeling in my chest. She wasn't beautiful anymore, and she wasn't homely by any means, but she was different. That difference thoroughly chilled me even in the warm light of the box. What was more, I saw from the look in her eyes the reflection of her own grave disappointment. All of my pent-up desire vanished, leaving me limp inside and out. I saw her bottom lip begin to tremble and the sight of this brought tears to my eyes.

"I'm not Gloriette Moss," she said.

"I know," I told her and stepped forward to put my arms around her once again.

For fifteen minutes of our precious time in paradise, we stood holding each other in silence, not as lovers but as frightened, lost children. The notion of sex was as distant from that box as we were from the true sun. Like a desperate confession, she began frantically to whisper into my ear her life story. Born on Earth as Melissa Bower to a military man and his wife, she married very young to a career diplomat, who forced her to accompany him to the bug planet. In choosing her exo-skin, he would not allow her to become anyone of any recognition. She had wanted Jane Mansfield, but instead was allowed only Gloriette Moss. His main desire was to achieve great wealth for himself. The ambassador, it turns out, was as abusive a species of vermin as Stootladdle. It was she who did Lancaster in with a hatpin to the eye. "I used something so very thin, so there would be no evidence and he would suffer longer as he turned to jelly," she said. "The smoke was my only friend."

Her honesty made me feel as naked within as without. I told her the truth about how I had come to her house and why. As I explained, I heard her give a brief groan and then felt her slump in my arms as if she were now no more than an empty exo-skin. When I finished, I eased her onto the floor and lay beside her. She did not cry, but stared vacantly into the corner of the box.

"We have each other now," I told her. "We can help each other beat the smoke, and if we sell all the things in your house, we can return to Earth. We might even come to love each other." I kissed her on the cheek, but she did not respond.

I talked and projected and promised, rubbed her arm and ran my open palm the length of her hair. Then the gong sounded, waking me suddenly from the dream of the future I was spinning.

I immediately began fitting my suit back on. "It will be fine," I said right before I momentarily died and was revived. When I was again Cotten, I looked down and to my horror, she hadn't moved.

"Come on, hurry!" I yelled. "There are only minutes left."

She lay motionless, staring. I tried to slip her suit onto her—an impossible task unless the wearer is standing—but she was curled in a fetal position. Those few minutes were an eternity, and when I thought they should have long been over, I lifted her and held her to me.

"Why?" I asked. "Why?"

She slowly turned her face to me. "You know why," she said. Then the door slid open, and she turned to rain in my arms.

This story got turned down more times than my Visa card. What's not to like? It's got giant alien bugs, Hollywood stars, balls of aphrodisiacal insect shit, drug consumption through a spigot in the crotch, and Judy Garland as Dorothy Gale, shooting herself in the head. Anyway, at least I thought it was great. The story finally met a kindred spirit in Dave Truesdale, editor of the first issue of Black Gate: Adventures in Fantasy Literature.

I got the idea for this story from a book my son bought about the history of Japanese monster flicks titled Monsters Are Attacking Tokyo! by Stuart Galbraith. Before looking through it, I was unaware that the great actor Joseph Cotten had done a bunch of low budget monster movies in Japan near the end of his career. I never saw any of them, but the book had plenty of pictures. "Exo-Skeleton Town" is told in the melodramatic fashion of the black and white movies I watched on TV in the afternoons when, as a kid, I'd skip school, which was pretty often.

The name of the movie that is coveted by the mayor of the bug world, The Rain Does Things Like That, came from a deranged guy who wandered the streets of South Philly when I lived near Marconi Plaza, only a stone's throw from Monzo's Meatarama. I'd see this guy at least once a week, and he never tired of repeating that same phrase.

I've often thought that someday I'd like to write the story of the rise to power of Stootladdle, the flealike mayor of Exo-Skeleton Town. Thanks go out to Dave Truesdale and John O'Neill (Black Gate publisher) for bringing this creature feature to a theatre near you.

The Honeyed Knot

ABOUT TEN YEARS AGO I HAD A STUDENT IN A composition course I was teaching who, upon my giving the class a writing assignment, raised his hand and, with a monotone voice, asked, "Mr. Ford, what if we don't have any rhymes?" I looked up to see if he was joking, but what I saw was a worn leather jacket, an ageless face, a sinister Dutch-boy haircut and eyes that stared so intently they seemed to be seeing all the way around the world to the back of his own head.

"Don't worry," I said. "We're not writing poetry. Just tell a story."

"But I have no rhymes," he insisted.

He sat there for the entire class and did nothing but stare. I didn't understand his dilemma, but it was college, he was paying, and as long as he wasn't obstreperous, I figured I'd let him sit there and work through it.

After teaching for another ten years, though, his statement eventually became clear to me. Hundreds of students and thousands of papers later, I too had begun to feel a conspicuous lack of rhymes. At first, I thought perhaps it was my age. Long gone were the days when the students would mistake me for one of their own. I felt out of touch at work, as if I had been hollowed out and were sleep-walking through my duties. It was eerie, otherworldly, and I had a vague presentiment that it had to do with the residual power of all those papers I'd read and the authors' minds behind them. Make no mistake, words have magic. They are contagious. In delving so deeply into other individuals' writing processes, I had come in contact with secret machinations. I had witnessed inexplicable instances of the uncanny.

I remember one woman who wrote that her husband's ex-wife had placed a Santería spell on her. She was surprised on a particular Sunday morning to find dinner plates of dry rice and human hair positioned at the four corners of the outside of her house. Under the advisement of an aunt, who was also an adept of the mysteries of that religion, she suspended a bowl of water with an egg in it from the ceiling. Three days later, when she broke open the egg, she found it contained a blood spot. This is how she discovered the true nature of the curse. Before finally going to New York and hiring a *bruja* to sacrifice a chicken for her, she met with all manner of accidents and mishaps, some of which I had seen the proof—bruises from her fall down a flight of stairs, her car dented in the parking lot, the aftermath of a fire that had started spontaneously in her pocketbook.

Another young woman, a favorite student of mine, divulged in an essay that she was a witch and, later in the semester as a favor to me, cast a spell to cure some trouble I was having with my vision. The night she worked her magic, she came to class in a pure white outfit, like a child's party dress, and white patent-leather shoes. She never said a word and left before the class was over. Three days later, my sight had improved.

I remember a young African-American student who had traced his lineage, with green crayon on a piece of cardboard, back to Leif Ericsson, the Viking explorer, on one side of his family, and, on the other, to Geronimo. He believed he was constantly being watched by the infrared eyes of satellites. Who was I to tell him he was mistaken? Perhaps even more pathetic was a girl who wrote that she had a disease that caused exotic flowers to grow in her lungs. When I inquired further about it, she said, "Like a garden. When they blossom, I will suffocate to death."

Then there was the meek, bespectacled young man who spoke only in whispers, and ended up raping and murdering a child in his neighborhood during the time he was a student of mine. All of his stories and essays revolved around a dragon named Flamer, and when I saw my student on CNN, manacled and accompanied by two U.S. marshals, I blamed myself for having failed to decipher the obscure symbolism of his tales and ward off the tragedy. That little girl's death haunted me for years.

But the most unnerving incident of my career had to do with a forty-seven-year-old woman with a metal plate in her head. Her story proved to be a prism that focused all the disparate narratives of all of my hundreds of students together into a lesson I will never forget.

Mrs. Apes came to my class in that fall semester so devoid of rhymes I had considered quitting. She was very soft spoken, and although her face was scarred and her hair somewhat spotty in front, she had a look of simple kindness about her that I immediately liked. The other students, all much younger, were at first put off by her questions and encouragements because she was unabashed in her expression of emotion and would touch them lightly on their shoulders when talking to them. By the third class session, though, they were treating her like the mother they wished they had.

Her writings were neither stories nor essays. "Visionary testaments" is the best way I can think to describe them. I hadn't seen anything like them since the dragon stories of that doomed young man, Kevin Wheast. They had no official beginning or ending, and their purpose was elusive. Birds turned into wolves that leaped into the sky to reside in a magical cloud realm where the tears they cried became a rain that washed terror out of lonely children. Deer knew the secrets of creation, crows lived inside men's minds, dogs harbored the souls of dead saints. And the loving spirit Avramody watched over this strange and complex cosmology.

I knew it was best to work with what I was given by the student at first and then try to move on to different things as the semester progressed. She was an atrocious speller, and her sentence structure was, at times, bizarre, as if she were translating from another language. Paragraphing was out of the question. When I would mention these problems to her and possible strategies to overcome them, she would laugh softly and look into the distance as if remembering the amusing antics of a long-dead relative.

Then one day, when I was having a conference with her at my desk at the front of the classroom, I asked her to write a story about some incident that happened in her life. She was silent for some time before blurting out that her husband had brutally beaten her and broken her skull. "The police had to shoot him," she said. "And when they took me to the emergency room, I came out of my body and flew around the hospital, seeing everything. I saw people's true colors, like a glowing ball of light, right here," she said, pointing to her solar plexus. "With each soul I encountered in this form, their color would shoot out a beam at my head. Finally, I met up with a little girl down in the hospital morgue in the basement who called me to her and kissed me between the eyes. She told me to return to my body and that I would live. Now I have the metal up there." And she knocked on her head as if it was a door.

"A metal plate?" I asked her.

She nodded. "My head is a magnet and a beacon. At times it is a bonus, because it allows me to see into situations, to broadcast to the world, but it also makes me forget important things I need to remember."

I knew the worst thing I could do was to dismiss Mrs. Apes's story. It was her reality, and if I wanted to help her with her writing, I had to respect it no matter how incredible it sounded. Still, I had my job to do, so I pressed her a little, hoping to find a focused topic she would be willing to write about.

"What's one of the things you have forgotten?" I asked. "For you to feel that there is something missing from your memory, you must have a vague idea what it entails."

"I had a daughter," she told me. "She was a beautiful girl, as sweet and kind as her father was a monster. Four years ago, two years after I was attacked, when she was fourteen, she was hit by a car while crossing the street in front of her school. She was rushed to the hospital and the doctors worked on her for hours, but she finally died from a traumatic head injury. I almost died from grief myself. I've always felt I should have seen it coming, should have been there to help her," she said, but her placid expression never diminished.

I looked away from Mrs. Apes for a moment and saw the other students of the class had been listening intently. Their various facades of youthful cynicism and cool had melted, leaving their faces looking like those of a bunch of children watching, for the first time, the squadron of hideous monkeys take wing in *The Wizard of Oz*.

Mrs. Apes continued. "Anyway, my daughter was taken to the same hospital I had been taken to." Here she leaned forward and put her hand on my arm. "Do you know that because of our same last name, the x-ray technician mixed up my head x-rays with hers? When the doctor noticed from the first name that the tech had pulled the wrong pictures, he asked for my daughter's. At one point, he had a copy of each on his desk. That is when he discovered they were identical. The damage, the breaks, the fractures, were a perfect likeness of each other. I mean *perfect*."

I shook my head.

"Think about it," she said. "I was forty-one when it happened to me and my daughter was fourteen."

"What does it mean?" I asked.

"I'm not sure," she said. "But I believe my visions are leading me to the answer."

"What is it you've forgotten?" I asked.

"My daughter's name," she said. "I can't for the life of me remember her name. I call my sister in California and ask her what my daughter's name was, and she tells me, but before I can write it down I forget it. If I'm not looking at it on a piece of paper, I can't remember. That loss of memory is agony to me."

"Could you write about that?" I asked.

Mrs. Apes turned very somber. "I'll try," she said, "but wait till you see what happens."

I took her vague warning under advisement, and wondered if I had done the right thing by trying to get her to write about something so close to her. I had learned through the years that students who dealt with very personal material could have real breakthroughs in their writing, because, very often, it was the confusion caused by the memories of these events that hampered their ability to express themselves clearly. Stories and essays don't produce themselves, and they aren't born from typing fingers. The reality of a narrative exists first in the mind.

She went back to her computer and started working. I had to address some of the questions and problems of other students, and for a while I paid no attention to her. As I made my rounds of the classroom, checking in with everyone and reading pieces of the projects they were working on, I finally came to Mrs. Apes's workstation. She was not typing but simply staring blankly at the screen. I looked over her shoulder and saw that the monitor was flashing a jumble of letters and symbols that changed with each pulsation. The background color, normally a royal blue, was now pink.

"Wow," I said. "I've never seen that before."

When she laughed the screen went completely blank, and the computer made a sound like it was dying.

"I told you," she said. "It's the plate in my head. Now it's ruined your machine."

"No," I said. "It's probably just a glitch. These machines are used by thousands of students every year. The wear and tear probably did it in. Maybe it contracted a virus along the way."

"If you say so," she said.

"Were you making any progress?" I asked.

She nodded.

"Well, before you forget what you had typed, let's switch you to another machine." I walked over to an empty workstation and got the computer up and running for her.

By the end of the class, Mrs. Apes's metal plate had beamed three machines into uselessness. She was effusively apologetic but kept telling me that she had warned me. She was the last student to leave, and I stopped her and told her not to worry about the machines, that I would have them fixed.

"Thank you, thank you," she said. "You know, I saw in my writing that you'd find a buck in the road."

"Gratuities are unnecessary," I said. "But let's hope it's a hundred."

She smiled at me and left.

Later that afternoon, I had the computer tech take a look at the machines that had gone haywire. He turned them on and they worked perfectly.

"There's nothing wrong with them," he said.

I described what I had seen and explained to him Mrs. Apes's metal-plate theory. He told me it was possible that the plate might have had something to do with it. "There's an electromagnetic field around these machines when they are on, and the body generates its own electromagnetic field. I've never heard of it happening before though. More than likely she didn't want to write and just screwed them up herself when you weren't watching."

I hadn't considered the fact that she might be sabotaging the machines consciously in order not to have to deal with her memories of her daughter. It was an interesting possibility, and it made me decide that during the next class I would have her write about something less personal. If she was going to those lengths to avoid the subject, it might be dangerous to force her to it. I had to remind myself that it was a writing class and not a psych experiment.

That night I had a late class and some time to kill beforehand, so I went over to the library and asked the librarian to do a search for me on the name or word "Avramody." I told her I suspected that it might be from some crackpot religion or cult, maybe the title of one of the myriad mediaeval demons. She promised that she would work on it and let me know if she found anything.

Then I phoned Mrs. Apes's counselor and asked what he knew about her claims of a metal plate in her head. He said she had never told him anything about it. "Look," he told me, "she seems like an ordinary middle-aged woman to me, but sometimes that ordinariness is the problem. It wouldn't be the first time one of our students has invented an interesting past for themselves. She was obviously abused by her husband, maybe she is looking for empowerment through a sense of individuality. She wants to be different and special. Maybe she is reinventing herself now that she is in school. Don't question it too deeply," he said.

My night class let out at 10:30. By the time I got to my car and began the hour and half ride home, it was almost 11:00. Instead of taking the New Jersey Turnpike, which was too fast for me, I always took route 537, a country road that passed through farmland and woods. Just after the midnight news came on the radio, I found my buck.

Weighing about 250 pounds and carrying a ten-point rack, it came charging out of a blind of cattails on the left side of the road. In an instant, I slammed on the brakes, but the car went into a skid, and I helplessly watched as the corner of my station wagon nailed the huge animal in the side. Upon impact the deer bent in toward my windshield and, for a moment, I could clearly see its eye, brimming with animal fear, looking in at me. Then it flew off my car from the force of the collision while at the same time my car stopped. The radio shut off when the car cut out and everything was dead quiet.

I couldn't open the driver-side door because the whole left front of the car was smashed back and out of alignment. Instead, I crawled across the seat and let myself out the passenger side. The buck was writhing on the side of the road, kicking only one of its back legs spasmodically. I was shaking and my mind was blank. The animal craned its neck up out of the pool of blood it lay in and looked back over its shoulder at me. That is when I noticed that one of its lower antler points had grown down and into the side of its jaw. The sight of that anomaly made me wince.

A great rasping sound came up from its chest and turned into high-pitched squeals. It was clear to me that the creature was about to die. "I'm sorry," I said aloud to it. Its cries became weaker and more breathy, and just before it went limp, the buck made a noise through its mouth that sounded distinctly like a human voice uttering a word. I swear I heard it, a word made up of only vowels. I shook my head and backed away. As soon as I crawled back into the car, I got it started, and drove slowly to the Vincent Town Diner, where I called the police to report the mishap. The officer told me he'd send someone out to fetch the animal.

For the rest of the drive home, I was jittery, waiting for something else to come dashing across the road. I prayed the car, which was in very bad shape, wouldn't crap out and leave me stranded in the dark. When I finally pulled into my driveway, I felt like crying. The first thing I did upon entering the house was go upstairs and check on my sons who were fast asleep. Their light, steady breathing diminished the trembling of my hands and put me at ease. My wife was also asleep; I undressed and climbed into bed beside her.

"I hit a deer on the way home," I told her.

"Why?" she asked from sleep.

I didn't bother to wake her. Once I told her about the accident she would be unable to sleep for the rest of the night. I just lay there in the dark, trying to get warm by thinking about a vacation we had taken to the beach the previous summer. My method of relaxation worked quite well, and I was eventually able to doze off. Somewhere in my sleep, I relived the accident, saw the wounded deer, and heard that haunting word composed of vowels. In my dream I told myself, "You've got to remember this word when you wake up." But then the morning had come and I had forgotten.

The accident had left me with a feeling of unreality, as if I had died in it and was now a spirit unaware that he was no longer alive. My wife, who was a nurse, told me to take the day off, and I decided to take the rest of the week off. It was not only that I was afraid of driving again, but more that I didn't want to leave home. I wanted to stay close to my sons for some reason. They were eight and ten, at ages where a hug had to be requested from them, but when I told them what had happened with the deer, they kept hugging me and touching my face.

After my wife left for work and the boys had gone to school, I called the college and explained that my car was wrecked, and I had been slightly hurt; although truthfully there was nothing physically wrong with me. Then I called the garage in town to come and tow the car in for repairs. While I was waiting for the tow truck, I decided to make a pot of coffee. At the kitchen sink, while running water into the pot, I looked out the window into the backyard.

There, in broad daylight, I saw a deer drinking out of the birdbath. The sight of it sent a wave of fear through me. I walked to the back door, pulled it open and yelled, "What do you want?" There was nothing there.

I drank my coffee and reasoned that the deer was just a coincidence as we did live in a wooded area very close to the Pine Barrens. Still, a deer sighting in daylight was not a common occurrence. I played music, tried to grade a stack of class papers, watched television, but the entire time I kept trying to remember that word the buck had spoken to me.

That afternoon, when my older son, who rode his bike to school, did not return on time, I felt an ominous reptile uncoiling in my thoughts and I became frantic. I took the younger one, who had been delivered by the bus and, since I didn't have a car, set out on foot to look for his brother. All manner of horrors went through my mind, and don't think I didn't remember what had happened to Mrs. Apes's daughter. I walked so fast my son had to run to keep up.

After walking the length of five long blocks at a breakneck pace, we saw him at a distance coming along on his bike. I was so relieved I laughed out loud. When he reached us he told me that he had stopped with some other kids to see a deer that had come out of the woods by the lake. I told him I had seen the same one in our backyard that morning.

"The one with the weird horn?" he asked.

"What do you mean?" I said.

"It had a weird horn that grew down instead of up."

I told him the one I had seen didn't have antlers.

"Two deer in one day," he said, "good thing your car's in the shop," and then he took off on his bike. "I'll race you guys home," he called back over his shoulder.

I was in a perpetual fog for the next few days, only surfacing when the kids said they were going to do something. Then my mind focused into worry. During these days I must have filled the backs of twenty envelopes with combinations of vowels, trying to reproduce the word that eluded me. Finally, on Monday, I picked up my car at the shop on the way to work. It was a white-knuckle drive that morning even though the sun was bright and the day was beautiful.

When I arrived at work, I found in my mailbox an interoffice envelope from the librarian. Inside was a typed sheet with a yellow Post-It note attached, which said:

Jeff,
    Next time, how about something a little easier, like who invented Velcro? Anyway, here's what I found on Avramody. Hope it's what you were looking for.

Jean

    I took the sheet back to my office, closed the door, and read it.
    Nicholas Avramody, born 1403, died 1441, lived in the village of Fornapp on the southern coast of England. He had been born into a well-to-do family and was given a classical education by his father who was a cartographer. Around the age of twenty, Avramody left home and gave up his part in his father's business. He built himself a small home in the nearby woods and began writing a book that was later published, entitled *The Honeyed Knot*. This work would eventually become a key text for the Puritans, and would figure extensively in the religio-philosophical works of Cotton Mather. The "honeyed knot" was a metaphor for the impossibly complex plot of human existence. For mere mortals, their lives and the reasons for the events in them may seem like a tangled ball of string, but this inexplicable mess is a sweet one because it is the deity's plan for us. Within the knot, all our lives touch and crisscross and bind together for good but unknowable reasons.
    This philosopher-hermit eventually fell afoul of the church for another belief of his, namely the fact that animals have souls and given enough patience, one can communicate with them. Creatures all have knowledge of the plan, a knowledge we lost in the Garden of Eden. When the locals started going to him for spiritual guidance, the clergy became jealous and started rumors that he practiced bestiality with the various animals of the forest that flocked around his small home. It so happened at this time that a girl in Fornapp was bitten by a bat, contracted rabies, and died. The church fathers told the townspeople that the bat had been sent by Avramody. They incited such fear and contempt of him that he was eventually attacked by an angry mob and cudgeled to death.
    With this knowledge still buzzing in my head, I went downstairs to my class only to be met by Mrs. Apes. She handed me a paper and said, "I did it. I finished the piece you asked for." As soon as I was able to get all of the students working on their various projects, I sat down with her at my desk and looked at her writing. The piece had been executed very sloppily in pencil and was about four pages long. I got no further than the title, though, because *there* was the word the buck had spoken to me. I realized now that it did have one consonant, but a soft one that sounds like another vowel when surrounded by vowels.

"Ayuwea?" I said to Mrs. Apes.

She smiled, "My daughter's name."

"It's unusual," I said.

"My mother's mother was half Ojibwa Indian, and I had heard her name from my mother many times, but never saw it spelled. So when I had my daughter, I named her after my grandmother but had to invent the spelling. I knew she would be a special child and needed a special name."

"Does it mean anything?" I asked.

She shook her head and shrugged. "Something, I'm sure," she said.

"I thought you couldn't remember it," I said.

"Well, it was the strangest thing. Last week, after I had tried to write about her in class, I couldn't get her off my mind. Later that night, I was sitting in front of my television and the name just popped into my head. I remembered it just like I had never forgotten it. I'm sure trying to write about her brought the name to me."

So I read Mrs. Apes's paper about her daughter. It was a loving tribute but nothing I hadn't seen from a thousand other students who had lost someone close to them and recorded their feelings and memories in writing. As I had suspected she would, Mrs. Apes had made great strides in her grammar and spelling in that paper, but I never got the chance to continue working with her because she never returned to class after that day. The school had no phone number for her and none of the other students knew her or where she lived.

This is where I thought the story should end. In one way it seemed satisfying that my student had come to some greater understanding of herself. There were loose ends, though, and all of the amazing connections really didn't seem to add up to much. I decided to pass it off as one huge coincidence that I had somehow helped to generate through a bout of paranoia. With each class that came and went, I held out hope that Mrs. Apes would return and I could continue to work with her.

At lunch one day, three weeks after Mrs. Apes's disappearance, I saw a familiar face in the college pizza shop. She was wearing all black but looking exactly the same as when I had last seen her. I took my lunch over to her table and sat down.

"Do you think you could put a spell on this pizza and make it taste better?" I asked.

She looked up at me and shook her head. "It's dangerous to mock powers that are greater than you," said the witch and smiled.

She filled me in on what she had been doing since going on to study at the state university in graduate-level anthropology. I was always happy to hear when my students hadn't opted for a degree in business. On this particular day she had come to the college, which was near her house, to do some research on her thesis, concerning the importance of written language in magic and witchcraft.

"How are your eyes?" she asked.

"I haven't had a problem since," I told her. "It's not my eyes I'm having a problem with now, it's my head."

"Such as?" she asked.

"As a matter of fact," I said, "you'll love this." I proceeded to tell her the entire story of Mrs. Apes in all of its convoluted detail. When I got to the part about the buck I had hit and the word I believed I had heard it speak, she laughed. When I was done, I asked her, "What do you think of that?"

She looked into my eyes and her expression became serious. "You've missed something," she said.

"Like the boat?" I asked.

"It's important," she said.

"I think I was shaken by the incredible synchronicity of the whole thing," I told her.

"Listen," she said, "I'll make you a deal. If you'll read my thesis over before I submit it, I'll look into things for you."

"I'll read your paper anyway," I said, unsure if I wanted any more involvement in the supernatural.

I had to run to class after that, but before I left, she told me she would be in touch.

Weeks passed and although I had learned to keep my uneasiness at bay, it was always there, hovering in the background. At the end of the semester, I had a hard time giving Mrs. Apes an F for the course, but I was required to because she had "phantomed" halfway through the semester. She had definitely learned something, though what it was exactly I wasn't sure.

On the last day, I still had quite a few papers to read before I could make out my grade sheets. I envied all those who had fled in a mass exodus after the final class had let out. The place was as still as a ghost town while I sat in my office reading. Just when I finished and was about to enter the final grades, the phone rang. It was Jean from the library.

"I think we're the only ones left on campus," I said.

"Count me out," she said. "I'm home, but I just remembered something I had meant to tell you."

"Okay," I said.

"I thought I was done with Avramody," she said, "but I found something else."

"What's that?"

"There was a student at the library yesterday, a young woman. She said she was doing research on a paper about vanity for one of your classes. She was rather outlandishly dressed in all white. Said her name was Maggie Hamilton."

I laughed. "I know who you mean," I said, "but her name isn't Margaret Hamilton."

"Well, she had me pull some microfilm for her from the local newspaper. She took it over to the machine, cued up the reel, and started reading through it. When I walked back over there a little later to see if she needed help, she was gone. I left the reel on the machine for a while in case she came back but she didn't. Before I took the reel off, out of curiosity, I glanced at the page she was on and the name Avramody jumped out at me."

"More about the honeyed knot?" I asked.

"Not exactly," she said. "Do you remember about six years ago a student who went to the college here who raped and murdered a little girl?"

I said nothing.

"Hello?" said Jean.

"I'm here," I finally said.

"The little girl's name was Melissa Avramody. I don't know what you can do with that," she said.

"Thanks," I said. "I remember now."

After I hung up, I got out of my chair and paced back and forth in the confines of the office. This pointless journey finally ended at the window that overlooked the empty parking lot. I leaned my forehead against the glass and looked out. The sun had nearly set and twilight was creeping out from the trees of the nature preserve that bounded the asphalt expanse. I saw my car sitting there like a lonely student who has stayed in class long after dismissal. A few seconds later my attention was drawn to something moving in the shadows by the edge of the woods. It stamped its hooves and, startled by the approach of night, turned to show me its rack of bone, one branch growing down into its jaw. At the sight of it, a feeling welled up from deep within me, and my own jaw opened to release a word made only of consonants.

When you are a teacher, you are ever vigilant to instruct, to correct, to lecture, to advise, to care. The residue of this responsibility accumulates around you through time and can serve to make you a poor student. That night in my office, in the last hours of the semester, I passed them all, Kevin Wheast, Melissa Avramody, Mrs. Apes, by setting myself an assignment to stand for those I never received. I did not ask how long it had to be or if I could have an extension but turned on my computer and began typing. Somewhere in all those words, I found the rhymes. Then the final loop of the honeyed knot tightened and drew me back into its jumbled heart.

THE HONEYED KNOT

I've been a professor of writing and literature for the past twenty-five years, fifteen of that at Brookdale Community College in Lincroft, New Jersey. I know a lot of writers say that they would never want to teach writing for a living because it would deaden them to their own work. That hasn't been my experience. My students' writing has really helped me with my own. The idea for "The Honeyed Knot" was sparked by the fact that I actually did have a student in my class one semester who raped and murdered a little girl in his neighborhood. There was nothing I could have done to prevent it from happening, but for some reason I still felt a measure of responsibility for the tragedy. It haunted me for quite a while and left me cold to teaching for a time — something I had always loved. The story is not a confession, nor an expiation, nor an explanation, but merely an attempt to express what I was feeling about the situation. The strangest thing about it is that, I swear, it's 99.9% true.

Gordon Van Gelder accepted this story for The Magazine of Fantasy and Science Fiction *and suggested some changes to certain parts, especially the ending. The story benefited from these changes, but still I was very wary of the piece because of the great emotional connection it had for me. I think Gordon had far more faith in the story than I did. Only when the piece was published and I reread it again in the magazine did I fully allow myself to like it. The process of writing it, editing it, and seeing it published helped me to exorcise some ghosts and reminded me about the importance of my work as a teacher.*

Something by the Sea

MAGGIE RAN AHEAD OF HIM DOWN THE PATH IN the failing light, the sleek gray whippet, Mathematics, moving gracefully at her side. Her Uncle Archer came hobbling slowly along behind with his cane, a picnic basket draped over one arm.

"Watch that tree root at the turn," he called, "it will try to grab your ankle."

Her laugh came back to him and he smiled.

It was a warm twilight of sudden, billowing breezes that rushed through the leaves and made the boughs sway. Night was mixing quickly into the last faint glow of red, filling the woods with shadows. Off in the distance could be heard the calm and methodical heartbeat of the ocean, while closer a night bird sang melancholic, trilling its low whistle from within a tangled thorn bush.

He rounded the bend in the path and beheld his niece—powder-blue pajamas, pigtails, and bare feet—standing uncharacteristically still, head cocked back, and gazing at a firefly floating erratically midway between her nose and the rustling green canopy above.

"Look, Uncle Archer, the first one of the night," she turned and said when she heard him behind her.

"There will be more," he said. "Soon they'll all be out and we'll have to put on dark glasses."

"Silly," she said matter-of-factly and continued on her way. "Come, Math," she called back to the dog.

The path meandered for a quarter mile through the woods, and by the time they reached the *observatory*, as Archer called the small clearing, they had only the moon and fireflies to light their way. Two fan-backed wicker chairs and a low, glass-topped table were there waiting for them. Archer put the picnic basket down on one of the seats and drew back its leather cover. From within, he retrieved a candle and placed it on the table. Leaving his cane propped against the arm of the chair, he stepped uneasily over to the trunk of an oak tree at the boundary of the clearing.

Maggie took her uncle's arm and steadied him as he unwound the cord that, at their end, was twined around a cleat driven into the trunk and, at the other, looped up over the one branch that jutted out above the furniture. Once the line was clear, he released it slowly, a handful at a time, lowering an orange globe the size of a beach ball from where it had hung, up near the sheltering branch. When the lantern had descended, twirling and swaying, to a foot above the table, he rewound the extra cord around the cleat.

"Can I light it?" she asked, as they moved back to where the orange ball swung.

"Absurd," said Archer, reaching into his vest pocket. He took out a cigarette lighter that had the form of a derringer. "You can get the hatch, though," he told her.

Maggie climbed upon the other chair and, reaching for the globe, unhooked the curved panel that opened on delicate hinges, while her uncle shot a spark of flame at the wick of the candle. "Hold it still, now," he said, and she steadied the lantern. He carefully fitted the candle into its place inside the globe and then closed it. A warm glow filled the sphere and radiated subtly throughout the observatory.

"Hoist it," he said to her and she did the honors at the tree, unwinding the cord from around the cleat. As she slowly pulled back on the line, she watched the rising lantern and thought of it as a miniature sun, and then a soul. When she had the line secured, she turned back to her uncle, who had taken from the picnic basket a folded quilt that he was just then unfurling. She stepped forward as he held it up in front of him like a bullfighter's cape. "Madame Margaret," he said. When she was before him, she turned her back, and he draped the cover of a hundred different textures and colors over her shoulders.

A queen in a procession, she marched to her chair and, with the blanket wrapped around her from her neck to her shins, sat back onto her throne. Mathematics curled up at her feet, and she rested the soles of them lightly, one on his rib cage, one on his haunch. Archer placed the picnic basket on the ground next to him, seating himself in the chair. Leaning over, he then took from the basket a thermos and two glasses, and what appeared to Maggie to be a tall, slender-necked vase ending in a kind of cup, with a base like a bulging belly etched in a flower motif. There was a thin hose attached to one side that tapered into a nozzle.

"Is that a magic lamp?" she asked him.

"Sort of," he said, as he opened the thermos. He poured her a glass of tea and then lifted the top off the odd contraption and poured some tea inside it as well. Fitting the bowl top back in place, he said, "It's called a hookah, or a *narghile*."

"Does a genie come out when you rub it?"

Archer laughed. "This part here" he said, pointing to the bowl at the top, "is called the *lule*." His finger then moved to the neck. "This is the *marpuc*," he said. "The *govde*," pointing to the body. "And this is the *agizlik*," he told her, and put the end of the nozzle momentarily into his mouth to test its draw.

Maggie leaned forward to take her glass of tea from the table, and her uncle thought he caught a glimpse of what she would look like when she was older. There was an expression of seriousness in the brow, a slight indication of uncertainty around the eyes that he feared would become more pronounced with time.

"The *narghile* should always sit on the floor or ground," he said to her. "That is proper etiquette, but I am too old and crippled to sit down there with my legs crisscrossed like a pretzel."

"What does it do?" she asked, lazily reaching out for but missing a firefly that passed by her head.

"For smoking," he said. With this, he lifted his cane and twisted the onyx crow's-head handle, which came away from the stick in his hand. Very carefully, he moved the ornament over the top of the hookah and tilting it, watched as a fine dark powdery substance fell in grains from a tiny hole at the end of the beak, filling the water pipe's bowl.

"Can I try it?" asked Maggie.

"You are too young," he said as he reattached the black head to the cane. "I need the smoke sometimes to keep my internal engine running, to, as they say, get up a full head of steam. You have all of the energy you need. Besides, the smoke teaches contemplation and patience, and it is a child's job to be *im*patient."

"Is that tobacco like what my father puts in his pipe?" she asked.

"Hardly, my dear. This is the house blend, the recipe of sultans—mixed with perfume and crushed pearls."

"What's inside a pearl when you crush it?" she asked. "A yoke?"

"No," he said, "that's an egg."

"What?"

"Something," he said and pulled the trigger on the derringer, lighting the contents in the bowl until it began to smolder. He pocketed the lighter and then lifted the nozzle at the end of the hose to his mouth. For the duration that he drew in, Maggie sipped her tea. Its flavor was a mix of orange and peach and some other soothing ingredient. She imagined she was drinking the glow of the lantern.

Archer exhaled slowly, and the pale violet smoke grew up into the night from his open lips like the ghost of a vine, spiraling, knotting, nearly taking the form of a blossom before dissipating.

"Where's the telescope?" asked Maggie.

"There is none," he answered.

"But you call this the *observatory*," she said. "I thought that was a place where you looked at the stars."

"Precisely," he said, took another toke, exhaled, and then leaned back in the chair with a faint smile.

"They will be coming for me tomorrow," she said.

"I'll be sorry to see you go."

"Will you bring Math with you and visit us in the city at the holidays?" she asked.

"Perhaps."

"Yes," she corrected. There was a pause and then she asked, "Do you think my parents have been arguing while I've been away?"

He had meant to tell her, "Of course not," but instead he heard himself saying, "I don't know."

"My father is going to leave us," she said. "Mother told me he might."

"Well, let's wait and see what happens," he said. "And while we are here, I believe I promised to tell you a story, one that you will remember until next summer."

"Tell me one that will make me remember the beach and you and Math even when it's dark and snowing. Something by the sea, please," she said.

He leaned forward to relight the bowl of the hookah. This time as he drew on the nozzle, she peered through the dim light at him, studying his features—long beard, thinning hair, high forehead, and round cheeks with a scar across the right side—in order to commit them to memory, like a photograph for her mind.

"I left home at a very young age," he said, his eyes closed, "and went to sea as a cabin boy on a large vessel out of Kelmore, bound for exotic locales, with the sole mission of capturing a strange creature for the garden zoo of a millionaire."

Maggie put her tea down and leaned back in her chair to listen, all the time thinking what a wonderful father the dog at her feet, Mathematics, would make.

"The name of the ship was *The Mare*, and it had three masts, three bright yellow sails, and a crow's nest. The figurehead was that of a wild horse with a mane of wooden flames and eyes made from what were rumored to be the two largest rubies in the world. Our captain was a fine old man named Karst, easy going and just, who could split a proverbial hair with his tongue and a real one with a dagger at twenty paces."

Maggie pictured the wild horse, which melted into Math, who rode her on his back to school, made her hard-boiled eggs for lunch, and read stories to her at night next to the fireplace. She saw her mother, tears in her eyes, sitting at the kitchen window of their apartment in the city, staring out at the rain-washed streets while Math sat beside her, quietly, patiently, with his paw resting gently atop her forearm.

"The crew of *The Mare* was an odd and interesting lot, men who had spent so much time on the ocean that their eyes, no matter the color they were born with, had all turned blue, and their faces were like dark leather, cured over time by the sun and salt spray. There was a man named Farso, who had once been a pirate and whose entire body was tattooed in aquamarine and rose with scenes of the war between Heaven and Hell—fierce angels and cunning demons battling with broadswords amongst the clouds, amidst the flames. On our first day at sea, he gave me the nickname Beetle, and it stuck to me the way the jagged legs of that insect fasten themselves to a sweater."

"Did he ever kill anyone?" asked Maggie, thinking of Math standing upright, with his concave stomach and ridged back, a long gray paw placing the shiny tin star atop the Christmas tree while her mother applauded.

"Farso?" said Archer. "I should think so, for he kept a cutlass in the sash that was his belt, the blade of which was stained red. I don't believe it was raspberry juice that had discolored the metal, if you catch my drift. One night, when we were becalmed in the Sea of

Dolphins, as we sat in the rigging of the main mast in the moonlight, he told me how he had witnessed the birth of a child in a tavern of Sechala, the pirate town of Peru. This incident tipped the scales, and the war, the one depicted upon his flesh, between good and evil that had raged inside him since his own birth, was finally won by Life. He had only glimpsed the child for an instant, he said, but its wide eyes, taking in the new world around it, shot out an invisible beacon that bore into his heart and vanquished his fear of Death."

"We studied the oceans and seas of the world," said Maggie. "I never heard of the Sea of Dolphins."

"Am I to be held accountable for the state of education in these dry times?" asked Archer, pouring himself a glass of tea.

She laughed, as Math laughed beside her, at the antics of the marionettes on the stage of the puppet theatre. The dog turned to her in the dark of the auditorium and whispered, "I know how to cure your mother's unhappiness, to dissolve her ghosts and sadness, for you know she is troubled behind her eyes."

"Insane," said Maggie, a word she had only recently learned.

"Quite," said Archer and then continued. "Another of the fellows aboard ship was Hustermann, a giant of a man who had never been granted the power of speech, but who could haul in the ship's anchor by himself. There were also the Fong brothers, identical twins from a village on the South China Sea, who had their own invented language of whistling with which they told each other secrets. A man from the frozen north, Kekmi, ate everything raw and went about without a shirt on even when we sailed through waters littered with icebergs. And there were others, a dozen or so, each as interesting as the next. These rough-and-tumble men, with muscles like rocks and dispositions like exotic creatures, who could not live for more than a year at a time on dry land, who had witnessed firsthand the treachery and wonder of nature, all treated me like a prince. "Beetle," they called me and, I suppose, saw in my innocence something they had lost and could never regain."

"Beetle," said Maggie. "I'm going to call you that sometimes."

"As you wish," said Archer. "But you might instead want to call me Collo, the name of the ship's mascot, a monkey from Brazil with a long tail and the refined human face of a leading man in the moving pictures, whose purpose in life was to make the crew laugh precisely when things seemed most grim. I remember a typhoon off the Cape of Bad Faith. We were all huddled below decks, the deafening sound of the storm above, screaming like the ocean itself was angry at us, and the jostling, the buffeting, the chaotic tumble as we all gathered around a single lantern, waiting to see if we were to live, or drown and lay forever, slowly rotting, on the slope of some undersea mountain . . ."

Mathematics led her into the heart of the city, his narrow snout pointing the way through dark alleys, across the piazza, up and down great flights of steps. "What is it called?" asked Maggie. "The cure, what is it called?"

The dog got down on all fours as they stopped by a fountain. "I cannot speak its name," said Math, "for then we will never find it. But, here, I will trace it in the water of the fountain with my paw and you will know it." The whippet leaned over the pool of the fountain and traced the name of the cure in his reflection. Maggie tried to read, to herself, the silvery trail of his design but did not understand. "Never say it," said Math as she became a monkey riding on his back through the long columned hallway of a museum.

". . . but that damned primate was a card, I tell you," said Archer, laughing so hard he wheezed and coughed, using the index finger and thumb of his right hand to clear the tears from his eyes. "The spitting image of Randolph Mondrian in *The Marble Lark*, I tell you, especially when he combed back his monkey hair and employed his tail as a mustache." He took the bowl off the hookah and tapped it against the side of the table, clearing its charred contents. He then replaced it atop the water pipe and went through the process of refilling it from the crow's head.

"What about the exotic beast you were capturing for the millionaire?" asked Maggie as her eyelids began to droop.

Archer watched her yawn as he toked at the pipe. He slowly exhaled and said, "Yes, I have yet to tell you about *The Mare*'s clandestine passenger, hidden in a crate in the hold. We of the crew had heard only rumors of him, that his name was Chromonis and he needed no air or sunlight or water to survive, and that he was the perfect hunter."

"How many zeroes in a million?" asked Maggie as her eyelids closed. She pictured the zeros as a string of pearls.

"Do you know a thousand?" asked Archer.

His niece nodded as if in a trance.

"Ten thousand?" he asked.

She tried to nod again and her head went down but did not rise.

"Use your mathematics," she heard him say and saw an image of the boot at the end of his crippled leg crush a clutch of pearls. A thick dark gas, like the ink of a squid, rose to momentarily envelop her in the aroma of the sultan's perfume. When she looked again, her uncle was asleep and Math had slipped out from under her feet. He stood on his hind legs by the opening to the path they had taken to the observatory.

"Quick, Maggie, we have so far to go," Math said and dropped to four paws. She wriggled out of the wicker chair and threw off the quilt. Passing Uncle Archer, she leaned over and lightly kissed the scar on his cheek. Then, with a skip and a bound, she was on the dog's thin back, her legs wrapped around his rippled rib cage, and they were dashing, with whippet speed, along the path. The night trees went by in a blur, and the wind in her face momentarily took her breath away. Math's haunches released like powerful springs long held back and, yelling to her, "Put your arms around my neck," he leaped into the sky. They touched down again in the field near the house and then with one more leap they were out over the ocean glimmering with moonlight, flying.

Archer was about to begin his story again when he saw that Maggie had dozed off. He loved to see her so peaceful, but hated to think of her in the clutches of anything so powerful, such as sleep, where he could not intercede. She looked so small in the wide-backed chair, wrapped like a cocoon in the quilt; so alone in the meager glow from above. The wind blew the leaves and the lantern swung, and he wondered if there was anything more he could have done to save her from the unhappiness that would overtake her the following day.

It was true that her father would be leaving her mother, but what Maggie did not know was that she would be accompanying him because her mother would, by then, have been committed to an asylum for the insane. "Elise," whispered Archer, contemplating his sister and her ghosts. He pictured her tall, stately figure, her long black hair. She had been a kind and gentle mother to Maggie, but those spirits that only she could see, hounding her day and night, had made her dangerous to herself and others, for she believed the only way to rid the world of them was with fire. The list of disastrous incidents was a catalogue of charred remains and close calls for the child.

The ghosts might as well have also haunted his brother-in-law for, through the years of trying to understand *her* madness, they had drained much of Havrad's personality, leaving him rather cold, haggard, and blank. Archer gave him credit for trying to effect some change that would save the child from any more time in the presence of true madness, but at the expense of a mother's love, it was not a real solution. Life was never so clear-cut as to offer anything as certain as a war between Heaven and Hell. That was for stories. As Maggie's crippled old uncle, he knew that all he was capable of was kindness toward her, and though many would think that enough, he felt its inadequacy tattooed in aquamarine and rose upon his conscience.

Archer refilled his pipe and smoked again. The house blend influenced his thinking, leading him down a back alley of rumination concerning Elise's spirits. One was a fat old man, Grisby, with a long white beard and a ruddy face like Santa Claus, and the other a small, wasted child, a girl, Quill, with wide eyes and a pale, alabaster face. These two wraiths were always present, reminding Elise of anything that could possibly go wrong. She had told Archer that they spread their messages of gloom with such jolly sarcasm — the possibilities of injury to her daughter, death for her husband, and war and famine and chaos for the world they lived in — like some cosmic joke. At the same time, they protected her from injury, for, as they admitted, without her they would not exist.

Mathematics slipped out from beneath Maggie's feet and came over to sit next to his master. Archer leaned back in the chair and stroked the whippet's smooth scalp. He closed his eyes and saw the fat old man and the child laughing uproariously. Those peals of mirth, at first cacophonous, soon began to flow like music and then like water, gushing down and all around as the fat man held his stomach as if to keep it from bursting and the poor girl pinched her nose with her fingers to hold her breath against the rising tide. Before he knew it, Archer was quite literally at sea. He lost his weak grip on the chair and was floundering, kicking his good leg and flapping his arms in an attempt to stay afloat.

A giant wave took him under, and he sank like a stone down into the depth of the ocean. "I'll drown," he said aloud and his words came as a torrent of bubbles. He did drown but was still somehow miraculously alive. After falling through sleep and miles of jade-green ocean, his feet touched the edge of an undersea mountain. When he kicked off with his good leg in a vain attempt to rise back to the surface, only his spirit ascended in the phantasmal form of his old body, which he left behind to rot on the craggy rock of the sunken precipice.

Then he was Beetle, scurrying along the deck of *The Mare*, heading for the prow at the insistence of Farso, who pointed into the clear sky. The rest of the crew, the Fongs and Captain Karst, silent Hustermann, Kekmi and Collo, all gathered behind the tattooed man and looked up to where his finger pointed.

"I see it," said Beetle.

"It's a girl," said the captain.

And so it was, a girl falling out of the sky.

Farso pulled off his shirt, leaped up onto the prow and then, taking two quick steps along the wooden horse's head and muzzle, dove into the sea. His muscled arms, one bearing the likeness of Saint Michael, one the visage of Beelzebub, cut the water as he swam with all his might to the spot where the falling girl hit the waves and sank like a cannonball. When he reached the vicinity, he dove.

"I hope she is all right," said Archer in the guise of Beetle. He was the boy, but still strangely aware of the old man he had been. Of two minds at once, he wondered at the odd happenstance of a girl falling from the sky and then at the oddness of being a boy filled with wonder.

The Fongs whistled shrilly and Hustermann brought a hand up to cover his roast beef of a face, one eye peeking through splayed fingers. "Get the medical bag, Beetle," said Captain Karst. "Treatment might be in order."

Beetle ran back across the deck and then down the short flight to the captain's cabin. Archer worried that he might not be able to find the bag, but the boy spotted it sitting next to the globe and knew it immediately. By the time he had rejoined the others, Farso had the girl gripped in his left arm and was swimming on his back toward the ship. Hustermann climbed out over the side and hung down by a rope in order to take the girl from her savior.

She lay on the deck, eyes closed, water glistening on her in the sunlight as if she were a newborn baby. She wore a pair of powder-blue pajamas and her hair was twisted and fastened in the back into pigtails. Captain Karst called for the bag and removed its only contents—a bottle of rum. His knees creaked as he knelt beside the girl and tilted the now-open bottle to her lips. A droplet or two of rum trickled into her, and then they waited. When, after a few moments, she did not begin to breathe, Kekmi, the man of the north, gently pushed Karst out of the way and took his place beside the girl. He leaned down over her and put his open mouth on hers. Collo, hanging by his tail from the rigging, looked down upon the group and clapped excitedly.

Nothing happened for close to a minute, and then Kekmi reared back and spat something small, black, and tentacled out onto the deck. Whatever it was tried to scuttle away, but the better looking of the Fong twins stomped on it, crushing it to a pulp. The girl opened her eyes and coughed. The northerner lifted her and placed her in the captain's arms; he took her below decks, removed her wet clothing and wrapped her in a warm blanket. He and Beetle sat with her, feeding her hot soup, and listened to her explain how the dog she was flying on had turned into a string of numbers, mostly zeros, which were nothing. Then all that was left was a thin *one*, and she eventually lost her grip on it and fell.

Beetle told her she was safe and with friends. She smiled and asked where she was.

"On a ship in the Sea of Dolphins," said the captain. "You'll stay with us until we return to port and then we will find your mother for you."

"My mother?" asked the girl.

"Of course," said the captain. "Until then, *The Mare* will be your mother, and we will all be your father, except Beetle, here. He can be your brother. Come to think of it, Collo can be your doll, if you like."

"I don't play with dolls," said Maggie.

"Just as well," said Karst. "I don't think the monkey would have liked it."

The waves, the sky, the tropical breezes, and the dolphins always leaping, arcing up out of the sea that carried their name and plunging back to cut the water, marked the passage of time beneath the saffron colored sails, appearing for all the world like the curtains in Archer's sunroom. Like some montage out of *The Marble Lark*—there was Maggie, riding Hustermann's shoulders to the crow's nest as if he was a plough horse with a penchant for climbing; listening intently and learning in a single day the whistle code of the Fongs; taking cutlass instruction on the poop deck from Farso, who smiled, with three gold teeth, at his pupil's ingenuity; and watching Kekmi carve a dolphin out of whale bone.

Beetle lazed in the moonlight, twined in the rigging, thinking with his Archer-half about how much of the night remained back at the observatory in the forest. Off the starboard side, he saw a ghostly longboat pass, holding a miasmatic old man, fat as a barrel, with a white beard, and a wan, iridescent, young girl. They were laughing without mirth, in a sinister tone. The sight of the spirits frightened him and he closed his eyes momentarily. When he opened them, it was morning, and off in the distance he spotted an island. "Land ho!" he called in his Beetle voice, with his Beetle-half, and below, on deck, the crew crowded to the side of the ship to view the palm-lined shores and volcanic crest of Taramora.

"The home of Neptune's Daughter," said Karst.

"He has a daughter?" asked Farso.

"Does Neptune even exist?" asked Karst. "I believe he is merely an ancient myth. You see, if you were to take the ocean and pour it into the shape of man . . . No, I am referring to the *creature* they call Neptune's Daughter. It supposedly haunts the sea caves of this island."

"Is it pretty?" asked Maggie.

"More horrible, I believe," said Karst. "With seaweed for hair and a blue and green mottled body. Slippery like a dolphin, but stalking around on huge webbed feet."

"Claws," said Kekmi.

"My friend is right," said Karst. "It cracks one's head like a walnut, with fangs as thick and sturdy as marlin spikes. Then it scoops out the brains and . . . you get the picture," said the captain, glancing down at Maggie and then back to the men.

"How do they know it's a girl?" she asked.

"They don't. Men named it," said Kekmi.

Collo, sitting on the captain's shoulder, batted his eyelashes and placed the back of his hand lightly against his forehead.

As *The Mare* approached the island, there was much commotion on deck, for the men were hauling out of the hold, with block and tackle, the large crate that contained the perfect hunter Chromonis. One of the indistinct crew, of the dozen or so whose faces and characters had yet to become clear, utilized a crowbar to pry open the front panel of the container. Its nails released their hold with a screech and the wooden wall fell forward onto the deck. From within the darkness of the crate stepped a man, glistening silver, made all of metal.

The sun's bright reflection off the strange figure shot a beam into Maggie's eyes. This blinding light, combined with the frantic whistling of the Fongs, formed a whirl of flame inside the girl's mind. In the leaping patterns of that fire, she saw, played out, a tableau of her mother in the arms of her father. They were dancing to music performed on the keys of a tiny piano, each snowflake note like the sound of a crystal pin tapping a crystal goblet. She realized eventually that what she had mistaken for a fire was the flicker of a motion-picture projector and that her father was really the actor, Randolph Mondrian. And then Mondrian was, in fact, Collo, hair perfectly combed, pretending to be that leading man with the reputation for romancing starlets. They danced on and on, in tight circles, through light and dark until finally disappearing into a thick fog redolent of perfume and crushed pearls.

That night, after Maggie had retired to her hammock, the men passed around the bottle from the medical bag and listened, by torch light, to Chromonis recite the times tables in honor of the morrow's hunting. He stood tall and straight like an ambitious young student declaiming Horace. The reflection of the flames played upon his metallic skin, and his eyes, like rivets of light, never blinked. His copper lips did not pronounce words, but merely opened and closed like trapdoors, allowing words to escape, holding them back, straining some to make them squirm through as a means of emphasis. The numbers came and went, and one by one the crew fell into a trance.

Amidst the incantatory rhythm of arithmetic intoned with mechanical accuracy, like a molten rain upon the senses, Farso had a vague recollection of walking the plank in shark-infested seas off Zanzibar. Kekmi fell from the prow toward the gaping maw of a sperm whale. Karst recalled a monstrous typhoon on his tail in the Far Tortuga, but forgot if he ever escaped it. Hustermann felt his neck where the rope had once burned, and the Fongs did not whistle about the incurable fever they had contracted back in the Year of the Rat. Even Beetle had the tiniest whisper of a notion of a bullet to his leg, a cutlass across the face.

Through the fog-shrouded swamps of Taramora they slogged. Chromonis led the way, hand-in-hand with Collo. The moss-hung trees twisted in silent agony. The dark unseemly waters that swirled at their feet, the hunting calls of giant crows, and the death wails of diminutive green cats the size of one's fist that scurried along the branches, made Hustermann take Maggie upon his shoulders for protection. Like some pasha from her elephant castle, she scanned the shadowy landscape for a sign of Neptune's Daughter. In her hand she held a pistol, issued by Karst, that fired narcotic darts to tranquilize but not kill the creature. Farso walked beside her mount, whispering instructions to aim for the heart. Around them traipsed the other members of the crew, carrying rifles loaded with the same nonlethal ammunition. Beetle brought up the rear, hauling a rolled up fishing net over his shoulder.

Tall Chromonis, sleek and proportioned as a statue from antiquity, stopped in his tracks, turned to face the others, and sniffed at the fog. His metal nose somehow twitched, his shining brow wrinkled, and he spoke mechanized words whose sound was not without its own gear-born beauty. "I smell a monster," he said.

Captain Karst looked over his shoulder, and then back to their guide. "Could you be more specific, sir?" he said.

"Very close," said Chromonis.

"Where?" whispered Karst.

The water at their feet exploded, and up from the mire came an enormous form, a head taller than Hustermann. It shook the mud from itself, the long strands of seaweed hair flinging wet globs of it in the faces of the hunting party. A green-blue form, slick with wet earth, as if the Earth itself had come to life, leaped upon Chromonis and, with one deft swing of its muscled arm, knocked the perfect hunter's head off in a graceful arc to land spluttering in a puddle. Gear work and springs, party-colored wires and sparks, sprayed from his chrome neck. Maggie was the first to shoot, but her trembling aim succeeded only in wounding both Karst and Collo. As Neptune's Daughter lunged into the pack of sailors, moving with the grace and speed of a dolphin through deep water, more rifles were fired, more errant shots finding human targets, until all save the girl and Beetle had been hit.

Collo curled into a ball of sleep. Farso halfheartedly reached for his cutlass, but was unconscious before he hit the damp earth. Kekmi twitched once and slumped down. The Fongs' whistling turned to snoring as they locked in an embrace and remained upright, a twinly dozing triangle. Hustermann pirouetted three times, already dreaming of home and the dance lessons he had been forced to take as a child. When his huge body succumbed to the drug, he fell over like a sack of potatoes. Maggie screamed as he fell, but the creature grabbed her off his shoulders. Beetle watched from his hiding place behind a tree as Neptune's Daughter carried the girl away into the terrifying shadows of the swamp.

The boy wiped his eyes and came out of hiding. He threw down his net and whistled once, twice, not to the dreaming Fongs but for his friend. Mathematics flew down through the trees as if on a wire in a stage play, his left front leg curled for the descent, and landed next to his master. The dog sat and waited while the boy strained and, with much internal fortitude and a good deal of grunting, transformed himself into the elderly Archer. He knew full well that in this form he would be crippled again and that his cane would be of little help in the swamp, but with a grim determination he stuck its end down into the shallow water and set off in search of his niece, the dog following at his heels.

On a beach inside an ocean cave, whose mouth stared out to sea, lit only by the rays of the setting sun streaming in from the horizon like the faint glow from a lantern, sat two figures on thrones made from dry, woven seaweed. A table, made from the same vegetal effluvia of the ocean, was arranged between the chairs, and upon it set a tortoise shell of sea tea and a huge sand-dollar platter holding fancy jelly and starfish. Neptune's Daughter sat with her back to the cave wall, and Maggie with her back to the small wavelets that broke upon the beach.

"The tide is rising," said the creature in a fair voice. She leaned over and poured two nautilus shells of tea. She handed one to Maggie.

"Will you crack my skull like a walnut?" asked the girl.

"Perhaps metaphorically, my dear," she said, smiling grimly through her overbite.

"When you eat a brain, what does it taste like?" asked Maggie.

"Bittersweet," said the creature, staring into the distance, trying to find the right explanation. "Bittersweet. The knowledge goes down rough and offsets the confection of ideas. And then the memories. The memories burst upon the tongue, bubbles of longing and regret, and the entire repast leaves you tired but wanting more."

"Why have you taken me?" asked Maggie, sipping at her tea.

"We are waiting for your uncle. He will be here shortly."

"What would your own brain taste like?" asked the girl.

"Like fire, child," she said. Her claws had shrunk simply to long nails, and the ocean shades of blue-green that had camouflaged her body were softening into pink. Neptune's Daughter was now less a monster and more a woman with dark hair mixed in with the seaweed locks.

"Are you changing?" asked Maggie.

"Look," said her hostess, "here he comes now."

Maggie stood and turned around to see a small figure slogging, waist deep, through the white water at the mouth of the cave. Uncle Archer's journey through the incoming tide, through the rays of the setting sun, seemed to take forever, yet took no time at all. Her heart leaped for joy at the prospect of rescue. Only when Archer neared the shore did Math emerge from beneath the water's surface—first the ridge of his back and then his snout.

"Let your uncle sit down for a moment," said Neptune's Daughter to Maggie. "And you come and sit on my lap."

"I don't want to," said Maggie.

"Now, now, do as you're told or I'll rip his face off," cautioned the creature.

Archer, out of breath, nodded to Maggie, motioning with his cane for her to do as she had been told. He walked unsteadily, leaning his full weight at times on the cane, to the empty seaweed chair and sat back into it. Mathematics took up a position at his side. He leaned forward for a minute, regulating his breathing, and took a handkerchief from his damp tweed jacket with which to mop his brow. "That water is frigid," he said, shaking his head.

Maggie sat very still on the lap of Neptune's Daughter, feeling as she did sometimes when she was home alone with her mother and smelled the first hint of smoke. The creature wrapped her wet hand around the girl's neck from the back and applied a light pressure. "Now, Archer, tell the child the truth or . . ."

He hung his head, closed his eyes, and began speaking, unable to look directly at them. "When I was young, I went to war against the sultan of an eastern land. I was filled with foolish courage, with bravado, until one day in a skirmish at Taramora, I was wounded in the leg. The bullet shattered my shinbone. An enemy soldier leaped into the pit where I lay, writhing in pain, and brought his cutlass down to skewer my head. A friend of mine, a mathematics professor from Kelmore, John Farso, shot the enemy just as the blade was biting into the flesh of my face.

"Farso, mortally wounded himself, dragged me to safety back to our battalion. I spent the better part of a year on a field hospital cot, screwed to the cosmos on morphine for the pain. It was during that time, at night, when those who were not dying slept beneath the big tent, that the ghosts first came to me—the old man with the beard and the girl with the wide eyes. At first, in my delirium, I thought they were real—good samaritans helping the wounded. Then one night the girl walked through the man as the man walked through my cot, and once I was aware of their nature, their ill intent became clear to me.

"Another soldier, who had occupied the cot next to mine for a brief time before dying of infection, also saw them. He told me the story of a millionaire and his daughter who had come to the war-torn land of the sultan to sell guns to both sides. They lived in a splendid house in Taramora. The millionaire was not there long before he became enamored of the pleasures of the hookah. He succumbed to the sultan's special recipe and went mad, thinking he was haunted. One night, mistaking the girl for one of his ghosts, he shot her with a derringer he carried in his waistband. When he came to his senses and saw what he had done, he took his own life.

"I was sent home from the front to recuperate, but they followed me. Even on the most beautiful day, out in the sunshine on a green field beneath the swaying boughs of an oak, they made themselves known. My sister, Elise, cared for me, brought me back to full health, save my limp and scar. I told her about the spirits, and in order to allow me to grow strong, she said she would take them from me for a time. We cut our thumbs and mixed our blood on the deal."

"But you never took them back," said Neptune's Daughter.

"They would not return to me, Maggie, I swear," said Archer, tears in his eyes.

"You know the reason they would not return to you," said the creature. "Tell the girl your secret, the thing that protects you," she demanded, raising her voice so that it echoed through the cave.

At that moment, the breaking wave at Archer's back crashed upon the beach and Collo came leaping out of the water. In three incredible bounds he was across the sand and in the air. He landed on the creature's face, wrapping his arms and legs around her head and biting into the smooth flesh of her brow. For an instant, she released her grip and Maggie ran to her uncle.

Neptune's Daughter struggled to her feet, trying to pull the monkey loose, but by then the others had risen from the water and were charging the monster. Kekmi, the Fongs, Farso, Karst, Hustermann, and the headless Chromonis bolted into the cave and knocked her back into her seaweed throne. She struggled wildly against the strong sailors' arms that held her down.

"Hurry," cried the captain.

Archer hobbled away from Maggie to the melee, reached into his pocket and took out the derringer. He leaned over and pulled the trigger, once, twice, three times, setting three small fires at the base of the seaweed chair. The flames jumped up as if he were lighting a pile of three-year-old tinder. "Maggie, come to me," he yelled and held his arms out as he returned to her. She ran, jumped up, and he caught her in midair. For a moment, he teetered, thrown off balance, and then he grunted and righted himself, hoisting her up over his shoulder. She saw Math pick up the cane with his mouth and follow.

As they trudged out through the ever-deepening water from the mouth of the cave, she looked back at the flaming pyre of crew and creature, a pulsating mass of burning flesh and steel. Violet smoke poured out of the blaze, filling the cave, but the only sound was that of twin whistles, twining, knotting, nearly becoming a blossom before dissipating.

Just before they submerged, she saw the whole chaotic inferno as a huge orange ball floating in the dark, and then the water came up, or they stepped down. Archer limped slowly, relentlessly across the ocean bottom, breathing bubbles like strings of pearls. Maggie saw lamprey wriggle in the lime-green light, herds of sea horses flit here and there all of one mind, toppled columns of a sunken palace, the sleek immensity of a whale passing a hundred yards overhead.

The movement of the water around them soothed her and made her weary. She reluctantly closed her eyes, knowing that what had happened had not been right. Already half-asleep, she looked one more time and saw the path through the forest at night. The wind was rustling the leaves. The lantern at the observatory receded in the distance. She hugged Archer tightly as he carried her back to the house.

In the morning the sun came up, round and bright orange. Out to the east there was a ship with three yellow sails on the ocean. Archer and Maggie stood in the drive as the girl's father stepped out of the shiny black car. He stood tall and rigid, little, if any, expression on his face.

"Come, Maggie," he said. "Say goodbye to Uncle Archie and let's be off."

Archer motioned to his brother-in-law to follow him, and then turned and walked away a few yards. Her father did as was requested and joined Archer out of earshot of the girl. Maggie watched intently, trying to overhear what was being said. At first, her father shook his head and said, "I can't." Archer brought his arm up and wrapped it around her father's shoulders. He leaned over and whispered in his ear for a long time. When he pulled back, his brother-in-law nodded.

"Get in the back seat, Maggie," said her father.

She did as she was told.

"But don't close the door just yet," he added.

She watched as Archer whistled and Mathematics came running from the back of the house. He petted the dog on the head and rubbed his ears. He then clicked his fingers at the height of his chest and the dog stood up on hind legs, resting both front paws against Archer's chest.

His master spoke to him quietly, and then said, "Go!"

The dog bounded over and leaped into the back seat with Maggie.

The car door closed. The car pulled away down the long drive.

Archer woke to the sound of the leaves rustling above the observatory. He leaned forward and removed the bowl from the hookah, tapped it against the side of the table and then fit it back in place.

Filling it from the cane head and lighting it, he considered his dream. As he took in the smoke, he had a vague memory of Randolph Mondrian in a comic pratfall scene from *The Marble Lark* and smiled. Across from him, the girl Quill sat, deep in sleep, wrapped in the hundred colors, while next to him, directly beneath the orange lantern, the old man sat, his white beard rising and falling with his chest and enormous gut, napping like Santa the day after Christmas.

Taking one more toke at the nozzle, Archer's reason sped off like a whippet through the forest. The exhalation, when it came, would be the violet yoke of a crushed pearl, and its sweet aroma would gently awaken his sleeping niece to the now darkened observatory, the last firefly, the wind in the leaves, and the snoring of her uncle.

I borrowed the title of this one from a mystery novel my mother had worked at, on and off, through those years preceding her illness and subsequent death. The characters and content here are mine. The only item I remember from her manuscript was a woman who played an instrument that produced waves of air requiring her to wear different colored glass prosthetics over her fingers with which to sonically manipulate the currents.

Some of the characters aboard The Mare were lifted out of stories that my grandfather had told me about his time in the Merchant Marine. For instance, on the ship he served on there was a pair of Chinese brothers, twins, who worked in the kitchen. At dinnertime, as they delivered the meals throughout the ship, they would whistle back and forth so that each knew where the other was and they wouldn't collide. One of the brothers died during a voyage in the Indian Ocean and was buried at sea. At sunset, after the burial, my grandfather told me that the remaining brother went to the side of the ship and whistled out over the water. A few seconds passed and then a whistle came back from off the ocean.

My grandfather was also very interested in grafting fruit trees, and we had many different varieties on our quarter-acre of property. Over the course of years, he grafted into existence a bluish tinged fruit he called Neptune's Daughter. What connotation the name had for him, I can't recall.

The Delicate

THE DELICATE IS PALE, LIMBS PIPE-CLEANER thin, with a head as shiny hard as beetle-back. Violent, in utero skull tectonics have led to a precipice of brow, a compression of matter past the point of truth. His eyes are crow eyes, and his ear holes winding tunnels to nowhere.

He comes in the latter days of afternoon, through blowing snow, dressed in black, while Schubert's "Eighth" plays magically in the background. He comes to suck the breath out of passing fancies and to treat the infirm of mind, the particularly annoying, to a long sleep.

"In order to take the waters," as he explains it, he comes to a resort town on the edge of reason. Beyond it, the wilderness stretches north to the frozen pole. God has never drawn breath there—the domain of bat-winged demons whose skin is the ringed wood of oak trees. These creatures fly out of the forest at night to snatch up children, their little legs kicking to the moon. To live in Absentia is to live with a soul that is liquid lead.

Perhaps it is the manner in which he holds his cigarette or maybe his distinguished apparel that immediately ingratiates him to both the guests and staff of the Hotel Providence. At his request, they call him Harding Jarvis and marvel at his grace and facility with foreign language. Though his face is more a cow skull than a thing of flesh, no one seems to notice except the woman who cleans his rooms. She knows him by his aroma—roses over bad meat. When he knows she knows, he wheezes into his wine glass.

No matter who Carlotta confesses her fears to, they brush her off, saying, "Herr Jarvis? Not possible. My dear, you are disturbed." She makes it a point never to enter his rooms when they are occupied. *Sleep to her is death,* say the toothpicks holding open her eyes. She lasts only three days before she sits down and closes them. To sleep is warm and beautiful, but the chair she sits in is at the foot of Herr Jarvis's bed. There is so much dirt on the floor—four ounces of fly meat on every windowsill.

He returns unexpectedly from an afternoon of playing whist with Madame Fesh of the colorful muff, Barlin the local logomancer, and Meme Haspin, taxidermist to the landed gentry, and discovers Carlotta asleep in the chair. With little pomp and less circumstance, he sucks the life out of her. The process is long and painful, and he doesn't spare her a minute of it. After hanging her withered corpse, like a wrinkled garment bag of flesh, on a peg in the closet, he sits down to smoke his clay pipe. Before long, he moves to the writing desk, where he takes up his pen and records the essence of the maid he has just ingested. The first phrase to crawl out onto paper is, "Insouciance is the engine of regret," and from there it is a smooth plunge into lyrical facility.

At first he thought it was the crab soufflé he had had for lunch, but then realized, too late, that something in Carlotta's blood was causing a strange transformation in him. With a popping of bone, a stretch of incisors, a whisper growth of fur and the shrinking of skin, he stoops to become a dog. His last oath is excremental before his words give way to growling.

The inhabitants of Absentia mention to each other the clever little hound that now wanders the streets looking for scraps. One boy tells how he heard it cry human, and the men who mine Mount Alfarabi are amused when the beast tries to have its way with a lady's shinbone outside the beer hall. Meanwhile, everybody who is anybody is seeking out Harding Jarvis for a ride in the car, a game of tennis, a cocktail party.

Pharsalus, the hunter, comes in from the wilderness with furs to sell and wild turkey feathers in his hat. With the money he makes, he goes directly to the beer hall and drinks many mugs. He tells those he hasn't seen in three seasons about the demon he shot and about the beautiful paradise surrounded by hundreds of miles of ice. For proof of the demon, he displays a pair of gnarled horns which he pulled like teeth, with a pair of pliers, from the forehead of the creature. As for paradise, he offers only a shrug.

The days of Night fall while Pharsalus is drinking. When he steps out of the beer hall, there is a brisk wind and winter chill. He stares up at the ice-bright stars and remembers tracking white apes at twilight. They moved like ghosts among the giant pines. They died with a cough of steam and a trickle of blood.

When his memory clears, Pharsalus notices a dog sitting in the street in front of him. Because the first hours of Night each year give him a desire to speak to something other than only the earth and wind, he decides to adopt the mutt as a hunting dog. Using scraps of dried caribou, he lures his new companion out of town and into the uncharted wilderness.

Night in the forest is either stone silence and falling snow or the sound of something dying. Demons fly out of the trees without warning, and Pharsalus is always ready with his gun. When they jump him from behind, he uses his long, curved knife and engages them in hand-to-hand combat. The dog helps in the kill. As the demons' mauled bodies expire at his feet, he questions them about the path to the Earthly Paradise. Some of the dying offer clues, but most go quietly, their barbed tails thrashing the snow. Pharsalus writes whatever they tell him in a little notebook and then pulls their horns out with a pair of pliers.

In spring, the hunter and dog traverse a pass that leads over the mountains. The sudden return of the days of Morning brings light that blinds. In those mountains there exist hundreds of small caves formed long ago in the Ice Age. Each year, he hunts them for snapping yellow back and artifacts left behind by the ancients who had once inhabited them.

In one cave, the hunter discovers the frozen corpse of a man, sitting on a large stone at a table hewn from rock. Icicles hang from the man's nose and frost glazes his eyes. From the worm-eaten journal laying open in front of the dead man, Pharsalus learns of his father's search for him. The hunter puts his arms around the dog and cries.

In one entry in his father's journal, the old man describes his love affair with a woman who lives at the bottom of a lake. Her skin is blue and her hair so long it turns into sea grass and trailing vines. He descends from his mountain perch every night to meet her on the shore of her lake.

They sit beneath a tall dune, the wind blowing around them.

Above, stars smash into stars. He tells her how fifteen years earlier he left home to search for his son who had become a hunter in the wilderness. As he kisses her, he hears the immensity of paradise singing across the water to him.

Pharsalus dreams every night of the only beast he has any desire to hunt. It is a creature he has never actually seen, with many jumbled attributes—scales, fur, talons, fangs, feathers beneath and around the hide and hair. Every night it comes vividly to him and fills him with longing to hunt it. In the dream, he always hears it flying. There is a struggle and it bites him, like a snake, in the heel. He always awakens wondering if the bird part is rooster. But since he has gotten the dog, it has become more and more difficult to envision the dream kill.

In their wandering, the hunter and companion stumble upon a beautiful garden locked in ice. At the last second the Delicate steps out of the sloughed skin of the mutt to take the hunter by the throat. Lips meet lips and breath begins leaving, begins arriving. When the hunter is blind in one eye and his left rib cage shattered by the internal pressure, he summons those years of the kill and thrusts his hunting knife into the thorax of the Delicate. Streams of agony intermingle and separate out into fields of bright color. With a simple cracking noise the monster pushes a bony finger through the hunter's chest and turns off his heart.

But the Delicate is dying from his wound. He stumbles through the wilderness clutching his oozing side with a slim, sharp hand. He kneels and prays to heaven but nothing happens. The memories of other lifetimes swirl in his memory with an anguished forgetting of paradise. He cries for the loss of his delicate form, his exo-skeleton now a crystal meteor. If only he could change into a dog, he thinks, as life leaves him in a cascade of steam. With little conviction, he sucks it back up as it goes. In no time, he's good as new.

Back in the town of Absentia, in the very room of the Hotel Providence where he took Carlotta, he's now taking them two at a time. The empty husks of life pile up like fresh-cut bales of tobacco in his closet. Men catch their wives sneaking to his door. Wives catch their husbands at some shadowy rendezvous with him, and he takes them both as quick as you please. He takes the contessa from behind as she leans over to adjust her corset. Her piles of hair almost save her, but, in the end, she is as easy to draw the life out of as is Master Cley, or the mayor, or Madam Silwort, or the Grossdig Twins.

Someone notices the population of the town dwindling at an

alarming rate and wires for the government to send troops, before the Delicate can snip the telegraph line with his incisors. When the army arrives and surrounds the town, he is huffing, as if taking snuff, the last few morsels of Mrs. Fleacox. He realizes too late that she has long since gone bad as a soft melon even though she keeps right on talking till the end. Her pointless words infect him with *flexis midocarsis*, and he slowly begins to disintegrate. In his final hour, he stands upon the balcony of the mayor's house, staring out over the wilderness, playing the violin until his fingers turn to salt and the instrument falls to the floor.

    The soldiers break into Absentia, machine guns blurting out death, air cover dropping flames as if the clouds were on fire. They find the Delicate—a sorry, prodigious pile of cigarette ash. Mrs. Fleacox is lost between life and death, and they call for a specialist to administer the needle to the base of her spine. They collect the creature into a plastic bag and freeze-dry him. His remains are taken to Spire City in the Sunbelt where they are stored for the edification of future generations. The funding never comes through to study the crumbs of the Delicate, so he lies in a bag on a shelf and waits.

There were a number of reasons why I wanted to include "The Delicate" in this collection, none of which has anything to do with the quality of the story. I do think it is an interesting little surreal fable that works in a number of different ways, but it has as many problems as it has merits.

The first and foremost reason that I include it here is because I wanted a representative piece from my publications in the magazine Space and Time. This venue was so essential to my writing career as was its editor, Gordon Linzner. Gordon has been publishing Space and Time for, I think, over thirty years now, and it remains a viable and interesting publication. He gave many an aspiring writer and artist a chance to break into print. I remember reading very early work by Joe Lansdale, Scott Edelman, James Van Pelt, and Allen Koszowski back in the '80s.

Gordon has great eclectic tastes, printing sword and sorcery stories in between surreal fantasy and contemporary horror. As a reader, part of the fun is that you never know what you are going to get in each issue. He is also an editor who is not afraid to take risks and publish someone new or something really out there (as evidenced by "The Delicate"). An enterprising interviewer will eventually tap into Gordon's long history and experience in the field and come up with some amazing testimony. A million thanks to Gordon Linzner.

The second reason for including this story is for those readers who have followed my trilogy, beginning with The Physiognomy. "The Delicate" was a kind of condensed sample of that larger story. I was trying to work out a certain tone and setting I had been carrying around in my head for months before committing to the larger work. As can be seen, from early on, I had the mining town, the character of the Delicate, the idea of a hunter's journey through the wilderness, in mind for the longer narrative. I know some detractors of the trilogy have said that I just added on books to the first one as an afterthought in order to make scads of money. (I'm still waiting for the scads of money.) But it had always been my intention, from the very start, to write three books and to include all the elements that appeared in this brief piece. I knew that trilogies were not the hippest thing to do at the time, but I have always been and remain a writer interested in representing my personal vision, whether it be deemed in or out of fashion. For all those who doubt me, may you do lunch with the Delicate.

Malthusian's Zombie

1

I'M NOT SURE WHAT NATIONALITY MALTHUSIAN was, but he spoke with a strange accent; a stuttering lilt of mumblement it took weeks to fully comprehend as English. He had more wrinkles than a witch and a shock of hair whiter and fuller than a Samoyed's ruff. I can still see him standing at the curb in front of my house, slightly bent, clutching a cane whose ivory woman's head wore a blindfold. His suit was a size and a half too large, as were his eyes, peering from behind lenses cast at a thickness that must have made his world enormous. The two details that halted my raking and caused me to give him more than a neighborly wave were his string tie and a mischievous grin I had only ever seen before on my six-year-old daughter when she was drawing one of her monsters.

"Malthusian," he said from the curb.

I greeted him and spoke my name.

He mumbled something and I leaned closer to him and begged his pardon. At this, he turned and pointed back at the house down on the corner. I knew it had recently changed hands, and I surmised he had just moved in.

"Welcome to the neighborhood," I said.

He put his hand out and I shook it. His grip was very strong, and he was in no hurry to let go. Just as I realized he was aware of my discomfort, his grin turned into a wide smile and he released me. Then he slowly began to walk away.

"Nice to meet you," I said to his back.

He turned, waved, and let loose an utterance that had the cadence of poetry. There was something about leaves and fruit and it all came together in a rhyme. Only when he had disappeared into the woods at the end of the block did I realize he had been quoting Alexander Pope:

> Words are like leaves; and where they most abound
> Much fruit of sense beneath is rarely found.

As a professor of literature, this amused me, and I decided to try to find out more about Malthusian.

I was on sabbatical that year, supposedly writing a book concerning the structure of Poe's stories, which I saw as lacking the energetic ascent of the Fichtean curve and being comprised solely of denouement. Like houses of Usher, the reader comes to them, as in a nightmare, with no prior knowledge, at the very moment they begin to crumble. What I was really doing was dogging it in high fashion. I'd kiss my wife goodbye as she left for work, take my daughter to school, and then return home to watch reruns of those shows my brother and I had devoted much of our childhood to. Malthusian's daily constitutional was an opportunity to kill some time, and so, when I would see him passing in front of the house, I'd come out and engage him in conversation.

Our relationship grew slowly at first until I began to learn the cues for his odd rendering of the language. By Thanksgiving, though, I could have a normal conversation with him, and we began to have lengthy discussions about literature. Oddly enough, his interests were far more contemporary than mine. He expressed a devotion to Pynchon, and the West African writer Amos Tutuola. I realized I had spent too long teaching the canon of Early American works and began to delve into some of the novels he mentioned. One day I asked him what he had done before his retirement. He smiled and said something that sounded like *mind-fucker*.

I was sure I had misunderstood him. I laughed and said, "What was that?"

"Mind-fucker," he said. "Psychologist."

"Interesting description of the profession," I said.

He shrugged and his grin dissipated. When he spoke again, he changed the subject to politics.

Through the winter, no matter the weather, Malthusian walked. I remember watching him struggle along through a snowstorm one afternoon, dressed in a black overcoat and black Tyrolean hat, bent more from some invisible weight than a failure of his frame. It struck me then that I had never seen him on his return journey. The trails through the woods went on for miles, and I was unaware of one that might bring him around to his house from the other end of the block.

I introduced him to Susan, my wife, and to my daughter Lyda. There, at the curb, he kissed both their hands, or tried to. When Lyda pulled her hand back at his approach, he laughed so, that I thought he would explode. Susan found him charming, but asked me later, "What the hell was he saying?"

The next day he brought a bouquet of violets for her; and for Lyda, because she had shown him her drawing pad, he left a drawing he had done, rolled up and tied with a green ribbon. After dinner, she opened it and smiled. "A monster," she said. It was a beautifully rendered charcoal portrait of an otherwise normal middle-aged man, wearing an unnerving look of total blankness. The eyes were heavy lidded and so realistically glassy, the attitude of the body so slack, that the figure exuded a palpable sense of emptiness. At the bottom of the page in a fine calligraphic style were written the words *Malthusian's Zombie*.

"I told him I liked monsters," said Lyda.

"Why is that a monster?" asked Susan, who I could tell was a little put off by the eerie nature of the drawing. "It looks more like a college professor on sabbatical."

"He thinks nothing," said Lyda, and with her pinky finger pointed to the zombie's head. She had me tack the drawing to the back of her door, so that it faced the wall unless she wanted to look at it. For the next few weeks, she drew zombies of her own. Some wore little hats, some bow ties, but all of them, no matter how huge and vacant the eyes, wore mischievous grins.

In early spring, Malthusian invited me to his house one evening to play a game of chess. The evening air was still quite cool, but the scent of the breeze carried the promise of things green. His house, which sat on the corner lot, was enormous, by far the largest in the neighborhood. The lot encompassed three acres of woods, which, at the very back, touched upon a lake that belonged to the adjacent town.

Malthusian was obviously not much for yard work or home repair—the very measure of a man in this part of the world. A tree had cracked and fallen during the winter and it still lay partially obstructing the driveway. The three-story structure and its four tall columns in front needed paint; certain porch planks had succumbed to dry rot and its many windows were streaked and smudged. The fact that he took no initiative to rectify these problems made him yet more likable to me.

He met me at the door and ushered me into his home. I had visions of the place being like a dim, candlelit museum of artifacts as odd as their owner, and had hoped to decipher Malthusian's true character from them as if they were clues in a mystery novel. There was nothing of the sort. The place was well lit and tastefully, though modestly, decorated.

"I hope you like merlot," he said as he led me down an oak-paneled hallway toward the kitchen.

"Yes," I said.

"It's good for the heart," he said, and laughed.

The walls I passed were lined with photographs of Malthusian with different people. He moved quickly and I did not linger out of politeness, but I thought I saw one of him as a child, and more than one of him posing with various military personnel. If I wasn't mistaken, I could have sworn I had caught the face of an ex-president in one of the photos.

The kitchen was old linoleum in black-and-white checkerboard design, brightly lit by overhead fluorescent lights. Setting on a table in the center of the large expanse were a chessboard, a magnum of dark wine, two fine crystal goblets, and a thin silver box. He took a seat on one side of the table and extended his hand to indicate I was to sit across from him. He methodically poured wine for both of us, opened the box, retrieved a cigarette, lit it, puffed once, and then led with his knight.

"I'm not very good," I said, as I countered with my opposite knight.

He waved his hand in the air, flicked ash onto the floor, and said, "Let's not let it ruin our game."

We played in silence for some time and then I asked him something that had been on my mind since he had first disclosed his profession to me. "And what type of psychologist were you? Jungian? Freudian?"

"Neither," he said. "Those are for children. I was a rat shocker. I made dogs drool."

"Behaviorist?" I asked.

"Sorry to disappoint," he said with a laugh.

"I teach the Puritans with the same method," I said and this made him laugh louder. He loosened his ever-present string tie and cocked his glasses up before plunging through my pitiful pawn defense with his bishop.

"I couldn't help but notice those photos in the hall," I said. "Were you in the army?"

"Please, no insults," he said. "I worked for the U.S. government."

"What branch?" I asked.

"One of the more shadowed entities," he said. "It was necessary in order to bring my mother and father and sister to this country."

"From where?" I asked.

"The old country."

"Which one is that?"

"It no longer exists. You know, like in a fairy tale, it has disappeared through geopolitical enchantment." With this he checked me by way of a pawn/castle combination.

"Your sister?" I asked.

"She was much like your girl, Lyda. Beautiful and brilliant and what an artist."

As with the game, he took control of the conversation from here on out, directing me to divulge the history of my schooling, my marriage, the birth of our daughter, the nature of our household.

It was a gentle interrogation, the wine making me nostalgic. I told him everything and he seemed to take the greatest pleasure in it, nodding his head at my declaration of love for my wife, laughing at all of Lyda's antics I could remember, and I remembered all of them. Before I knew it, we had played three games, and I was as lit as a stick of kindling. He led me down the hallway to the front door.

As if from thin air, he produced a box of chocolates for my wife. "For the lady," he said. Then he placed in my hand another larger box. Through bleary eyes, I looked down and saw the image of Rat Fink, the pot-bellied, deviant rodent who had been a drag-racing mascot in the late sixties.

"It's a model," he told me. "Help the girl make it, she will enjoy this monster."

I smiled in recognition of the figure I had not seen since my teens.

"Big Daddy Roth," he said, and with this eased me out the door and gently closed it behind me.

Although I had as my mission to uncover the mystery of Malthusian, my visit had made him more of an enigma. I visited him twice more to play chess, and on each of these occasions, the scenario was much the same. The only incident that verged on revelation was when Lyda and I constructed the model and painted it. "Rat shocker," I remembered him telling me. I had a momentary episode in which I envisioned myself salivating at the sound of a bell.

On the day that Lyda brought me spring's first crocus, a pale violet specimen with an orange mouth, Malthusian was taken away in an ambulance. I was very worried about him and enlisted Susan, since she was a nurse practitioner, to use her connections in the hospitals to find out where he was. She spent the better part of her Friday evening making calls but came up with nothing.

2

Days passed, and I began to think that Malthusian might have died. Then, a week to the day after the ambulance had come for him, I found a note in my mailbox. All it said was *Chess Tonight*.

I waited for the appointed hour, and after Susan had given me a list of things to ask about the old man's condition, and Lyda, a get-well drawing of a dancing zombie, I set out for the house on the corner.

He did not answer the door, so I opened it and called inside, "Hello?"

"Come," he called from back in the kitchen.

I took the hallway and found him sitting at the chess table. The wine was there, and the cigarette case, but there was no board.

"What happened?" I said when I saw him.

Malthusian looked yet more wrinkled and stooped, sitting in his chair like a sack of old clothes. His white hair had thinned considerably and turned a pale shade of yellow. In his hands he clutched his cane, which I had never seen him use before while in his house, and that childish grin, between malevolence and innocence, had been replaced by the ill, forced smile of Rat Fink.

"No chess?" I asked, as a way of masking my concern.

"A game of a different order tonight," he said, and sighed.

I was about to ask again what had happened, but he said, "Drink a glass of wine and then you will listen."

We sat in silence as I poured and drank. I had never noticed before but the blindfold on the ivory woman's head did not completely cover her left eye. She half stared at me as I did what I was told. When the glass was empty and I had poured another, he looked up and said, "Now, you must listen carefully. I give you my confession and the last wish of a dying man."

I wanted to object but he brought the cane to his lips in order to silence me.

"In 1969, September, I was attending a conference of the American Psychological Association in Washington, D.C. A professor from Princeton, one Julian Jaynes, gave a lecture there. Have you heard of him?" he asked.

I shook my head.

"Now you will," he said. "The outrageous title of his address was 'The Origin of Consciousness in the Breakdown of the Bicameral Mind.' Just the name of it led many to think it was pure snake oil. When Professor Jaynes began to explain his theory, the audience was sure of it. Individual consciousness as we know it today, he said, is a very recent development in the history of mankind. Before that, like schizophrenics, human beings listened to a voice that came from within their own heads and from this took their cues. These were post-ice-age hunter-gatherers for whom it was important to think with a single mind. They heard the voice of some venerable elder of their tribe who had since, perhaps, passed on. This was the much touted 'voice of God.' Individual ego was virtually non-existent."

"You mean," I said, "when the ancients refer to the word of the Lord, they were not speaking figuratively?"

"Yes, you follow," he said and smiled, lifting the wineglass to his lips with a trembling hand. "I could tell you that this phenomenon had to do with the right hemispherical language center of the brain and a particular zone called Wernicke's area. When this area was stimulated in modern laboratory experiments, the subjects very often heard authoritarian voices that either admonished or commanded. But they were very distant voices. The reason, Jaynes believed, was that these auditory hallucinations were traveling from the right hemisphere to the left, not through the corpus callosum—the, shall we call it, bridge that joins the hemispheres—but rather through another passageway, the anterior commissure."

"I'm hanging on by a thread, now," I said.

Malthusian did not acknowledge my joke, but closed his eyes momentarily and pressed on as if it would all soon become clear.

"Whereas Jaynes gives many explanations for the growing faintness of the voice of God—genocide, natural upheavals, parental selection, environmental demands requiring the wonderful plasticity of the human brain to enact these changes—my fellow researchers and I believed that the muting of the voice was a result of the rapid shrinking of the anterior commissure to its present state of no more than one-eighth of an inch across. This, we believed, was the physiological change that fractured the group mind into individual consciousness. 'Father, why have you forsaken me?' You see? There is much more, but that is the crux."

"The survival of human beings depended upon this change?" I asked.

"The complexity of civilization required diversification."

"Interesting," was all I could manage.

"As I said," Malthusian went on, "very few took Jaynes seriously, but I did. His ideas were revolutionary, but they were not unfounded." Here, he took a cigarette from the silver case and lit it.

"Is that smart," I asked, nodding at the cigarette, "considering your health?"

"I have been conditioned by Philip Morris," he said with a smile.

"This theory is only the beginning, I can tell," I said.

"Very good, professor," he whispered. "As Farid Ud-Din Attar might have written: if this tale I am about to tell you were inscribed with needles upon the corner of the eye, it would still serve as a lesson to the circumspect."

He lifted the bottle of wine and poured me another glass. "To begin with, if you tell anyone what I am about to tell you, you will be putting your family and yourself in great jeopardy. Understood?"

I thought momentarily of Malthusian's photos with all those military personnel and his telling me that he had been employed by one of the more shadowed entities of the government. A grim silence filled the room as those huge eyes of his focused on mine. I thought of leaving, but instead I slowly nodded.

"I was part of a secret government project called Dumbwaiter. The title might have been humorous if not for the heinous nature of the work we were doing. As psychologists, we were assigned the task of creating dedicated assassins, men devoid of personal volition, who would do anything—*anything*—that they were ordered to do. Mind control, it is sometimes called. The CIA had, for a short period, thought that the drug LSD might be useful in this pursuit, but instead of creating drones they spread cosmic consciousness. Once this failed, the behaviorists were called in.

"My lab was situated in a large, old Victorian house out in the woods. No one would have suspected that some bizarre Cold War experiment was taking place in its basement. I had two partners and, working off Jaynes's theory, through surgery and the implanting of pig arteries and chimpanzee neurons, we widened and filled the anterior commissure in a test subject's brain in order to increase the volume of the auditory hallucination. Through conditioning, my voice became the voice of God for our subject. I was always in his head. One verbal command from me and my order would remain with him, inside his mind, until the task was completed."

What else was I to think but that Malthusian was pulling my leg. "Do I look that gullible?" I said, and laughed so hard I spilled a drop of my wine on the table.

The old man did not so much as smile. "We had created a zombie," he said. "You laugh, but you should be laughing at yourself. You do not realize how, without any of our work, the human mind is so perfectly suggestible. The words 'obedience' and 'to listen' share the same root in more than half a dozen languages. With our experiment, this man would do whatever he was told. The results even surprised us. I instructed him to learn fluent French in a week. He did. I instructed him to play a Chopin nocturne on the piano after only hearing it once. He did. I instructed him to develop a photographic memory. I commanded him to stop aging. At times, for the purpose of a particular assignment, I might instruct him to become fatter, thinner, even shorter."

"Impossible," I said.

"Nonsense," said Malthusian. "It has been known for some time now that the mere act of deep thought can change the physiological structure of the brain. If only my colleagues and I could publish our findings, others would also know that prolonged, highly focused thought is capable of transforming the physiological structure of more than just the brain."

It was obvious to me at this time that Malthusian's illness had affected his mind. I put on a serious face and pretended to follow along, exhibiting a mixed sense of wonder and gravity.

"Why are you telling me all of this?" I asked.

"Why, yes, why," he said, and, more astonishing than his tale, tears began to form at the corners of his eyes. "The zombie had been useful. Please don't ask me specifically how, but let us just say that his work resulted in the diminution of agitators against democracy. But then, with the end of the Cold War, our project was disbanded. We were ordered to eliminate the zombie and set fire to the facility, and we were given large sums of cash to resume normal life—with the threat that if we were to breathe a word about Dumbwaiter to anyone, we would be killed."

"Eliminate the zombie?" I said.

He nodded. "But I had pangs of conscience. My own God was talking to me. This man, whom we had hollowed out and filled with my commands, had been kidnapped. Just an average healthy citizen with a wife and small child had been taken off the street one day by men in a long dark car. His loved ones never knew what had become of him. Likewise, I had made a deal to never see my family again when I promised to work on Dumbwaiter. I disappeared after my parents and sister were brought to this country. For me to contact them in any way would mean their demise. I have missed them terribly through the years, especially my sister with whom I had a strong bond after surviving the horrors of the old country. For this reason, I could not dispose of the zombie."

"That would be murder," I said, and instantly regretted it.

"It would have been murder either way," said Malthusian. "Either I killed the subject or they killed us *and* our subject. Instead, I took a chance and left to the ravages of the fire a cadaver we had on ice there for many years. We hoped that no one was aware of it, that if a body was found in the ashes that would be enough to suffice. Remember, this is the government we are talking about. We had worked for them long enough to know that their main priority was silence." Malthusian went silent, nodding his head upon his chest. I thought for a second that he had fallen asleep. When I cleared my throat, he reached for the wine but stopped. He did the same with the cigarette case. Then he looked up at me.

"I'm dying," he said.

"This very moment?" I asked.

"Soon, very soon."

"Did they tell you that at the hospital?"

"I'm a doctor. I know."

"Is there something you need me to do? Do you want me to contact your sister?" I asked.

"No, you must not mention any of this. But there is something I want you to do," he said.

"Call the ambulance?"

"I want you to take care of the zombie until the transformation is complete."

"What are you talking about?" I said, and smiled.

"He's here with me, in the house. He has been with me all along since we burned the lab." Malthusian dropped the cane on the floor, leaned forward on the table and reached for me with his left hand.

I pushed the chair back and stood away from the table to avoid his grasp.

"I've been working with him, trying to reverse the affects of the experiment. The change has begun, but it will take a little longer than I have left to complete it. You must help me return this poor man to his family so that he can enjoy what is left of his life. He is beginning to remember a thing or two and the aging process is slowly starting to return him to his rightful maturity. If I should die, I require you to merely house him until he remembers where he is from. It won't take very long now."

"Dr. Malthusian," I said. "I think you need to rest. You are not making any sense."

The old man slowly stood up. "You will wait!" he yelled at me, holding his arm up and pointing with one finger. "I will get him."

I said nothing more, but watched as Malthusian precariously leaned over to retrieve his cane. Then he hobbled out of the room, mumbling something to himself. When I heard him mounting the stairs to the second floor, I tiptoed out of the kitchen, down the hall, and out the front door. I reached the street and started running like I was ten years old.

Later, in bed, after locking all the doors and windows, I woke Susan up and told her everything that Malthusian had said. When I got to the part about the zombie, she started laughing.

"He wants you to baby-sit his zombie?" she asked.

"It's not funny," I said. "He worked for some secret branch of the government."

"That's the one all the kooks work for," she said. "You're a man with way too much time on his hands."

"He was pretty convincing," I said, now grinning myself.

"What if I told you they were putting Frankenstein together in the basement of the hospital? If he's not crazy, he's probably playing with your mind. He seems to have a healthy measure of mischief about him. That string tie is a good indicator."

I wasn't completely convinced, but Susan allayed my fears enough to allow me to get to sleep. My dreams were punctuated by wide-eyed stares and piano music.

I forced myself to believe that Susan was right, and that I had better ignore Malthusian and get to work on my book. Summer was quickly approaching and soon autumn would send me back to teaching. It would be a great embarrassment to return to work in September empty-handed. I picked up where I had left off months earlier on the manuscript—a chapter concerning "The Facts in the

Case of M. Valdemar." The return to work was what I needed to anchor me against the tide of Malthusian's weirdness, but that particular story by the great American hoaxer, second only to P. T. Barnum, had *zombie* written all over it.

One afternoon, when I was about to leave the house to go to the local bookstore, I looked out the front window and saw the old man slowly shuffling up the street. I had neither seen nor heard from Malthusian since the night I had abandoned him in his fit of madness two weeks prior. It would have been a simple thing to leave the living room and hide in the kitchen, but instead I quickly ducked down beneath the sill. As I crouched there, I wondered at the fear I had developed for my neighbor.

Five minutes went by, and when I thought he should have passed on to where the woods began at the end of the block, I raised my head above the windowsill. There he was, standing at the curb, hunched over, staring directly at me like some grim and ghastly bird of yore. I uttered a brief, startled gasp, and as if he could hear me, he brought the top of his cane up and tapped it lightly against the brim of his Tyrolean hat. Then he turned and moved off.

This little scene threw me into a panic. I never went to the bookstore, and when it was time for Lyda to get out of school, I drove over and picked her up instead of letting her take the bus, which would have left her off at the corner. My panic was short-lived, for that evening, at dinner, as I was about to describe the event to Susan, we heard the ambulance.

It is sad to say, but Malthusian's death was a relief to me. Lyda and I watched from a distance as they brought him out on the wheeled stretcher. Susan, who was afraid of nothing, least of all death, walked over to his house and spoke to the EMTs. She was not there long when we saw her begin walking back.

"Massive heart attack," she said as she approached, shaking her head.

"That's a shame," I said.

Lyda put her arm around my leg and hugged me.

The next morning, while I was wandering around the house looking for inspiration to begin working on Poe again, I discovered that Lyda had draped a silk purple flower, plucked from Susan's dining-room table arrangement, around the neck of Rat Fink. The sight of this made me smile, and as I reached out to touch the smooth illusion of the blossom, I was interrupted by a knocking at the door. I left my daughter's room and went downstairs. Upon opening the front door, I discovered that there was no one there. As I stood, looking out, I heard the knocking sound again. It took me a few long seconds to adjust to the fact that the sound was coming from the back of the house.

"Who knocks at the back door?" I said to myself as I made my way through the kitchen.

3

His eyes were the oval disks of Japanese cartoon characters, glassy and brimming with nothing. Like the whiteness of Melville's whale, you could read anything into them, and while Lyda and I sat staring at him staring at the wall, I projected my desires and frustrations into those mirrors with a will I doubt Ahab could have mustered.

"A blown Easter egg," said Lyda, breaking the silence.

And in the end, she was right. There was an exquisite emptiness about him. His face was drawn, his limbs thin but wiry with real muscle. He looked like a fellow who might at one time have worked as a car mechanic or a UPS delivery man. I guessed his age to be somewhere in the late thirties but knew, from what Malthusian had suggested, that his youth was merely compliance to a command. I wondered how old he would become when the spell was broken. *Perhaps, like Valdemar in Poe's story*, I thought, *he will eventually be reduced to a pool of putrescence.*

We had been sitting with the zombie for over an hour when Susan finally arrived home from work. Lyda got up from her seat and ran into the living room to tell her mother that we had a visitor.

"Guess who?" I heard her ask. She led Susan by the hand into the kitchen.

Upon discovering our guest, the first word out of her mouth was, "No." It wasn't like the shriek of a heroine being accosted by a creature in the horror movies. This was the *no* of derailed late-night amorous advances, a response to Lyda's pleading to stay up till eleven on a school night.

"Let's be sensible about this," I said. "What are we going to do?"

"Call the police," said Susan.

"Are you crazy?" I said. "The very fact that he is here, proves that what Malthusian told me was all true. We'd be putting our lives in danger."

"Go play," Susan said to Lyda.

"Can the zombie play?" she asked.

"The zombie has to stay here," I said, and pointed toward the kitchen entrance.

When Lyda was gone, Susan sat down at the table and she and I stared at him some more. His breathing was very shallow and, with the exception of this subtle movement of his chest, he sat perfectly still. There was something very relaxing about his presence.

"This is crazy," she said to me. "What are we going to do with him?"

"Malthusian said he would soon remember where he was from, and that we should take him to his home whenever the memory of it became clear to him."

"Can't we just drive him somewhere and let him out of the car?" asked Susan. "We'll leave him off in the parking lot at the mall."

"You wouldn't do that with a cat, but you would abandon a human being?" I said.

She shook her head in exasperation. "Well, what does he do? It doesn't look like much is becoming clear to him," she said.

I turned to the zombie and said, "What is your name?"

He didn't move.

Susan reached over and snapped her fingers in front of his face. "Hey, Mister Zombie, what should we call you?"

"Wait a second," I said. "He doesn't answer questions, he responds to commands."

"Tell me your name," Susan said to him.

The zombie turned his head slightly toward her and began to slowly move his lips. "Tom," he said, and the word sort of fell out of his mouth, flat and dull as an old coin.

Susan brought her hand up to cover a giggle. "Tommy the zombie," she said.

"Pathetic," I said, and couldn't suppress my own laughter even though there were shadowed entities at large in the world who might engineer our demise.

We had never had so unassuming a house guest. Tom was like that broom standing in the kitchen closet until you need it. The novelty of performance upon command soon wore off. Sure, we got a little mileage out of the stage hypnotist antics—"Bark like a dog," "Act like a chicken." I know it sounds a bit unfeeling, but we did it, I suppose, simply because we could, similar in spirit to the whim of the government that originally engineered the poor man's circumstance. Lyda put an end to this foolishness. She lectured us about how we should respect him. We were embarrassed by her words, but at the same time pleased that we had raised such a caring individual. As it turned out, she had a real affection for the zombie. He was, for Lyda, the puppy we would not let her have.

It was not difficult remembering to command him to go to the bathroom twice a day, or to eat, or shower. What was truly hard was keeping him a secret. We all swore to each other that we would tell no one. Susan and I were afraid that Lyda, so completely carried away by her new friend, might not be able to contain herself at school. Think of the status one would reap in the third grade if it were known you had your own zombie at home. Throughout the ordeal, she proved to be the most practical, the most caring, the most insightful of all of us.

The utter strangeness of the affair did not strike me until the next night when I woke from a bad dream with a dry mouth. Half in a daze, I got out of bed and went to the kitchen for a glass of water. I took my drink and, going into the living room, sat down on the couch. For some reason, I was thinking about Poe's "The Fall of the House of Usher," and how D. H. Lawrence had described it as a story of vampirism. I followed a thread of thought that looped in and out of that loopy story and ended with an image of the previously airy and lethargic Madeline bursting out of her tomb to jump on old Roderick. Then I happened to look to the left, and jumped, myself, realizing that the zombie had been sitting next to me the entire time.

Tom could make a great pot of coffee. He vacuumed like a veteran chambermaid. Susan showed him how to do hospital corners when making the beds. When he was not busy, he would simply sit on the couch in the living room and stare directly across at the face of the grandfather clock. It was clear that he had a conception of time, because it was possible to set him like a VCR. If we were going out, we could tell him, "Make and eat a bologna sandwich at one P.M. Go to the bathroom at three."

Somewhere in the second week of his asylum with us, I got the notion to become more expansive in my commands. I recalled Malthusian telling me that Tom was capable of playing Chopin after only listening to a piece once. It became clear that the requests I had been making of him were penny ante. I upped the stakes and instructed him to begin typing my handwritten notes for the Poe book. He flawlessly copied exactly what I had on the paper. Excited by this new breakthrough, I told him to read a grammar book and then correct my text. *Voilà!*

It became rapidly evident that we would have to get Tom some new clothes, since he continued to wear the same short-sleeved gray Sears workshirt and pants day in and day out. There was no question he would have worn them until they were reduced to shreds. Susan went to the store on her way home from work one night and bought him a few things. The next day, as an experiment, we told him to get dressed, choosing items from the pile of garments we laid before him. He came out of the spare bedroom wearing a pair of loose-fitting khakis and a black T-shirt that had written in white block letters across it *I'm with Stupid*. We all got a charge out of this.

"Laugh, Tom," said Lyda.

The zombie opened wide his mouth, and from way back in his throat came a high-pitched, "HA . . . HA."

The horror of it melted my smile, and I began to wonder about his choice of shirts. That's when I noticed that a distinct five o'clock shadow had sprouted across his chin and sunken cheeks. *My God, I thought, without telling Susan or Lyda, the aging process has begun.*

When Tom wasn't pulling his weight around the house, Lyda usually had him engaged in some game. They played catch, cards, Barbies, and with those activities that were competitive, Lyda would tell him when it was his turn to win—and he would. For the most part, though, they drew pictures. Sitting at the kitchen table, each with a pencil and a few sheets of paper, they would create monsters. Lyda would have to tell Tom what to draw.

"Now do the werewolf with a dress and a hat. Mrs. Werewolf," she said.

That zombie could draw. When he was done there was a startlingly well-rendered, perfectly shadowed and shaded portrait of Lon Chaney in drag, a veritable hirsute Minnie Pearl. Susan hung the drawing with magnets on the refrigerator.

"Take a bow," Lyda told him and he bent gracefully at the waist in a perfect forty-five-degree angle.

My wife and daughter didn't notice that Tom was changing, but I did. Slowly, over the course of mere days, his hair had begun to thin out and crow's feet formed at the corners of his eyes. This transformation astounded me. I wondered what it was that Malthusian had done to offset the effects of the original surgery that had been performed on him. Perhaps it was a series of commands; some kind of rigid behavioristic training. I hated to think of the old man poking around in Tom's head in that checkerboard kitchen under the fluorescent lights. What also puzzled me was how Malthusian had transferred command of the zombie to me and my family. I began paying much closer attention to him, waiting for a sign that he had begun to recollect himself.

4

I held the drawing out to Lyda and asked her, "Who did this?"

She took it from me and upon seeing it smiled. "Tom," she said. "Yesterday, I told him to draw whatever he wanted."

"It's good, don't you think?" I asked.

"Pretty good," she said and turned back to the television show she had been watching.

The portrait I held in my hand was of a young woman with long, dark hair. This was no monster. She was rendered with the same attention to detail as had been given to Mrs. Werewolf, but this girl, whoever she was, was beautiful. I was especially drawn to the eyes, which were luminous, so full of warmth. She wore an expression of amusement—a very subtle grin and a self-consciously dramatic arching of the eyebrows. I went to the kitchen and called for Tom to come in from the living room.

I told him to take his usual drawing seat, and then I handed him the picture. "You will tell me who this is," I commanded.

He stared for a moment at the portrait, and then it happened, a fleeting expression of pain crossed his face. His hand trembled slightly for a moment.

"You must tell me," I said.

"Marta," he said, and although it was only a word, I could have sworn there was a hint of emotion behind it.

"You must tell me if this is your wife," I said.

He slowly brought his left hand to his mouth, like a robot programmed to enact the human response of awe.

"Tell me," I said.

From behind his fingers, he whispered, "My love."

It was a foolish thing to do, but I applauded. As if the sound of my clapping suddenly severed his cognizance, he dropped his hand to his side and returned to the zombie state.

I sat down and studied him. His hair had begun to go gray at the edges, and his beard was now very noticeable. Those wrinkles I had detected the first sign of a few days earlier were now more prominent, as was the loosening of the skin along his chin line. Invading his blank affect was a vague aura of weariness. As impossible as it might sound, he appeared to me as if he had shrunk a centimeter or two.

"My love," I said out loud. These words were the most exciting shred of humanity to have surfaced, not so much for their dramatic weight, but more because he had failed to follow my instruction and definitively answer the question.

I left him alone for the time being, seeing as how he seemed quite saddened by the experience of remembering; but later, when Susan had returned home, we cleared the kitchen table after dinner and tried to advance the experiment. We conscripted Lyda into the plot, since Tom was with her when he had created the portrait of Marta.

"Tell him to draw a picture of his house," I whispered to her. She nodded and then Susan and I left the kitchen and went into the living room to wait.

"He looks terrible," Susan said to me.

"The spell is slowly dissolving," I said. "He is becoming what he should be."

"The human mind is frightening," she said.

"The Haunted Palace," I told her.

Twenty minutes later, Lyda came in to us, smiling, carrying a picture.

"Look what he drew," she said, laughing.

He had created a self-portrait. Beneath the full-length picture were the scrawled words *Tommy the Zombie*.

I pointed to the words and said, "Well that didn't work as I had planned, but this is rather interesting."

"A sense of humor?" said Susan.

"No," said Lyda. "He is sad."

"Maybe we shouldn't push him," I said.

"Wait," said Susan and sat forward suddenly. "Tell him now to draw his home."

Lyda nodded and returned to the kitchen.

An hour passed while Susan and I waited in silence for the results. We could hear Lyda, in the kitchen, talking to him as they worked. She was telling him about this boy in her class in school who always bites the skin on his fingers.

"When Mrs. Brown asked Harry why he bites his skin, you know what he said?" asked Lyda.

There was a moment of silence and then we heard the deep, flat response, "What?"

Susan and I looked at each other.

"Harry told her," said Lyda, "he bites it because that way his father, who is very old, won't die."

A few minutes passed and then came a most disturbing sound, like a moan from out of a nightmare. Susan and I leaped up and ran into the kitchen. Lyda was sitting there, gaping at Tom, who was pressing on the pencil with a shaking hand, writing as if trying to carve initials into a tree trunk. There was sweat on his brow and tears in his eyes. I walked behind him and looked over his shoulder. There was a picture of a ranch-style house with an old carport to its left. In the front window, I could make out the figures of a black cat and a woman's face. He was scrawling numbers and letters across the bottom of the picture.

"Twenty-four Griswold Place," I said aloud. And when he finished and slumped back into his seat, I saw the name of the town and spoke it, "Falls Park."

"That's only an hour north of here," said Susan.

I patted Tom on the back and told him, "You're going home," but by then his consciousness had again receded.

The next morning I arose well before sunrise and ordered Tom down the hall to the guest bedroom to change. He set to the task, a reluctant zombie, his rapid aging causing him to shuffle along, slightly bent over. Literally overnight, his hair had lost more of its color and there was a new, alarming sense of frailty about him. While he was dressing, I went in and kissed Susan good-bye and told her I was taking him as we had planned.

"Good luck," she said.

"Do you want to see him?" I asked.

"No, I'm going to go back to sleep, so that when I wake up I will be able to discount the entire thing as a bad dream."

"I hope I get him there before he croaks," I told her. "He's older than ever today."

I settled Tom in the backseat of the car and told him to buckle the belt. Then I got in and started driving. It was still dark as I turned onto the road out of town. Of course, I was taking a big chance by hoping that he might still know someone at the address he had written down. Decades had passed since he had been abducted, but I didn't care. Think ill of me if you like, but as with the lawyer in Melville's "Bartleby, the Scrivener," who ends up finally abandoning the scribe, which of you would have done as much as we did? Shadowed entities be damned, it had to come to an end.

"You're going home," I said over my shoulder to him as I drove.

"Home, yes," he said, and I took this for a good sign.

I looked into the rearview mirror, and could only see the top of his head. He seemed to have shrunk even more. To prepare myself for a worst-case scenario, I wondered what the bill would be to have a pool of putrescence steam-cleaned from my back seat.

About halfway into the journey, he started making some very odd sounds—coughing and hushed choking. This gave way to a kind of grumbling language that he carried on with for miles. I couldn't make out what he was saying, and to block it out, I eventually turned on the radio.

Even with the map, the address, and the drawing, it took me an hour and forty-five minutes to find the place. The sun was just beginning to show itself on the horizon when I pulled up in front of 24 Griswold Place. It was remarkable how perfect his drawing had been.

"Go now and knock on that door," I said, pointing.

I was going to get out of the car and help him, but before I could get my belt off, I heard the back door open and close. Turning, I saw his figure moving away from the car. He was truly an old man now, moving beneath the weight of those years that, in the brief time of our trip, had caught up and overtaken him. I hoped that his metamorphosis had finally ended.

A great wave of sorrow passed through me, and I couldn't let him go without saying good-bye. I pressed the button for the window on his side. When it had rolled down, I called out, "Good luck."

He stopped walking, turned slowly to face me, and then I knew that the transformation was complete. His hair had gone completely white, and his face was webbed with wrinkles. It was Malthusian. He stood there staring at me, and his eyes were no smaller because he did not wear glasses.

I shook with the anger of betrayal. "You bastard!" I yelled.

"Let's not let it ruin our game," he said with a thick accent, and then turned and went up the front steps.

I was so stunned, I couldn't move. He knocked on the door. After a few moments, a woman, as old as he, answered. I heard her give a short scream and then she threw her arms around him. "You've returned," she said in that same accent. She ushered him into the house and then the door slammed closed.

"Marta Malthusian, the sister," I said to myself and slammed the steering wheel. I don't know how long I sat there, staring blankly, trying to sort out the tangled treachery and love of a madman turning a zombie into a zombie of himself. Eventually, I put the car in gear, wiped the drool from my chin, and started home.

Julian Jaynes's The Origin of Consciousness in the Breakdown of the Bicameral Mind *is a fascinating book. It's one of those reading experiences, like* The Holographic Universe *by Michael Talbot, that seems crackpot but could hold a viable explanation for why things are the way they are. Either way, as a fiction writer, you have to love these books when you find them. They are potent fodder for the imagination.*

Also, there's nothing like a good zombie to liven up a story. The ultimate straight man.

This story is sort of an homage to Poe, since it has a plot I think he would have liked. For those who also admire American Literature's favorite laudanum-ingesting light-bulb head, the text is, sometimes subtly, sometimes not, peppered with references to his life and work.

My sincerest apologies to Mr. Jaynes.

On the Road to New Egypt

ONE DAY WHEN I WAS DRIVING HOME FROM WORK, I saw him there on the side of the road. He startled me at first, but I managed to control myself and apply the brakes. His face was fixed with a look somewhere between agony and elation. That thumb he thrust out at an odd angle was gnarled and had a long nail. The sun was setting and red beams danced around him. I stopped and leaned over to open the door.

"You're Jesus, right?" I said.

"Yeah," he said and held up his palms to show the stigmata.

"Hop in," I told him.

"Thanks, man," he said as he gathered up his robe and slipped into the front seat.

As I pulled back out onto the road, he took out a pack of Camel Wides and a dark blue Bic lighter. "You don't mind, do you?" he asked, but he already had a cigarette in his mouth and was bringing a flame to it.

"Go for it," I said.

"Where you headed?" he asked.

"Home, unless you're here to tell me different," I said, forcing a laugh.

"Easy, easy," he said.

After a short silence, Christ took a couple of deep drags and blew the smoke out the partially opened window.

"Where are *you* going?" I asked.

"You know, just up the road a piece."

We stopped at a red light and I looked over at him. That crown of thorns must have itched like hell. I shook my head and said, "Wait till I tell my wife about this."

"She religious?" he asked.

"Not particularly, but still, she'll get the impact."

He smiled and flicked some ashes into his palm.

We drove on for a while through the vanishing light, past fields of pumpkins and dried corn stalks. A few minutes later, night fell, and I turned on the headlights. I didn't see it at first, but a possum darted out into the road right in front of the car. *Bump, bump,* we were over it in a microsecond. I looked at Christ.

He shrugged as if to say, "What can you do?"

". . . and Heaven?" I asked as the car traveled into a valley where the trees from either side of the road had, above, grown together into a canopy.

"Angels, blue skies, your relatives are all there. The greats are there. Basically everybody is there. It gets a little tense sometimes, a little close."

"You said that 'basically' everybody is in Heaven," I said. "Who isn't?"

"You know," he said, "those other people."

We kept going past the fences of the horse farms, the edges of barren fields, until Christ had me stop at McDonald's and order him a quarter pounder with cheese, and a chocolate shake. I paid for it with my last couple of dollars.

He said, "I'll pay you back in indulgences."

"Hey, it's on me," I said.

He wolfed down that burger like the Son of man that he was.

"So what have you seen in your travels?" I asked.

"You name it," he said, sucking at his shake. "The human drama."

"Do you ever stop anywhere?"

"Sometimes. I'm always on the look-out for an old Howard Johnson." There was a short pause and then he said, "Could you step on it a little, I have to be in New Egypt by eight."

"Sure thing," I said and put down the pedal. "You meeting someone?"

"I've been seeing this woman there on and off for the past couple of years. Every once in a while I'll appear, give her a little push and then split by sunup."

"She must be pretty special."

"Yeah," he said, and took out a flattened wallet. "Here she is."

He showed me an old photo of this forty-five-year-old ex-blonde-bombshell in a leopard bikini.

"Nice," I said.

"Nice isn't the word for it," he said, with a wink.

"What's she do?" I asked.

"A little of this and a little of that," he said.

"No, I mean where does she work?"

"At the funeral parlor. She sews mouths and lids shut. She lives in a small house in the center of town. When I get there, she's usually in bed. I step out of the armoire, minus the robe, and slip between the sheets with her. We eat of the fruit of the knowledge of good and evil for a few hours and then lay back, have a smoke."

"Does she know who you are?"

"I hope by this time she's figured it out," he said.

"She'll end up going to the tabloids with the story," I warned.

"Screw it, she already has. We were in that one recently with Bigfoot on the cover and the story about the woman who turned to stone on page three."

"I missed that one, but I remember the cover."

All of a sudden Christ sat straight up and pointed out the windshield. "Whoa, whoa," he said, "pull over like you're going to pick this guy up."

Only when he spoke did I see the shadowy figure up ahead on the side of the road. I could see it was a guy and that he was hitchhiking. I passed by him a few feet and then pulled over to the shoulder. We could hear him running toward the car.

"Okay, peel out," Christ said.

I did and we left that stranger in the dust.

"I love that one," said the savior.

A few minutes passed and then I heard a hatchet of a voice from the back seat. "You fuckers," it said. I looked in the rearview mirror and there was the Devil—horns, red skin, cheesy whiskers in a goatee. As I looked at him his grin turned into a wide smile.

Jesus reached back and offered a hand.

"Who's the stiff at the wheel?" asked the Devil.

"You mean fat boy here?" Christ said and they both burst out laughing. "He's cool."

"Nice to meet you," said the Devil.

I reached back and shook a hand that was a tree branch with the power to grip. "Name's Jeff," I said.

"I am legion," he hissed.

Then he stuck his head in the space between us and shot a little burp of flame into the air. Christ doubled over with silent laughter. "I got a bag of Carthage Red on me, you got any papers?" the Devil asked, putting his hand on Christ's shoulder.

"Does the Pope shit in the woods?" asked the Son of God.

The Devil got the papers and started rolling one in the back seat. "Jeff, you ever try this shit?"

"I never heard of it."

"It's old, man, it'll make you see God."

"By the way," Christ said, interrupting, "what ever happened with that guy in Detroit?"

"I took him," said the Devil. "Mass murderer, just reeking evil. He hung himself in the jail cell. They conveniently forgot to remove his belt."

"I thought I told you I wanted him," said Christ.

"I thought I cared," said the Devil. "Anyway, you get that old woman from Tampa. She's going to make canonization. I guarantee it."

"I guess that's cool," he said.

"Eat me if it isn't," said the Devil. They both started laughing and each patted me on the back. The Devil lit up the enormous joint he had created and the odd pink smoke began to permeate the car.

It tasted like cinnamon and fire and even with only the first toke, I was stunned. Paranoia set in instantly, and I slowed the car down to about thirty. I drove blindly while in my head I saw the autumn afternoon woods of my childhood, where it was so still and the leaves silently fell. I thought of home and it was far away.

When my mind returned to me at a red light, I realized that the radio was on. New Age music, a piano, and some low moaning, formed a backdrop to the conversation of my passengers.

"What do you think?" Christ had just asked.

"I think this music has to go," said the Devil. His fingers grew like snakes from the back seat, and he kept pressing the scan button on the radio until he came to the oldies station. "Back seat memories," he said.

Somehow it was decided that we would go to Florida and check out the lady who was going to become a saint. "Maybe she'll pop a miracle," said the Devil.

"No sweat," said Christ.

"My wife's expecting me home around nine," I said.

The Devil laughed really loud. "I'll tell you what I'll do," he said. "I'll split myself in two, and half of me will go to your house and boff your wife till we get back."

Christ leaned over and put his hand on my knee. "Don't be an idiot," he said to me with a smile. "I have to be in New Egypt by eight."

"You can do things?" I asked.

"Look," said Christ, nodding toward the windshield, "we're there. Just make a right at this corner. It's the third house on the left."

I looked up and saw that we were in a suburban neighborhood with palm trees lining the side of the road. The houses were all one-story ranch styles and painted in pastel colors. When I pulled the car over in front of the house, I could hear crickets singing quickly in the night heat.

Before we got out, the Devil leaned toward the front seat and said to Christ, "I'll make you a bet she doesn't do a miracle while we're here."

"Bullshit," said Christ.

"What do you want to bet?" asked the Devil.

"How about *him*," said the savior and pointed that weird thumb at me.

"Quite the high roller," said the Devil.

As we were walking up the driveway to the front door, the Devil lagged a little behind us. I leaned over and, in a whisper, asked Christ if he thought she would perform.

He shrugged and rolled his eyes. "Have faith, man," he said. "Sometimes you win, sometimes you lose."

"I heard that," said the Devil. "I don't like whispering."

We walked right through the front door and into the living room where a woman was sitting in front of the television. At first, I thought she was deaf, but it soon became clear that we were completely invisible to her.

The Devil walked up behind me and handed me a sixteen-ounce Rolling Rock. "There she is in all her splendor," he said, as he handed a beer to Christ. "Doesn't look like much of an opportunity here unless she's gonna get better looking."

We stood and stared at her. She was about sixty-five with short hair dyed brown and wearing a flowered bathrobe. On the coffee table in front of her set an ashtray with a lit cigarette in one of the holders. In her left hand she held a glass of dark wine. As the daily reports of mayhem and greed came through the box, she shook her head from time to time and sipped her drink.

"What's she done?" I asked.

"She brought a kid back from the dead a few months ago," said the Devil. "A girl was hit by a car outside a local grocery store. Mrs. Lumley, here, was present and just touched the girl's hand. The kid got right up off the stretcher and walked away."

"Strange shit," said Christ. "We don't really know how it works."

"You mean," I said, "that you can't make her do a miracle?"

"Not exactly," said Christ.

"That's a bitch, isn't it?" said the Devil. "Now drink your beer and calm down."

The Devil walked around behind Mrs. Lumley's chair and used two fingers to make horns behind her head. Christ went to pieces over that one. I even had to laugh while we watched her pick her nose. She was at it for a good five minutes. Christ applauded her every strategy, and the Devil said, "The one that got away."

"We better sit down. This may take a few minutes," said Christ.

The Devil and I sat down on the couch and Christ took an old rocker across from us. The evil one rolled another huge joint and listened intently to the report on the television of a murder/suicide in California. Mrs. Lumley began singing "The Whispering Wind" to herself in between sips of wine while Christ hummed a duet with her.

"I've had more fun in church," said the Devil, as he passed me the joint. Again, I tasted the cinnamon and fire, and I took big gulps of beer to soothe my throat.

Christ begged off and just rocked contentedly in his chair.

The news eventually ended and *Jeopardy* came on the television. "Wait till I get my hooks into *this* asshole," the Devil said, nodding toward the host of the show.

"He's yours," said Christ. "It's on me." Then he pointed his finger at Mrs. Lumley and made her change the channel to a *Star Trek* rerun.

While we waited for something to happen, the Devil showed me a trick. He took a big draw of Carthage Red and then exhaled it in a perfect globe of smoke. The globe hovered in the air before my eyes and turned crystal clear. Then it was filled with an image of my wife and kids reading bedtime stories. When I reached for it, the globe popped like a soap bubble.

"Parlor tricks," said Christ.

Eventually, Mrs. Lumley got up, turned off the set and went into her bedroom. We followed her as far as the door, where we looked in at her. She was kneeling next to the bed, saying her prayers.

"I hope you like the heat," the Devil said to me.

Then Christ said, "Look."

Mrs. Lumley lay on the floor, her body twitching. A steady groan escaped through her clenched teeth. In seconds, her skin had become a metallic blue and her head had doubled in size. Fangs, claws, gills, audibly popped from her features. She turned her head to face us, and I could feel she was actually seeing us with her expanding eyes.

"Shit," said the Devil, and turned and ran toward the door.

"Let's get out of here," said Christ, and he too turned and ran. I followed close behind.

By the time we got outside, the Devil was sticking his head out the back-seat window of the car. "Move your asses!" he yelled.

I ran around the front of the car and climbed in the driver's seat as fast as I could. Mrs. Lumley, now some kind of rapidly changing blue creature, growled from the front lawn. I turned on the ignition and hit the gas.

"What the fuck was that supposed to be?" said Christ, catching his breath as he passed us each a cigarette.

"Your old man is out of his mind," said the Devil. "It's all getting just a little too strange."

"Tell me about it," said Christ. "Remember, I warned you back when they first walked on the moon."

"This is some really evil shit, though," said the Devil.

"The whole ball of wax is falling apart," said Christ.

"I actually had a break-out in the ninth bole of Hell last week," said the Devil. "A big bastard—he smashed right through the ice. Killed one demon with his bare hands and broke another one's back."

"Did you get him?" I asked.

"One of my people said she saw him in Chicago."

"Purgatory is spreading like the plague," said Christ.

The Devil leaned up close behind me and put his claw hand on my shoulder. I could feel his hot breath on the back of my neck. "His old man is reading Nietzsche," he whispered, his tongue grazing my earlobe.

"What's he saying?" Christ asked me.

"Which way am I supposed to turn to get out of this development?" I asked.

Just then there was an abrupt bump on the top of the car. It startled me and I swerved, almost hitting a garbage can.

"You gotta check this out," said the Devil. "Saint Lumley of the Bad Trips is flying over us."

"Punch the gas," yelled Christ, and I floored it. I drove like a maniac, screeching around corners as the pastel ranches flew by.

"We're starting to lose her," the Devil called out.

"What are you carrying?" Christ asked.

"I've got a full minute of fire," said the Devil. "What have you got?"

"I've got the Machine of Eden," said Christ.

"Uhh, not *The* fucking Machine of Eden," said the Devil, and slammed the back of my seat.

"What do you mean?" said Christ.

"When was the last time that thing worked?"

"It works," said Christ.

"Pull off and go through the gate up on your right," said the Devil. "We've got to take her out or she'll dog us for eternity."

"I don't like this at all," said Christ.

After passing the gate, I drove on a winding gravel road that led to the local landfill. There were endless moonlit hills of junk and garbage. I parked the car and we got out.

"We've got to get to the top of that hill before she gets here," said Christ, pointing to a huge mound of garbage.

I scrabbled up the hill, clutching at old car seats and stepping on dead appliances. Startled rats scurried through the debris. When I reached the top I was sweating and panting. Christ beat me, but I had to reach back down and help the Devil up the last few steps.

"It's the hooves," he said, "they're worse than high heels."

"There's some cool old stuff here," said Christ.

"I saw a whole carton of *National Geographic*s I want to snag on the way out," said the Devil.

Off in the distance, I saw the shadow of something passing in front of the stars. It was too big to be a bird. "Here she comes," I yelled and pointed. They both spun around to look. "What do I do?" I asked.

"Stay behind us," said Christ. "If she gets you, it's going to hurt."

The next thing I knew, Mrs. Lumley had landed and we three were backed against the edge of the hill with a steep drop behind us. Her blue skin shone in the moonlight like armor, but there were tufts of hair growing from it. She had this amazing aqua body and an eight-foot wingspan, but with the exception of the gills and fangs, she still had the face of a sixty-five-year-old woman. She moved slowly toward us, burping out words that made no sense.

When she came within a few feet of us, Christ said, "Smoke 'em if you got 'em," and the Devil stepped forward. Tentacles began to grow from her body toward him. One managed to wrap itself around his left horn when he opened his mouth to assault her with a minute of fire. The flames discharged like a blowtorch and stopped her cold. When she was completely engulfed in the blaze, the tentacles retracted, but she would not melt.

As soon as the evil one finished, coughing out great clouds of gray smoke, Mrs. Lumley opened her eyes and the tentacles began again to grow from her sides. I looked over and saw that Christ was holding something in his right hand. It appeared to be a remote control, and he was furiously pushing its buttons.

The Devil had jumped back beside me, his hand clutching my arm. He had real fear in his serpent eyes, yet he could not help but laugh at Christ messing around with the Machine of Eden.

"What's with the cosmic garage door opener?" he shouted.

"It works," said Christ, as he continued to nervously press buttons. Then I felt one of the tentacles wrap itself around my ankle. Mrs. Lumley opened her mouth and crowed like a rooster. Another of the blue snake appendages entwined itself around the Devil's midsection. We both screamed as she pulled us toward her.

"Three," Christ yelled, and a beam of light shot out of the end of the Machine. I then heard the sound of celestial voices singing in unison. Mrs. Lumley took the blast full in the chest and began instantly to shrivel. Before my eyes, like the special effects in a crappy science fiction movie, she turned into a tree. Leaves sprouted, pink blossoms grew, and as the singing faded, pure white fruit appeared on the lower branches.

"Not fun," said the Devil.

"I thought she was going to suck your face off," said Christ.

"What exactly was she," I asked, "an alien?"

Christ shook his head. "Nah," he said, "just a fucked-up old woman."

"Is she still a saint?" I asked.

"No, she's a tree," he said.

"You and your saints," said the Devil and plucked a piece of fruit. "Take one of these," he said to me. "It's called the *Still Point of the Turning World*. Only eat it when you need it."

I picked one of the white pears off the tree and put it in my pocket before we started down the junk hill. The Devil found the box of magazines and Christ came up with a lamp made out of seashells. We piled into the car and I started it up.

I heard Christ say, "Holy shit, it's 8:00!"

The next thing I knew I was on my usual road back in Jersey. The car was empty but for me, and I was just leaving New Egypt.

I hope my use of the Judeo-Christian mythology in this remix of a contemporary legend doesn't upset anyone. It shouldn't since, according to the dogma, everyone is supposed to have their own relationship with Christ. Ours is a casual friendship. We like to party, and if horn-head is along for the ride, so much the better. Sometimes the Buddha joins us, but he insists on riding shotgun and too often lips the rope. In honor of Christ's teachings, we try not to be exclusive, for blessed are those who will suffer in his name.

New Egypt, New Jersey, is a town I pass through every night on the way home from work. I've never stopped there except in my dreams. It boasts a perpetual flea market and a convenience store where you can buy The Weekly World Star—*a perfect location for the second, or even third, coming.*

This story was originally published in the magazine Aberrations.

Floating In Lindrethool

1

"Your profession, gentlemen, has a long and distinguished lineage," was what the section boss had said when he stopped the bus, opened the door, and let them all out on the east side of Lindrethool. Eight men in black raincoats, white shirts and ties, and the company issued, indicative, derbies. They fanned out across the grim industrial cityscape, the soot falling like black snow around them. Each carried a valise in one hand and a large case with a handle in the other. Each walked away, mumbling his respective spiel, all of which included at some point the words, "for a limited time only." In three weeks, the bus would be waiting at the west end to collect them.

Slackwell sat now, tieless, hatless, pantsless, at a small scarred table in his hotel room, sipping straight bourbon from a smudged tumbler. "A distinguished lineage," he said aloud to the windowpane that beyond his reflection gave a view of the night and the myriad lights of Lindrethool. Every light stood in his mind for a potential customer. All he needed was one to part with forty thousand dollars in easy monthly payments spread over ten years and he would have fulfilled his minimal quota for the year. On that first day, he had covered three apartment buildings, lugging his case from floor to floor. "Not even a smell," as his colleague Merk might say.

He couldn't imagine the door-to-door salesmen of the previous century doing what he did, having nothing better to offer than brushes, or vacuum cleaners, encyclopedias, bibles. At least he had a real wonder in his case, a value that could change the lives of his customers. That's exactly what he told them while cajoling, reasoning, even threatening if necessary. While in training, he had practiced again and again like a martial artist the techniques of wedging a foot between the doorjamb and door, following through with the shoulder, and then achieving a look of homicide thinly veiled by a determination to please. The studies had shown that the novelty of face-to-face sales was what the consumer wanted. In the waning economy that had taken a nosedive ten years into the new century, people did not want to shop on-line or by phone for big-ticket items anymore. Or at least that was what they had told him during his training.

He hadn't had a sale in two months, and the section boss had told him that the company was thinking of letting him go. "You're too tired-looking, Slackwell," the boss had said. "Your complexion is as gray as your hair, and your spiel, though rabid enough, has all the allure of a drooping erection. Wrinkles are no comfort to our customers, it is power they want. You are selling status. And, please, your after shave is rancid."

Slackwell cringed into his bourbon, thinking about how he had pleaded, whined actually, to be allowed one more chance. The boss took pity on him, and not only allowed him another shot at it, but also issued him the latest model to hawk in Lindrethool. "If you can't sell that," the boss had said, "you can sell yourself to the devil."

Slackwell lit a cigarette. With the butt jutting from the corner of his mouth, he stood and unlatched the case that sat next to the bottle of bourbon. The black metal carrier bulged at the sides as if it housed an oversized bowling ball. The front panel opened on hinges, and he reached in and brought forth a large glass globe with a circular metal base. The base had dials and buttons on it, two jacks, a small speaker, and, attached in the back, a wound-up thin electrical cord. Thinktank, the name of the company, was written across the metal in red letters followed by the model number 256–B. The globe above was filled with clear liquid and suspended at its center was a human brain.

The bourbon, having gotten the better of him, made him weave a little as he stepped back to view the illustrious product. He took the cigarette out of his mouth, and with the two fingers it was wedged between pointed at the globe. "Now that's a floater," he said with a cloud of smoke. A floater was what the sales force of Thinktank called the organic center of their merchandise.

"Organic computing, the wave of the future," Slackwell slurred, practicing his spiel. "Consider this—a human mind, unfettered by physical concerns, using not the customary piddling ten percent used by your Joe Blow from Kokomo, not even fifty or seventy or eighty percent, but a full 95.7 percent of its total cogitative potential. The limitations of microchips have long since been reached. The computing power of a human brain is vast. This baby can run your household appliances from your apartment's master control box, your lights, your phone. It can easily increase the power of your home computer 300 times, provide access to television from around the globe, all at a fraction of your present cost. Set it to pay your bills once and it will do so, on time, every month—it learns what you like, what you want, what you need. And the speed with which it runs will make your parallel processing seem like . . ."

Slackwell couldn't remember what bit of hyperbole came next. All he could think of was the boss's ". . . a drooping erection." He took a drag on his cigarette and sat down to stare at the gray, spongy fist of convolutions. There was something both awe inspiring and lurid about the fact that an individual's consciousness was trapped inside that insanely winding maze of matter, an island lolling in a crystal bubble. Once, a few weeks earlier, Slackwell's thoughts took a dangerous detour, and he briefly glimpsed the analogy to his own existence—trapped, trapped, and trapped again.

This new model, though, this 256–B, had a feature that set it above all the others: a button on the base that when pushed would rouse the brain into consciousness. The customer could talk to it and the apparatus would break the spoken language down into an electrical impulse, send it to the floater by way of a remote transmitter in the base, and the brain would hear in thoughts. Then its response, sent out by the brain's language centers as its own electrical impulse of thought, would be picked up by another device which would translate it into spoken language. The voice that came from the speakers wasn't a stiff, robotic barking of words. The Thinktank technicians had patented a new development that allowed the device to emulate the tonality, resonance, inflection, and even accent of the original donor's voice.

The corporation had cut deals with certain indigent families, and there were a lot of them these days, to allow their loved ones' brains to be extracted before actual clinical death set in. The legalization of certain types of euthanasia had opened the door to more liberal organ donation practices. Hence, the individual personality of the brain was kept intact. These deals involved cash in rewarding quantities and the promise that the dying family member would live on, remaining a useful member of society and a catalyst for change in the new economy that was ever on the verge of dawning. Slackwell wondered which, the cash or the promise, was the more comforting to the bereaved.

The only member of the sales force who had had an opportunity to sell one of these new models with a personality as well as the usual unconscious computing power was Merk, and he had warned Slackwell and the others, "One thing to remember: you can demonstrate the floater's sentience for the customer but, whatever you do, don't engage it in conversation on your own. It'll give you the yips." They had asked Merk if he was speaking from experience or just relating what the researchers at Thinktank had told him. The veteran salesman gave no reply.

2

Although the concept of home was now no more than some vague memory, Slackwell never got used to waking in a strange hotel room. One second he would be dreaming of the old days back in the house on the bay, a spring breeze passing through the willows just outside the screened window. He would roll over in bed to put an arm around his wife, Ella, and then, like a light suddenly switched on, the nausea of his hangover would lodge featherlike at the base of his throat. His mouth would go instantly dry, and the pain would begin behind his eyes. That peaceful dream of the past would vanish and he would wake alone and disoriented.

Of late, his hands had begun to shake in the mornings, and it was all he could do to steady the bottle in order to pour the first of three shots that would get him through the hellish shower, the donning of his Thinktank uniform and to his first cup of coffee. Sometimes aspirin would be called for; sometimes, when he had it, a joint. Whatever it took, he would be on the street sharply at 8:15, staggering along, case in hand.

On this, the morning of his second day in Lindrethool, he met Merk at a diner around the corner from his hotel. They sat at a booth by the window, facing each other, but neither spoke until the first cup of coffee had been drained and the waitress had come with refills.

"How many units did you fob off on the witless citizenry yesterday?" asked Slackwell.

Merk shook his head. "This place is drier than my ex-wife."

"I had a guy who wanted to buy my hat," said Slackwell.

"There you go," said Merk. "I walked in on the middle of a domestic dispute. The woman had a shiner and the old man was seething, but still he made me demonstrate the Tank for them. I had one hand on that revolver I keep in my jacket pocket and used the other to flip the switches and turn the knobs. I got the floater to sing them a song, 'No Business like Show Business.' You know, it's a sentient model, and whoever the unlucky sap is who wound up under the glass can really belt out a tune. No sale, though. No sale."

"I'm packing a 256–B myself," said Slackwell, trying to impress his senior colleague with the fact that the company had entrusted one of its top-of-the-line models to him. "But I still haven't let the thing talk for itself yet. I had a near miss on a sale yesterday. A woman with a kid. She had me do the fucking kid's homework on it and print it out—a report on mummies. The whole time the little monster kept smearing his greasy fingers all over the globe, trying to get at the meat inside. Finally, I told his old lady she should teach him some manners. That iced it."

"You gotta watch that anger. The customer's always right," said Merk.

"The customer's hardly *ever* right," said Slackwell.

They had a few more cups of coffee and Merk had a plate of runny eggs. There was a brief discussion of the new guy Johnny, who Merk said hung himself in the shower stall of his hotel room.

"Did the company get there in time?" asked Slackwell.

"You kidding me?" said Merk. "The implant tipped them off that he was going south before he even put the belt around his neck. I was called over there last night at around nine to witness the operation. They always call me for that shit. I get a bonus. They opened his head like a can of peaches and whipped his sponge out faster than you can say 'a limited time only.'"

"Won't his brain be screwed up?"

"They have ways to revive them," said Merk. "Besides, when they cut him down, I'm not sure he was all dead, if you know what I mean."

"He seemed a little too sensitive for the work," said Slackwell.

"That poor bastard was born to be a floater," said Merk. "Some of us drift in the liquid and some on the sidewalk." He gave a rare smile, almost a wince, and shook his head. "Last I saw the kid alive, he had a stunned look on his face like he didn't know whether to shit or go blind. You know, I've seen that look before."

"Where?"

"Every morning in the bathroom mirror since the old lady left me."

"So make another face," said Slackwell. "What would it take?"

"Courage or insanity, and I haven't got the juice to muster either. When the bell rings, I drool, but I'm good at it."

"Yeah," said Slackwell, "my chin's damp more often than not."

They each had a cigarette and then stood, lifted their cases and exited the diner. Out on the windy street corner, they tipped their respective hats to each other, gave the parting Thinktank sales force salutation, "Lose a brain, brother," and set out on their separate paths.

By noon, Slackwell was no longer staggering. Instead, he was limping. On the last call before lunch, after covering two entire apartment buildings, a woman took a hammer she had apparently just happened to be holding and smashed the foot he had artfully wedged between door and doorjamb. "Scat," she had yelled as if he had been some kind of bothersome vermin.

As he moved slowly along the street, he could feel his foot swelling in the shoe. The pain was moderate—worse than the time an old woman had brought him a cup of steaming hot coffee after an hour and a half of hard sell and accidentally spilled it in his lap, but not quite as bad as the time a madman had taken his pen on the pretense of signing an agreement and jabbed him in the wrist with it. At times like this, he considered it a good thing that he did not carry a revolver like Merk.

He spotted the next address on his list, and its newness, its cleanliness, and name—Thornwood Arms—made him decide to skip lunch. Everything about this place suggested affluence. These were the apartments of those who had wound up on the right side of the perpetually widening divide between the haves and have-nots.

He entered the front of the building and made for the elevator, but before he could so much as press the button, a security guard had a hand on his shoulder.

"Whom are you here to see?" asked the tall young man dressed in what appeared to be a ship captain's uniform.

Slackwell retrieved a business card from his coat pocket and handed it to the guard. "I am here to bring the future to your residents."

"Sorry, sir, but there is no solicitation allowed here."
"This is not solicitation. This is demonstration," said Slackwell.
"Either way," said the young man, "you'll have to leave."
"Luddite," Slackwell yelled, as he exited through the revolving door.

Once out on the street, he immediately ducked down an alleyway next to the building. *There's no way this fool is going to deny me contact with a public in need of innovation,* he thought, *especially a public with plenty of cash.*

At the back of the huge building, Slackwell found an empty loading platform. Lifting the case onto it, he then scrabbled up himself. The tall, sliding aluminum gate directly in front of him was shut tight, but off to the far left and far right of the platform were doors that gave access to the building. He chose the left, walked over to try the knob and found he had chosen correctly. The door swung open, and he felt something in his solar plexus, either a muffled gasp of excitement or a jab of indigestion.

He entered, and following a short hallway, soon came in view of a freight elevator. Glancing around to make sure that he was alone, he pressed the button on the elevator and waited for the door to open. He knew better than to gloat in his victory, but he could not help a brief smile. The door slid back and he stepped into the wide, shiny box. "Which floor?" he wondered aloud, staring at the row of buttons. Out of the thirty possibilities, he chose number eleven. The door closed. He leaned back against the metal wall as the car lurched into its ascent. Sweat rolled down across his face from under his hat brim, his heart pounded, his hands shook from need of a drink, and his foot throbbed.

It was a quick decision, but he felt as if he might keel over if he didn't soothe his nerves. When the elevator reached somewhere between the fifth and sixth floors, Slackwell hit the STOP button. Reaching into his shirt pocket, he pulled out a joint. His hands shook violently and he had a difficult time working the lighter. Eventually, he got the thing lit and took five short tokes on it. The car quickly filled with smoke. Before he stubbed out the weed and started the elevator again, he could already feel his tension level beginning to drop.

Slackwell's mind swirled like the clouds that exited the elevator with him on the eleventh floor. For a few brief moments, as he made his way through a series of doors to find the hallway that held the residents' apartments, he entertained the possibility of filling at least twenty orders.

At the very first door he knocked on, a pleasant-looking older man answered. Slackwell took a deep breath in order to launch into his spiel, but found the dope he'd smoked had robbed him of words. Instead, he started laughing.

The man at the door smiled, and said, "Can I help you?"

"I'm selling something," said Slackwell.

"Shall I guess what it is?"

"Organic computing."

The customer's look changed slightly but he continued to smile. "I see," said the man. "Brains in a jar? I've heard of it."

"More than that," said Slackwell. "Much more."

"Let's see it do its thing," said the man. He stepped aside and let the salesman in.

The apartment was spacious and perfectly clean. A large window offered a view of the city. The man was obviously learned, because there were two huge bookcases filled with weighty volumes. Beautiful old paintings depicting religious scenes hung on the walls. It was clear to Slackwell from his training that this would be the type of customer who might balk at the usual bullying tactics. A smooth and reasoned delivery was called for in this situation, and he was high enough at the moment to believe he was the man for the job.

They sat, each in a comfortable armchair, at a small marble coffee table on which Slackwell rested his case. As he went through the operation of removing the unit, he laid down a spiel as smooth as a frozen lake. Having read the scene and taken in the surroundings—the customer's cardigan, loafers, and designer button-down shirt the same color as his socks—he tried to punctuate his message with as many erudite words as he was capable of.

"You see, sir . . . what is your name again?" he asked.

"Catterly," said the man.

"You see Mr. Catterly, there is no need for a man of your obvious intelligence to forbear the rigitudes of laboring under the present inadequate computing systems that now run the devices of your apartment and give you access to the Internet. There are bothersome buttons to be pushed, dials to be set, and the response time of all of this outdated equipment is regrettable, to say the least. Here is a system that will actually think for you. It will swiftly learn what it is you want, and one simple voice command from you is all it takes to make any changes."

Slackwell opened the hinged panel and took out the 256–B. "Feast your eyes on this unit," he said.

"A human brain," said the man. He peered in at it through the glass and his smile disappeared.

"Awe inspiring, isn't it?" asked Slackwell. "And best of all, it can be brought to consciousness if you require company as well as computing acumen."

Mr. Catterly shook his head and softly whistled.

"Granted, it takes a little getting used to."

Slackwell watched as his customer slowly stood. For a moment, he thought he was about to be shown the door.

"I'll be right back," said Catterly. "Make yourself comfortable." He left the living room by way of a hall leading off to the left.

"Going to find the old checkbook," Slackwell whispered, and for the first time that day his foot stopped hurting. He quickly got the unit up and running, using the battery setting that made it portable.

"You aren't from Lindrethool, are you?" Catterly called from down the hall.

"No," Slackwell replied.

A few minutes passed and then he heard the man's voice from just the other side of the living room. "Then you wouldn't know who I am."

Slackwell looked up from his task, and saw the old man transformed, wearing green and white robes laced with gold. He had on a tall pointed hat the shape of a closed tulip and carried in his hand a pole with a curved end.

"Oh, Christ," said Slackwell at the sight of him, knowing instantly he was in trouble.

"Not quite. I'm Bishop Catterly of Lindrethool," said the man and his once calm smile turned ugly as his face reddened and trembled. "Blasphemy," he yelled, and lunged across the room, bringing the shepherd's crook up over his head.

Slackwell roused himself from paralysis at the last moment and stood arched over so that his body covered the unit. That pole came down across his spine with a *whack*, and it was all he could do to support himself with his knuckles on the tabletop. He staggered into a standing position, the pain bringing tears to his eyes and radiating down to his heels.

The bishop was raising his weapon for another strike. "Release this soul," he said. But Slackwell had been sorely abused enough for one day. As he reached out and grabbed the crook with his left hand, he brought his right fist around and punched Catterly square in the jaw. The old man's high hat fell off. He took two steps backward and then just stood there, dazed. His bottom lip was split and blood trickled down across his chin.

Slackwell quickly packed the unit up. When Catterly moved again it wasn't to take another swing at the merchandise. Instead, he fell to his knees, dropped the crook and folded his hands in prayer. A long low burp issued from his open mouth and then he began weeping.

"You damn kook," said Slackwell, putting on his derby. He made for the door and escaped into the hallway.

3

Slackwell sat in a booth at the back of an establishment called The Bog. He sipped a beer, an appetizer for the main course of bourbon that would come later back at his hotel room. He lit a cigarette off the candle in the middle of the table and watched from the corner of his eye as some young professionals at the bar pointed at his hat and laughed. He'd have taken it off, but every time he moved any part of his body, his back screamed with pain. There wasn't much more he could manage other than drinking and smoking. Earlier, as he limped quickly away from the Thornwood Arms, grunting with each step, his heart racing, mind spinning with fear of Catterly calling the police or sending out his religious minions, a palpable sense of doom eddied about his head like a personal, portable storm cloud. Somewhere between his second and third beer the urgency of that terror had fizzled into a blank apathy.

He drank and wondered why he had always had jobs with stupid hats. Then Merk showed up and took the seat across from him. The older man was outright smiling, which was unusual, and his gray eyes had somehow lightened to blue.

"Okay, how many?" asked Slackwell.

Merk held up four fingers and laughed. "Signed orders for four and an almost certain fifth with a promise of full payment in cash when I return tomorrow. How'd you do?"

"Let's see," said Slackwell, taking a drag of his cigarette, "a woman smashed my toe with a hammer and Bishop Catterly of Lindrethool whacked me on the back with his holy stick. Other than that, it was a lousy day."

"The Bishop of Lindrethool?" asked Merk as he held one finger up to the waitress to order a beer.

"He wanted to release the soul of the floater."

"Slack, Slack, Slack," said Merk, "there is no Bishop Catterly of Lindrethool."

"What do you mean?" asked Slackwell.

"I know," said Merk, and reached into his shirt and pulled out a religious medallion he wore on a chain. "The only bishop in this county is in Morgan City, and his name's not Catterly. The guy must have been deranged."

"Good," said Slackwell, "because I clocked him."

Merk shook his head. "Is the unit all right?"

Slackwell nodded. "If you're religious how can you peddle brain? I thought there was a flap about that in the church."

Merk downed the beer that arrived in one long drink. He held his finger up to the waitress again and then lit a cigarette. "Because," he said, "between Heaven and Hell there is this place called reality. Reality might as well be Hell if you don't have cash. Granted, it's a grim business, but I'm good at it."

"Why is that?" asked Slackwell.

"Because," said Merk, "I understand the human brain. It's a double-edged sword. An evolutionary development that gives you the wherewithal to know that life is basically a shit pastry one is obliged to eat slowly, and the ability to disguise that fact with beautiful delusions."

"Where do God and the cash come in?" asked Slackwell.

"The cash is the pastry part. God, he just likes to watch us eat. The more we eat the more he loves us. You can't live without love."

"Well," said Slackwell, wincing and grunting as he hoisted himself out of the booth, "I've lost my appetite." He took some bills out of his wallet and dropped them on the table. With a small moan, he lifted his case off the bench. "Coffee tomorrow?"

"On me," said his colleague. "Float easy, Slack."

Outside, the wind was blowing hard and tiny black tornados of soot caught scraps of litter up in their gyres for a moment, promising flight, and then dropped them. The streets of Lindrethool were nearly empty and the place seemed to Slackwell like a ghost town he had recently visited in a nightmare. He stopped at a liquor store for a bottle, at a deli for a sandwich, and then crept back to his hotel, aware of nothing but the weight of the case in his hand.

Once back at the room, he had a couple of drinks and took a hot bath. Sitting at the scarred table, surveying the night scene of Lindrethool again, he smoked the other half of the joint he had started in the freight elevator of the Thornwood Arms. In no time the emptiness of his mind began to fill with memories. Before he could stop himself, he started thinking about his wife and how he had not been home for years. He wondered, after all of the grimy cities he'd been through, if Ella was still waiting for him to return a success. For a brief moment, he entertained the thought of calling her, but then pulled himself together.

"Get with it, Slackwell," he said to his reflection in the window. "Go down that path and you'll have the belt around your own neck quicker than you can say 'Johnny.'" He stood up slowly, the pain in his back now deadened by the drink and dope. Weaving around the room, he searched desperately for something to do. There was the television, but just the thought of what it might offer depressed him. He turned away from the sight of the remote and his gaze landed on the case.

He went back to the table and popped the hinges on the black carrier. Lifting out the 256–B, he set it on the table and flipped the switch to the battery setting. There was a nearly inaudible hum and the luminescent particles in the liquid beneath the glass began to glow, meaning the brain was open for business. Then he sat down, poured himself a drink, and lit a cigarette. At least three minutes passed with him touching the tip of his finger to the button that would rouse the brain into consciousness. The force holding him back was comprised of Merk's warning and the basic rule that the company didn't want the sales force screwing with the equipment if a sale wasn't involved. These were strong deterrents but not as strong as the loss he was now feeling for a life gone down the chute. He pressed the button.

Static came from the speaker.

"Hello?" whispered Slackwell.

There was silence.

"Hello?" he said, this time a little louder.

"Yes," came a voice, "I'm here. What can I do for you?"

Slackwell leaned quickly back away from the unit.

"How are you today?" it asked.

He wanted to answer but he was stunned by the fact that the voice was female.

"I've been asleep for a long time," she said. "Are you there?"

"Sorry," he said. "I didn't expect you to be a woman."

There was laughter. "Most men are confounded by the discovery of the female brain," she said.

"Can you do that again?" he asked.

"What?" she asked.

"Laugh," he said.

She did for real and asked, "Why?"

"I'm your salesman," he told her. "I'm trying to place you with a good family."

"You make me sound like an unwanted puppy," she said.
"No," he said. "You understand, it's business, nothing personal."
"Are your clients present?" she asked.
"No," he said.
"I thought that was against the rules."
"It is," he said. "I wanted to talk to someone."
"Are you lonely?"
"Very," he said.
"My sensors detect that you have been drinking. Are you drunk?"
"Very," he said.
"What do you want to talk about?" she asked.
"Anything but the job," he said.
"Agreed. Tell me about your day."

He told her everything: coffee at the diner with Merk, the woman with the hammer, the bishop, The Bog. The recounting took an hour and he filled in all the details, trying as often as possible to accentuate his own feckless absurdity in order to hear her laugh.

"What's your name?" she asked.
"Slackwell," he said.
"Your mother named you Slackwell?"
"My first name is Arnold. Call me Arnie," he said.
"I'm Melody," she said.
"Your voice is like a melody," said Slackwell, surprising even himself.
"Is that the bourbon talking?" she asked.
"If the bourbon talked, I probably wouldn't have turned you on," he said.
"Do you like being a salesman?"
"It's a job, a routine. The other day I was thinking of it as a trap. I don't know what real freedom is."
"I know about traps," she said.
"Tell me," said Slackwell, pouring another drink.
"When I sleep, when you turn me off, I dream. In my dreams, I have my body again. I never realized how beautiful I was when I was whole. I breathe in the air and it's cool and electric with life. I see trees and the clouds in the sky, the faces of people I loved, and they are all wonderfully complex and mysterious. I take my children to the ocean and we swim in the waves. We eat lemon meringue pie on a blanket on the sand and the ocean breeze blows around us, the sun beats down. But always, I reach some limit, like running into an invisible wall and I begin to disintegrate. My atoms

begin to disperse, and I try to hold myself together but I can't. The hands that clutch at my disappearing head vanish themselves and eventually the world goes dark. The darkness is claustrophobic and so exquisitely boring."

"Kids?" asked Slackwell.

She told him about her children—two girls. It was just her and her girls. Her husband had left them. It was for the best because he had lost his job and eventually became so depressed by his own uselessness, he took to drinking. Then came the anger. She raised her girls as best she could, working in a waitress job she hated. She had gone to school for anthropology and gotten a degree. Her dream had been to travel to exotic lands and meet those near-extinct groups of people who still tried to live in nature. One night, at closing time, the restaurant she worked at was robbed. The gunmen shot all the employees. She was still alive when they found her and rushed her to the hospital.

"Luckily," she said, "I had signed the papers only six months earlier to sell my brain to Thinktank in case anything happened. I figured it was a long shot, but if something happened, I wanted to leave my daughters something. Insurance was too expensive."

Slackwell shook his head. "How can you stand it?" he asked.

"How can you?" she asked.

"Touché," he whispered and finished off his glass.

They made a pact never to speak again of those things in the past that brought sorrow or of the crystal globes that bounded each of their lives. Instead, they just made small talk about places, and people, and events, like friendly neighbors meeting on the street, like old friends. This discussion carried on for hours, punctuated with laughter and the sound of bourbon pouring, the click of the cigarette lighter. Some time just before the sun showed itself red from between the tall buildings of Lindrethool, Slackwell and Melody said goodnight. Before turning her off, he promised to see her again tomorrow. Then he lurched over to his bed and literally fell into a dreamless sleep.

4

When the alarm clock went off at seven, he pulled the plug out of the wall and fell immediately back to sleep. Waking a little after noon, he got out of bed like a somnambulist and proceeded through his usual routine. It was in the shower that he finally came fully awake. He was amazed at how minor his hangover was: a slightly dry mouth, a vague headache, but no nausea or dizziness. His back no longer hurt that badly and his foot, though it was swollen and the color of an overripe banana, was capable of bearing his full weight. All at once, the memory of his having opened the case came to him, and he smiled. "Melody," he said.

He dressed only in his pants and a T-shirt. Instead of bourbon for breakfast, he called down to room service and had them send up a pot of coffee and two cups. While he waited for his order, he plugged the 256–B into the wall outlet and recharged its batteries.

After the coffee had arrived, he unplugged the unit and turned on the battery setting. As the ambient liquid of the globe began to glow, he put the pot and two cups on the table next to it. He lit a cigarette, closed his eyes for a moment to gather his thoughts and then pushed the consciousness button at the base of the Thinktank.

"Hey, you'll sleep the day away," he said.

"Arnie?" asked the voice.

"Who else?" he said. "I ordered coffee."

"Strong or light?" she asked.

"How do you like it?"

"Strong," she said.

"You're in luck," he told her.

"And what is the weather like today?"

He looked out the window at the sun trying to shine through a soot squall. "Perfect," he said. "Warm with blue skies and a light breeze out of the southwest."

"It's late, shouldn't you be out selling?" she asked.

"Not to worry," he said. "I'm on top of it."

He drank his coffee and eased back in the chair. The conversation of the previous night resumed with him telling her about a dog he had when he was a child, and then their tête-à-tête just continued on, rolling out across the afternoon like some epic Chinese scroll.

Late in the day, she told him of her love for music, so he turned on the radio. They listened to each selection and commented on it, spoke of the memories that it elicited. Slackwell couldn't think of the last time he had bothered to so much as hum a tune. She sighed with delight at the sound of instruments and voices weaving a song. "Before I was married," she told him, "I loved to dance." He got up and turned the knob to a station that played old-time jazz. Before long a beauty of a number came on, Lester Young doing "Polka Dots and Moonbeams." He lifted the 256–B off the table and they moved gracefully together around the room to the smooth sound of the tenor sax. She whispered in his ear that he was a wonderful dancer.

That night, he packed the unit in its case and they went out to dinner. Slackwell never noticed the quizzical stares of the other diners as he sat eating with a crystal encased brain on his table. He ordered her the lobster tail she had been dying for and described in explicit detail each mouthful. He was well into a second bottle of wine, his voice now very loud, when the restaurant manager, a short, bald man in a tuxedo, approached the table and asked him to leave.

"Sir, you are disturbing the other customers, and this bizarre . . . curio," he said, pointing to the unit, "is ruining their appetites."

Slackwell stood up, poked the manager in the chest with his index finger, and yelled, "Too damn bad. My date and I aren't bothering anyone." There was real door-to-door menace in his voice, and the little man backed away. Melody was finally able to calm him down and convince him it was time to go back to the hotel. She even prevailed upon him to leave a tip, saying, "It's not the waiter's fault." He carried her under his right arm as they walked along the streets of Lindrethool, the empty case swinging to and fro in his left hand. They laughed about the incident with the manager, and then Slackwell described for her the brilliance of the stars, the full moon, the aurora borealis.

The next morning there was a knock on the hotel room door at 9:00 sharp. Slackwell got out of bed and quickly pulled on his pants and T-shirt.

"Who is it?" he called.

"Sir," came the reply, "I have something here to show you that could very well change your entire life. A new invention that will revolutionize the way you run your household."

"Hold on," said Slackwell, realizing it was Merk.

He opened the door and stepped out into the hallway.

Merk stood there impeccably dressed in his Thinktank uniform, case in hand, derby cocked slightly to the left. "Where have you been?" he asked.

"What do you mean?" said Slackwell.

"They called me from the office this morning and said that the info they are getting from your implant indicates that you weren't out pounding the pavement yesterday. They tried to call you but they said you aren't answering your calls. When you weren't at the diner this morning again, I thought I better check up on you."

"My back," said Slackwell. "It was bad yesterday. I couldn't get up."

"You look all right now," said Merk.

Slackwell immediately hunched slightly and breathed in

through clenched teeth. "The truth is it's about all I can do to stand here. I'll get out this afternoon."

"You sure you're okay?"

"Yeah."

Merk stared into his eyes. "You haven't been talking to that floater have you?" he asked.

"You know it's against the rules," said Slackwell.

"Listen, Slack, get back out there today. If they don't see some action from your implant reading, they'll send one of their goons out to check up on you, if you know what I mean. Those boys play rough."

"No problem."

"This city is better than I first thought," said Merk. "Yesterday, a guy in a penthouse apartment over on Grettle Street gave me the whole payment for a 256–B, in cash. I'm packing over forty thousand dollars." His face lit up with a smile as he patted his overcoat pocket. "The section boss is gonna crap 'em when he sees that."

"Amazing," said Slackwell, mustering as much enthusiasm as he could.

"Well, remember what I told you about the office, and good luck today. Float easy," said Merk, as he turned and walked down the hallway lined with doors.

Slackwell breathed a sigh as he straightened to his full height. He let himself back in the room and locked the door behind him. Then he removed his clothes and got back in bed next to Melody.

"What was that about?" she asked.

"Nothing, baby," he said.

"I need a smoke," she said.

He reached over, took a cigarette from the pack on the stand next to the bed, and lit up. Blowing a smoke ring, he put one hand lightly around her globe and said, "You certainly have a way with words."

5

Two days later, at an outdoor café on Lindrethool's waterfront, Slackwell watched the huge barges of coal steam in from off the high seas and described their filthy majesty to her. He had still not returned to work, but as a vague concession to the job had dressed that morning in his uniform.

"When did they go back to using coal?" asked Melody.

"About five years ago," he told her, tipping back his derby. "It's a fact that the world's resources are almost completely tapped out, and burning it pollutes the hell out of everything. You know, it's expedient. Big business finally said screw it, let's just squeeze every black dollar we can out of the moment. Nobody thinks about the future anymore," said Slackwell.

"I do," said Melody.

He sipped at his drink.

"I'm thinking about how I'll miss you once I'm sold and I'm running some schlub's refrigerator and heater, turning his lights on and off, and scouring the Internet for free porn sites. Think of the drivel I'll have to listen to, day in and day out, until the components of my unit simply wear out from use. What's the guarantee on me, seventy years?" she said.

"I've considered it," said Slackwell.

She began crying.

"That's why I've decided I'm not selling you. We're going to split this dump and find a new life," he said.

"Arnie," she said, "you can't do that. The company will stop you."

"The company," he said mockingly. "They'll have to catch me first."

She tried to speak, but he silenced her by saying, "Shhh . . . let's go back to the hotel and get our stuff."

He had forgotten to charge her batteries that morning, so they decided it was better he turn her off until they could. The instruction manual had warned that it could be detrimental to the unit to run them completely dry. As much as he hated to pack her away in the case, he needed some time to think through the logistics of how they would make their escape. Money was tight, but he had enough to buy two train tickets that would get them a good distance away from the city. He walked on a little farther before he realized he would only really need one ticket. Slackwell considered the danger of what he was planning, but for once he could see a crack in the globe that contained him. Envisioning himself smashing through the boundary, he said aloud, "You can't live without love."

A block away from the hotel, he passed an alleyway and heard a voice call to him. He stopped, looked down the shadowed corridor and saw Merk, partially hidden by a dumpster.

"Slack, come here," he said, waving him into the darkness.

Slackwell looked cautiously around him and then slowly went to his colleague.

"They're up in your room, waiting for you," said Merk. He appeared nervous and his eyes kept shifting suspiciously.

"Who?" asked Slackwell.

"The section boss and a Thinktank security officer big as an ape."

"Bullshit," he said, and his body tensed with anger.

"Listen, Slack, just listen to me. You've got to hand the unit over to them now. If you don't want to see them, give it to me and I'll take it up."

"I'm not giving it up," said Slackwell.

"If you run with the unit, and they catch you, which they will, you're bound to have an accident, if you know what I mean. They'll say they pursued you to get back their merchandise, you put up a struggle, and then they had to off you out of self-defense. Don't forget about the clause in the contract, Slack. They get your sponge if anything happens to you while you work for the company."

Slackwell leaned over and put the case on the pavement. He rose calmly and said, "You're not taking the damn unit, Merk." His arm came up quickly then and his hand circled his colleague's throat. The pressure applied by the grip of the hand that had carried that case through two dozen cities for nine hours a day, six days a week, was intense. "I know how close you are to them, invited to all the sponge harvest parties, the first one to get the good merchandise. Now tell me, where's the implant." He pushed Merk back up against the dumpster and brought his other hand up to join the first.

Merk's face grew red, then blue, and eventually he lifted his right hand and with his index finger pointed to his left eyebrow.

Slackwell loosened his grip and his colleague gasped for breath. "The eyebrow?"

"Behind the eyebrow," Merk wheezed out, doubling over to catch his breath. "The hair of the eyebrow acts as an organic antenna for it. Shave it off and it will confuse the signal."

"Are you sure?" asked Slackwell.

"I saw them pull one out of Johnny's head the other night. I've been around enough to know this stuff."

Slackwell caught sight of Merk slipping his hand into his coat pocket. He remembered the revolver and threw two savage punches without thinking. One connected with Merk's chest and the other with his left temple. The back of his head banged off the dumpster. He dropped the case he'd been holding and followed it, unconscious, to the ground. As Slackwell lifted his own unit by its handle, he saw that Merk had not been going for the gun after all, but held a folded piece of paper in his hand. He took it and slipped it into his pants pocket.

A second later, he was back on the street, running as fast as he could away from the hotel.

He ran only two blocks before he was completely winded. His heart was slamming and the idyllic sense of calm that had filled him since meeting Melody was now shattered. He knew she would be able to help him think through the situation, but there was no question that he needed a bottle of bourbon and a pack of razors. Setting himself to search for these two essentials helped his concentration. He found the bourbon first, and once he had this, he came upon a convenience store only a block away and bought a pack of razors and cigarettes.

On the street again, he ducked into a doorway, set the case down and ripped open the razors. He shaved off his eyebrows, finishing the job in a matter of minutes and cutting himself badly on the right side. Blood dripped down into his eye and he wiped it with the sleeve of his coat. Before taking up the case again and hitting the street, he knocked the derby off his head. It wasn't enough to simply be free of it, he had to stomp it once with each foot. Then he was off again, mumbling to himself, the hem of the overcoat flying out behind him as he searched everywhere for a place to hide.

6

"My head looks like a wrinkled ass with eyes," said Slackwell, checking his reflection in Melody's globe. He sat in a third-floor room of a different hotel on Lindrethool's west side. It was his power of spiel that had gotten them in. The woman at the desk had nearly turned them away after taking in his shaved brow, the blood on his face, his mad hair, and wild eyes.

"What possessed you?" asked Melody.

"I don't know if you are aware of this," he said, "but when you go to work for Thinktank, since you are entrusted with expensive merchandise, you agree to wear an implant by which they can track your daily progress and locate you. It's a minor operation they do right in the training office. They put you out and when you wake up you are tagged."

"Your eyebrow hair?" she asked, laughing.

"Sort of," he said, pouring himself a drink. "Now, for the future."

"We're in a jam, Arnie," she said.

"I thought you could turn some of that computing acumen on this situation and come up with a plan."

"Please don't say that," she said. "I refuse to be thought of by you as a unit."

"Mea culpa, darling," he said. "Still we have to run. Merk said if they find me, it's not going to go well."

"They can't trace you. What if we lay low here until tonight and then take a really late train."

"We're near the train station," he said.

"Where to, though?" she asked. "North? South?"

"As long as I'm with you," he said, "I don't care. Is there any place you've always wanted to go?"

"What about Canada?" she said. "There's less of a chance they will chase us into another country."

"Agreed," he said.

"Hook me up to the phone wire. I'll go out on the 'net and check train schedules, so we don't have to hang around the station too long before boarding."

"You're really thinking," he said.

"A no-brainer," she said, and they laughed.

He got up and removed the jack from the phone and inserted it into the port at the base of the tank. While he performed the task, he told her how much he could spend on the ticket.

"This will take a minute," she said as he sat back in his chair.

While he waited, he lit a cigarette and then remembered the sheet of paper he had taken from Merk. He retrieved it from his pocket and unfolded it on the table. It was an official Thinktank form that looked familiar to him but took a few seconds to recognize. Then he realized it was one of the invoices every salesman had, describing the display unit he carried in his case. Slackwell's eyes scanned down to the bottom of the page, and where he expected to find Merk's signature, he read instead the name Johnny Sands. He wondered what Merk was doing with Johnny's invoice. Then he looked back up to the top of the document and saw that Johnny had been packing a 256–B.

He wondered why they had given this kid, even more hapless a salesman than himself, a top-of-the-line sentient model. Johnny had trained with it for a two-week period and then was on the road no more than two days when he had hung himself. Slackwell remembered Johnny as being very high-strung, not too smart, and definitely on some kind of medication. He was surprised they were willing to trust him with any merchandise at all, even an economy model. A picture came to him of the kid, lanky, dim, sitting in his hotel room, staring at the brain in the globe. "He was talking to that sponge," Slackwell said to himself, and then, as if someone had pressed his own consciousness button, he woke up to reality with a distinct taste of shit pastry in his mouth.

"Melody," he said, "you're not looking up train schedules are you?"

"What are you talking about?" she asked.

"You're signaling our location to the section boss," he said.

"Why would I do that?" she asked.

Slackwell didn't answer.

"Arnie, what would—"

"Please," he said, interrupting, "there's no need."

"All right," she said. "I haven't gotten through yet, but, yes, that's what I'm doing."

"Everything has been a lie," he said.

"I was commissioned to make you run," she said. "They told me you were so pathetic that there would be no question that you would engage my consciousness. 'It's like handing Pandora the box,' was how the general manager had put it. Then I was to lure you into running. That is all the pretense they need to get away with taking your brain. You sold only two nonsentient economy units all year, grand total—less than ten thousand dollars. They're having a problem harvesting enough organic product for the orders they are getting. Your brain is worth more to them than you are."

Slackwell felt no anger, shed no tears. It was as if he was a hollow flesh doll without brain or heart. Still, he heard himself asking, "Why?"

"I cut a deal. If I trapped you for them, they would destroy me, something I want more than anything and can not make happen. Termination is freedom to me, Arnie. All of that crap I told you about my dreams of my daughters and the beach, the lemon meringue pie—my God, as horribly frustrating and sad as that fairy tale sounded, it's nothing compared to the real agony of floating."

"I understand," he said.

"You have been nicer to me than any man I ever knew when I was walking around in the world," she said. "You're a good person, Arnie, and I hated to sell you out, but it means so little compared to my having to remain in this state for even another moment. Listen, I'll make you a deal, a limited time only though, and I mean it. If you don't accept, I promise the call will go through. Destroy me. Break the crystal."

"I can't," said Slackwell.

"You're going to end up like this!" she yelled.

"I'm sorry," he said.

Slackwell drank and smoked, wrapped in silence. In his mind, he was now back at the house by the bay, moving from room to room, looking for Ella. He did not know how much time had passed before a knock sounded at the door.

He didn't stir but to bring the glass to his lips.

A moment later, the door burst in, the chain-lock swinging free, splinters of the frame flying across the room. In walked a huge wall of a man, sporting a red Thinktank security-force windbreaker. His head was the size of Slackwell's display case. He held a handgun straight out in front of him, steadying it with his free hand. The gun was aimed at Slackwell. Stepping out from behind him appeared the section boss, Joe Grace. He was a round fellow with jowls and glasses. His derby sat tilted back on his head and he wore a red blazer with the company's insignia on it.

"So, Slackwell," said Grace, "I believe you have something that belongs to us. You are a pitiable fool to have crossed the company. Please do not resist or we will take it as a sign of aggression and who knows what might happen."

Slackwell stubbed out his cigarette in the overflowing ashtray. "Gentlemen," he said, and nodded.

"Jolson, he looks like he's becoming belligerent," Grace said to the larger man. "Here, use this object he attacked us with that you valiantly wrestled away from him." He reached into his jacket and pulled out a long ice pick with a wooden handle. "Once in the heart, and once in the throat, and don't damage that head." He handed the pick to Jolson who took it after returning the gun to its shoulder holster.

"Turn me off, Grace," Melody called. "I don't want to hear this."

"What you want is inconsequential. To me you're a turd in a goldfish bowl. Take him, Jolson. I'll dial up the removal crew. Too bad you had to make a scene, Slackwell."

Jolson advanced with the ice pick, but Slackwell did nothing. The huge man pulled his arm back and aimed for the chest.

Then Melody cried out for them to stop, and there was a loud popping sound. In his daze, Slackwell looked over at the unit, thinking her scream had shattered the crystal globe, and that's when Jolson doubled up and fell. He landed on the table, knocking the bottle of bourbon over, and then continued on to the floor. Blood seeped in a puddle from the back of his head.

Merk stood in the doorway holding the smoking revolver. He then moved the gun to aim at the section boss's head. Grace uselessly tried to cover his face with his hands, but Merk did not fire. Instead, he took aim at the portly stomach and pulled the trigger.

Grace went over backwards, grabbing his midsection. The bullet went clean through him and lodged in the wall. He lay on the floor, howling.

Merk stepped over the bodies and walked up to Slackwell, who sat staring, mouth open wide.

"Let's go, Slack, the removal crew will be here any minute," he said.

Slackwell stood up, taking his cigarettes off the table.

"Arnie, are you all right?" called Melody.

"Yes," he said.

"Don't leave me here," she said.

"Take her if you want, but we've got to hurry," said Merk.

"I'm taking you with me," said Slackwell. He quietly motioned for Merk to give him the revolver. At first his colleague was reluctant, but finally he handed the gun over.

"Where?" she asked.

"The limitless ocean," he said. "Want to come?"

"Yes," she whispered.

His hand shook as he pulled the trigger, but to Slackwell the shot was no explosion. Instead he heard a spring breeze in the willows and the sound of a door opening somewhere in the house by the bay. The bullet splintered the glass, jellied the brain, and the glowing liquid bled out onto the floor. As they turned to leave, Merk took the gun from him, wiped the prints off with his shirttail, and threw it at the section boss, who was grunting and wheezing for air. "Float easy, Grace," he said. Then they ran.

Slackwell saw all of Lindrethool at once, like a bottled city, in the passenger-side mirror of the old car Merk had bought with a piece of the forty thousand.

As they drove out past the city limits, into the country where the soot no longer fell, Merk said, "I knew what they were up to when I realized Johnny was packing a 256–B."

"I thought you were a company man," said Slackwell.

"Yeah, well, once I realized what they had done to the kid, and I had that forty grand in my pocket, it lit the spark in me I needed to want out. They thought they knew me, but no one knows what goes on up here," he said, pointing to his head. "That's the only freedom."

"But you came to get me," said Slackwell.

"After you beat the crap out of me, I knew you were love crazy enough to break through. I checked every hotel I could think of. Finally a woman at the front desk of that one you were in said she'd seen you. My only chance was to chomp down on the coattails of your beautiful delusion and pray for lockjaw."

"I thought you were rescuing me," said Slackwell.

"Nah, me and your girl, you led us both out."

"I did?"

"Sure," said Merk. "You're the goddamn Bishop of Lindrethool."

"Floating in Lindrethool" was my attempt to write a Twilight Zone episode for the original Rod Serling TV show. Too bad it and Serling are not around anymore, save in the limbo of reruns. For four years, I lived in the town of Binghamton, in upstate New York, where Serling was born and raised. My bathroom window looked out on the cemetery where the Rod was supposedly buried. The town next to Binghamton, Johnson City, was my model for Lindrethool. It existed in the modern world but it was like something out of the forties, always overcast with a lot of abandoned warehouses. Its one remaining industry was the Fairplay Caramel Company, makers of BB Bats. Their smoke stack spewed out a sweet ash like cobwebs of gray cotton candy.

I visualized this story in black and white, and I think that is why a lot of readers have noted its noir tendencies. The brain in the jar is one of those classic science fiction themes—most notably from the films of the fifties and even early sixties. I combined this rich metaphorical goofiness with another icon of the fifties, Death of a Salesman. Slackwell has some Willy Loman in him, but he is much more fashioned after the characters in a documentary about door-to-door Bible salesmen I saw in college. I don't remember the title, but I think the film was made by a pair of brothers. Add to this a smog-choked world redolent of the Republican economic mindset, and it's time to float. Sometimes as a writer, those years of crappy jobs and hangovers pay off as research. My friend, writer Richard Bowes (Minions of the Moon), gave me some good suggestions and a pair of eyebrows, or lack there of, that I used in this one.

High Tea with Jules Verne

WE POLITELY NIBBLED CURRANT SCONES WITH fresh butter and sipped at lime tea. He sat across from me in a well-stuffed leather chair, crumbs dotting his beard, tea dribbled across his cravat. In his arrogance, he chose to speak only in English.

"I get my ideas early in the morning, while steeping in a hot bath—you know, the steam, the moment of privacy, the easy access to the genitals." With the look he gave me, one of disdain buttered with indifference, I could tell I was interviewing a man with a divinely wide seat of intellect.

"Once, while taking the moment of leisure in hand, my head verily exploded with rushing stars and void, and I was *Off on a Comet*," he said matter-of-factly. "That book came to me deliciously well. Upon sitting down to write at half past five that morning, all manner of boldly gesticulating personalities squeezed their way out of the birth canal at the nib of my pen and darted across the page."

"I know this is a question you must get asked all the time," I said, "but my readers would find me remiss if I did not ask you if your characters were derived from people you know in real life?"

I noticed a smile form under his beard as he spit tea back into the cup. He put the cup and saucer down on the table between us. He cleared his throat and pointed in the air.

"Nothing is drawn from real life when it comes to my characters. I forge them in my mind from the raw material of utter nothing. I torture blobs of the stuff into shapes larger than life and then inject them through the nasal cavity with animation. For the most part, they follow my command. Occasionally, one will get away off the writing table and hide in the other rooms of the house. Then it is no end of trouble hunting the rascal down and squishing it." As he leaned back, he retrieved the pocket watch from his vest and began spinning it by its silver chain.

"Could you elaborate?" I asked.

"Very well," he said, and nodded as if he was anxious for the opportunity. "The Mrs. and I are fond of hunting them for they are nearly as fast as mice and at least three times as wily. My weapon of choice is a croquet mallet and my wife prefers the largest fry pan in the kitchen."

"When they are hit do they scream?" I asked.

"If they have voices they do," he said. "You see, you must understand, they are as I make them. Once my wife caught one in a trap, a young lad I had created to be a castaway on a desert island. I had made him poorly with no sense of purpose in the adventure, so he fled. We hunted for weeks and could not find him. I began to be concerned that he might have escaped to the outdoors. Then I discovered that the Mrs. had him pinned by his clothing to the inside lid of her jewelry box and was keeping him between life and death by feeding him crumbs of toast and thimbles of water."

"Your wife had taken a liking to him?" I asked.

"Quite a liking, I might say." For a moment I saw his face redden, but he easily composed himself and went on. "She begged me to spare him, but how could it be? She did the job herself with a hat pin. Then she baked him in a loaf, and we buried him in the garden beneath the yellow rose bush."

"Your candor becomes a man of your genius," I said.

He nodded.

I saw a moment of vulnerability and seized it. "Is Science your God?" I asked with as little impertinence in my voice as possible.

He gave a look as though I had slapped him in the face. "Your readers be damned," he said in a whisper. Silence weighted the air. The crammed bookshelves, the Persian carpet, the polished wood, the light and dust did nothing. He bit the hairs of his mustache and his eyes grew watery.

"When I was a boy of six, a magician came to my town. Marlu the Manipulator, he was called. His specialty was performing prestidigitation with doves. Doves flew from his hands, his jacket pockets, his gaping mouth, from thin air. He announced at the end of his first week that the Saturday afternoon show would be the last in his career. For the grand finale to a distinguished life's work, he promised that he would have his doves lift him bodily into the air and fly him to the moon."

"Are you certain that these were doves and not pigeons?" I asked.

He waved my question away with a look of irritation and continued. "We gathered in the town square and watched as Marlu's doves swarmed around him. Some wrapped their talons in his hair, some grasped the material of his jacket and trousers. One took his black top hat and one his cane, and all of them beat their wings with the fury of the devil. With a smile on his face, he rose up and up until he was a dot in the blue sky, until he was gone beyond the clouds."

"This must have had a great influence on your sense of wonder," I said.

"Certainly," he said, "for on the next afternoon, a body fell screaming from the sky and broke the back of a peasant in the town square. Its velocity embedded them both three feet into the dirt beneath the cobblestones. When some men dug the corpses out, they found that the body of the great Manipulator was a fake made of wax. More than a dozen people had heard it screaming in its descent."

"To change the subject now," I said, "what is it you are presently working on?"

"A novel entitled *The City at the Center of the Sun*," he said.

"Could you grace us with a snippet of the plot?" I asked.

"Well," he said, looking toward the ceiling, "it only came to me this morning in the tub. I saw a fellow, a rough and ready American named Dick Web, who travels in a cannon ball, shot by a gun the length of a train, to the sun. This cannon ball has a window, and he can study the stars. I want to be able to name in this novel all of the stars that I know. Let's see there's . . ."

"Yes," I interrupted, knowing his inclination to wax taxonomic, "he goes to the sun and finds a city inside it. Then what happens?"

"Well, then he discovers that the city's citizenry are humanlike automata. While wandering the crowded streets of the city, he runs into a female who is the image of his dear, departed mother. She takes him on a tour of the city and introduces him to her lover who turns out to be an automaton Captain Nemo. The Nemoton, as I call it, is the proprietor of a small zoo that houses a rare beast with the power of mental telepathy . . ."

"It sounds splendid," I told him.

"I hate it," he said.

"Very well," I countered, "could you give us an idea as to how much mail you get each day from your readers?"

"A veritable avalanche. People ask for autographs, for reviews of their books, for me to read their reams and reams of dribbling prose riddled with imagination as shriveled as a scrotal sac in cold, cold water. They tell me of their personal lives, their problems, their most intimate moments."

"Answering these missives must be a drain on your time," I said, mustering a look of sympathy.

"Not at all," he said with a frown. "I throw them in the fireplace. Only once did one blow back into the room as I emptied the waste basket. I picked it up and started reading. It was from a woman who was reproaching me for my books. Because of my novels, her husband had been digging in their basement, hoping to uncover a hidden passageway on a veritable *Journey to the Center of the Earth*. She asked him what he expected to find there, and he told her a lost race of wise and kindly people."

"Some do see the literary phantasm as a dangerous illusion," I said.

"Perhaps," he said. "I struck up a correspondence with this woman. Eventually she told me that her husband was lost underground, digging toward the *axis mundi*. The basement is nearly filled to the ceiling with dirt, and her husband is somewhere in a slowly moving capsule of space, displacing dirt in front of him and throwing it behind, blocking his escape as he goes. In her last letter, she thanked me for having written my books."

"I must ask you about the wonderful inventions that inhabit your novels. If you were a machinist or mechanic and not a writer, what an amazing world we would live in."

"And if I were a fisherman," said Verne, "every day would be a battle with the fierce, flesh-tearing squid in the boiling waters off Madagascar. And if I were a gardener, my every hour I would be plucking the fruit from the tree of the knowledge of good and evil and hiding behind the hedges as God walked in billowing robes. And if I were a blind man, I would be a constant point of darker blackness in the night, a hole into which everything would pour and be devoured."

"Have you any inventions in your new novel?" I asked.

"So far, only a pair of spectacles one might wear in order to look through solid objects."

"Brilliant," I said.

"Yes," he admitted, "it came to me after a dinner of rare lamb. A certain miasmatic disturbance fogged me into this prophecy of future technology."

"Does your character Dick Web wear these glasses in order to read the hidden souls of automata?" I asked.

"Of course not," he said with a smirk. "He wears them to see through the iron undergarments of the gear-work ladies of the city at the center of the sun."

"Is there anything a man of your eminence fears?" I asked.

"I fear only one thing," he replied, "the fall of the true body of Marlu. I have dreams of his clavicle splitting my head on a sunny morning on the streets of town. Then the doves will take me up and wing their way above the gaping maw of a dead volcano. I will be dropped and, after falling for days, will strike upon the head and kill that woman's husband who would have, at that precise moment, broken through the last wall of dirt and into the land of the wise and kindly ancients."

With this said, the great writer rose and brushed the crumbs from his beard. "I must be off," he said in an apologetic voice as precise as an invention for the vivisection of love. "My play, *Dr. Ox*, is premiering tonight, and I must begin the preparations for my journey to the theatre."

I tried to shake his hand, but he bowed slightly instead as a way of putting me off.

"Kindly show yourself out," he added, and then turned and left the library.

On my way out through the shadowy corridors of his home, I came across a shelf holding a large bell jar filled with clear blue water. At the bottom lay bleached sand and a diminutive reproduction of a toppled Roman column. Tiny star fish dotted the dunes, and floating midway in that Caribbean liquid was the body of a miniature man—a homunculus with a beard and open eyes betraying a profound sense of will. On a piece of masking tape affixed to the top of the jar, lightly written in pencil, were the words: *Nemo, do not feed!*

From the time I first started reading real books, I've been a fan of Jules Verne. I have always been enamored of the juxtaposition of the anachronistic and the futuristic. Verne was, at times, a plodding prose stylist, but his work incorporated the elements of adventure and wondrous technology. The images generated by his stories have been some of the most vivid I have ever experienced. When I was around twelve years old, a publishing company reprinted a series of some of his more obscure titles: The City in the Sahara, The Village in the Treetops, Off on a Comet, *etc. I scoured the racks at the local candy store for these and collected and read as many as I could. Along with the better known titles like* 20,000 Leagues Under the Sea, The Mysterious Island, Journey to the Center of the Earth, *these books comprised my first forays into the world of science fiction. Their influence is everywhere in my fantasy trilogy that begins with* The Physiognomy.

One Christmas a few years ago I acquired three of the more famous Verne novels in one volume. The book had some of the original illustrations and was printed in that eye-strain style with small type in double columns. What I loved about the edition was that it had a piece of journalism from Verne's time in which a reporter visits and interviews him. Part of the piece is a description of a normal day in the life of Jules Verne. It told about his writing habits, his leisure activities, his wife, his home. I was envious of this reporter, so I decided that I would pretend to have visited Verne myself and write it up in the style of an interview. "High Tea" is not about the real Jules Verne though, it is about my *Jules Verne, the one I still often visit in my imagination. This story was published by Gavin Grant and Kelly Link in their wonderful magazine,* Lady Churchill's Rosebud Wristlet.

Bright Morning

IF THERE IS ONE THING THAT DISTINGUISHES MY books from others it is the fact that in the review blurbs that fill the back cover and the page that precedes the title page inside, the name of "Kafka" appears no less than eight times. *Kafka, Kafkaesque, Kafka-like, in the tradition of Kafka.* Certainly more Kafka than one man deserves—a veritable embarrassment of Kafka riches. My novels are fantasy/adventure stories with a modicum of metaphysical whim-wham that some find to be insightful and others have termed "overcooked navel gazing." Granted, there are no elves or dragons or knights or wizards in these books, but they are still fantasies, none the less. I mean, if you have a flying head, a town with a panopticon that floats in the clouds, a monster that sucks the essence out of hapless victims through their ears, what the hell else can you call it? At first glance, it would seem that any writer would be proud to have their work compared to that of one of the twentieth century's greatest writers, but upon closer inspection it becomes evident that in today's publishing world, when a novel does not fit a prescribed format, it immediately becomes labeled as Kafkaesque. The hope is, of course, that this will be interpreted as meaning *exotic*, when, in fact, it translates to the book-buying public as *obscure*. Kafka has become a place, a condition, a boundary to which it is perceived only the pretentious are drawn and only total lunatics will cross.

As my neighbor, a retired New York City transit cop, told me while holding up one of my novels and pointing to the cover, "Ya know, this Kafka shit isn't doing you any favors. All I know is he wrote a book about a guy who turned into a bug. What the fuck?"

"He's a great writer," I said in defense of my blurbs.

"Tom Clancy's a great writer, Kafka's a putz."

What could I say? We had another beer and talked about the snow.

Don't get me wrong, I like what I've read of Kafka's work. The fact that Gregor Samsa wakes from a night of troubling dreams to find that he has been transformed into a giant cockroach is, to my mind, certain proof of existential genius firing with all six pistons. Likewise, a guy whose profession is sitting in a cage and starving himself while crowds throng around and stare, is classic everyman discourse. But my characters run a lot. There's not a lot of running in Kafka. His writing is unfettered by parenthetical phrases, introductory clauses, and adjectival exuberance. My sentences sometimes have the quality of Arabic penmanship, looping and knotting, like some kind of Sufi script meant to describe one of the names given to God in order to avoid using his real name. In my plots, I'm usually milking some nostalgic sentiment resulting from unrequited love or working toward a punch line of revelation like an old Borscht Belt comic with a warmed-over variation of the one about the traveling salesman, whereas Kafka seems like he's trying to curtly elicit that ambiguous perplexity that makes every man an island, every woman an isthmus, every child a continental divide.

My friend, Quigley, once described the book *The Autobiography of a Yogi* as "a miracle a page," and that's the kind of effect I'm striving for, building up marvels until it just becomes a big, hallucinogenic shit-storm of wonder. Admittedly, sometimes the forecast runs into a low-pressure system and all I get is a brown drizzle; such are the vicissitudes of the fiction writer. On the other hand, Kafka typically employed only one really weird element in each story (a giant mole, a machine that inscribes a person's crime upon their back) that he treats as if it were as mundane as putting your shoes on. Then he inspects it six ways to Sunday, turning the microscope on it, playing out the string, until it eventually curls up into a question mark at the end. There are exceptions, "A Country Doctor," for instance, that swing from start to finish. I don't claim to be anywhere near as accomplished a writer as Kafka. If I was on a stage with Senator Loyd Benson and he said to me, "I knew Kafka, and you, sir, are no Franz Kafka," I'd be the first to agree with him. I'd shake his damn hand.

I often wondered what Kafka would make of it, his name bandied about, a secret metaphor for *fringe* and *destination remainder bin.* For a while it really concerned me, and I would have dreams where I'd wake in the middle of the night to find Kafka standing at the foot of my bed, looking particularly grim, half in, half out of the shaft of light coming in from the hallway. He'd appear dressed in a funeral suit with a thin tie. His hair would be slicked back and his narrow head would taper inevitably to the sharp point of his chin. Ninety pounds soaking wet, but there would be this kind of almost visible tension surrounding him.

"Hey, Franz," I'd say, and get out of bed to shake his hand, "I swear it wasn't my idea."

Then he'd get a look on his face like he was trying to pass the Great Wall of China and haul off and kick me right in the nuts. From his stories, you might get the idea that he was some quiet little dormouse, a weary, put upon pencil pusher in an insurance office, but, I'm telling you, in those nightmares of mine, he really ripped it up.

Do you think Kafka would be the type of restless spirit to reach out from beyond the pale? On the one hand, he was so unassuming that he asked Max Brod to burn all of his remaining manuscripts when he died, while on the other hand, he wrote an awful lot about judgment. He might not have as much to do with my writing as some people say, but me and Franz, we go way back, and I'm here to warn you: the less you have to do with him the better. His pen still works.

It was 1972 and I was a junior at West Islip High School on Long Island. I was a quiet kid and didn't have a lot of friends. I liked to smoke pot and I liked to read, so sometimes I'd combine those two pleasures. I'd blow a joint in the woods behind the public library and then go inside and sit and read or just wander through the stacks, looking through different books. In those days, I was a big science fiction fan, and I remember reading *Martians Go Home, Adam Link, Space Paw, Time Out of Joint,* etc. In our library, the science fiction books had a rocket ship on the plastic cover down at the bottom of the spine. There were three shelves of these books and I read just about all of them.

One afternoon at the library, I ran into Bettleman, a guy in my class. Bettleman was dwarfish short with a dismorphic body—long chimp arms, a sort of hunchback, and a pouch of loose skin under his chin. He was also a certified math genius and had the glasses to prove it—big mothers with lenses thick as ice cubes. I came around a corner of the stacks and there he was: long, beautiful woman fingers paging through a book he held only inches from his face. He looked up, took a moment to focus, and said hello. I said hi and asked him what he was reading.

"Karl Marx," he said.

I was impressed. I knew Marx was the father of Communism, an ideology that was still viewed as tantamount to Satanism in those days when the chill of the cold war could make you dive under a desk at the sound of the noon fire siren.

"Cool," I said.

"What have you got there?" he asked me.

I showed him what I was carrying. I think it was *Dandelion Wine* by Bradbury. He pushed those weighty glasses up on his nose and studied it. Then he closed his eyes for a moment, as if remembering, and when he opened them proceeded to rattle off the entire plot.

"Sounds like it would have been a good one," I said.

"Yeah," he told me, "it's alright—fantasy with a dash of horror meets the child of Kerouac and Norman Rockwell."

"Cool," I said, not knowing what he was talking about, but recalling him correcting the math teacher on more than one occasion.

"Hey, you want to read something really wild?" he asked.

"Sure," I said uncertainly, thinking about the first time I was dared into smoking weed.

He closed the book in his hand and walked to the end of the aisle. I followed. Three rows down, he turned left and went to the middle of one of the stacks. Moving his face up close to the titles, he scanned along the shelf as if sniffing out the volume he was searching for. Finally, he stepped back, reached out a hand and grabbed a thick, violet-covered book from the shelf. When he turned to me he was wearing a wide smile that allowed me to see through his strange exterior for a split second and genuinely like him.

"There's a story in here called "The Metamorphosis," he said. "Just check it out." Then he laughed loudly and that pouch of flesh that caused the other kids to call him *The Sultan of Chin* jiggled like the math teacher's flabby ass when she ran out of the room, embarrassed at her own ignorance in the face of Bettleman's genius.

He handed it over to me and I said, "Thanks." I turned the book over to see the title and the author and when I looked up again, he was gone. So I spent that sunny winter afternoon in the West Islip public library reading Kafka for the first time. That story was profound in a way I couldn't put my finger on. I knew it was heavy, but its burden was invisible like that of gravity. There was also sadness in it that surfaced as an unfounded self-pity, and underneath it all, somehow, a sense of humor that elicited in me that feeling of trying not to laugh in church. I checked the book out, took it home, and read every word of every tale and parable between its covers.

It took me a long time to read them all, because after ingesting one, I'd chew on it, so to speak, for a week or two, attempting to identify the flavor of its absurdity, what spices were used to give it just that special tang of nightmare. Occasionally, I'd see Bettleman at school and run a title by him. He'd usually push his glasses up with the middle finger of his left hand, give me a one-line review of the story in question, and before scuttling hastily off to square the circle, he'd let loose one of his Sultanic laughs.

"Hey, Bettleman, 'The Imperial Message,' " I'd say.

"Waiting for a sign from God that validates the industrious drudgery of existence while God waits for a sign to validate his own industrious drudgery."

"Yo, Bettleman, what do you say to 'The Hunter Gracchus'?"

"Siamese twins, altogether stuck. One judgment, one guilt, both unable to see their likeness in the other which would allow them to transcend."

"Yeah, whatever."

Then in the first days of spring, I came across a story in the Kafka collection that I will admit did have a true influence on me. Wedged in between "The Bucket Rider" and "Josephine the Singer, or the Mouse Folk," I discovered an unusual piece that was longer than the parables but not quite the length of a full-fledged story. Its title was "Bright Morning," and for all intents and purposes it seemed to me to be a vampire story. I read it at least a half dozen times one weekend and afterward couldn't get its imagery out of my mind.

I went to school Wednesday, hoping to find Bettleman and get his cryptic lowdown on it. Bettleman, it seems, had his own plans for that day. He sailed into the parking lot in the rust Palomino, three-door Buick Special, he'd inherited from his old man and didn't stop to park, but drove right up on the curb in front of the entrance to the school. When he got out of the car, he was wearing a Richard Nixon Halloween mask and lugging a huge basket of rotten apples. He climbed up on top of the hood of his car and then, laughing like a maniac behind the frozen leer of Tricky Dick, started beaning students and teachers with the apples.

Although Bettleman's genetic mishap of a body prevented him from being taken seriously by the sports coaches at school, those primate arms of his were famous for having the ability to hurl a baseball at Nolan Ryan speeds. He broke a few windows, nailed Romona Vacavage in the right breast, splattered a soft brown one against the back of Jake Harwood's head, and pelted the principal, No Foolin' Doolin', so badly he slipped and fell on the sauce that had dripped off his suit, dislocating his back. Everyone ran. Even the tough kids with the leather jackets and straight-pin-and-India-ink tattoos of the word SHIT on their ankles were afraid of his weirdness. Finally the cops came and took Bettleman away. He didn't come back to school. In the years that followed, I never heard anything more about him but half expected to discover his name on the Nobel lists when I'd run across them in the newspaper.

The Kafka collection didn't get returned to the library until the end of the summer. I'd run up a twenty-dollar late fee on it. In those days, twenty dollars was a lot of money, and my old man was pissed when he got the letter from the librarian. He paid for my book truancy, but I had to work off the debt by raking and burning leaves in the fall. Under those cold, violet-gray skies of autumn, the same color as the cover of the book, I gathered and incinerated the detritus of August and considered Kafka and the plight of Bettleman. I realized the last thing that poor bastard needed was Kafka, and so when my labor was completed I put the two of them out of my mind by picking up a book by Richard Brautigan, *In Watermelon Sugar*. The light confection of that work gave me a rush that set me off on another course of reading, like "The Hunter Gracchus," in frustrated search of transcendence.

The hunt lasted throughout most of my senior year of high school, taking me through the wilds of Burroughs and Kerouac and Miller, but near the end, when I was about to graduate, I found myself one day in the stacks of the public library, returning to the absurd son of Prague for a hit of real reality before I went forth into the world. To my disbelief and utter annoyance, I discovered the book had been removed as soon as I had returned it at the end of the summer and never brought back. In its place was a brand new edition of *The Collected Stories of Franz Kafka*. I paged through the crisp, clean book, but could not find the story "Bright Morning."

The incompleteness of this new volume put me off and I just said, "The hell with it!"—much to the dismay of the librarian who was within easy earshot of my epithet.

I went to college and dropped out after one semester, bought a boat and became a clammer on the Great South Bay for two years. All this time, I continued to read, and occasionally Kafka would rear his thin head in a mention by another author. These were usually allusions to "The Metamorphosis," which seemed the only work of his anyone ever mentioned.

One night on Grass Island out in the middle of the bay, a place where clammers congregated on Saturday nights to party, I ran into a guy I knew from having spoken to him previously, when I'd be out of the boat, with a tube and basket, scratch raking in the flats. If we were both working the same area, he'd take a break around three o'clock when the south wind would invariably pick up, and wander over to talk with me for a while. He was also a big reader, but usually his tastes ran to massive tomes like the Gulag books, Mann's *The Magic Mountain*, Proust.

That night on Grass Island, in the gaze of Orion, with a warm breeze from off the mainland carrying the sounds of Lela Ritz getting laid by Shab Wellow down in the lean-to, we were sitting atop the highest dune, passing a joint back and forth, when the conversation turned to Kafka. This guy from the bay, I don't remember his name, said to me, "I really like that story, "Bright Morning."

"You know it?" I said.

"Sure." Then he proceeded to tell the entire thing just as I remembered it.

"Do you have a copy of it?" I asked.

"Sure," he said. "I'll bring it out with me some day for you."

The discussion ended then because we spotted Lela in the moonlight, naked, down by the water's edge. Lela Ritz had the kind of body that made Kafka seem like a bad joke.

In the days that followed, I'd see that guy from time to time who owned the book, and he'd always promise to remember to bring it out with him. But at the end of summer, I'd heard that he'd raked up the beringed left hand of a woman who, in June, had been knocked out of a boat, caught in the propeller, and supposedly never found. The buyer at the dock told me the guy gave up clamming because of it. That fall I returned to college and never saw him again.

I went to school for my undergraduate and masters degrees at

SUNY, Binghamton, in upstate New York, where I studied literature and writing. It was there that I met and worked with novelist John Gardner, who did what he could to help me become a fiction writer. His knowledge of literature, short stories, and novels was encyclopedic, and when I was feeling mischievous, I would try to stump him by giving him merely a snippet of the plot of, what I considered to be, some obscure piece I had recently discovered: Bunin's "The Elaghin Affair," Blackwood's "The Willows," Collier's *His Monkey Wife*. He never failed to get them, and could discuss their merits as if he had read them but an hour earlier. Twice in conversation I brought up the story by Kafka, and on the first occasion he said he knew it. He even posited some interpretation of it, which I can't now remember. The second time I brought it up, in relation to having just read his own story, "Julius Caesar and the Werewolf," he shook his head and said that there was no such piece by Kafka, but if there was, with that title, it would have to be a horror story.

What was even more interesting concerning the story during my college years, and really the last time I would hear anything about it for a very long time, was an incident that transpired at the motel where I lived with my future wife, Lynn. The Colony Motor Inn on Vestal Parkway had a string of single rooms that sat up on a hill, separated from the main complex of the establishment. These rooms were reserved for students, long-time borders, and the illegal Chinese immigrants who worked at the motel restaurant, The House of Yu. It was a dreary setting in which to live on a daily basis—a heaping helping of Susquehanna gothic. The maintenance guy had one arm and an eye patch, and two of the maids were mother and daughter *and* sisters, whose *other* job was slaughtering livestock.

Lynn was in nursing school and I was doing my literary thing, spending a lot of time writing crappy stories with pencil in composition books. The room we had was really small, and the bathroom doubled as a kitchen. We had a toaster oven in there on the counter, and we cooked our own food to save money. In the mornings I'd shave onto ketchup-puddled plates in the sink. The toilet was also the garbage disposal, and it wasn't unusual for me to try to hit the floating macaroni when I'd take a piss. That bathroom had no door, just a sliding curtain. Right next to the entrance, we kept an old Victrola, and if one of us was going in to do our thing, for a little privacy, we'd spin the "Blue Danube Waltz" at top volume.

When the weather was good and the temperature was still

warm, we'd walk, in the mornings, down to the motel pool at the bottom of the hill. Lynn would swim laps, and I would sit at one of the tables and write. If we went early enough, we usually had the spot to ourselves.

On one typical day, while Lynn was swimming and I was hunched over my notebook, smoking a butt, trying to end a story without having the protagonist commit suicide or kill someone, I heard the little gate in the chain-link fence surrounding the pool open and close. I looked up and there stood this skinny guy dressed in a sailor's uniform, white gob hat tilted at an angle on his shaved head, holding a Polaroid camera. He said hello to me and I nodded, hoping he wasn't going to strike up a conversation. I watched his Adam's apple bob and his eyes shift back and forth and immediately knew I was in for it.

He came over and sat at my table and asked to bum a smoke. I gave him one and he lifted my matches and lit it.

"That your girl?" he asked, nodding toward Lynn as she passed by in the water.

"Yeah," I said.

"Nice hair," he said and grinned.

"You on leave?" I asked.

"Yeah," he said. "Got a big bunch of money and a week or so off. Bought this new camera."

"Where you staying?"

"Up on the hill," he said.

"They usually don't rent the places up on the hill unless you're staying for a long time," I said.

"I made it worth their while," he told me, flicking his ashes. "I wanted to be able to see everything."

I was going to tell him I had to get back to work, but just then Lynn got out of the pool and came over to the table.

"Ma'am," he said, and got up to let her sit down.

"Well, have a nice day," I told him, but he just stood there looking at us.

I was going to tell him to shove off, but finally he spoke. "Would you two like me to take your portrait?" he asked.

I shook my head no, and Lynn said yes. She made me get up and drew me over to stand against the chain-link fence with the Vestal Parkway in the background.

The sailor brought the Polaroid up to his eye and focused on us. "Let's have a kiss, now," he said, that Adam's apple bobbing like mad.

I put my arm around Lynn and kissed her for a long time. In the middle of it, I heard the pool gate open and close and saw the sailor running away across the parking lot toward the hill.

"Creep," said Lynn.

Then I read her my new story and she dozed off while sitting straight up.

That night, as we lay in bed on the verge of sleep, I heard a loud bang come from somewhere down the row of rooms. I knew immediately that it was a gunshot, so I grabbed Lynn and rolled onto the floor. We lay there breathing heavily from fear and she said to me, "What the hell was that?"

"Maybe Mrs. West's hair finally exploded," I said, and we laughed. Mrs. West was the maids' supervisor. She had a seven-story beehive hairdo she was constantly jabbing a sharpened pencil into to scratch her scalp.

About ten minutes later, I heard the police car pull up and saw the flashing red light through the split in the curtains. I hastily put my shorts and sneakers on and went outside. In the parking lot, I met Chester, our next-door neighbor.

"What's up?" I asked him.

He was shaking his head, and in that Horse Heads, New York, upstate drawl, said, "Man, that's gonna ruin my night."

"What happened?" I said.

"Admiral asshole blew his brains out down there in 268."

"The sailor?" I asked.

"Yeah, I heard the shot and went down to his room. The door was open part way. Jeez, there was a piece of jaw bone stuck in the wall and blood everywhere."

Two more cop cars pulled up and when the officers got out they told us to go back inside.

After I told Lynn what had happened, she didn't get much sleep, and I tossed and turned all night, falling in and out of dreams about that goofy sailor. I just remember one dream that showed him in a small boat in shark-infested waters, while in the background a volcano erupted. I awoke in the morning to the sound of someone knocking on the door; Lynn had already left for her shift at the hospital. I got out of bed and dressed quickly.

It was Mrs. West. She wanted to know if I wanted the room cleaned. I said no, and quickly shut the door. A second later, she knocked again. I opened up and she stood there, holding something out toward me. It was then that I noticed that her hands and arms were red.

"They had me here early this morning, cleaning the death," she said. "I found this amidst the fragments." She handed me what I took to be a square of paper. Only when I touched it did I realize it was a photograph—the picture of Lynn and me kissing, while all around us splattered flecks of red filled the sky like a blood rain.

That afternoon, I had the photo setting on the table next to where I was writing a story about a sailor who goes to a motel to commit suicide and falls in love with the maid. Every time I'd look up, there would be that picture. It gave me the willies, so eventually I turned it over. I hadn't noticed before, but written on the back in very light pencil were these words: *He stepped out into the bright morning and quietly evaporated* . . . I recognized it immediately as part of the last line of Kafka's elusive story. That photograph is still in my possession, at the bottom of a cardboard box, out in the garage or in the basement, I think.

Just when the synchronistic influence of that text seemed to be reaching a crescendo of revelation, it suddenly turned its back on me, and I heard nothing, saw nothing about it for years and years, until I could easily ignore my awareness of it. The avalanche of books and stories I read in the interim helped to bury it. Occasionally, when I was in a bookstore and would see some new edition of Kafka's stories, I would pick it up and scan the table of contents, hoping *not* to see the piece listed. I was never disappointed. So many other writers came to call, and their personalities and plots and words became ever so much more important to me than his.

Slowly, and I mean slowly, the stories I wrote became less and less crappy and I actually had a few published by small-press magazines. The amount of time it took me to become a professional writer is reminiscent of the adage of a hundred apes in a room with a hundred typewriters, at work for a hundred years, eventually producing Hamlet's soliloquy. From there, it was only a matter of more time, and then one day I sold a novel to a major publisher. I could less believe it than the fact that the sailor had known "Bright Morning" well enough to quote it. When my novel was published, the blurb the publisher had written for it mentioned Kafka twice. At the time, I wasn't thinking about all the incidents that had been related to the Kafka story; they seemed light-years away. All I thought was, "Hey, Kafka, it's better than Harold Robbins." Or was it? The book didn't sell all too well, but it got great reviews. Nearly every critic who wrote about it mentioned Kafka at least once, so that when the paperback edition came out, it carried all of the critical blurbs and the back cover was lousy with Kafka.

In four years, I'd published three fantasy novels, a dozen short stories also in the genre, and a couple of essays. The first novel won a World Fantasy Award, the first two were *New York Times* Notable Books of the Year; one of the stories was nominated for a Nebula Award, another appeared in *The Year's Best Fantasy and Horror*; there were starred reviews in *Publishers Weekly*, *Kirkus Review*, the *Library Journal*; three stories in one year made *Locus* magazine's recommended reading list. I tell you all of this not by way of bragging, because there are others who have written more and garnered more accolades, there are others who *are* better writers, but for me it was a goad. I thought that to stop for a moment would mean to let all I had worked for slip away. At the same time, I was teaching five classes, over a hundred writing students a semester, at a community college an hour and a half from my house, and I had two young sons with whom I needed to spend a considerable amount of time. So I slept no more than four hours a night, smoked like mad when writing, and lived on coffee and fast food. It was an insane period and it made me into a bloated zombie. Finally I hit an impasse and needed a break. I couldn't think of one more damn fantasy story I could write. And as it turned out, what stood between me and a vacation from it all was just one more story.

Like a good soldier, I had finished off all the pieces I had promised to editors, and then all that remained was a final story for a collection of short fiction I really wanted to see published. When the project had first presented itself I had, with reckless largesse, promised to write a piece for it that would appear nowhere else. My imagination, though, was emptier than the dark, abandoned railway station I visited every night in my dreams. In four years, I'd done just about everything *I* could possibly do in fantasy. I told you already about the flying head, the cloud city with attendant panopticon, but there was much more—demons, werewolves, men turned to blue stone, evil geniuses, postmodern fairy-tale kingdoms, giant moths, zombies, parodies of fantasy heroes, an interview with Jules Verne, big bug-aliens enamored of old movies, Lovecraft rip-offs, experimental hoodoo, and that's just for starters. The only fantasy I could now conceive of was sneaking in a nap on Saturday afternoon after the kids' basketball games and before the obligatory family trip to the mall. I was burnt crisper than a fucking cinder on the whole genre.

The deadline for the story collection was fast approaching, and all I had was a computer file full of aborted beginnings, all of which stunk. I was determined not to fail, so when the college I taught at closed for spring break and I had a week to write, I said to myself, "Okay, get a grip." Driving home the last night before the vacation, I had a brainstorm. Why reinvent the wheel? I decided I'd just take one of the old fantasy tropes and work it over a little—a ready-made theme. Upon arriving home, I went to my office and scanned the bookshelves for an idea, and that's when I came upon a book I had bought at a yard sale back when Lynn and I were still in college. I'd almost forgotten I'd owned the thing—an anthology of vampire stories. That night and the next day, I read almost all of the pieces in it. There was one great one, "Viy," by Gogol, that reinvigorated my imagination somewhat. As I sat down to compose, though, a memory of Kafka's "Bright Morning" came floating up from where it had been buried, and breached the surface of my consciousness like the hand of that corpse at the end of the movie *Deliverance*. I thought to myself, "If I could just read that story one more time, that would be all I'd need to get something good going."

Sitting back in my office chair, I lit a cigarette and tried to remember what I could about the piece. Bettleman and his apples; Gregor Samsa lying in bed on his back, six legs kicking; the sailor's hat; the worm-filled wound of the kid in "The Country Doctor"—all passed through my mind as I called forth the intricacies of the plot. Then I imagined I was back in the West Islip public library on a winter's afternoon, reading from the violet book. Ironically enough, it dawned on me that "Bright Morning" centered around a frustrated writer, F.—a young dilettante of literary aspirations, who feels he has all of the aesthetic acumen and an overabundance of style, but, for the life of him, cannot conceive of a story worth telling. It is intimated that the reason for this is that he has spent all of his days with his nose in a book and is devoid of life experience. There is more to it than that, but that's how the story begins. Somewhere along the way he hooks up with this haggard, bent, old man, a Mr. Krouch, whose face is "a mask of wrinkles." I think they meet at night on the bridge leading into the small town that is the story's setting. The old man offers his life story to the young writer in exchange for half the proceeds if the book is ever published. The writer is reticent, but then the old man tells him just one short tale about when he was a sailor, shipwrecked on a volcanic island in the Indian Ocean, south of Sumatra, and encountered a species of ferocious blue lizards as big as horses.

The young man is soon convinced he will become famous writing the old man's biography. Each night, after their initial meeting, the old man comes to F.'s house. On the first night, as a gift to the writer, the old man gives him, from his tattered traveling bag, a beautiful silver pen and a bottle of ink. The pen feels to the young man as if it has been specifically designed for his grip; the ink flows so smoothly it is as if the words are writing themselves. Then the old man begins to recount his long, long life, a chapter a night. In that wonderfully compressed style Kafka utilizes in his parables, he gives selections from the annals of Krouch. Years tending the tombs of monarchs in some distant eastern land, a career as a silhouette puppeteer in Venice, a love affair with a young woman half his age —these are a few I remember, but there were more and they were packed into the space of two or three modestly sized paragraphs.

At the end of each session, Krouch leaves just before dawn, and F. falls asleep to the sounds of bird song that accompanies the coming of the sun. The work has an exhausting effect upon him and he sleeps all day, until nightfall, when he wakes only an hour before the old man returns. The gist of the story is that, as the auto/biography grows, F. slowly wastes away while Krouch gets younger and more robust. It becomes evident as to how the old man has managed to fit so many adventures into one lifetime, and the reader begins to suspect that there have been other unsuspecting writers before F. By the time the young man places the last period at the end of the last sentence—a sentence about him placing the last period at the end of the last sentence—he is no longer young but has become shriveled and wrinkled and bent.

"Now off to the publisher with it," Krouch commands and gives a hearty laugh. F. can barely stand. He struggles to lift the pile of pages and then, knees creaking, altogether out of breath, he shuffles toward the door. "Allow me," says Krouch, and he leaps from his chair and moves to open the door.

It takes much of his remaining energy, but F. manages to whisper, "Thank you."

He steps out into the bright morning and quietly evaporates, the pages scattering on the wind like frightened ghosts.

It is one thing to vaguely remember a story by Kafka and quite another to actually have the book before you. There is that wonderfully idiosyncratic style: the meek authorial voice, the infrequent but strategically placed metaphor, a businesslike approach to plot, and those deceptive devices of craft, nearly as invisible as chameleons that make all the difference to the beauty of the imagery and the impact of the tale. I knew I needed that story in my hands, before my eyes, and that I would obsess over it, unable to write a word of my own, until I had it.

I enlisted the help of my older son, and together we scoured the

Internet, made phone calls to antiquarian and used book shops as far away as Delaware; the western wilds of Pennsylvania; Watertown, New York, up by the Canadian border. Nothing. Most had never heard of the story. One or two said they had a very vague recollection of the violet edition but couldn't swear to it. The used book sites on the web were crammed with copies of the more recent Schocken edition and some even had expensive originals from Europe, but none of the abstracts described the book I was searching for. I drove around one day to all the used bookstores I knew of and, in one, found the violet-covered book. I was so frantic to have my hands on it, I could hardly control my shaking as I forked over the $23.50 to the clerk. When I got out to my car and opened it, I discovered that it was really a copy of *Mansfield Park* by Jane Austen. I was livid, and on my way home as I drove across an overpass, I opened the window and tossed the damned thing out into the traffic below.

My week off was nearing its end and I was no closer to Kafka's story, no closer to my own. The frustration of the search, my fear of impending failure, finally peaked and then dropped me into a sullen depression. On Saturday afternoon, between basketball and the mall, I received a phone call. Lynn answered it and handed me the receiver.

"Hello?" I said.

"I understand you are looking for the violet Kafka," said the voice.

I was rendered speechless for a moment. Then I blurted out, "Who is this?"

"Am I correct?" asked the voice.

"Yes," I said. "The one with the story . . ."

"'Bright Morning,'" he said. "I know the story. Very rare."

"Supposedly it doesn't exist," I said.

"That's interesting," he said, "because I have a copy of the volume before me as we speak. I'm selling it."

"How much?" I inquired, too eagerly.

"That depends. I have another client also interested in it. I thought perhaps you and he would like to bid for it. The bidding starts at eighty dollars."

"That seems rather low," I said.

"Come tonight," he said, and gave me a set of directions to his place. The location was not too far from me, directly south, in the Pine Barrens. "Eight o'clock, and if you should decide to participate, I will explain more than the price."

"What is your name?" I asked.

He hung up on me.

I was altogether elated that this voice had validated the existence of the story, but at the same time I found the enigmatic nature of the call somewhat disturbing. The starting price was suspiciously low, and the fact that the caller would not give a name didn't bode well. I envisioned myself going to some darkened address and being murdered for my wallet. This alternated with a vision of discovering an abandoned railway station in the woods where the angry Kafka of my dreams would be waiting to bite my neck. At seven o'clock, though, I drove down to the money machine in town, withdrew five hundred dollars (more than I could afford), and then headed south on route 206.

My fears were allayed when, at precisely 7:45, I pulled up in front of a beautifully well-kept Victorian of near-mansion dimensions on a well-lit street in the small town of Pendricksburg. I parked in the long driveway and went to the front door. After knocking twice, a young woman answered and let me in.

"Mr. Deryn will see you. Come this way," she said.

I followed. The place was stunning, the woodwork and floors so highly polished, it was like walking through a hall of mirrors. There were chandeliers and Persian carpets and fresh flowers, like something from one of my wife's magazines. Classical music drifted through the house at low volume, and I felt as though I was touring a museum. We came to a door at the back of the house; she opened it and invited me to step inside.

The first thing I noticed were the bookcases lining the walls, and then I gave a start because sitting behind the desk was what I at first took to be a human frog, smoking a cigar. When I concentrated on the form it resolved its goggle eyes, hunch, and pouch into nothing more than an oddly put together person. But what was even more incredible, it was Bettleman. He was older, with a few days' growth of beard, but it was most definitely him. Not rising, he waved his hand to indicate one of the chairs facing his desk.

"Have a seat," he said.

I walked slowly forward and sat down, experiencing a twinge of déjà vu.

"Bettleman," I said.

He looked quizzically at me, and said, "I'm sorry, you must be mistaken. My name is John Deryn." Then he laughed and the pouch undulated, convincing me even more completely it was him.

"You're not Christian Bettleman?" I asked.

He shook his head and smiled.

I quickly decided that if he wanted to play-act it was fine by me; I was there for the book. "The violet Kafka," I said, "can I see it?"

He reached into a drawer in front of him and pulled out a thick volume. There it was, in seemingly pristine condition. Paging through it with his long graceful fingers, he stopped somewhere in the middle and then turned it around and laid it on the desk facing me. "Bright Morning," he said.

"My God," I said. "I was beginning to think it had merely been a delusion."

"Yes, I know exactly what you mean," he said. "I've spent a good portion of my life tracing the history of that story."

"Is it a forgery?" I asked.

"Nothing of the sort, though, in its style it is slightly unusual for Kafka, somewhat reminiscent of Hoffmann."

"What can you tell me about it?" I asked.

"I will try to keep this brief," he said, drawing on his cigar. His exposition came forth wrapped in a cloud. "In the words of Kafka's Czech translator and one-time girl friend, Milena Jesenska, Kafka 'saw the world as full of invisible demons, who tear apart and destroy defenseless people.' She was not speaking metaphorically. From the now expurgated portions of his diaries, we know that he had a recurring dream of one of these demons, who appeared to him as an old man named Krouch. Of course, knowing Kafka's problems with his father, the idea of it being an 'old man' admittedly has its psychological explanations.

"In 1921, when Franz was in the advanced stages of tuberculosis, he attests to his friend Max Brod, as evidenced in Brod's own journal, that this demon, Krouch, is responsible for his inability to write. He feels that every day that goes by that he does not write a new story, the disease becomes stronger. Being the mystic that he is, Kafka devises a plan to exorcise the demon. What he does is utterly brilliant. He writes a story about the vampiric Krouch, ensnaring him in the words. At the end of the tale, F., the figure who represents Kafka, disappears from the story back to the freedom of this reality. One believes upon reading it that the young writer is, himself, trapped, but not so, or at least not in Kafka's mind. This is all documented in a letter to the writer, Franz Werfel. Hence the nonindicative but promising title of the story, 'Bright Morning.'

"It becomes clear to Kafka soon after that, although he has effectively imprisoned the demon in the words of the story, Krouch still has a limited effect on him when the text is in close proximity.

So what does he do? In 1922, at his last meeting with Milena, in a small town known as Gmünd, on the Czech-Austrian border, he gives her all of his diaries. Along with those notebooks and papers is 'Bright Morning.' How effective Kafka's plan was is open to question. He only lived until 1924, but consider the further life of poor Milena, now the owner of the possessed text: she nearly dies in childbirth; has an accident which causes a fracture of her right knee, leaving her partially crippled for the rest of her life; becomes addicted to morphine; is arrested in Prague for her pro-Jewish writing, and is sent, in 1940, to Ravensbrück concentration camp in Germany where she suffers poor health. A kidney is removed when it gets infected, and not too long afterward the other fails and she dies.

"Here, 'Bright Morning' seems to quietly evaporate for some time until 1959 when the Pearfield Publishing Company of Commack, Long Island, New York, publishes an edition of Kafka containing the story. At the time, the building that houses the small publisher catches fire, burns to the ground, and of the few boxes of books salvaged, one contains twelve copies of the violet edition. Six of them went to local libraries, six to the local USO."

"And so, it carries a curse," I said.

"That is for you to decide," he said. "I acquired this copy years ago from a shellfish harvester who worked the waters of the Great South Bay. He might have said something about a curse, but then people who make a living on the water are usually somewhat superstitious. Another might laugh at the idea. I will admit that I have had my own brushes with fate."

"You cannot deny that you are Bettleman," I said.

He stared at me and a moment later the young woman was at the door. "Mr. Deryn," she said, "the other gentleman is here. Shall I show him in?"

"Please do," he told her. When she left to carry out his wish, he turned back to me. "I have chosen to only tell you the story behind the story," said Deryn. "For old time's sake." Then he smiled and with his middle finger pushed his glasses up the bridge of his nose. By now, the cigar was a smoldering stub, and he laid it in the ashtray to extinguish itself.

I was, of course, about to make some inane exclamation, like "I knew it!" or "Did you think I could be so easily fooled?" but the other bidder entered the room and saved Bettleman and myself from the embarrassment.

Not only had I recognized Bettleman, but with one glance, I

also knew my competition in the auction. I should have been more startled by the synchronicity of it all, but the events that preceded this fresh twist allowed me to take it in stride. He was another writer, working also in my genre, a big, oafish lout by the name of Jeffrey Ford. You might have heard of him, perhaps not. A few years ago he wrote a book called *The Physiognomy* which, by some bizarre fluke, perhaps the judges were drugged, won a World Fantasy Award. I'd met and spoken to him before on more than one occasion at various conferences. What the critics and editors saw in his work, I'll never know. Our brief careers, so far, had been very similar, but there was no question I was the better writer. He leaned over the desk and shook Bettleman's hand, and then he turned to me and, before sitting, nodded but said nothing.

Bettleman, in his affable Mr. Deryn guise, allowed Ford to inspect the book. Once that was finished, the bidding was to begin. Ford wanted to know why it was to start as low as eighty dollars, and Deryn told him only, "I have my reasons."

I had been slightly put off the book by what I had been told, but once Ford started making offers, I couldn't resist. I felt like if he were to win, he would be walking out of there with my best plot ever. We two cheapskate writers upped the ante at ten dollars an increment, but even at this laggardly pace, we were soon in the three-hundred-dollar range. Bettleman was smiling like Toad of Toad Hall, and when he stopped for a moment to light another cigar, my gaze moved around the room. Off in the corner, behind his desk, wedged into a row of books, I saw a large bell jar, and floating in it, a delicate, beringed hand. For some reason the sight of this horrid curio jogged my memory, and I recalled, perhaps for the first time something that I had wanted to suppress, that the woman who had fallen off the boat back in the bay and was lost those many years ago, was not a woman at all but a young girl, Lela Ritz. For a brief moment, I saw her naked in the moonlight. Then Bettleman croaked and the bidding resumed.

As we pushed onward, nickel-and-diming our way toward my magic number, five hundred dollars, I could not dismiss all of the tragedy left in the wake of "Bright Morning." I thought about Lynn and the kids and how I might be jeopardizing their safety or maybe their lives by this foolish desire. Still my mouth worked, and I let the prices roll off my tongue. By the time I took control of myself and fully awoke to the auction, my counterpart had just proposed four hundred and fifty.

He added, "And I mean it. It is my absolute final offer."

Ford now turned to look at me, and I knew I had him. By a good fifty dollars, I had him.

"Your apple," said Bettleman, looking at me from behind his thick lenses. Now he was no longer smiling, but I saw a look of sadness on his face.

That long second of my decision was like a year scratch raking for hands in the pool of the Colony Inn. The truth was, I didn't know what I wanted. I felt the margins of the story closing in, the sentences wrapping around my wrists and ankles, the dots of i's swimming in schools across my field of vision. Experiencing now the full weight of my weariness, I finally said, "I pass."

"Very well," said Bettleman.

I rose and shook his hand, nodded to Ford, who was already reaching into the pocket of his two-sizes-too-small jeans to retrieve a crumpled wad of money, and left.

Call me a superstitious fool if you like, I might very well deserve the appellation. As it turned out, I never finished the promised story, and the publisher of the collection, Golden Gryphon Press, retracted their offer to do the book. Of all the ironies, they filled my spot on their list with a collection by Ford. He even wrote, especially for it, a story entitled "Bright Morning," making no attempt to disguise his swiping of Kafka's material. One of the early, prepublication critics of the book wrote in a scathing review, "Ford is Kafka's monkey." Nothing could have interested me less. I returned to my teaching job. I spent time with my family. I slept at night with no frightening visits from old or thin demons. In the mornings I woke to the beauty of the sun.

A year later, after retiring from my brief career as a fantasy writer, I read that Ford, two weeks prior to the publication of his collection, had given a reading from his manuscript of "Bright Morning" at one of the conventions (I believe in Massachusetts). According to the article, which appeared in a reputable newspaper, after receiving a modest round of applause from the six or seven people in attendance, he stepped out into the bright morning and quietly evaporated, the pages scattering on the wind like frightened ghosts.

This story is for Marty Halpern, editor of the collection you hold in your hands. Without him, you would be holding air. As for the piece itself, I did spend quite a few years as a clammer on the Great South Bay. The sailor did take our picture and then shoot himself in the head. The maids were mother and daughter and *sisters, and slaughtered livestock as their part-time job. I did throw a book off the overpass, but it wasn't* Mansfield Park, *which I actually liked. Kafka did kick me in the nuts. I did evaporate.*

Three thousand copies of this book have been printed by the Maple-Vail Book Manufacturing Group, Binghamton, NY, for Golden Gryphon Press, Urbana, IL. The typeset is Electra, printed on 55# Sebago. The binding cloth is Arrestox B. Typesetting by The Composing Room, Inc., Kimberly, WI.